G. S. CIFUENTES

Glass Hearts

Book 1

Second edition

ISBN: 979-8-9998253-1-5

This book was professionally typeset on Reedsy.
Find out more at reedsy.com

Acknowledgments

I'd like to thank my soulmate, with whom this work would have never happened. Thank you for being such a loving, caring, and creative person. I'm blessed to be your husband. You're the mac to my cheesiness.

My friends and family who helped me out throughout the process and listened to me go on and on about plots, sequences, and character development, your patience is greatly appreciated.

To my aging computer: I found you abandoned behind some stairs and gave you a new life, and despite all the long hours, you still function. Thank you for being more than a solitaire-playing machine.

To my patient editor who helped me make this story cohesive. Thank you for guiding me through my unfamiliarity.

And to you, dear reader, who picked up this book, you've made a decade's worth of work worth it. Thank you.

1

The First Day of June

It was a hot sunny day as pedestrians went about their lives. Over the rooftop of a run-down, five-story building in the heart of New Jersey, shadowy figures scurried into position.

June Romero walked into her building and toward the elevator. She picked at the paint that was peeling off of the button when the doors opened with a metallic clank.

"Hi there, child. Butterscotch?" June Romero's neighbor smiled as they passed each other.

"No thanks, Mrs. Jones, I just got my lavender tea from the coffee shop."

"Oh, you kids and your fancy drinks nowadays. Well, be safe, deary."

"Will do."

She resented her petite stature. At five-foot-nothing, June constantly felt she was treated like a child despite turning eighteen in a few days. She knew her baggy outfit didn't help her look any older.

I can't wait till I graduate and get out of here. June sighed and pressed the elevator button. *Why does she always pick places like this? I could be working at a better job. Hell, I should probably threaten her with selling feet pics online again...* She chuckled to herself as the elevator doors opened again and her elderly neighbor holding a pet-carrying case stood on the other side.

"Hey there, kid. How was school?" the man said, smiling with deep-set wrinkles as he walked into the elevator.

"Mr. Jameson, it was okay. I can't wait for summer vacation. How's Mrs. Whiskers?"

"Oh, right." He waved his hand dismissively. "The vet said I need to stop giving her ham. But she likes it."

"Doctor's orders, Mr. Jameson. Have a good day." June waved goodbye as the doors closed after stopping on her neighbor's floor. Her phone rang and she answered to hear the familiar nagging voice.

"Yes, Mom. ... I know, Mom. ... It's fine, I was just grabbing some tea at the corner. ... No, Mom, I'll be home quick. It's gonna be summer, can't I just go out for a little while on my own? ... It's fine, I'll let you know if my stalker dad shows up. ... I'm kidding. ... No, Mom, you know I don't know what my dad looks like, right?" She held her phone down and sighed deeply before lifting it up to her ear again. "Yes, Mom, I'm aware I'm insane for drinking hot tea on a hot day. Please, if you'd just let me go gro— Ugh, fine, I love you too, Mom. I'll see you soon." The elevator doors opened and June took a sip of her tea as she made her way down the dimly lit hallway.

She returned to her apartment and fixed the books she knocked over when she bumped into the shelf before leaving earlier that day. She noticed the crack on the shelf where she bumped into it and picked up the steamy romance novels that toppled over and stood them up against the book ends. "How'd my mom let me read this steamy trash at the age

2

of eleven?" June thought aloud as she placed each romance novel on the shelf. She knew they weren't poor, though June wondered where all the money came from. Somehow her mother always found the shadiest apartment buildings in whatever city they ended up in. She sighed and dropped off her small wallet and keys on the table and was about to take off her boots before a shadow by the window caught her eye, but before she could examine it, she heard the door.

"Mom? Is that you?"

"No," a man's voice answered from the living room. June's heart raced as the footsteps grew closer. She was about to scream when he walked into the hall and pulled out a badge unlike any she'd ever seen.

"William Saturnino. I'm with B.R.I.C. It's a government agency that helps people like you."

The tall, light-skinned man with thinning hair and an average build wore a suit so nice, June thought he might have just come from a wedding.

"What do you mean, people like me?" June said, eyeing the kitchen knives that were a bit too far for her to run to.

"People with, uh, a unique biology."

"So, not because my mom is running away from a deadbeat stalker?"

He blanched then sauntered toward June with his hands splayed open. "I know you must have a million questions, June, but I'll answer it all if you just come with us peacefully. I'll tell you all about your past and why you never really get hurt."

June analyzed the cracked shelf from earlier. "My past, huh? Like, am I an alien that crashed-landed on Earth or some shit?"

William smirked at that. "No, no, it's much more boring than that."

June glanced out the window to see an armed man in military gear hanging from what she assumed was the roof. "So, what am I then?" Her voice trembled.

"A genetic anomaly," he replied in an honest tone, looking her in the eye as he walked toward her. "There are others like you. My agency has been finding them all over the world. Children who need help, medicine, and a guiding ha—"

"So, we're mutations, and you're here to put me away, huh?"

"Something like that," sighed William, "but it's more complica—"

"Yeah, yeah, more complicated. I get it!" June lost her nerve a bit. She felt her hands trembling as William got closer to her and slowly put his hands on her shoulders.

"You're definitely your mother's daughter."

June pulled back and squinted at him. "Don't touch me. And don't talk to me like you know me! You've got S.W.A.T. outside waiting to just snatch me like... like... some criminal!" June backed away and threw her hands up. "And you want me to trust you!? You're insane. When my mom comes home, you guys are gonna hear about it! I'm calling the cops; you guys can't be in here! You don't even have a warrant. This is bull—"

William yelled into his wrist, "Stand down. I got this." June's eyes widened in panic, knowing she could be snatched at any moment and probably never heard from again.

William's voice snapped her out of it. "It'll be okay, June. I guess I should start with the truth. Melody is not your real mother. She took you from us when you were very little."

4

"Wha—"

"We found you in a house explosion in California. There were no survivors except you." William's brow furrowed. "A newborn baby girl completely unscathed, just lying there in the rubble."

"That's bull..."

"When was the last time you were really hurt?" William gave her a knowing stare. "Last time you stubbed your toe? Hit your funny bone? Last time you banged your head and felt anything other than a slight discomfort?"

"I..."

"You haven't. It bothers you, sometimes there's a little bit of discomfort, but it never bruises or lasts longer than a moment."

June eyed the cracked bookshelf once more and touched the back of her head. No pain.

"I know. You're not the only one," William continued. "We've taken in many with your ability. The agency helps people like you. Lost, confused, and unsure of what to do with their power."

"What do you want from me?"

"To help, to give you the tools you need to survive in a world that would be terrified if they knew of your existence. This is a lot to take in, I know. This isn't my first recruitment, but it is the first time it's taken me years to find the person I've been looking for."

June cocked her head in confusion.

"Melody, or Agent Romero, has eluded us for as long as she could because of her training, but everyone has a digital fingerprint." June glanced at her phone on the shelf and cursed under her breath. "We finally tracked her down because she was transferring money again into a new account. I suppose she was getting ready to move again. Didn't help you got yourself tea and used your real name."

June's heart sank and she let out a loud sigh. William tried to change the subject.

"Your kind is stronger than normal. Invulnerable to most injuries and heals surprisingly fast. I need you to come with us so we can help you hone those skills and join the agency to help find and protect others like you."

June snickered. "So, basically, you're saying I'm a wizard, and you're taking me to the fortress of mutants to fight for the fate of the world?"

William gave her a surprisingly caring smile at her intentional butchering of pop culture. "Yeah, in a way," he said softly. "Come on, kiddo. The world is a scary place." She studied him for a moment and scanned the room. "Come with us. Leave this life of running away from place to place and help us help you."

June glanced again at the broken shelf and pondered for a moment before cuttingly replying, "So, what you're saying is..." She shot him a mischievous grin. "I can kick all of your asses?"

William chuckled as he backed away from June, expressing friendliness. "Yeah, kid, and I would still very much like for you to come peacefully."

"Okay..." she said, looking up slowly to catch his eye "... make me."

"DON'T!"

As she charged, the house was immediately covered in gray smoke and shattering glass all around them. Everything went dark.

6

June didn't feel herself hit the floor.

***

Melody Romero, a woman of petite stature and lean build with tan skin, dark hair, and dressed casually, looked up at her apartment with brown eyes similar to June's. Her jaw clenched and her fists tightened around her shopping bags. She knew she was in trouble.

Helpless to do anything, she could only watch as a small crowd formed across the street from her corner apartment. She heard the shots and breaking glass. The smoke spewed from her third-story apartment. The police had prepared a perimeter. The best she could do now was to blend in, sneak away, and find her way to her emergency stash.

The grocery bags she held were now a needless burden. She regretted leaving June alone while she went to the store, but Melody knew someday this would happen. She knew June was becoming tired of being constantly questioned and followed, but it was foolish of her to think June could take care of herself against the agency and she took a deep breath, telling herself they were just two women against an entire government. It was only a matter of time. There had to be a way to save June, and she'd find it.

She did it once, she could do it again.

***

June awoke strapped to a slab in what looked to be a medical facility. The room was white and sterile, large and padded, and the door made of metal seemed heavy. She pulled on her restraints and almost felt them breaking before a voice came through a speaker hidden in the room.

"Don't! Don't do that. It's designed to shock. Its voltage won't knock you out, but it will be very uncomfortable."

"So tell me again, how are you the good guys?" June said firmly as she tried to hide her fear.

"We're trying to help, but like a lot of others, you seem to be very stubborn." William sighed. "I want to help you, but we have to take care of ourselves too."

June gave a puzzled stare and opened her mouth to speak but decided against it.

"You might not know it, but we've dealt with hundreds like you, and at first, we tried to be civil and reasonable, only to have Bricks smash through our people like butter. We've lost so many just because they couldn't control themselves or had no clue how strong they could be... or worse," William said with a severe tone. "They know what they're capable of and will joyfully destroy us without hesitation."

The braces on her arms and legs released with a whirring sound. June got up and sat on the slab, nursing her wrist.

"Look, I'm sorry, but you said you were gonna tell me about my past."

The door opened with a hiss and a whirring sound. William, flanked by two guards covered in heavy riot gear, walked in and he motioned his hands to let them know they could put their stun rods down.

"You can follow me. We're gonna have a long talk in my office."

June raised an eyebrow.

"I'll fill you in on all that I know. Also, I'll give you a quick tour. Come on, we have much to discuss, Mel—" William stopped mid-sentence, looked away, and shook his head. "Come, come. Let's go."

June followed behind, glancing out the door, and realized this would be a lot to take in. The long, large hallways were encased in walls of unpainted thick concrete with metal tubes running along the bottom. The signs posted showed around fifty floors. June fell behind as she tried to read the signs but hurried to follow him.

"What is this place?"

"Base Alpha," said William in a matter-of-fact tone. "We have bases all around the world, anywhere we can, anyway. We've been trying to help so many like you. The ones we can't, well, let's just say it's hard to tell the difference between a savage Brick and a terrorist explosion nowadays. A lot of the time, they're one and the same."

"So, I'm profiled and put in a camp..."

"No!" exclaimed William before June could finish her thought. "It's not like that, but we need to be careful. As I said before, we've lost a lot of good people..." William trailed off again.

The four of them turned a corner and June saw a door with a glass window at the end of the hall.

"Ah, that's us. That'll do, guys. Thank you."

William nodded at the guards as they straightened up and turned back to the direction they walked from.

"Come in, take a seat."

As June surveyed the large office, she noticed bookshelves covered in psychology and biology books, the occasional 'World's Best Boss' mugs of different styles, and one small picture of an infant in a crib toward the back corner of it all. On the other side of the office was a large window that showed

9

an area around three stories deep and cylindrical. Scratch and burn marks all over the walls caught June's attention.

"The hell is this?"

She was about to sit down, but straightened herself to get a closer look.

"This is the training area."

"For what? Kaiju?"

William smirked and sat down in his chair.

"No, it's clear you really have no idea what you're capable of. Bricks are..."

"You keep saying 'Bricks', what is that? Is that what you call people like me?"

"Uh, y-yeah, sorry. That's what the agency calls your species as code, and it kind of stuck. Strong, durable, like a brick." He paused for a second. "Tough skin like Kevlar..."

"Stop!" said June, frustrated. "Just... start explaining."

William turned his monitor to face her.

"Okay," he said, "get ready for the exposition dump."

June glared at him with a raised eyebrow. William cleared his throat, and his grin turned into a grimace as he noticed June wasn't in a joking mood.

"This is the Biological Research, Identification, and Containment division, aka B.R.I.C. We don't know when, how, or why it all started, but decades ago, a few doctors stumbled onto something strange. A, er, a gene, I suppose, that was within some of the population.

"It was hard to get samples since most of the skin is impenetrable, so saliva, tears, and waste were used. The subjects were people who survived an accident or a shooting or just came in for a checkup only to realize they are very, very durable. Hard skin, even the eyes are tough, though not completely impenetrable like the skin. You see here on this chart how a bullet can pierce skin with no resistance practically, and with a Brick's skin, it just bends, and the bullet is flattened."

June stared at the screen with her mouth agape. She nodded slowly.

"Okay, here's a video of a man getting bombarded with grenades filled with shrapnel. See, barely fazed. And here! Here is another video. Look—look at her, she just took the bus on the shoulder, and it just threw her back a couple of feet, then she got up like nothing happened. We tracked them down, ran tests, and they became some of our first agents." William took a breath. "And it's been like that for years. It's fascinating knowing there are so many—"

"William, focus!" June said sternly, noticing him rambling.

"Sorry." He shook his head. "Uh, anyways, yes, okay, so, you were found in a small town in Southern California. The whole apartment went up in flames. Family, uh... deceased, but you were in a collapsed crib, crying your lungs out like it was just dinnertime. Not a scratch on you despite the rubble and smoke. So, of course, we took you in, and we adopted you as our daughter.

"Our... Um, yes, Melody and I, we, uh, we tried to raise you ourselves. But she was too idealistic, or, well, I guess you can say we both are in different ways. She believed you should have a normal life, and I knew one day someone would push you a little too far, and we'd be picking up splattered children from walls and roofs, a—"

"Okay, so Mom was an agent too!? Also, you thought caging and brainwashing me into a super soldier would be best for everyone?"

11

"Ye— No," he sighed. "It's complicated. Not a super soldier, per se, just a..."

William struggled to find the words.

"...just not a menace to society."

"But don't I have aunts or grandparents or..."

"You might have, but we needed to protect you. Melody is the one who pulled you out and took you to the hospital. After that, she got the paperwork done. She was always good at that, and then you were ours."

June grew more and more uncomfortable with everything she was hearing.

"But we look so alike. How— How can you just sweep all of this under the rug... Also, how do Bricks die? If an explosion didn't kill a baby?"

"Poison, asphyxiation, uh, and electrocution mostly, maybe drowning, but who can hold your kind down for that long without any strength of their own? It's almost impossible, but doable," William said proudly, but he realized that June became even more severe than before. He trailed off into the next subject. "I know this is a lot to take in, but..."

"Are you serious? You're gonna tell me that not only are my real parents dead, I'm adopted, my 'mom'," she said with finger quotes, "is a rogue spy, and you're technically my adoptive dad, and you've got the nerve to tell me all of this, play yourselves the heroes, and expect me to join the cause as if the world needs me to save it?"

"Well..." William's gaze fell toward his desk. "...yyyeeesss." His shoulders slumped as he looked up at June. "This is important. You're a Brick, and if not us, someone would try to take you too, and with us, you have a chance to at least attempt to live a normal life. The alternative—"

"THERE'S AN ALTERNATIVE!?"

Leaning on the desk and visibly agitated, she seethed and stared at William.

He searched for a subtle way to say what he was thinking.

"There are groups, small for now but growing, made up of Bricks that are, for lack of a better word... dangerous."

June tilted her head with an expression that made William regret his choice of words.

"I'm scared. The world is changing, and as much as I want to trust you, you can join one of these groups because you like what they're selling, and there isn't much we can do to stop you."

He looked around, searching for the words as June stared at him with narrowed eyes.

"It's Armageddon. Melody and I found you and tried to raise you to be a good person. She just couldn't bear the fact that someday we would need you to fight this war for us. She took you from us using all her training. She hid you in plain sight."

William let out a long sigh. Both of them paused, processing the information.

"I held you as if you were my own, fed you, changed your diapers, but despite it all, where Melody and I differed is she wanted you to have a life, and I needed you to save lives."

June's gaze shot up. Her eyes watered from rage.

"My life was stolen from me, and you want me to be your savior? A stupid weapon to use to protect you from people who were born different... Special or..." June's eyes started darting around as she found the words. "Better than you?" She stared at William. "You wanted a baby orphan to go out into the big bad world and fight for you? Are you insane?! I mean, how the hell else do you explain this? I can't with this,

I just want to go home. I don't care if she was a rogue agent, Mom—my mom—cares for me."

"She's a criminal..."

"She's my hero."

June stood up abruptly and unintentionally, she watched the doors of the arena downstairs open. A group of six armored people walked in. Dressed in what seemed like riot gear and faces covered in something resembling scuba masks, June could see them making formations as one of them made hand gestures.

"Team Alpha," William said with a sigh of relief. June glanced up at him as he continued. "The team we send out when we know there's a dangerous Brick out there."

"You mean your own black ops team."

"How do you know—"

"I watch movies. You—" But before she could finish, large sliding doors opened above. "MISSILES?!"

"Well, RPGs and—"

"AND? There's more!?"

"And live ammunition." William smirked.

"What..."

June panicked and stared at William. Her heart raced as she looked down at the group.

"I don't want to see people get hurt or die! What is this shit? You'll kill them!?"

"Relax, this isn't their first rodeo."

William walked around his desk and stood next to June. He looked out the window and grimaced.

An alarm buzzed as the sound of a timer went off. They made a formation using themselves for cover, almost like a triangle. Three stood in front with two in the middle and one in the back. They took the spray of bullets as if it were simply raining. Then the two on each end spun around and pulled the person behind them up, throwing them about twenty feet into the air to block the incoming missiles with their bodies. The one on the right attempted to punch it, but at that moment, June could notice him missing and getting a face full of rocket. They stopped the rockets in midair while the others used their bodies as shields and to protect themselves from the hail of gunfire.

"This is the training exercise we do. Keep civilians safe, avoid heavy damage, and bring everyone back alive."

June looked out the window, mouth fully opened, and let out a low curse.

"So, when you say we're invulnerable..."

"I mean it."

"The world really is screwed..."

June was bemused. William seemed so much taller than her. She felt small, as if the world around her just grew exponentially.

"Yeah." William put his arm around her shoulders. "Unless people like us make a difference."

June looked away from the window and toward the picture of the infant on William's shelves.

"I'm here for a reason, then. I guess psychology isn't in my future."

William gave her a tender grin.

"I don't believe in destiny, but I believe in people. They can let you down, but they can also make things right."

He sat down in the chair next to her.

"Let me make it up to you. You'll train as a handler. I'll tell you about that later but, it's worth it, trust me. That's what I do. You'll serve with us for a couple of years, hopefully until you retire or..."

June suddenly felt both hopeful but also a sinking feeling.

"...we find a cure," William finished, snapping both of them back from the deep thoughts in their minds.

"A cure?" June said, surprised. "Is that even possible? Would anyone want that?"

She felt conflicted. She just found out she could punch a rocket and survive, but that power in the wrong hands could be terrifying. June missed the times when she would think a gun was the worst thing an individual could have. She noticed William pulling a key ring from his pocket and placing it on his desk.

"It was my panic switch. I press it, and the entire room gets knock-out gas."

June grinned sheepishly.

"I want to trust you, kid. Now, let's show you around."

***

The next day, June awoke with a sense of bewilderment and sat up in her bed. She looked around at people climbing out of their bunkers in what seemed to be a parking garage with all the thick concrete pillars and gray walls. It was a rough first night and the bags under her eyes were proof of that. She felt she just had to go with the flow and try to keep a low profile. In the morning, everyone got up, made their beds, and there were segregated boys' and girls' locker rooms with bathrooms and showers to freshen up, and then it was out into the hallways to pile in with the other hundred or so people forming a queue for the mess hall to get some breakfast. June saw people filling the massive mess hall that opened up to rows of metal benches all illuminated under even more fluorescent lighting. She still didn't know how far down underground they were, miles if yesterday's really loud, very explosive training was anything to go by. She waited about twenty minutes in line before she was able to grab a tray with a plate and see what they had in store for her. Fast food breakfast sandwiches and juice boxes.

"Thanks."

She reached for the fruits and yogurt, noticing there was some Tater Tots and orange slices also being served. She gave the server a weak grin and finally got a good look at most of the kitchen workers. Some were middle-aged but they all seemed to be retired military with the way they carried themselves, arms still muscular enough to crush an apple with just their bare hands. June chuckled to herself as the image amused her. She walked toward the dining area and glanced around. She felt like it was the first day of school again. With a sigh, June tried to find the least populated table to eat her meal.

"Yo! Newbie!" shouted a deep voice from across the hall.

June kept looking down, hoping it was not her they were calling, but no such luck.

"Mighty Mouse! Over here!"

June gave an exasperated sigh and looked up. The voice belonged to a handsome guy with thick eyebrows, deep hazel eyes, a strong jawline, and very unkempt curly hair. June snickered, but she walked toward him. She thought he was cute but felt flushed as she made her way toward his table.

"Have a seat with us, we haven't been formally introduced and William seems to be out on business. I'm Ken, Ken Bennett. This is the crew. William wanted us to show you the ropes."

The six sitting at the table reminded June of the type of friend groups she saw in every teen movie.

"This is Zoe, she's the heart of the group. She's only been here for a year."

Zoe raised herself up slightly off the chair to shake June's hand. June glanced around the dining bench with a wary smile.

"Hi, don't mind him, he's just excited to meet someone new who isn't trying to kill us."

June raised an eyebrow and noticed Zoe seemed to be a little older than her and roughly a few inches taller. Mocha skin and even darker hair kept short with the burgundy highlights giving her an interesting contrast that June found pretty. June admired her outfit and noticed a cute tattoo choker that seemed to have faded with time.

"Like our fearless leader here said, I'm Zoe Creed, been in the company for over a year now. They found me in Jersey. Long story short, I'm a Brick. Yes, I like it here, no I don't like what we do, and don't exactly know why we're like this. No one really does, but we do our best here to get along." Zoe smirked and turned to the young man sitting next to her, who seemed to be staring at June's clothes. "With no help from this one." Zoe quickly pointed at the guy next to her and sat down to take a bite of her sandwich.

"You know you need me! I'm the glue of the group!"

Zoe laughed and the young Japanese man stood up. He didn't reach for June as he gave a slight nod with his head. A tall, light-skinned man with spiky, dark hair. He was dressed in a designer shirt and pants, with a large brand name belt buckle June couldn't recognize but she couldn't look away until he spoke again.

"I'm Jin Kurosawa. Japanese descent raised in Cali. My family thinks I'm becoming a doctor in Oxford U. Also, girl, what are you wearing?"

He pointed at June's oversized long-sleeved plaid shirt over a black T-shirt and black leggings tucked into combat boots. June was wearing the same comfortable outfit she had when she got her tea. She glanced down at her clothes then back up at him and shrugged.

"Jin's also our resident stylist," Zoe said without a hint of irony.

"Girl, I'm fabulous and I need everyone around me to be too!"

June gave a dry chuckle, but she knew deflecting when she saw it. She'd done a lot of it in her life with school counselors and teachers when she really didn't want to talk about herself.

June looked around and noticed the others staring at her as well. June felt her face becoming flush.

"Anyways!" yelled Jin. "You're next!"

He pointed at the guy at the end of the table who seemed shy and seemed as interested in this interaction as June was.

"Fine," said the dark-skinned man in a Letterman jacket with broad shoulders built like a linebacker, wearing fitted jeans and a sports team T-shirt June couldn't make out. He stood up and towered over the others as he rubbed his shaved head. June figured he must have been almost, if not over, six feet tall. His voice seemed higher pitched than June would have imagined and he spoke shyly, but with a hint of pain in his voice.

"Name's Isaac." He cleared his throat. "Brown. My life sucked till I got here. I'm from Texas and..." He trailed off, pondering for a moment. "Will helped me before I did something stupid. It's nice to meet ya."

He sat back down and his lips ticked upward at June as he crossed his arms, then he looked at Jin and Zoe with concern, until the girl next to him nudged him with her elbow.

"You're damn lucky he did!"

Pale-skinned, ashen hair, blue eyes, and possibly as tall as Ken when she stood up. She gave Isaac a big hug and turned to June with a stern expression. Her billowy outfit resembled a retro hippy style with a modern elegant take. June wanted to admire it but then she pointed up and down at June with pursed lips.

"I've been here the longest. They call me Queen, but my name is Freya Solberg. You gotta earn our trust. We're a family here and we've been through some rough times. I know you got the welcome spiel from William and he awed you with our display." She stopped to analyze June. "You have to be careful around here. Because, if you turn on us or threaten any of us, I will personally beat your ass and have you sent to the block."

June was about to form the words but was stopped by the sixth member.

"Yeah, she's our matriarch, you'll have to forgive her."

Freya stared daggers at the nonchalant young man as he placed his book next to his meal and looked back up at June. He was clearly ignoring Freya and beamed like he was about to ask June on a date.

"William said someone important to him was coming and we should take you in."

"Yeah, something about him wanting you to join our team," Ken concurred.

"But he never elaborated," Freya said with a huff.

"Yup, so anyways..." The tanned-skin man dressed in a Vneck shirt and tight jeans stood tall, but he was a few inches shorter than Isaac and had much narrower shoulders. His hair was combed back with copious amounts of gel, and a scruffy stubble lined his chiseled jaw. With a strong handshake, June noticed he seemed to work out his arms quite a bit.

"I'm Hector Ramirez. The block is a prison where all the bad ones go and never come out, and I hail from the faraway land of Florida. Yes, to answer your question." He bowed sheepishly. "I may have wrestled an alligator or two."

June wanted to laugh but she could swear Ken was shooting daggers at Hector as he continued.

"How ya feeling being brought into the circus?"

June forced her lips into an upward curve and shrugged her shoulders thinking of what to say.

"I'm okay. It's nice to meet all of you."

She felt awkward with everyone staring at her.

"But, um, I don't want to be a bother, so I'm just gonna..."

She pointed with her thumb and tried backing away from them. Ken stood back up and put his hand on her shoulder.

"Nonsense. Join us, we wanna know all about you."

June felt her cheeks warm. She wasn't expecting him to be so forward.

"Um, sure, what's the harm?"

June sat down at the end of the table next to Ken.

"So, I'm June. It's nice to meet you all. I'm from California too... I guess. My family died in an accident and, apparently, I was raised by a rogue agent... until they found me."

The group grew silent and attentive. June felt flustered as she felt all eyes on her.

"I, er, so, I traveled a lot and it never occurred to me that I was different. I never had time, trying to always catch up at schools and stuff. Um, anyway, yeah, nice to meet you guys, I'll just get out of your hair—"

"You're her?" asked Freya. "The lost kid?" She looked concerned. "The lost kid who survived the building explosion, then was stolen from the agency?" Talking more to herself than the group, Freya glanced up at June. "That was you!?"

Jin's eyes dart back and forth between Freya and June. "Girl, there are rumors that the agent who stole you wants to eliminate the Bricks and used you to figure out effective ways to kill us."

June blinked and became defensive.

"No, she was my mom, she took care of me."

The group looked at each other.

"Stick with us," said Freya, "I'm sure she'll be back for you."

June felt hesitant with them. Ken studied Freya who seemed to soften up while he had a concerned look on his face.

"You think she'll try to take her again?"

"Maybe, but why?"

June felt conflicted. She loved her mom, but the way they talked about her, she questioned if she really knew Melody at all.

Ken held June's hand and stared her in the eye.

"It's all right, it's all right. We act tough but we stick together."

June couldn't help herself; she squeezed his hand back and then they all started talking, but it all sounded distant to June.

"If William thinks you're okay, then I guess we can trust you."

Freya's eyes darkened and she grew quiet as she finished her meal. June looked around at the group and did her best to join in their conversations.

After learning that her new friends were all around her age, June noted she didn't see any recruits that seemed much older than Freya; everyone was around twenty or under. At least from what she could see in the sea of about a hundred people in the mess hall.

"Are there any other people that are older than us?"

The team nodded and turned toward Freya as she finished her drink.

"Yeah, this is the young adult ward, younger ones are a few floors below, and older folk go up, though some might get sent to other bases to live or work until they're retired. I'm still not sure how that all goes about yet, I've only been here for a couple of years and am still learning something new every day," Freya said with a hint of spite in her voice before glancing up and seeing William rushing into the hall, panting. He spotted June at the table. June noticed he was dressed in a more casual suit than yesterday, but he seemed much more stressed. He hurriedly made his way toward them.

"Morning, troop," he said, exasperated and out of breath.

"Morning, boss," the group said in disorganized unison.

Catching his breath, he turned to June. "Sorry, I was supposed to help you with your routines today, but I couldn't. Something came up. Follow me, I've got stuff for you."

June put down her cold, half-eaten orange slice and got up to follow him.

"I'll clean up for ya," Hector said, grabbing her tray.

Ken raised an eyebrow and turned to June as she stood up and waved goodbye to them.

"See you in class, Mouse," said Ken.

June's eyes tighten with a cringe as she loathed being called that, but she forced a smile.

"How do you like the team?" William asked as he opened the door for June.

"They seem... nice."

2

School of Hard Bricks

June followed William back into his office. Once there, William placed a green duffle bag on his desk next to the large cardboard box that took up half of his equally large desk.

"This is yours, er..."

William searched for a box cutter and found it in his drawer while he tried to maintain conversation.

"We went back to your place and gathered a few of your things and..."

"Was my mom there?" June asked before she could stop herself. William stopped for a moment and shook his head.

"She wasn't there. We have no lead on where she might be," he said, while trying to hide his disappointment. "Ah, here!" he exclaimed. A photo frame with a picture of Melody and baby June. He opened it and pulled out the photo.

"What are you..." William unfolded the picture and showed it to June. Her eyes widened. It was him—it was the three of them together, smiling, when she was about a year old. "What..."

"This is what I meant by trying not to keep things from you.

The truth about your past. I raised you till you were about three or four, when Mel... Melody somehow had it all planned out. We were agents together working on Brick cases, and one day, without warning, I got home to find both of you missing."

William let out a deep sigh and glanced down at the picture with melancholy in his eyes.

"We have tighter security now because of that."

He handed June the picture, and she looked at it closely as William continued to speak.

"Everyone keeps eyes on each other and it's not great, but we haven't lost anyone since."

June sat down and stared at the picture, trying to process it all.

"We didn't want you to be a soldier, at least not unless you wanted to be. Half the people here just want to hide away and try to live normal lives. We give them schooling and online trade courses trying to get them adjusted so when they graduate, they can go up and live a semi-normal life, but things are, well..."

"So you actually let them out after..."

"No. Once deemed safe, they stay here or transfer to another base, working in data analysis or doing other office work for the FBI or the government."

June nodded with scrunched eyebrows. William seemed worried. Something else was on his mind, but June didn't want to push any more. The information was a lot to take in, especially with no sleep and barely any breakfast.

"Um, so now what?" said June, eyeing the box on the desk.

"This will go in your storage locker upstairs. Everyone has one. They keep books, clothes, personal artifacts, or whatever there, and you can access it whenever you want. Eventually, in a few years, you can live in the dorms upstairs, but for now, elevators are down the hall toward the left at the end. Use this key card to access it. You won't be able to go to any other floor for the time being. And... We'll talk about your future here later."

William handed her a blank white plastic card with her name on it and the same government logo as his badge.

It read:

B.R.I.C.

Biological Research, Identification, & Containment.

June raised an eyebrow and pocketed the card, smiling weakly at William.

"We brought you a few clothes here to get you started. We'll pack these in your locker. The rest we'll store. Laundry is next to the lockers, lunch is daily between noon and one, and dinner is at six. All in the same area. Classes are past the dining hall and your schedule will be in your locker along with your books. You can open it with your key card, should be number 225. If you feel like you're up for training, the playground's off limits unless you're training as a team, but we do have a gym near the classrooms."

"That is a lot to take in... Also, library or coffee place?"

June felt she needed a place to think if she was going to spend the next few years here, and she hoped for a quiet area.

William gave a nod. "Of course. That's past the classroom, coffee is in the mess hall but you have to ask for it.

"Well, I have to do a ton of paperwork. You can grab your things and head off. Don't lose your key. Getting a new one is a pain."

William walked around his desk toward June and awkwardly gave her a hug. June was frozen in confusion.

"Sorry, I... I've missed you and..." He trailed off. "...I should have asked first. I'm sorry."

"No, no, it's okay, this is all new to me, and it's weird knowing you were the crazy stalker dad that I pictured very differently in my head." June noticed William's confused face and changed the subject. "Hey, do you... I'm sorry, I don't know if I should ask, or even if you have any..." She sighed and dropped her shoulders. "My real parents. The ones who..."

William shook his head somberly. "Nothing left. Everything was lost in the fire. Or buried in rubble. I'm... I'm sorry."

June looked down at her feet as she nodded.

"Lester and Harmony Freeman. Simple folk, regular nine to five, nothing extraordinary from what their records showed."

"Is June my real name?"

"Yes." William walked back around the desk.

"June Freeman. We were gonna keep your name but Melody convinced me that it would be weird and a logistical hassle, and you became June Romero. We put you under Melody's name since she's the one who adopted you. I'm not too sure what she filled out, because we were just dating at the time and I had an important mission going on. It makes sense now. It made it easier to keep us from your scent, but I'm glad we found you before someone else did."

"Is that really everything you have on my parents? Just names?"

"Afraid so, kid. You probably should get to class, you need to learn about yourself and be ready for missions, so..."

"Class?" said June, realizing she wouldn't get the rest she needed.

"It helps with orientation and gives the others something to do. We want to keep your mind sharp while you're here and keep you posted with any new findings."

"Oh, okay," she said, furrowing her brow. "I'll go there now." She nodded and crossed her arms. "Do I... How do I..."

"Oh, right, back the way you came, showers and lockers for your clothes are on the right before the dorms. Classes are..."

"I've seen the signs, I'll just..." She pointed outward with her thumbs.

June walked away feeling heavy and not fully focusing. She didn't even say goodbye or hear what William said before closing his door.

***

She felt her lips purse as she stared at the locker room door and couldn't remember how she got there. The large locker room was filled with rows of standing lockers big enough to fit two of her inside. The red walls contrasting with the metal lockers and benches made this seem more like a gym than a school. It felt different from the rest of the base, breaking up the monotony of concrete walls. June searched for the locker with her number on it and opened it up with the key card William gave her. Some of her things were already neatly packed on the shelves while clothes hung on hangers. She grabbed a few things and headed toward the showers. Past the lockers were doorways on each side and the female showers were on her right. She wondered what the difference was and noticed the menstrual product dispenser on the wall. June shook her head and took a deep breath as she tried to keep her influx of different feelings at bay. She walked past the enclosed shower rooms and noticed the gray tiles lining the sectioned showers. She placed her clean clothes on the bench, took off her boots and socks, and walked into the stall. June opened the door and placed the clothes she was wearing in a small basket to the right of the shower. Noticing the generic brands of body wash and hair products, June sighed and turned the water on.

***

Walking out of the steaming shower, June grabbed the clothes she left on the bench and reminisced about shopping for them with her mom. June wanted to put on something less baggy so as not to appear too childlike to her peers. She hated it, though, but Melody convinced her how much more mature she looked in her crop tops and skinny jeans. June still put on her favorite boots out of spite. She resented her size, but remembered all the times Melody would try to convince her it was an advantage. *"The more your enemies underestimate you, the easier you'll destroy them,"* she would say to June. June nodded to herself, realizing how much that meant now knowing who Melody truly was. She threw on her plaid shirt to keep her back from getting cold and sat down on the bench across from her locker. She put her hands on her face as she failed to hold back her tears.

***

William sat down at his desk and answered his ringing cell-phone.

"Director McAfee, yes, she seems to be acclimating. It's always a process. I know she'll do well. ... Well, we don't have any leads and we are on high alert, sir. ... I understand. We'll catch her. As for Villalobos's Zealots, we're monitoring their progress. ... Undercover agent hasn't contacted us either. ... No, sir." William's voice hardened. "We can't afford to lose any more, sir."

After a pause, William took a deep breath and turned back to the family picture of the three of them.

"Sir, we have no idea where she is, but as far as we know, she hasn't made contact. We are monitoring the Purist group closely and I'll keep you updated. Plus, the South American cult is being closely monitored. ... She hasn't, sir. She's only a child, but she didn't know anything. She thought they were just running from an abusive husband. ... Yes, sir. Didn't even tell her about me, apparently. The apartment had nothing on any collaborations, just signs of the two of them trying to get by. ... Understood. I will. She'll be key. If what we know is true, then she's very special and we can't lose her again."

William closed his eyes and hung up the phone. He pulled out a box of files from a pile toward the back of his office and began to work on all of June's paperwork. He sighed as he lifted his cup of coffee to drink, but it was empty.

***

June had spent the good portion of an hour just holding her head in her hands. She walked to the sink and washed her face. She stared at herself in the mirror and noticed how puffy her eyes were and how red her nose was. She sighed deeply and splashed water on her face again in the hope that it would calm down. She dried her face with a paper towel and walked away without glancing at herself in the mirror. June closed her eyes and pinched the bridge of her nose as she saw the stacks of books that were already placed inside her locker along with a schedule. She peered at the schedule and up at the clock on the wall. Math was next in room one hundred two.

Letting out a frustrated sigh, she grabbed the required book and a notepad, then walked toward the classrooms. Passing the dining hall, she noticed the staff getting ready for lunch. Meatballs getting carted in from the kitchens and bread being prepared to toast. She passed the mess hall and was hit with high school. The doorways, the lockers, the motivational posters. She shook her head and tried to remember she was miles underground and that everyone here could take a rocket to the face. None of this was normal, no matter what coat of paint it had. June found room one hundred two and walked in as quietly as she could but already felt all eyes were on her. She gave a quick smile and tried to find a seat quickly. The teacher, a burly man who seemed more suitable as a lumberjack than a math teacher, stopped what he was writing and walked up to her.

"Hi, you must be June. They told me you were coming in today. Surprised you actually did, since new recruits usually have an existential crisis for a few days. I'm Benjamin, Axel Benjamin. You can call me Mr. B. There's a chair on the right back there for you.

"I'm told you're in your senior year, so I hope you know what I'm covering. If you need help, just raise your hand. We're here to help. It's not like we're going anywhere."

June tried to appear pleasant and glanced around the classroom but didn't recognize anyone. She made her way to a desk while everyone else seemed much more interested in writing notes and keeping their faces in their books. June raised her hand and Mr. B, confused but impressed she was communicating, called on her.

"So, do we have class all throughout summer here?"

The class gave a chortle as Mr. B beamed and replied, "This is to test how well you're doing and apply knowledge into everyday life. The better prepared the student, the quicker they move on to the next phase of job placement."

June nodded but didn't fully understand.

Mr. B called on her to answer a question, but she was so bewildered she didn't even know what he was talking about.

"Uh..." She looked at the board and saw a garbled mess of letters and numbers. "The square..."

Mr. B grinned. "It's okay. The first day is always over-whelming. You need to find X. What's the process? You remember PEMDAS, right?"

June rested her elbows on the desk and her head in her hands and let out a sigh as the professor continued.

***

June left the class and looked at her schedule. "Science..." She opened her locker and realized she left the books back at the shower locker. "Crap." The bell rang and she grabbed her notebook and made her way toward class. She stood at the doorway, noticing the long tables with plastic chairs that reminded her of her chemistry classes in high school. Jin and Zoe smiled and waved at her. She mirrored the gesture and was about to wait until everyone else sat down to find her place, but the duo rushed up and grabbed her by the arms and sat her down with them.

"Forgot your book?" Jin shook his head. "Happens to us all

the time. How can we be expected to do school and save the world all at the same time?"

Zoe let out a dry chuckle while rolling her eyes.

"Save the world?" June asked, unsure of his sarcasm as she prepared her notebook on the table. Zoe noticed and put her hand on June's back.

"Don't mind him. We do have to do a lot, but not everyone does. If you're on a team like ours, it's difficult, but they cut us some slack. School here is all year round."

"So, you do go on black ops missions?"

"Yeah, we need to be a little hush-hush about it, but we get to go out compared to everyone else. They're kind of stuck here until they get to move on..."

Zoe shrugged and pulled out her books. She placed them on the table and turned to glance at Jin's notes, giving a quick nod before continuing.

"Everyone else kind of ages out like in an orphanage. We usually get called out for a few days at a time, and when we come back the teachers fill us in so we don't fall behind. It helps, but..."

Jin looked at Zoe with concern, then he turned to June.

"Girl, my first few classes here were tough, but thanks to her and Freya and meeting the others, we've been on top of each other to do better. That's why I want you to know, we know how it is. We seem nonchalant about this whole situation, but trust me, Mighty Mouse, your big puppy dog eyes are gonna be safe with us."

June let out a small groan.

"You're such a sap."

Jin and Zoe chuckled and turned to June, who was looking down at her blank notepad, lost in thought. Zoe held her hand.

"You're gonna be okay."

She nodded and they glanced up as the teacher was just walking in.

"Good morning, class. Is... ah, there you are. Ms. Romero, pleasure to have you in class."

June's eyes widened as she was not expecting to be called out so suddenly.

"Like I told everyone here at some point, do not be afraid to ask. We're here to help you live a normal life... even if we're miles underground and have indestructible skin. So, feel free to raise your hand and I'll try to help any way I can. Oh, and you can call me Ms. Carter."

The short-haired woman of average stature, with dark skin and light brown eyes, appeared more like a model than any of the science teachers June ever had. She felt compelled to raise her hand.

"That was quick, Ms. Romero. How can I help?"

"Are... you..." June paused, searching for the right words. "Is everyone here, teachers included, like, indestructible?"

Ms. Carter sniffed as she grabbed a book from her bag and placed it on the podium.

"Here's the thing, and don't worry, you're not the first to ask this and probably won't be the last."

Ms. Carter's eyes looked down toward the left as if disappointed in the answer she was about to give.

"What we know is that a lot of us, yes, myself included, have developed a Kevlar type of skin. Impact makes it tighten together and the atoms on our skin creates an indestructible barrier that makes penetration or impacts nigh impossible. I've had some students graduate and move on to study what we are, but it's all so new. Probably a little over a few decades since its discovery and less since the agency was formed as a task force to find and deal with anomalies."

It all sounded rehearsed to June but the disappointment in her voice was pretty clear. She had probably said this speech countless times. Somehow, knowing the adults also had some things they were unsure of made June incredibly uneasy. June gave a tight-lipped nod and looked down at her notebook.

"Ms. Romero, we're all in this together. We have Dr. Glendale, our head of research, working around the clock making new discoveries and studying our anomalies as best she can, so please be patient."

June nodded softly and placed the pen on her notebook as Ms. Carter clasped her hands.

"And now let's catch you up on this week's studies. Page two hundred ten, chapter fourteen, the digestive tract."

June glanced around the room, and everyone was focused on their books.

"What we know about this is that the outer layer of the skin is flexible, durable, and almost indestructible. Inside, from what we have gathered, it is equally strong at its first layer and weaker as it goes. The organs, particularly the stomach, kidneys, and gallbladder have a thinner lining, similar to the heart, that in many cases are almost normal and require a little more force than usual to penetrate. They can still withstand deadly explosions." The teacher pointed at someone near June.

"Yes, Mark."

A scruffy-looking young man had his hand raised with a puzzled face.

"You said the heart is the most delicate part of the body, how is it more delicate than the rest of these?"

Ms. Carter gave an acknowledging nod and replied, "The heart is delicate because, despite it still having a stronger lining, the arteries and veins that flow through are much thinner and much more susceptible to damage. A well-placed shock with no protection can cause them to burst and it's the closest to walking dead an anomaly can be before the heart expires."

Mark nodded as he took notes.

"Kidneys and other thin tubes can also experience such damage but because of the distance from the heart, a person may recover. Remember in chapter eight, we talked about rapid healing and how slow anomalous cells die despite how quickly they reconstitute."

June was confused. She sat forward, putting her cheek on her hand, and felt an uncontrollable tear run down her cheek just as Zoe made eye contact with her.

"Teach, I gotta go... you know."

Zoe gave a quick nod toward June.

"Of course," said Ms. Carter with a soft expression. "Take Ms. Romero."

Zoe gave a quick knowing glance toward Jin as she got up and took June by the hand and walked her out of the classroom. June could hear Ms. Carter continue speaking to the class but felt dazed and her eyes became blurry as they filled with tears.

June and Zoe made it to the restroom down the hall when Zoe put her hands on June's shoulders.

"It's okay. We've all been there. You can go to a stall and let it out. I'll be here if you need me."

June was confused but felt the tears swelling up uncontrollably.

"We miss home. Triggers can come from anything. Even

if home wasn't the best, it's what we knew. Take your time, 'kay? I'll be right outside if you need me."

June nodded and walked into a stall. As soon as she heard the door close behind her, she sat there crying again. June shook her head and rolled up as much paper as she could around her hand as the tears wouldn't stop coming.

Zoe was sitting on the floor outside across from the door when June finally stepped out, eyes red and puffy. Zoe pulled out a water bottle from her backpack.

"Here, put this over your eyes on and off every few seconds to reduce the swelling, hon."

June grabbed the bottle and gently put it over her right eye first.

"Sorry, couldn't find an ice pack."

Zoe put her arm around June and they began walking down the hall.

"Listen, I know this sucks, like major suckage, but Ms. Carter is right, we're all here to help each other and..."

"And be weapons for them?" June cut her off with her voice trembling in anger. "Kidnap others like us? Keep us down here like... Like in concentration camps?"

June felt her hopeless rage boiling to the surface. Zoe could only offer her an empathetic look.

"We are guinea pigs to an agency that doesn't even know what we are and they treat us like weapons, like we're freaking black ops to, I'm assuming, topple governments and kidnap others like us, or even kill people like us who don't want to join?!"

June's voice cracked as she tried to step away from Zoe, but Zoe put her hands on June's shoulders.

"You have every right to question this. Yeah, this seems

wrong, on a lot of levels, but it could be worse. Other governments are trying to violently eliminate or dissect us. We're trying to keep some peace. It seems weird as heck, and wrong, but we are trying to make the world safe from people like us who feel like they can do whatever they want."

June's gaze lowered.

"I know you've just met me, but trust me when I say, I've been in your shoes, thinking about how this is the worst thing that could have happened to me, but once I saw how much worse it is out there, suddenly being an asset here doesn't sound all that bad and Imma be honest with you, I've seen some bad, traumatizing shit out there." Zoe's eyes watered before whispering, "The things I've seen them do, I won't let that happen again. If we can stop it, if we can create a world safe for us, I'll take it. I know you gotta feel your feelings, but know that you're a lucky one and the world needs people like us more than ever."

Her tight grip lessened around June's shoulders.

"Listen, we're not all agents or whatever, some of the others just want to hide and get by, but if we do become agents, we get a little better treatment and get some time outside. So, I think that's why William wants you to become one, but for now, let's just get back to class. We still got a few minutes left, and Ms. C's one of the more understanding of the teachers, probably 'cause she was like us once."

"I just, I'm sorry." June closed her eyes and shook her head. "I... My family's a lie, my real family's dead, and this is so much to take in."

Zoe took a deep breath and hugged June. She hesitated for a moment, but hugged her back tightly.

Back at the classroom's entrance, the two stood in front of

the door as June wiped away tears.

"If you need to go again, don't hesitate. Me and Jin are pretty good note takers, so we won't let you miss out on anything."

"Jin and I," corrected Ms. Carter as she opened the door. "Come in, please, and relax. You've got a few minutes before the next class starts. Swap whatever notes you can and be ready."

Zoe and June nodded and took their seats.

"You two okay?" The corner of Jin's mouth ticked upward.

Zoe nodded and turned to June who was focused on trying not to cry. Jin pursed his lips and slid his notebook toward Zoe. "You didn't miss much, something about a new enzyme, but I wrote it in there."

***

As June finished packing her books and gave back Jin's notes, the bell rang and they all prepared to move on to the next class.

"Wha— What's next?" June asked Jin and Zoe who were already packed and ready to go.

"Well," said Jin, as he looked at her schedule and nodded. "Baby girl, you're gonna wanna go to one o' eight for Dr. Drew's class. See you at lunch later." Jin put his hands on her shoulders and made an earnest face. "Do not hesitate to ask for help, 'kay? If you need to bolt from class and take some time, you just ask. Drew's pretty chill with that."

Zoe and Jin hugged June and went on their way, leaving June to find the class.

June walked into Dr. Drew's class and a plump, tall, jolly-looking man with balding gray hair and rosy cheeks welcomed the students as they came in before his eyes locked onto June.

"Welcome, dear, I'm sure you've already been introduced at the other classes so come, come, have a seat. If you need anything, just raise your hand, okay?"

He clapped his hands together and continued talking to the class.

"Welcome, welcome. Where did we leave off yesterday... Ah! Here we go into learning about the difference between Poe and modern writers who have taken inspiration from him. Your Kings, Koontz's, and Barkers. Poe created dread in short stories using the tools of his time. Here you will learn the basics of how literature can shape perception and how perception has changed us."

June raised concerned eyebrows and opened her notebook.

"Sup, Mighty Mouse?" whispered a voice from behind.

June turned to Ken and the rest of the group sitting behind her. She must have missed them when she walked in.

"Hey," June replied, trying not to get the teacher's attention and hurriedly taking notes.

"Horror has identified us from the dawn of time," the professor continued. "The cavemen of old would draw what's meaningful to them, what they hunted, and what hunted them. Their fears evolved into what we know today as fear of the unknown. Like how we spoke of Shelly yesterday and how science was an unknown. The possibilities were endless and she wrote one of the most enduring stories of all time. Poe, too, created timeless stories of fear, but not of science, of the supernatural kind. But it was a horror that reached inward. It wasn't vampires or werewolves, it was the human psyche. Terrors are often caused by the guilt of the wicked or conflicted

41

characters that could not handle their stress."

The professor paused and looked around the room with clasped hands.

"We are living in confusing times. Humanity is always confused, anything new is dangerous. Thus, instead of secluding ourselves such as in *The Tell-Tale Heart*, I want you all to partner up and use humanity's greatest weapon, the mind, to rationalize what some of Poe's characters could have done differently to avoid their fates. So find someone. I believe we're all evened out now, and two per group can handle this assignment."

June glanced back to see Ken smiling at her. She felt herself blushing.

"Sup, Mighty Mouse. You can relax, I don't bite... Why do people say that?"

June shrugged.

"Should ask the doc to see if that was a thing in 'ye olden times'. Anyway, you wanna team up?" he finished with clasped hands and a goofy grin. His face became softer when he saw June smirk and pull her hair behind her ear. June suppressed a laugh and looked back at the professor. He gave them a side-eyed glance before shaking his head and walked to his desk. June blanched until Ken put his hand on her back.

"June, you can relax here. This is a safe place and we won't let anything bad happen to you. It's all right, it's all right."

The honesty in his face made June want to cry and fall into his arms. June crossed her arms and stared at her book. She just held her elbows, before quickly glancing up at Ken.

"Th-thanks, I, er, have to..." She trailed off and focused on her notepad. Ken smiled and turned to the others.

"I'm gonna help her out. See you guys later?"

Issac nodded, and Hector was already up talking to another girl. Ken sat next to June.

"You really don't have to worry, we all started off like you. Scared, abandoned, in need of some TLC. 'Sides we need to work together soon, so why not start with some class work?"

June smirked while looking down at her book.

"Okay, but only 'cause everyone else is pretty much taken."

"All right." Smiling and scooting his chair closer, Ken said in a triumphant tone, "Hurrah for teamwork."

June felt her face blush and leaned closer to her book.

***

After class, June and Ken finished packing up and headed out. "See you at lunch, Mighty Mouse," Ken said with a glowing grin. June gave him a soft smile in return. Hector and Isaac waved at her. She waved back, trying not to blush.

June headed to her locker to leave her books. Along the way, she heard the familiar duo of Zoe and Jin calling her.

"Sup, June! So, girl, how was your last class?"

Jin beamed mischievously. Zoe gave him a nudge with her elbow and told him to be nice.

"He's just teasing. But for real, how's it going, lady?"

June's mouth quirked and got a little flustered about working together with Ken before snapping back.

"It's been good... Yeah, real good."

Zoe and Jin looked at each other and back at June. "So?" they said in unison.

"What?"

"How was class with Ken?" Jin smirked.

"I, uh..."

43

"We're just teasing. Come with us. We're heading toward lunch."

June nodded and followed them.

They had finally made it down the line and gotten their lunch when they heard Hector yelling from their usual table.

"Yo! Mighty Mouse joins us once more!"

"She's still not sick of us, yet!" Jin teased as he went around him to sit and gave Isaac a soft slap on the shoulder. The group began to eat and talk about their day. June just listened and noticed Ken glance at her. She took a bite of her salad as the others bit down on what she assumed was either a sloppy Joe or a meatball sandwich, and noticed Ken smiling at her. She tried to reciprocate, but she felt overwhelmed.

"So, how's your first day going?" Ken asked as the group looked at June.

"I-I... It's going," she replied, surprised at everyone staring intently at her.

"You're doing great," Zoe cut in. "She's doing great. This is a lot to take in."

"Yeah," Hector concurred. "It's not easy for us or anyone else here."

"God, you remember when Mark came..." Freya said in a whispered tone.

"He was bawling uncontrollably," said Ken, matching her tone.

"We just want to make sure you're doing all right, Mighty Mouse," Hector said as he bit into his sandwich. He gave June a wink then turned to Ken, whose face grew serious before Isaac spoke, drawing everyone's attention.

"This ain't a great environment; we're all different here but going through the same shit."

Isaac stared at the table where he hadn't yet touched his sandwich.

"It sucks, but we try to make our little support groups and help each other out since..."

June waited for him to finish. She noticed their faces grow somber. The awkward silence made Freya agitated.

"Fine, I'll tell her. His name is Ryan. Ryan..." She hesitated.

"Borden," said Zoe, a visible gloom over her face.

"Yeah, well, anyway, Ryan was the last new recruit we had before you. Same story: found by an agent, brought in, and had trouble adjusting. Turned out he *really* had a hard time adjusting."

"Not really our fault, though," said Jin, seemingly lost in his memories.

"He had issues way before he got here," Freya continued "He'd cry, say he's feeling trapped and he couldn't go back to his life's work. We thought he was really into selling hardware, or whatever it was he did at his shop. He somehow managed to be... charismatic, yet vulnerable. We all wanted to help him. This was probably a year or two ago; Zoe had just joined, so maybe two?"

She and Zoe agreed with a shrug.

"Anyway, Ryan would sob a few times during class and constantly go to the bathroom, and we just thought he was having a hard time transitioning. Like we all did." Freya swallowed and her eyes glistened as tears formed. "Then, people started disappearing."

June's eyebrows snapped up.

"It was kind of the last thing we expected. He targeted the normies first. Starting with Susan, the kitchen cook. They found her in the trash can that gets taken up to be disposed of, he... I'll save you the details, but he liked to take his time. When he got to his first Brick, well, we found out our necks can be snapped with enough force. He figured it out and..." Freya looked up, as if the memory was playing out in her mind, before continuing. "She was sixteen, a runaway, confused about her powers, and she wasn't in our group. She hung around with Tom and them over there." She pointed to a scrappy-looking slender man with a scruffy beard a few tables away. "They keep to themselves a lot nowadays."

"Definitely counting the days till they go up," Jin said, glancing at them sadly as Freya nodded and continued.

"Ryan shoved her body in a crevice he dug himself whenever he would go to a specific stall in the bathroom. Then he'd wait for lights out to retrieve it and put it in the dumpsters that would be taken up. Of course, when security noticed it, it was a matter of time before they closed in on him. William told us each individually so he wouldn't get wise. So that night we all hit the bunks and..."

Freya took a breath and June felt Ken's hand on her back. She wanted to look at him but was too invested in what Freya was saying.

"It was under the guise of a mission, that'd we'd all be together and get ready in the morning. We had our gas masks at the ready under the sheets, but Ryan had seen through the ruse, apparently. So when the gas was released, he quickly got up, put on Isaac's mask, who was the closest to him, and went for Hector next. The guards rushed in for him but they were no match. We didn't expect him to be so ready for us. Isaac and Hector down, Ken tried to talk to him while I was..."

June noticed Freya didn't want to say this part.

"I was crying and hiding under my bed," Zoe said, feeling

ashamed of herself. "I had just joined, and I was confused. Still trying to get used to this."

Freya's mouth twisted with a frown and she continued. "Ken tried to tackle him but he learned how to leap pretty high and took off his mask, then found Zoe and pulled her mask off. Then mine." Freya's glance lowered and Hector reached under the table to hold her hand. "And we were all out after that for a while. According to William, he killed about four more guards before Tom and his group came in to help when they heard the commotion... and it took everything they had not to kill Ryan on the spot." Freya swallowed, trying to hold back her seething anger. "After that, um... Well, Ryan's being held in the prison below us."

Ken rubbed June's back to make her feel better, but it wasn't working.

"So, we've been wary of newcomers. We were scared of you at first but, seems like you've had a lot going on. Ryan, turns out, was wanted for the murder of several women before he was brought in here."

Hector got closer to Freya, and she leaned her shoulder against his. Ken took his hand away and turned toward June. June gave him a concerned sigh and glanced down at her plate of salad. She had lost her appetite. She then looked up at everyone and didn't really know what to say. Jin, who had been uncharacteristically quiet for a while, finally spoke.

"Well, life sucks and we never know when it's our time. So, we gotta stick close and love who you love!" Jin gave Zoe a big hug. Zoe hugged him back without saying a word.

"Come on, we have a few minutes to finish this slop and get to class. June, what's your next class, baby girl?" Jin waited for June to reply. June noticed them, seemingly uncomfortable with the memory.

"I, uh." June pulled out her schedule from her pocket. "Calculus?" she said, feeling unsure.

"Gomez," said Isaac. "I got him next, too. You can come with me. I'll show you where it's at."

"Thanks." June's cheek twitched. The mood was definitely heavy after their story. Her mind raced until she heard the bell. It was time for the remaining classes. She cleaned up after herself and followed Isaac to class. He was just as quiet and solemn as he was in the lunchroom.

"So, how did you end up here?" she asked cautiously.

Isaac shrugged his shoulders and pointed with his chin toward their classroom. June sighed and braced herself for a long class.

***

Later that evening, the team met up in the mess hall and sat down for dinner. Everyone started talking a little more cheerfully, trying to forget lunch's macabre story. June noticed Ken sitting a little closer to her and trying to include her more into their conversations.

"Mighty Mouse, what was your favorite movie growing up?"

June took a second to remember, her life seemed like a distant memory despite living it just a day ago.

"I wanna say *North by Northwest*," she said after giving it a thought.

"Whoa! Mouse hitting hard with Hitchcock!" said Ken, surprised.

"You and Hector should pass notes. Dude loves *Psycho*!"

They laughed as Hector turned to June with a wide grin.

"I do, I love Hitchcock, the man ran a ridiculously tight ship, but he got the results he wanted. He even made birds scary, bro!"

Zoe sighed loudly and threw her head back. "Y'all are basic. Hitchcock knew suspense. But his characters were all the worst humanity had to offer. Dude was making nihilistic cinema. I like having something with a little more realism and slightly more hopeful. Life sucks too much. I don't wanna leave a movie feeling worse than I went in."

Jin chuckled and looked at Zoe with a raised eyebrow. "And that's why you like the movies made by the mouse. Horrifying ethics, but at least their movies make you feel good."

Zoe slapped his arm. "I'll have you know, sir, I like Disney and I like *Shrek* 2, and I have no qualms about it!"

"Is that why you emulate him down to the smell?"

Zoe gasped and grabbed a book from her bag, before slapping Jin in the arm with it.

"How dare you, sir. I. AM. A. DELICATE. FLOWER!" Zoe said in a cheerfully, violent manner.

The group laughed wholeheartedly except for Isaac, whose shoulders bounced as he chuckled softly. June felt it was right to ask what his favorite movie was.

"What's your favorite, Isaac?"

"Er, I don't watch movies," he said dryly.

Freya cut in, giving Ken a quick glance. "Well, my favorite movie is *Legally Blonde*. It's clever, funny, speaks volumes about society while also having a realistic yet happy ending, but I do also love *The Princess Bride*."

Ken beamed as he crossed his arms and leaned back in his chair. "I'll give you that one. It's a good movie, the other one, though..."

"What do you—"

June was cut off by the team when they suddenly stared behind her. William walked up to the table, catching his breath. "We need you. Alpha, get ready. We leave tomorrow at o' six hundred."

The team stopped smiling and nodded their heads.

"Yes, sir," Ken said, wiping his mouth with a napkin.

"June, you'll be with me. It's time to start training you in what you're gonna be doing here. I hope I can count on you, but..." He sighed. "It's your choice." He then lingered over the table without saying a word and palmed June on the head before walking off.

June nodded her head and looked around to see if anyone else was going to say anything.

"Good," said William. "Six a.m. Okay. You guys will meet at my office for mission details. Get some rest." William quickly pulled his hand back as if realizing he didn't mean to do that.

"Good night," he said and quickly walked away.

"What the hell was that?!" said Jin.

Freya was just as confused. "I've never seen him like that."

June raised an eyebrow.

"He usually just tells us the time he wants us, makes a quick comment about what it might be, and leaves. He straight up gave you a dad pat and wants you to join us?" Ken said as he studied June, crossing his arms again.

"Dude still thinks he's your dad?" chuckled Hector.

"He 'hopes he can count on you'?" repeated Jin, making air quotes.

"That... That was new," Freya said, taking the last bite of her steak.

"Well, let's finish up here and call it a night soon, then," Ken said with a sigh.

"It's probably going to be a long flight, and an emotionally damaging experience soon," said Jin sarcastically.

June wanted to ask but couldn't find the words. Freya looked at her and knew June felt lost.

"Mission time is usually us, Team Alpha, going in, capturing a rogue Brick, or stopping some terrorist group, or at the very least, convincing someone like you to join us."

"Who brought me in?" asked June impulsively.

"Delta, if I'm not mistaken."

"Oh."

"They're up near Jersey."

June shook her head and continued her original train of thought. "Anyway, I figured that, it's just..." June's eyes darted as she tried to form the words. "Well, I thought we'd have more time to have, like, a meeting, and then, like, suit up or something. You know, like in the movies?"

June shrugged. Ken and Freya gave each other knowing looks before turning back toward June.

"It's definitely *not* like in the movies, mostly 'cause it's on a time frame. They tell us things on the fly. That's why people like William, and Quinn from the Texas base, run around like chickens with no heads. It's chaotic as new sightings occur, or attacks, so they have to do everything and have it all set up before we go in. Later, on the way, they fill us in and we need to come up with a plan on the spot."

"Which is why today was weird," said Zoe. "We got a heck of a heads-up. So, just eat and rest. It's gonna be a long day tomorrow."

June nodded, slowly letting it sink it. The team became quiet again and continued to eat their meal.

3

Gods or Monsters

The following morning, June was startled awake with Zoe looming over her. She placed a finger on her lips and shushed June. June rubbed her eyes and sat up. Freya beckoned her to follow them toward the lockers.

"Hey, rookie, dress comfy. I think it's gonna be a long flight."

"Where're we going?"

"Not sure. William hasn't told us yet. The guys are gonna meet us here soon, and then we'll head out to his office."

"Yeah, have you ever flown before?"

June glanced at Freya and shook her head. Freya waved a hand and they headed toward the showers to change.

"You'll be fine. If your ears hurt, try popping them... Where's my... Oh." Freya grabbed a mask and added it to the pile of black clothes she was holding on to that caught June's eye.

"What's that?"

"It's a padded balaclava-style mask with built-in air filtration for gasses, and the visor has night vision goggles made of bulletproof fog-resistant lenses. Helps during raids where we set off the gasses and detain our target. It's all got light Kevlar padding 'cause, you know, we really don't need a lot, but reinforced joints help protect our sensitive bits." Freya chuckled, but June looked concerned.

"The zipper here in the chest is covered by this pack. It's got four slim pockets for storage." Freya slipped on the black vest. June noticed the belt along the waist with soda can-sized pockets. Freya continued explaining as she adjusted the straps. "These contain the sleeping gas canisters, a military knife in the slit back here," she pointed under the belt on the back, "and a stun gun." She pointed at the pocket above it, then lightly patted the sides of her thighs. "Legs contain pouch pockets on each side and foot coverings, and it's all made of the thermal regulating lining, so we're okay in any weather. Oh, and we have regular military-style combat boots." Freya chuckled. "But you've already got that covered."

June smiled at how her black boots were similar to the ones Freya and Zoe were wearing. Freya placed the mask on to do a check, and June noticed the small breathing apparatus on the cheek. It made sense to June after hearing the story of the serial-killing Brick. The goggles seemed very thick and had circuits surrounding them. Zoe walked back out from getting fully dressed as Freya patted her shoulder and walked into the showers to put on the suit. Zoe grinned at June, and an awkward silence filled the room.

"So, um…" Zoe started.

"How often do you guys do this? Missions, I mean."

Zoe scratched her head with a gloved hand. "Maybe once or twice a month, though sometimes we can go a few months without any incidents or, like, one after another."

"Is it, like... dangerous?" June knew it was a stupid question, but she felt she had to kill time since she had already finished getting dressed. She kept her leggings on and threw on her oversized plaid shirt over her William tank, rounding off the outfit with athletic socks under her favorite boots. Zoe answered. "It's usually pretty chill. Sometimes, like I told you before, we see some shit that would make your skin crawl. Girl, there is so much I wish I could unsee."

"Do you regret it? Being here?"

"No, not really..." Zoe sighed. "I regret not being able to help more. I used to do so much back in my community—"

"Yo! Ya ready?" Jin yelled as the rest of the guys walked in.

Freya stepped out of the showers, rolling her eyes. "Yeah, yeah. We're ready."

"Good, we got about fifteen minutes before spaghetti strap expects us at his office."

"Relax, Ken, you always get like this. We're ready, let's go."

The group walked out to Isaac and Hector, waiting for them in the hall. They all dressed in the same suits, making June feel like she was in a comic book.

"All right, team." Ken clapped his hands and led the way. "Back into the fray."

June swallowed. She paused for a moment, falling behind from the group.

Jin watched June with a raised eyebrow and shook his head with a sigh.

"Let's go, Mouse," he said with an eye roll.

June tensed up. "I don't like it when you guys call me that," she said, shocking herself. "Sorry, I just, I don—"

"Say no more. We gotcha," Freya said proudly. "Come on,

we don't wanna be late on your first mission."

June tried to hide her embarrassment, but Zoe held her arm out and gave her an approving nod. "You're gonna be fine, sis."

"All right, you heard the queen, we can't be late," Ken said. The team walked out toward William's office and June realized they were checking each other's suits for openings.

***

The team arrived with William already waiting for them. He was dressed in an all-black casual suit with aviator sunglasses on his head. He was waiting with two other guards.

"All right, let's get started."

William nodded, and the soldiers checked the team's gear, ensuring there weren't any gaps in the suits. After the all clear, the men gave William a thumbs-up, and they made their way down a hallway June hadn't been through before. They stopped at the large elevator doors. June hadn't seen this elevator, and as it opened, she noticed it even had benches on each side glowing in a metallic blue sheen. June couldn't tell if the paint or the lights gave off that color. The team climbed in and sat along the sides, with William sitting closest to the door. He tapped his key card against the panel and pressed a button. He crossed his arms, looked up, and leaned against the wall before remembering June was there.

"Oh, hey, kid. How... Did you sleep okay? The ride's long, so you can relax now. I'll explain everything in a bit." William turned to address the team. "Okay, team. We tracked a problematic Brick in South America. Should be about an eight-hour flight before we reach the destination. Remember, once the target is located, make sure to keep witnesses and collateral damage to a minimum. Intel shows our target likes to live like a king and has taken a drug lord's compound and all of his assets by force. *Do not* engage in a fight if he is out and about. We are going to the compound. We'll drop about seven miles out in the jungle and head east toward his location. I'll give you more details on the flight."

William rubbed his eyes and pulled out his phone, turning his attention to June and noticing the unamused expression on her face.

"I want you to see what we do firsthand."

He went to reach out for her hand, but stopped himself.

"I want you to know that I..."

He looked around the elevator, and all eyes were on them.

"I want to train you to be my successor."

June's face must have seemed incredibly shocked because William immediately started to stumble on his words.

"I—we—the plan was—the... No. Okay." He took a deep breath. "I want a leader—no, I want someone I can trust to carry out my—no..."

He gave an exasperated sigh. "I need a number two."

Hector stifled a chuckle, and Freya quickly gave him a nudge.

"I need someone to be my eyes and ears up front. Ken and his team are amazing, and I'd like for you to learn what I do, but be there for them more closely. I didn't think you'd take with them as quickly as you did. I'm glad this is working out. You're getting to know each other, and that's great, to an extent, but regardless..." William beamed at the team. "We always say stick together and be there for each other, and it'll be easier on me and everyone to have a leader on the ground to manage intel. If anything happens to me, you can run this operation just as well as I can."

June was annoyed but felt like the spotlight was on her, and she didn't know how to react.

"Five minutes," said a guard after letting go of his earpiece.

"Thanks," replied William. "You'll see what I do, and we'll see what happens from there. You're gonna stick with me."

June nodded but felt like this was moving so fast. She looked around at everyone sitting still and trying to get some rest, except for Ken, who was fidgeting with his hands. He smiled at her. June felt her cheeks blush, and she nervously averted her gaze when the elevator finally stopped at what seemed to be the letter *P* on the sign, but it was still dark. Everyone walked out, and June noticed a light opening up in the distance with a rush of wind coming in. The large cave-like structure seemed long and about twenty feet high, with an eerie red glow from rows of lights engulfed in the morning light from the opening doors. June then noticed a large matte-black plane coming out of a large storage bunker.

"I've never been on a plane before..."

"Once, when you were a baby, we brought you here," William said with a note of melancholy in his tone. "Anyway, you'll be okay. You're gonna sit with me in the front."

The small jet plane looked like something out of a spy movie. She noticed it had a cargo door under its tail.

The group made their way to the plane while the crew diligently prepared the aircraft. A metal ladder was rolled in and placed on the side while the copilot opened the door. William, June, and the team climbed in. The team made their way to the back while William took the seat behind the pilots, who were dressed in black with dark-visored helmets, so all she could see was half their faces. She gave them a small wave hello and was about to follow the others when she felt a hand tug at her wrist.

"Sit here." William pointed at the seat behind the pilot and handed her a headset with a microphone. She saw the rest of the team do the same as they strapped in the back along the benches before William waved at them and closed the cockpit door. The plane door closed behind her and it became dark inside, then a red glow came from the plane's rear.

"These help us communicate until we reach the DZ, er, drop zone. That's where the team is going to drop down... Team, check in," he said while pushing down the button on his headset.

"Queen, check," said Freya.

"King, check," said Ken.

"Brook, check," said Hector.

"Pawn, check," said Zoe.

"Bishop, check," said Jin.

"Knight, check," said Isaac.

"Grand-master, check. Guest secure," said William as he adjusted the seat belt and looked over to ensure June was strapped in.

The pilot flipped switches, and the plane began to roar and pick up speed. He spoke over the radio. "Clear for takeoff. ETA, eight hours."

June noticed the opening at the end of the runway getting bigger and bigger, and as they finally flew out of it, she realized they were high up. The plane only had two front windows, but all she saw was desert as the plane tilted and turned.

June felt the gravity pull her stomach down, and she fought to not get sick.

"Three thousand and climbing," the pilot said before flipping a few more switches. "We are clear for international airspace. Continuing to destination."

"Good," said William. "I'm hoping they'd approve this sooner, but we have little time to waste."

After a quick moment, the pilot came on the radio.

"Cruising at thirty-five hundred. ETA, two p.m., Pacific Standard."

"Good," repeated William, this time putting his hands down and grabbing the phone. "All right, team, listen up. Destination is Colombia. Our target is a dangerous man who has amassed a large amount of power in a short amount of time. His name is Cesar Villalobos. He's held up in what used to be a drug lord's compound; Ernesto Pérez, now deceased. Status of the family is unknown. Status of Cesar's family is also unknown, though all are presumed dead. There may be hostages. Cesar has accumulated a large following, claiming he is a god or chosen by God, and claims of his invulnerability are spreading. God or not, he has an army of followers, and they will die for this man. Your mission is to arrive in the river about seven miles away from his compound, swim your way toward it, observe, and wait until nightfall to infiltrate and capture the target."

June blanched nervously and he gave her a quick thumbs-up and continued.

"We've done what we can to remove videos on the internet and keep news coverage of him off the air, but there's only so much we can do. Making him disappear will make him look like another nut who gained power only to be eliminated by their own hubris. If all goes well, no one will even remember who he was by tomorrow. So, to summarize: arrive incognito, search for hostages, and retrieve the target. Get to the extraction zone that will be twelve clicks east of your location, and deposit the target with the Colombian team. They'll be waiting in an unmarked cargo truck. Then go for the yellow taxi van with dark tinted windows. Call sign fianchetto. Everyone got that?"

"Copy. Over," said Ken, with a bit of nervousness in his voice, over the radio.

William turned to June and forced his lips upward, and she returned the gesture. "They'll be fine," he said. "They do this all the time, you just have to pick up on what I do, and when we get there, learn a few ground tactics too, but we'll explain later."

There was a silence that grew over the crew as everyone braced for the long flight. After what felt like the longest hours of her life, June was getting sleepy when William began talking again.

"This is the map, we're currently over the fringes of the Amazon."

June watched as he held out his phone. On it was a digital map showing small lines and circles that seemed like they came from an old video game.

"The color gradients are the altitude-like mountains, the lines are bodies of water, and since it's all jungle, there's just plain gray in these areas."

June nodded, but she was still confused about why she'd been thrown into this mess.

"When they drop, you'll stop seeing these little red dots. They're going to go radio silent until they meet up with the extraction van."

June gave a confused nod, looking at William with a worried

expression.

"Relax," he said, "they're playful at the base, but out here, they're the reason I use them for the most difficult of missions."

June blanched as William continued to show her the images on his phone.

"There's a reason you haven't heard about Bricks on the news."

"Sir, Director McAfee is on the phone for you," interrupted the copilot.

William's eyes widened, and he turned around in his seat for a switch on the panel behind him. June couldn't hear him on the radio anymore. She could barely make out what was being said before the pilot came over the radio and announced, "Approaching uncontrolled airspace."

June saw multiple switches being flipped and the pilots shifting in their seats.

After a few minutes, William hung up the phone and scratched the back of his head. His lips curled nervously at June before switching on his radio headset again.

"The big man gave me an earful, but he's approved this mission and hopes for our safe return."

June, clearly confused, was about to ask before Ken cut into the radio.

"Sir, was this unsanctioned?"

"Not anymore." William gave a nervous chuckle. "The higher-ups were taking too long this time. I just merely moved things along." William gave June a mischievous smirk. "Well, ETA is six hours. Now is the time to use the restroom if you need to."

The plane dinged, and William got out of his seat and walked toward the cargo area. June was unsure of what to do, so she decided it was best to stay seated until William got back. She wanted to go back and see the group, but decided against it and sat holding herself. June felt out of place and rocked in her seat with anxiety before a warm hand held her shoulder.

"Hey you," said Ken with his deep, soothing voice. "First missions are always nerve-racking, but we're pros with more or less two years of experience and a heck of a lot of training. You don't have to worry; we do this kind of thing at least twice a month. There's always some maniac who thinks they're special and deserve to rule the world."

June blanched nervously.

"We'll be fine. Besides, we got you as a backup if it all goes south."

June's face quickly turned to shock before Ken laughed and waved his hands.

"It's all right, it's all right. Just a joke. We'd never throw a rookie into the deep end like this."

June's heavy breathing made Ken realize this was probably not the best time for such a joke.

"Hey, when we get back, we usually chill at a motel and get to hang out around town before heading back to base. Anything you look forward to eating? My treat."

Still recovering from Ken's poorly-timed joke, June blinked and slowly shook her head for a moment before blurting out, "I can go for some pizza." She cringed at the idea of going to a different country with so much culture and cuisine and choosing pizza, but that was all she could think of. Ken grinned and patted her shoulder.

"All right, pizza it is. I know just the place."

William came back into the cabin and gave Ken a confused

look. Ken smiled, nodded, and walked back into the cargo area. William turned to June and asked what that was about. June fought the urge to blush.

"Um, they invited me to eat after the mission."

"Oh," said William, in more of a fatherly tone than he wanted to. "Th–That's great. They really seem to like you, June. You're going to fit right in. Try to get some rest now, it's all clear sailing from here."

June focused on her hands and sighed in frustration. William noticed and turned in his chair while staring at his phone. June closed her eyes and slipped into a deep sleep.

***

"REACHING DROP ZONE! ETA, FIVE MINUTES!"

The voice startled June awake. The dark plane cabin felt disorienting as it shook.

"Welcome to the land of the living!" William nervously joked before pressing on his headset. "Go! Go! Go!"

June glanced back at the door that separated the cabin from the back, and she could hear the wind billowing strongly behind it.

"All right, cargo has been deployed. Heading to base. Radio silence from here on out."

June felt the plane turn hard to the left and turned to William with concern.

"They're gonna be fine. Now is the hard part for everyone. The waiting."

June opened her mouth to say something but couldn't find the words.

"Our job now is to make sure they get out of this country in one piece."

June, still worried, nodded back and turned in her seat to face forward.

"This is unreal," she whispered under her breath.

***

After another hour of flying, the pilot spoke over the radio.

"Approaching airstrip, sir."

"Copy that! When we land, just follow my lead, okay?" William told June over the radio. "We need to talk to the director of the Colombian base of operations. He's expecting us. The operation here is small and doesn't have as many Bricks, or agents, or even the funding that we do. That's why they called on us."

June was trying to listen, but the sound of her heart racing wasn't letting her focus much.

"I hope your Spanish isn't rusty. We need you to go into the market and pick up as much info as possible. It's not dangerous work, listen around to see if there are any other cases of Bricks or anything you can hear about our current target. Agent Zoila De Armas will accompany you."

June nodded nervously and gripped the armrest as the plane bounced during its descent.

The plane touched down on the tarmac with a bit of a bump that made June's eyes widen.

William chuckled when he looked over to see June's hands gripped tight to the seat's armrests as she stared out the window in a panic. He changed his tone to sound softer as he explained what was going to happen. "It'll be for a few hours, nothing big. I'll be here coordinating with Director Gutierrez to make sure everything goes without a hitch."

He reached into his pocket and pulled out earphones.

"These look like earphones, but they're two-way radios, so we can talk directly. Put them on when you're with Zoila."

June nodded and grabbed them from his hand while still trying to catch her breath, momentarily releasing one of her hands.

The plane finally came to a stop at a small airfield, and June let go of the armrests, leaving a dent where her fingers dug in. She followed William off the plane and took in the fresh, humid smell.

***

The airport seemed to be in the middle of nowhere. Jungle all around and mountains as far as the eye could see. June walked down the steps of the side of the plane, and agents were all working to refuel the plane and bring down bags from the rear. William walked toward a stocky-looking man with a wide frame. He had a bushy beard and dark glasses. Dressed in olive green military attire, he had several medals on his chest June couldn't make out.

William shook hands with him before he turned and pointed to June. She noticed him give her a nod, turn around, and wave toward a car, then back to June.

The car drove up to her and lowered its window. "Ms. Romero? Come in. I hear we're going shopping," the woman said with a thick Colombian accent. Zoila De Armas gave June a wink and motioned her head toward the passenger seat. June studied the fair-skinned woman with dark hair and thought she looked young despite the crow's-feet and strands of grays showing in her dark hair. She was pretty and poised and seemed to be more elegant and spunkier than June would have imagined an agent to be. Getting in the small silver sedan, Zoila drove away, and June turned back at William, who was getting into a military truck and driving in the opposite direction. She put on the headphones and immediately heard William.

"June, check in, testing, testing. One, two, one, two..."

"I'm here," she said.

"I'm here, too," Zoila added.

"Copy that," replied William. "June, you're gonna go with Zoila to the market area, do some 'window-shopping' and walk around, and remember to listen for keywords like *fuertes*, *dioses*, *invencible*, just anything along the line of superpowers. Copy?"

"Ten-four, boss." Zoila smirked and turned to June. "His accent is cute. He tries."

Zoila stifled a laugh as June heard an uncomfortable cough coming from her headphones.

"You seem like a good kid," said Zoila. "So pretty, how did they get you into this?"

June didn't know how to reply, especially with William listening in.

"She's the child from the California incident," said William dryly.

"Oh," Zoila said, mildly surprised. "And you immediately put her to work? William, I thought you would have compassion for your baby girl?" Zoila gave June a mischievous wink.

"I—we—uh, Zoila, focus, please," William said, flustered. "There are more pressing issues right now..."

Zoila just smiled as she continued to drive.

"A-and besides, it's none of your business. June is a very capable young woman."

June felt uncomfortable in this conversation about her that wasn't really including her. Zoila let out a loud, obnoxious sigh. "Fiiiiine, Williaaaam. But for the rest of this trip, she's going to be my friend and pretending to be my daughter." She turned to June again with a more mischievous expression than before.

"Zoila. I know you get a kick out of busting my balls. So, I'm just gonna agree with whatever you do. Just as long as you keep her safe."

Zoila threw her head back with a silent laugh. "Yes, Daddy!" She snickered.

William groaned loudly. June felt confused and out of place. Zoila seemed to be very free-spirited and armed with a brutal sense of humor. June did not feel prepared for this. She thought it would be all *yes sir's* and *copy that's*. Zoila was making herself laugh and enjoying every minute of it. Until she toned it down and looked at June more softly, now having driven to a small town.

"William and I go way back. Probably over a few decades of working on missions together. I knew Melody too."

Zoila paused for a moment, probably waiting for William to react.

"She seemed really nice, incapable of what she did. Was she... How did she treat you? If you don't mind me asking?"

"She was wonderful. A little overbearing, but protective. I don't know why you guys think she's a monster. She did what she had to, to protect me... But I guess she was just keeping me away from this world."

There was a long, awkward silence between the two adults until Zoila finally spoke up.

"She was always sweet. And she saved me more than once from deep trouble." She looked around as she kept driving. "We should be there in about an hour."

William cleared his throat. "Good. Alpha should be arriving soon as well. Keep me posted, and you know our emergency channel, just in case."

Zoila agreed, and June gave a very unsure, "Ten-four?" That made Zoila and William chuckle.

"Good, I'll see the two of you soon. The director and I will be at HQ," William said before a pop sound notified them that he had turned his radio off.

"Guess we can chill now." Zoila dropped her shoulders and drove with one hand now. "The girl who lived, huh?"

June contorted her face in confusion.

"Harry... oh, never mind. There's a big mystery about you. No one knows who tipped William and Melody about you, but it was before the explosion. Don't tell William, but as much as he likes to pretend he knows everything, he's just as confused and lost as the rest of us. He's a good man, a little stuck in his ways, but he means well. He's been at this job for way longer than he cares to admit."

"Was he... Did he..." June couldn't find the right words.

"He loved Melody very much," said Zoila, piecing together what June was trying to ask, and smiled softly at June as she drove calmly through the rough dirt road.

"They met very young, probably five or six years before they found me. And it's said she saved him from an attacking Brick by jumping on his back and exploding a gas canister in the Brick's face just before he was about to snap William's neck.

She was a police officer, I think. She transferred shortly after. William is a little harder to pinpoint. He and the scientists go way back."

June questioned Zoila. "Scientists?"

"Yes, Dr. Weiss and his successor, Dr. Glendale, work with William to find ways of..."

She took her other hand off of the steering wheel and waved them around as she searched for the right word, causing June's eyes to widen with anxiety for a moment.

"Restraining Bricks. Dr. Weiss retired or passed away, I'm not sure." She put a hand back on the wheel.

June felt a little sad at the thought that probably more work was being done to restrain her kind than curing diseases, but she'd rather not get into it at the moment.

Zoila smacked the wheel almost as if reading June's thoughts.

"Billions spent on knockout gas that won't damage brain tissue, but we can't cure cancer, unbelievable."

June's eyes widened.

"No offense," said Zoila quickly. "Just that, it's hard to imagine people's priorities when you, yourself, have been a cancer survivor and see how little has been done in that front, but we can send trash into space!" she said with a sarcastic tone.

June, again unsure how to approach Zoila, asked, "So, you're not a Brick?"

Zoila let out a loud "Ha!" before explaining, "No, *mi niña*, I have been in the agency as an agent since the first recorded incident in Colombia, probably around 1997?"

She pondered for a moment. "Bah." She waved her hands before gripping the wheel again.

"Anyways, I was a young girl back then, probably about your age, living near a field of coffee. One day, this man comes into my house. The door was locked, and he just turned the knob until it broke. I remember *mi papá* ran to get his shotgun, and the man just stood there and laughed. I'll never forget the laugh." Zoila's face dimmed and she looked like she was vividly reliving that moment. "*Papá* yelled at the man to get out, get lost, that he'll shoot first and call the *policía* later. The man pulled a machete from his belt and swung it at *mi papá*. Next thing I know, shots were fired, and he laughed and laughed and laughed…"

Zoila paused for a moment and swallowed. June noticed Zoila's eyes water as she kept talking.

"My mother grabbed me and my little brothers, and we ran. I remember hearing another shot before the scream. We didn't stop running until a car pulled up. A very young William came out with his partner, and they both began to fire gas grenades at my house. The man came rushing at us but eventually fell. I was studying biology to be a doctor, but then I wanted to stop people like that monster. I have to admit, I wanted to rid the world of you, but the more I did this job, the more I saw normal people confused and lost, some with a willingness to help. William helped me see it was a lot more complicated than I thought it was. It was sweet, and it changed me." Zoila pursed her lips and leaned back in thought as the two sat at a busy intersection. "Anyways, I found it better to be happy and helpful than bitter and nasty to others."

June nodded her head. This poor woman just vented her entire life story, and June didn't know how to reply, but at least it killed time. The pair had made it to a small town where Zoila parked the car near an outdoor market, and they walked toward the shopping strip. "Okay. Spanish only from here on out, got it?"

June nodded and followed Zoila. She focused and surveyed the area. They walked around for a while, asking normal questions about the items they were looking at. June noticed how happy Zoila got when she found some mangoes that were to her liking.

"*Super Hombre!*" June heard someone say off in the distance. When she turned, she saw a young man wearing a towel around his neck and playing with some children. She moved to get a closer look while seeming very interested in some watches at a nearby store window. The owner came out and tried to sell her some oversized watches, and she just shook her head and tried to walk away without losing sight of the caped man. She finally got close enough to the caped man, and one of the kids threw a bottle at him, and it made contact with his face. He fell in pain on the floor, and the townspeople gathered around, trying to help him.

"That was a bust," said Zoila from behind, startling June. "Sorry, it's something you learn over time. Next time, don't seem too interested in store windows with shiny stuff. Some peddlers are always trying to push that trash on tourists." Zoila took a bite out of her mango and gave a contented moan. "We should head back. This place is dead today. A lot fewer people than usual. Could be the heat too."

They walked back to the car park and saw a man standing with a sign on the sidewalk.

"THE WORLD IS ENDING SOON!" he yelled in Spanish as he paced, causing Zoila to chuckle.

"The world is always ending. I'll miss the mangoes, though," she said before throwing away the seed in a nearby trash can.

June shrugged. She never really put much thought into the whole world ending.

"*Vamos*, we gotta head out if we want to beat the factory rush hour."

June had lost track of time wandering around the market. The anxiety never really went away, and she couldn't wait to hang out with the team in a setting that was much more normal than this.

"Not that one," said Zoila as June was walking to their car. "This one." Zoila walked up to a small red SUV with two doors. "We cycle through them in case the ones we arrive in are compromised," she explained as they sat in the car. June just shrugged it off and went with it, she had a lot to learn and didn't even know where to start.

***

The car ride back to the base was much quieter. June figured Zoila was just saving her strength to keep teasing William. This time they didn't turn toward the airstrip, they went the opposite way toward the edge of a forest at the foothills of a large mountain, following a dirt trail and into a closed-off cave. After a bit of darkness, they came into a large garage within the mountain, similar to the plane hangar they left from.

"We're here," said Zoila after finding a spot to park. "Come on, you have a lot to talk about with the director."

Zoila grabbed the bag full of mangoes, and the two walked toward the elevator guarded by two men in fatigues with heavy weapons. She greeted them and walked in, leaving June to just smile and nod as she walked past them. June and Zoila walked into the elevator, which was much smaller than the last one she was in, with nowhere to sit and a lot fewer floors.

"We're just a fraction of the main facility. There's a bigger base near Bogota where we keep—no, no, that sounds bad— we take care of the Bricks there."

June, now leaning against the wall with her arms crossed, looked at Zoila.

"Are there a lot of, you know, us in the world?"

Zoila nodded, folded her arms, and leaned against the wall, staring at June pensively.

"There are a lot, probably since the beginning of mankind, but we don't know, you guys just started showing up a lot a few decades ago. We studied all those family tree DNA swab tests and only found a few here and there." June's mouth opened to question that tidbit of information, but the elevator doors opened, and William was waiting on the other side.

"What happened to keeping me posted?" He sounded upset, but Zoila chuckled.

"There was nothing to report, but your little girl did very good work out there. The lead was a bust, but here," she reached into the bag and shoved a mango into William's chest, "we got you this!"

William stifled a laugh. "Oh, wow, thanks." He nodded at Zoila, then spoke to June. "Come, June, I want you to meet the director of this arm of B.R.I.C. Agency." He then turned to Zoila. "Thank you, Zoila. It was nice to see you again."

"Likewise, William," she said before turning to June. "*Adiós, preciosa*. It was wonderful to meet you finally." She waved as she walked away.

"So, how did you feel out there?" he asked, trying to figure out where to put the mango.

"It was, uh... It... was... freaking wild being flown into a foreign country, watching my friends parachute from a plane, and getting sent with a stranger to spy in a foreign market."

"Yeah, and you're surprisingly taking it well. For what it's worth, I am sorry. I wish you could have had a normal life, but being a Brick makes you..."

"A valuable asset?" June said dryly.

William sighed and stopped before some large double doors guarded by more soldiers with heavy weapons.

"The world is in shambles as it is. Imagine throwing super-powered people into the mix. They can barely handle the different races, let alone cultural differences. I need to protect you, the world..." William sighed heavily and held June's shoulder. "I have to protect them from each other."

June nodded understandingly.

"Now, let's do some bureaucracy."

William sighed as he opened one of the large double doors. Inside was a dimly lit room with monitors all around and a big round table in the middle where a few men in military uniform were seated, and two men in suits were talking with each other before they noticed William. "*Señor* Saturnino!" They gathered and began saying greetings in Spanish and pointing at the maps. June could make out some of the maps. It showed they were probably a few miles from the Atlantic side of Colombia. She wished her new friends were with her. She'd never felt this lonely. Even when she started a new school, she knew Melody was nearby waiting for her. She was lost in memories before hearing her name.

"June? You must be June," a suited man said, opening his arms to grab her by the shoulders. He looked her up and down.

"William, she's a woman now. June, you were maybe one year old the last time I saw you," the man said in his heavy accent. "You won't remember me. I worked with Melody in *México* on a case. She must have had you for a few months beforehand. William stayed behind on that case to take care of you."

William cleared his throat. "Well, what intel do we have? June will join us since she will be my number two and eventually an agent coordinator."

The men in the suits nodded at each other, and continued talking. "Okay, *Señor*, this is what we have on Villalobos."

The general sat down and reached under the table, pulling out his case of papers which contained a thick file.

"*Esté cabrón* has over a hundred followers. I'm not even sure how many are Bricks since all they do is sit down and watch him talk for hours. He's created his own religion and uses an old church near the edge of the town to gather offerings."

"And make dealings," said the other man dressed in camouflage with fewer medals on his chest than the other.

"Yes, we think he deals in people, maybe slaves or soldiers? Not sure who his dealer or supplier is, but all we know is that black vans appear, new faces appear, all looking terrified, and make the trade. Boxes are exchanged, and then they disappear into the jungle.

"Sometimes helicopters and planes can be seen leaving in the distance toward waters, but they're hard to track because they always go in different directions and very much try to stay clear of local airspace."

"Well, that's why I'm here." William turned to June. "They normally try to handle this on their own, but this Brick has become too dangerous and seems to be amassing a huge following and might even be dealing with international terrorists. We needed to quietly, and without the local government getting too involved, make him disappear before we have an international incident."

June nodded and, feeling a lot like it was bring your daughter to work day at school, glanced around the room at what she assumed were very high-ranking military men, then up at William.

"Why don't I join the church he goes to? I may be able to get some info."

William gave her a sad smile. "We tried. I don't know how they saw past our last agent that went in, but we never saw them again."

June's eyes widened and she regretted bringing it up.

"They were a Brick, too?" she asked, bracing herself for another morbid answer.

"No," said one of the suited men. "Alfonso was never seen again. Not even a body. Who knows what those animals did to him."

The doors opened, and all the men rose and saluted. The man William spoke to at the airport when they arrived walked in, and he told everyone to be at ease. Speaking in Spanish, William greeted the man.

"June, this is the director, Guillermo Gutierrez. Director, this is my trainee, June," William said before turning to him. "We'll have the target soon."

The man nodded, took a seat at the end of the table, and asked how long. William told him it would be a couple more hours before dusk, and then the team would have him. Director Gutierrez seemed pleased by this and grabbed the paperwork left by the other generals, and he began to read. The room became much quieter, and everyone mainly focused on the monitors. June felt even more out of place and fought back the urge to sit closer to William. William finally realized June was uncomfortable and started talking to her. "You like mangoes? I'll split this one with you, if you want."

June shrugged. She was never really had a mango. Living up north as she had, they were a little harder to come by, but she was desperate to make this whole awkward situation pass. William reached for a drawer under one of the monitors, grabbed some napkins, and pulled out a knife from his belt. All the generals glanced at him and then back at the monitors. He cut a slice off, gave it to June in a napkin, and then cut off another piece for himself that he just slurped up quickly. June really liked the smell, though the sliminess was a little off-putting. She took a bite of the fruit. She felt some of the fibers get stuck in her teeth, but the taste was so good she emitted a small moan that made the generals snicker and shake their heads.

"These are the best," said William, letting out a moan of his own. "Mmmm... Zoila knows how to pick 'em."

"Can't wait to eat mine when I get back to my office," said the director.

William gave her half of his mango and started eating the rest like an apple, and June did the same. Feeling much better, though incredibly sticky, William and June sat there eating and looking up at the monitors.

"Nothing's really happening. The police chatter is normal, and our agents have created a perimeter around the area." He pointed at a flat area on the map on the screen. The low tech surprised June; movies had spoiled her thinking every one of these rooms had holograms and super-focusing satellite imagery.

"The red dots here are the Colombian teams, mostly agents, and Edwin's team of Bricks."

June saw about nine dots in total.

"That's everyone they have on the field," William noted, almost with a hint of sadness.

"T minus thirty minutes," said a voice over the radio.

"Good, our extraction point is almost ready. Contact our flight coordinator and let them know it's a go," William said, and one of the generals got up and grabbed a phone behind him.

"It's happening."

Director Gutierrez and William exchanged concerned expressions, seemingly holding their breaths.

"Ya! Half an hour, sir, the plane will be ready," said the general hanging up the phone and retaking his seat. Everyone sat down and stared at the map. Another dot appeared farther away north of the others.

"Time to make the world safer," said William under his breath. June, seemingly holding her breath as well, could only imagine what was happening. The room was quiet, and then, the dots began to move. June, along with everyone else, seemed to lean forward in her seat.

"It's in God's hands now," whispered the director, crossing himself.

Everyone around him gave a slight nod and nervously kept staring at the monitors.

***

After an hour the radio came on, and through the static, June recognized Ken's voice.

"King to Grand-master. Checkmate. Fianchetto achieved. Heading to E 7."

June's sigh of relief was muted by all the men's applause. She looked around as they all got out of their seats and began to hug and congratulate each other.

"It's all good!" said William, turning to June with a triumphant smile. "We made the world safer."

He put his arm around her shoulders and gave her a side hug.

"They're coming home."

"That's great," she said, smiling up at William. "We get to go home now?"

William gave her a nod. "First paperwork, then home."

June nodded back and couldn't help feeling a happy relief.

***

After hours of tedious paperwork and hearing about how most of the followers were being arrested and detained for questioning, June asked what would happen to all the people that were arrested. William quirked his mouth at her interest and explained as they sat alone in a small office.

"So, they'll try to explain how it was all a hoax, and that Cesar was just a power-hungry theatrical major who knew special effects and was just starving for attention..."

June nodded and felt like she might have bought that story if she wasn't a Brick herself.

"The other Bricks will be processed and deemed as assets or placed in the bunker... Well, that's the last of it." William showed June how he did the reports and filed the paperwork into his suitcase. "Time to head out and meet up with the team."

June got up off her seat, and William noticed her genuine

smile.

4

The Greatest Lie

Clearly exhausted, and having been awake for almost twenty-four hours, June and William were on a car ride back toward the airport having a hard time staying awake. The ride was quiet as June saw the sun rising over the mountains and as soon as they got there, they were shuffled into a smaller propeller plane. They sat in the passenger seats in the back.

"This will take us to the Capitol. We'll land, meet up with the team there, and head to the motel. So, get some rest. It'll probably be about an hour-long flight."

June gave William an exhausted nod and sat back in her chair. He laid his head back and was asleep before the plane moved. She fought off the sleep as much as she could but the last thing she saw was the runway getting smaller before waking up as soon as they touched down. William, having been awake a little before her, seemed much more energetic and alert than she was.

"We're here, kid," he said, gathering his things. They got off and walked toward the terminal, where William provided the customs officer with their passports. June was a little confused but followed him, knowing she had a lot to learn about this secret agent life. He placed the passports back in his pocket and gave her a wink.

"How'd you get a passport picture?"

"I just used your yearbook photo."

He walked away and before she could ask anything else, she took in the sights. He got some distance and she hurried after him. She had never been to an airport before, let alone one so far from where she was used to living. Heading outside, she realized how humid this place was, living so far up north she'd never had to deal with so much of it before. Her hair felt frizzy and uncomfortable. She really wished she had packed a hat. William walked toward a small blue sedan and opened the rear door for June.

"It'll be about half an hour before our destination. So, if you need to use the bathroom, let me know."

June, realizing she hadn't really used the bathroom since they left the base, nodded and got in. William sat in front and greeted the driver. They drove toward a busy part of town with tall buildings and much more traffic and life than the small town she was in a few hours ago.

"We're here," said William, pointing to a smaller building that seemed old but well taken care of. "We'll be staying here for the night."

They both walked out of the car and that feeling of cold humidity made June shiver a little. In the motel it was warmer and dimly lit. William spoke to the concierge and grabbed a pair of keys.

"This is for you. I'm at the door across from you guys."

June took a second to realize she might be with the team much sooner than she thought and her lips curved upward.

"Okay, so when do we head out?"

"Tomorrow around ten in the morning. The van will pick us up and take us back to the airport." They both went up a flight of stairs and stopped at the third floor.

"This way," said William. "We're down here."

She followed him and he knocked before opening the door for her. Inside were Freya and Zoe talking.

"Ladies, I hope you're doing well," William said proudly. "You guys did a hell of a job."

"Thanks, boss," said Freya and Zoe simultaneously in a tired voice.

"I'll leave you girls alone for the night. Remember, if you leave, please let me know."

Zoe and Freya turned to William and bared their teeth mischievously.

He sighed. "Fine. Good night, ladies." William let out a big yawn that infected the group, and closed the door behind June.

"Girl, come here. You probably wanna hear all about it." Zoe pushed a chair out with her foot from the table they were sitting at. The motel room was cozy with old-timed floral wallpaper, an old tube TV wired to play HD television, and two queen-size beds with floral-print comforters. The small table near the window offered a little view of the busy streets below. They all sat in the chairs around it made of wicker.

"So," started June, a little nervous but very curious, "how did it go?"

The three of them could barely keep their eyes open, but Zoe began. "Well, we jumped off a plane and hit the ground hard."

"*You* hit the ground hard," said Freya with a chuckle. "I

aimed for the water."

"Yeah, I'm sure the parachute probably slowed the landing a bit, though, right?"

Zoe and Freya turned to each other and laughed.

"Parachutes? You think they'd announce us like that? Nah," said Freya, still having a laugh. We hit the ground hard. That's why we try to land in water and much farther away from our target location than anyone else. Very rarely do we need parachutes. If ever."

"Yeah. Sorry, I'm sure William forgot to tell you. He's so caught up on making things work he forgets he's human and just works like a machine," mused Zoe.

"Anyway..." Freya picked up from where Zoe left off. "We hit the ground—well, she did—we hit the water and Ken and the guys checked around to make sure there was no one around while Zoe and I made sure we weren't being followed."

June leaned closer on the table, holding her head up with her arms.

"The trek was long—oh, and a snake attacked Isaac."

Zoe gave a loud laugh. "He did not like that!"

They both laughed and Zoe continued the story.

"But, yeah, lady. Once it was pitch dark, we made it to that nasty-ass-looking mansion painted in some gross papaya color."

"Oh, my God, yes," agreed Freya. "Place looked like it was decorated by someone who doesn't know what colors are."

"For sure," continued Zoe. "But, yeah, got to that nasty-looking place with way too many rooms."

"Oh, my God, remember the tiger room?"

"Girl, yes, that dude did not see us coming."

June was confused and her eyes darted between them before

Zoe continued.

"We got there and looked around the rooms and found one with a dude sitting in a chair reading a magazine, and freaking tigers just chilling in a cage probably the size of a New York flat. It was huge."

"I was half tempted to let the tiger out just to see what happened, but I'd have probably gotten in trouble somehow," said Freya in a disappointed tone.

"Shit..." said Zoe. "You and me both. But, anyways." Zoe turned to June who was trying her hardest to stay awake. "We find the jerk. Like, in a room all the way on top, *Fifty Shades* style. It was disgusting. Whole playroom of torture devices."

Freya let out a disgusted sound.

"Those poor people. We freed them as soon as the knockout gas took hold. The ones living, anyways."

Freya gave a sad look to Zoe, then turned back to face June.

"And, yeah, we grabbed the disgusting monster and anyone else we could carry and made our way to the van. We told the survivors to never tell anyone about what they saw. That we were a rival gang and were going to cut his fake ass into so many pieces they'll never find him again."

"They seemed to like that a bit. One of them even gave Hector a hug and they ran as far as they could." Zoe let out a sigh.

"The lucky ones at least had some clothes on. But I can't imagine what they will say. All I know is that the media is gonna have a field day seeing all these naked people showing up out of nowhere, claiming Cesar is dead and his followers are full of shit."

Freya and Zoe gave a proud nod to each other and looked back at June.

"Girl, you must be exhausted and feel nasty. Use my anti-frizz shampoo when you take a shower. Don't worry about waking us, just get clean and freshen up. We're hitting the pizza place with the guys around seven."

June realized that's what she told Ken she wanted, and nodded.

"You two have to be, too. You guys are superheroes."

The two laughed and got up out of the chairs, making their way to the bed on the right.

"If we're superheroes," said Freya, "the world is screwed."

Zoe chuckled dryly and got into her side of the bed.

"Still, though," said June. "You guys saved those poor people. That's pretty epic in my book." June smiled and rocked a little in her feet before going into the bathroom.

"Well, that was embarrassing." She sighed to herself.

"Maybe we are superheroes," June overheard Zoe say. "Ain't no one doing what we do so well."

"We could be doing more." Freya gave a scoff and got into bed. "How many more people could have been in that compound that needed help, with people dying, heck, people like us being locked up or killed without mercy just because they might be a threat!? I hate all of this."

June listened through the bathroom door before she was about to get into the shower.

"We're not heroes, we're glorified trash collectors. Cleaning up a mess no one knows even started, and hopefully it will continue that way."

June felt stupid for being so naive. She turned on the shower and grabbed Freya's shampoo. She tried to wash off what felt like the longest day of her life. She couldn't help but be excited to spend more time with Ken later, but first that bed was the only embrace she wanted to feel right now.

Later that evening, June was shaken awake by Freya, Zoe, and Jin hopping on the bed.

"Okay, first, we need to make you look presentable."

June was about to ask what was happening.

"Shhh," Freya said, putting her finger over June's mouth. "Let the man work."

They took her to the bathroom and proceeded to get her ready and then to the small dining table so Jin could apply her makeup.

"I wasn't sure what size you were, so I picked a few outfits in different sizes. Try them on," said Jin as he set the clothes on a pile over the bed.

"Girl, we'll make you one of us yet."

"You didn't have to..." started June before Jin cut in.

"Listen, you're going to be happy with the result, Ken will be happy with the result, but me? I'm happy with the process. 'Kay? Let me be freaking happy. Last night was rough and I just want to get it out of my head and give you some shadowy eye makeup. Maybe with some winged eye liner." Jin contemplated that for a moment. "Yeah, yeah, I think wings will do. Well, no, maybe not. Might be a bit too much and send the wrong message. I wanna go for puppy love over Porn hub."

June's eyes widened and she began to blush. The others laughed as Jin sat down in front of June and opened his makeup bag.

"Oh, stop, now you're gonna make me blush... Ooh, let's start with some blush, shall we? What foundation should I use?"

June felt like a deer in the headlights. This was happening.

Someone other than Melody was applying makeup on her. She started to remember the first time, when Melody put a cute rose-colored lip gloss on her that she loved; she must have been seven or eight at the time. She thought of her mom as the most beautiful woman ever and wanted to live up to that before the stress of constantly moving made simple things like buying makeup and keeping up beauty routines become more and more difficult.

Afterward, Jin sat back in his chair, studying June up and down, and clicked his tongue.

"My finest work, if I do say so myself, ladies."

Freya was the first to lean in, in front of June and inspect her thoroughly.

"Yes, professor," she said sarcastically. "Truly, you have outdone yourself, this time."

Zoe chuckled behind her and said, "Lemme see." She took a look at June and put her hand on her chest. "Well, damn. If she ain't gonna be the belle of the pizza place."

"Har, har," said Jin, exasperated. "I know you like it. You don't have to be such dicks about it."

They all laughed and turned back toward June. Zoe scrunched her nose and said, "This is the way we unwind. Last time we gave Isaac the makeover treatment..."

Jin gave June a mischievous wink.

"While he slept!" laughed Zoe.

They all laughed, and June tried to picture Isaac covered in makeup.

"But you look beautiful, June. Ken will have to be an absolute blockhead if he doesn't fall for you," Freya said, standing behind June, looking at her in the mirror, and putting her hands on June's shoulders.

June, blushing slightly, said, "You guys are okay with this? Me liking..."

Freya cut her off. "Yes, we don't like to date amongst ourselves often but, sometimes, you see a couple that might work out and usually they do. Besides, don't tell him I told you, but Ken does not stop talking about you. He thinks you're the cutest, sweetest thing he's ever seen in his life. Come on, you had to have noticed how excited he gets when you're around and how he always tries to sit next to you when we eat."

June, feeling a little exposed now, gave a nod.

"I never wanted to assume anything. I just thought he was being really nice to a newcomer, and I, uh, well..."

Zoe cut in. "It's all right. If it doesn't work out between you two, it's not the end of the world. We'll just kick Ken's ass for being a dick, and hope we all get out of this place soon, alive, and retire to our own corners of the world."

June gave a small nod.

"You guys are too much. Sorry, I'm not used to this. I've been pretty alone all of my life."

Zoe and Jin put their hands on her shoulders.

"Girl, we got you. Now, come on, put on those battle armor greaves you call shoes, and let's go!"

***

The car ride was filled with stories of their past adventures and how much they wanted to start a new life when they got out, until finally they arrived at a small restaurant at the side of an old building much like the motel they were staying at. The others were already there waiting inside.

"Of all the places you chose, Ken, you picked a pizza place."

Jin gave June an obvious wink before reading the menu.

"All right, what flavors have they got? I better have some damn pork, one way or another."

Ken laughed, trying to hide his embarrassment.

"I miss home and just wanted something that'll, you know, remind me of something that makes me happy," he said, shooting a glance at June.

June felt a little bashful as she sat across from Ken at the long bench table. They all ordered off the menu, despite Jin getting angry that they couldn't put pork rinds on a pizza.

"You look..." Ken locked eyes with her. "Amazing." June felt like a protagonist in a romantic movie. Her yellow sundress with black polka dots paired with her combat boots well, and her hair felt soft and full. June was feeling cute, all the while loving the attention Ken was giving her. The way everyone was glancing at her made her feel pretty for the first time in her life. She was so used to always trying to blend into the background. Now, she was the *'belle of the pizza place'* and she felt happy.

***

The group kept talking about what crazy toppings they would have on their pizzas if they could, and Jin kept complaining about not having pork rinds as an option. Eventually the subject changed to how much longer they would have to keep doing this and the table grew silent. They knew they couldn't talk about their mission or who they are, so they kept it vague.

"We get sent on these jobs and there's always another job. Man, I just want to go home and do something else with my life," said Hector, frustrated. "I miss my family. As messed up as they are, we're a unit, bro. Large, Cuban, and loud. I miss that."

Everyone agreed except for Isaac, who simply said, "I just want a normal life, y'all. I ain't got a fam to go back to, but anything's better than... this stupid job."

A voice from behind spoke calmly, "Seven years of service guarantees safe passage to a quiet life in the country."

It was William, who managed to walk in unnoticed, carrying large grocery bags in his hand. He pulled out a bag of pork rinds that seemed freshly made and tossed it to Jin.

"You can't be... Oh my God! Hell yeah!" said Jin, taking a big whiff of the bag before digging in. He tossed a book to Freya, who seemed surprised but said nothing. Zoe got a beautifully multicolored choker with a topaz jewel hanging from it. Hector got a small replica ball signed by a player June had never heard of that made him almost squeal. Isaac got handed a beautifully carved replica of a Colombian double-decker bus that put a grin on his face, though his eyes seemed sad. William then turned to Ken and handed him a mango.

"Duuuude!" said Ken with wide eyes and a wider smile.

"Zoila left a note specifically to give you one," William said, clearly frustrated.

"Yes!" Ken pumped his fist. June caught herself smiling and looking around the table. She wondered if this was what a normal family was like but, before she could dwell on that thought any longer, William walked around the table to her and put his hand on her back.

"I hope you like it. I... I have to... I want to get to know you better."

June felt a little sad. This was her adoptive father and the more she got to know him, the more it seemed like he might actually be a good guy. June opened the bag and glanced down to see a necklace made of suede and a small heart-shaped emerald encased in a gold prong setting. It looked very expensive.

June stared up at him, surprised. "I-I can't accept this, it must have been so expensive."

William's mouth curved slightly and he helped her put it on.

"Think of it as a lot of years of missed Christmas gifts, kid."

June felt all the eyes around the table on them. Everyone collectively turned away nervously and became even more interested in their own gifts. June looked back up to William and he gave her a reassuring nod then he put his hand gently on her shoulder.

"I can see you're in good hands."

He cleared his throat and glanced at the team.

"You guys were amazing. The package should be arriving in a few hours, so enjoy and be ready to head out by ten a.m. tomorrow."

The team nodded.

"Yes, sir," said Ken after taking a big slurp of his mango.

Everyone chuckled and said their farewells before William left the restaurant.

The waitress leaned over between Jin and Zoe and placed a large pizza in the middle of the table. Freya leaned over and grabbed a slice before turning to June.

"He tries. Gift giving is his love language." She took a bite and, with pizza in her cheek, continued. "It's still manipulation, probably from high up to keep us happy." She swallowed. "But manipulation, regardless."

The team became stoic.

"I just want that damn normal life they dangle in front of us. Seven years, dammit. Seven years of being their black ops team."

"Shh," Freya shushed Hector with a stern face. "Careful, idiot, we're contractors. But, yeah, seven years kind of sucks. Most of us barely have two."

They all decided to change the subject because the mood was starting to become gloomy, when suddenly Ken turned to June.

"Hey, you, uh, you wanna go somewhere with me?"

June was shocked but tried to hide it.

"I, uh..."

She looked at Zoe and Freya who were failing to subtly give her two thumbs-up. Jin grinned and gave her a wink before pouring the rest of the contents of the pork rinds bag into his mouth.

She turned to Ken and tried to contain her glee.

"Yes, I'd like that."

Ken beamed. "You won't be disappointed."

A little while later, everyone went their separate ways and got into different taxis. Ken and June got in one and he told the driver in a surprisingly good accent, "Salto del Tequendama, por favor."

The driver gave a knowing nod. They drove a ways out of the city and arrived at what seemed like a hiking location for tourists. Ken gave the driver the money in cash and walked out. He held June's hand as she got out of the car. June looked at him for a moment and thought to herself how charming yet dorky he appeared. Who looks this good in the humidity? she mused to herself. Does he look more handsome now?

She kept glancing at him as she followed up the trail until

they finally made it to the sound of a roaring waterfall. The sight was majestic, especially during the setting sun. But her eyes kept sneaking glances at him and she noticed him looking at her a few times too. They stood by the rocks near the water and June caught herself with her mouth wide open, staring up at the waterfall.

"Beautiful, isn't it?" said Ken, staring at her with warm eyes.

June nodded.

"I've never seen anything like this. I usually just went from slum to slum with Mom and kind of figured the world really didn't have much to offer. I forget there are amazing things like this, you know?"

Ken let out a soft sigh and held her hand. "The world is a horrifyingly beautiful place."

June was puzzled, but she immediately understood what he meant.

"Yeah, I guess you're right."

They both looked back up at the waterfall. Ken let out a deeper sigh.

"We gotta head back soon. Try to get some sleep before the flight. The jet lag always sucks, and I hate flying commercial."

June cocked her head.

"Commercial? You mean we're flying back in a normal plane?"

Ken let out a dry chuckle.

"Yeah, we got to pretend we're normal here. Otherwise, we look like we did what we did. That means a long paper trail. We don't want anyone retaliating."

They both stood there, staring up and holding hands, and all the tourists around them seemed to disappear as the moment just became about the two of them in the presence of nature's majesty. June wondered if she'd ever feel this way again.

The next morning the team gathered in the lobby. June was unsure what to do. She expected William to greet them, but instead a man in a suite walked up to Ken and shook his hand. They had an exchange in Spanish and Ken turned to the others, motioning his head to follow him. They walked outside and a large black van was waiting for them. On their way to the airport, June kept peering out of the window but also noticed that Ken, sitting in the front passenger seat, kept peeking back at her every so often.

Zoe, who was sitting next to her in the last row, gave her a nudge with her elbow.

"So, lady, spill!" Zoe burst with excitement.

"Nothing much happened, he just took me to go see a waterfall and we held hands."

June felt her face blush, but Zoe's grin turned to a frown.

"Have you ever... Like, ever had a boyfriend? Girlfriend? Sex? No judging—myself, I'm waiting for the right person. Though, I'm always scared I'd make them look bad with my strength. So, you've never..."

June shook her head.

"How could I? I was always on the run and taught never to trust anyone. I wouldn't even know where to begin. I've had crushes but couldn't do anything, and my mom just told me boys are trouble. So, I dropped the subject quickly."

"Well, there's no instructions on the subject, but I'll make you my project and get you to, at the very least, first base."

June flinched in confusion.

"Kiss, lady," whispered Zoe. "I mean kiss. If you really like him, and I think he really likes you too, y'all gonna be sneaking off to make out all over the base."

June felt her face flush and tugged on her hair.

"You know I'm teasing. We don't get out much, and seeing people genuinely happy at the base just doesn't happen often. I am happy for you, though. If you really like him, then I wish the best for you both. I haven't found anyone I really like—I mean, Jeremy from Team Delta is kind of cute, though I only ever see him during meals, and that was a while ago. Also, Kim, but I heard she's mean."

June gave Zoe a sheepish grin. The rest of the drive to the airport was normal with stories from other missions and what they'd each do as soon as they got back. June imagined how wonderful it would be to take a shower in peace at her own house before remembering the shared showers she was going back to. June just wanted to forget this whole ordeal. Waiting to hear from her friends, having to sit with generals and government men, and having to spy in public, June was ready to leave all of this behind.

June frowned, thinking, William and the agency are going to train me to do this more often, and be the head of several departments and teams, and be just as flustered as he is, juggling so many teams and governments and... June's thoughts were interrupted.

"We're here," said Freya from the middle row.

The team made it through customs, even June, who had her passport and ID in her bag along with other necessary paperwork that William had provided. Boarding the plane, they were all sat separated. June got a middle seat and nervously held on to the chair's armrests through most of the flight, while a child kept kicking her seat and misbehaving the entire journey. Landing was a little bumpy but June finally let out a sigh of relief, then she got out of her seat and made eye contact with the mother behind her who blanched apologetically. Once off the plane, June saw William meeting up with Ken at the end of the terminal and the others met up soon after. It was past midnight on June seventh and June could almost see the Vegas lights as they drove from the airport but the van they all got into drove the opposite way toward the desert. June saw the mountains off in the distance and wondered which one they flew out from.

The phone rang for William. He answered and became infuriated. "What do you mean that wasn't him? How many others can possibly look like him and do what he did?!" William took a deep breath and tried to calm down. "I understand. I'll call the director now. We need to coordinate with Colombia as well. I'll let the team know."

Everyone stayed nervously quiet until he hung up. William put the phone in his front pocket and turned to the team. "Guys, this is gonna sound pretty bad, mostly because it is, but we messed up."

Ken spoke up, his voice cracked as the anger caused his fist to shake. "What do you mean we messed up? We found him!"

William put his hand up and tried to calm Ken down. "You did nothing wrong. He looks like him, he talks like him, but apparently during transport the restraints were too tight and cut his wrist. He was a look-alike. We don't know how, where, or when there might have been a switch. And I know the Colombian team searched the property thoroughly... What I'm saying is, we were either duped, or worse, baited."

Just then, an explosion happened on the side of the mountain.

"What's happening?" Freya, leaning up and trying to peer

out the front window, said frantically.

"Faster, Charlie!" urged William, pulling out his phone and searching for a number in a panic. "Pick up, pick up, pick up..."

Sirens could be heard off in the distance.

"Jane! Jane, is that you!? What's happening? What's... Who? Jane? Jane!?"

William stared at his phone as the line went dead.

"We're under attack. This is bad. The Cesar look-alike must have had a tracker under his skin or something, maybe... The Zealots must have followed us. We got faulty intel... I thought we had them all! Ahhh!"

William began to yell and punch the side of the door.

"We're always so careful. How?! How did no one notice anything!?"

The team was silent and June felt scared. The one place she thought she'd be safe, if imprisoned, just became the center of an attack.

Arriving at the scene, helicopters were circling overhead, and the fire department began showing up. They were miles from the nearest city, yet it seemed like services were coming out of nowhere. William ran out of the van and spoke to an officer who was just staring at the mountain on fire.

"Where's the chief? Officer, where's Chief Dugan?"

The officer shook his head, glanced at William, then continued to look up as the helicopters dropped water on the side of the mountain that was burning up. June stood behind the team and wondered what they were going to do.

Ken turned to her.

"All right, we know what we gotta do. June, you stay in the middle. We don't know who's attacking but I'll guard the front and Freya will watch the rear."

Before she could ask any more questions, Ken opened a hatch beside some rocks a little ways from where they parked near a tall cactus and some bushes. That's when June noticed they were going to climb down what seemed like a service tunnel with just enough space to go in single file.

"Girl, go, we got you," said Zoe, putting her hand on June's shoulder and nudging her gently to the ledge.

"Come on!" Jin yelled as he was already making his way down. "We'll protect you, but we might need your help!"

June climbed down the long ladder and made it to the bottom where red emergency lights had activated. She could barely make anything out in the darkness, but she followed Jin, trying to listen for anything. They walked for a while before coming to a stop.

"Here!" said Ken, reaching the ladder. "This takes us up. We'll be right under the training facility. I used this once just to see where it went and, yeah, William and a crew were waiting for me by the cactus. Which makes me wonder what the hell happened tonight."

Hector gave Ken a push to go up the ladder, gritting his teeth.

"I dunno, man, but this is messed up. How the heck did they find us, man? Who found us? Was it Cesar's people?" He looked back down as Issac followed. "I wouldn't mind busting some of those freak Zealots' heads, man. The shit they did to those people, monstrous, dude."

Ken paused for a moment. "Yeah, man, I don't wanna keep thinking about it. Let's just hope our people are okay."

They came out of the hatch near a corner inside of the training area. It seemed like it was recently used. Grenades had gone off and burn marks were everywhere. June walked to a mark near the massive doors opposite of the hatch and noticed a lot of dark red stains, then heard Zoe's voice cracking.

"Is that a shoe?" She gasped. "No, no, no, no, no, no..." Zoe fell on her knees, fighting back tears.

"Kevin from records. This looks like it was Ben from the cafeteria and Marta and..." Zoe put her hands over her mouth.

Isaac punched the doors, but they didn't seem to move much. Zoe began crying, and Freya, with tears running down her face, turned to Ken.

"They grabbed every normie and shoved them in here. They massacred them using our own weapons... THESE BAS-TARDS!"

Ken's face hardened and he grabbed the other guys by their arms and walked toward the door. June saw him making a plan as the guys nodded, but she couldn't hear him through the alarm buzzing and the sounds of distant explosions. Jin whistled to Zoe, who was still standing over what remained of the people she knew. She saw the guys and moved out of the way. Freya grabbed June by the arm and pulled her close. Then the guys began making a line with enough space between them to start running. Jin in the front followed by Isaac, then Ken, and in the back was Hector. They all ran in a single file until they reached the door. Jin hit it with his shoulder first and immediately Isaac crashed into him, then Ken, and finally once Hector landed, the door bent open just enough for them to squeeze through.

"Come on, there's hell to pay," said Ken, trying to budge the crack further.

"We need our gear," Freya, trying to peer past the gap into

the hallway, said. "It seems pretty clear. A lot of smoke, though."

June, still in shock from the bodies all around her, felt Zoe grab her by the arm and they both squeezed out first. Freya followed them. "That way!" She pointed, and the three ran down the hall.

"What about the rest?" Zoe asked.

"They're gonna head to security first and look for survivors. If there's anyone left, we'll grab the gear and meet up back here to find them. If not..."

Freya went quiet, her face contorted trying to hold back a quivering lip. She shook her head and ran toward the lockers, Zoe giving June an exasperated sigh before following Freya. Once there, they saw what appeared like another explosion had happened. Everything was in ruins and Freya and Zoe desperately tore the lockers open and tried to find gear that wasn't destroyed.

"Here!" Zoe tossed June a suit. "They're dusty but they'll do."

Freya began to suit up and stopped to yell at June.

"Today, Bambi! You're like a deer in the headlights," said an angry Freya.

June grimaced.

"The hell do you expect me to do? I've only been here a couple of days and now we're under attack, and I would have been happier living my normal life outside of this!"

"We all would!" said Freya back. The three women looked down and took deep breaths.

"Sorry, June, I know this is all new to you, and frankly, we've never been attacked before. So, sorry if I'm... I just have..."

"Sorry too, you've..."

Freya waved her hand. "Don't. We need to go. Hurry up and get dressed. I need to find my..."

Zoe, still focused on the floor, interrupted, "Well, glad that's settled." She put on her mask and started running. "Let's go."

June put on the rest of the suit and followed them back out into the hallway.

"Here, hold these." Freya handed her the suits for the guys. "I'll go ahead." She turned to Zoe and motioned to her with her head. "Zoe, watch the rear." Just then, the fluorescent lights went out completely and the red emergency lights flickered on.

"Great, it's like being in the shaft again," said Freya, frustrated.

"Keep going." Zoe nudged the two of them to keep walking. "Night vision option is inside above your left ear, June. Just dig in and you'll feel the button."

June reached up and searched for a second before feeling the button under the strap that held the goggles in place inside the cowl.

"All right, ladies, quiet from here on out. Try to move quietly," Freya said before an explosion shook the foundation.

"I don't think it matters," said Zoe, looking up. "How long do you think it would take us to climb up out of this rubble?"

"Don't," said Freya angrily. "We'd suffocate from lack of oxygen before we make it to ground level."

Zoe regretted asking as she crossed her arms and hugged herself, as if imagining the amount of rock between her and the surface. June clenched the suits tighter and walked faster.

"June's got the right idea, we gotta move. If they plan on burying this place, they're probably working fast," Freya said, picking up the pace, too. Just then, the three were blinded by a flash of light.

"June! Is that you!? Hurry, follow me, sweetheart!"

June blinked and desperately tried to turn off the night vision when she recognized the voice.

"Mom!?" June pulled off her mask. "How'd you know where to find me?" The three stood holding their masks, squinting toward the flashlight aimed at them.

"Honey, we need to hurry. These maniacs are rampaging now on the upper floors and it won't be long..."

"Before you bury us?" said Freya angrily. "How could you do this to us, Melody!?"

"I didn't, okay? I just want my daughter back, Freya. You and the agency are free to do whatever you want, but just give her back to me."

The desperation in her voice made Freya take a step back.

"Mom, I..."

"I know, sweetie. Now come on, we need to head out. You girls are welcome to follow, but we split up at the surface."

"Yes!" said June, running toward her and giving her a hug. Zoe and Freya glanced at each other, confused, but shrugged and followed them.

"How did you find us, ma'am?" said Zoe, putting on her mask again and picking up the guys' suits June dropped in her excitement.

"The security office. It wasn't terribly ransacked. They just dragged Joe out of it and..."

Melody let out a deep sigh.

"They used it to gather up the others."

"Have you seen my..." Freya said with a shaky voice.

Melody shook her head somberly.

Freya let out a curse and punched the wall. June could hear her softly sobbing behind her mask.

"Child, now is not the time. We need to go."

"What's the point?" said Freya, stepping back and pulling off her mask. "What's the point of keeping the world safe if we can't keep ourselves safe?"

Melody walked up to her and gave her a hug.

"Listen, I've been keeping an eye on this place since June came in. I saw the plane take off and tried to sneak my way in. I listened to all the transmissions for any word on you guys. Something happened, though, with your mission. That Cesar fellow came in and despite being in a coffin..." She turned to June. "Coffins are these blocks where we keep Bricks under sedation using gasses, anyway..." Melody glanced back at Freya. "I heard that he was bleeding from one of the constraints. From there it seemed like he might have been an impostor, and he might have held a tracker under his skin. So, whoever planned this, planned big and ahead. What gets me is how long it took them to notice that. I know it's not your fault, but someone had to have noticed. That's why you fight and why the agency exists. We didn't see eye to eye on a lot of things, especially June's future, but you guys are trained for this. So I need you to step up and be the leader I know you are."

Freya wiped her face with her forearm, sniffed heavily, and put her mask back on.

"Good, now let's go. You meet up with the guys and June and I will escape, understood?"

Freya nodded and Melody glanced at Zoe and June. "Understood?"

They both nodded and the four of them headed back to the

training facility. They continued down the hall while more explosions could be heard.

"We should wait for the guys." Zoe hesitated.

"Okay then, this is it. This is where we part. Do not find us again. Take care of yourselves."

She began to fiddle with a panel she forced open next to the heavy doors, and suddenly they began to open slowly.

"That would have been helpful," Freya said, a little impressed and glancing at the bent door.

"No panels on the inside. Only a safety hatch and an interior isolated fire suppressant system, that's also attached to knockout gas," Melody said dryly.

"I take it this place didn't take kindly to us at first," Freya said, crossing her arms.

"You have no idea," said Melody as she grabbed June by the hand and they walked in past the damaged door.

"Take ca..."

Melody was suddenly lifted off of the ground. She desperately tried to reach for the canister of gas attached to her belt. Two large men were inside. The one holding Melody by the neck, lifting her off the ground, started laughing.

"These idiots think they're escaping?!" They spoke in Spanish.

The two men laughed, and the other man faced June, Zoe, and Freya, then said, "You thought you could escape? Judgment Day has come for you!"

He put on a gas mask, and the guy holding Melody put his on too, turned, and nodded his head at the man.

"Eliminate them." The man twirled Melody closer to him. June could see he was easily two feet taller than her, and she pulled out the canister and opened it, releasing smoke, but the men just laughed.

"Finish this now," said the shorter man, also speaking Spanish, preparing to fight Freya and Zoe.

"June!"

Melody reached out her hand at June, but before June could reach her, the man snapped her neck and let her body drop at June's feet. June dropped to her knees and stared at Melody's lifeless body.

The mask hid June's tears. Freya yelled and rushed at the tall man. Zoe turned and charged at the other man. Freya began attacking by trying to drop the man using two leg sweeps then diving into a butterfly kick. The man just kept jumping back, laughing. He waved his hands around, feigning fear. Meanwhile, Zoe used a different tactic with the other man. He was taller than her by a foot. They both got into boxing poses. He struck first, but Zoe managed to block with her forearm and saw he was going in with his left. She parried and weaved under his left hook, coming up and aiming for his face, but hit his shoulder as he blocked.

June was paralyzed. She couldn't move, she didn't know what to do, but she knew she had to do something. She held Melody in her arms. She wanted to give her a kiss but knew she couldn't take the mask off because of all the gas that was surrounding the room. June could see the others fighting. She'd never had to fight someone, let alone someone who knew how to fight. Melody gave her pointers for being attacked by a mugger or the like, but these were Bricks, Bricks who seemed to want to destroy everything. The very thing William, and this whole organization, was fighting. June stood up and watched as the large man grabbed Freya by her collar and flung her to the floor and the other guy tackled and dropped Zoe to the ground, punching her while she tried to block him with her arms. Just then June ran up and pushed the guy on Zoe so hard, he flew through the air and landed on the other guy, who was trying to pull off Freya's mask. The two men landed with a loud thump against the wall before rolling violently on the floor. The taller man began to panic as he noticed his gas mask had a crack in the glass.

"Vamos, Vamos!" said the other guy as he helped him up and they both ran toward the hatch and dropped in. June looked back at Freya, who was being helped up by Zoe, and the three huddled together as Freya and Zoe hugged June tightly. They heard the fans turn on and the gas was sucked up.

"Someone activated the system... The guys!?" questioned Zoe as they made their way toward the door.

"Freya!? Zoe!?" they heard Isaac calling from down the hallway.

"We're here!" Zoe said halfheartedly.

"Is the gas gone?" Hector asked, getting closer to the door.

June pulled off her mask and took a deep breath.

"Yeah," Freya said in shock, not expecting June to be the first one to take off her mask.

"It's safe, plus we got your gear." Zoe walked back and held up the suits.

More rumbling occurred and soon the group gathered up around Melody.

"She came back?" said Ken. "Why?"

"For June," said Freya with a somber look on her face. "They wanted to escape."

Ken turned to June, unsure of what to say.

"I'm sorry."

The room continued to shake with explosions.

"I know this is a bad time, but we seriously have to get out of here," said Jin. "Or we're all dead."

"Yeah," said Hector. "We got a helluva climb, let's go!"

"I'm guessing no one else," said Freya with pain in her voice.

"No," Ken confirmed as he put his arm around her. "No sign of Tabby or Seb. They could have made it out."

He hardly believed it himself. Freya shook her head with a distraught expression on her face and they all made their way down the shaft and back up the ladder. They were all quiet and didn't bother putting on the suits. On the surface, they all sat around the cactus that, June just noticed, was made of metal.

"We gotta find William," Ken said as he stood up.

"You guys stay here with Freya and June. Hector, grab your suit and follow me."

Hector nodded and tucked the suit under his arm as they both walked off toward the ambulances. The group sat around the floor as Freya was softly sobbing while Jin and Zoe held her. Isaac sat with his hand on his head, rocking, and June looked around at the helicopters flying overhead. She felt numb, like these past few days had been a nightmare and she wasn't waking up anytime soon. How could all of this happen, how did she go from wanting a bit of independence from an overbearing mother to watching the halfheartedly secret agent she called Mom get killed right in front of her? Her world felt like it was literally coming down around her. June stared up at the mountain that was erupting from random holes along the sides as smoke silhouetted against the rising sun. Her anger burned inside her like the mountain.

It's horrifyingly beautiful.

After a long moment, Ken came back along with Hector and William. William appeared disheveled and red in the face, like he'd been screaming this whole time.

"Well, we've been compromised, casualties are..." William stopped for a moment and turned to June. "High, to say the least. If any of them managed to get out, they're long gone because we've done a perimeter search and found no traces, what we did find, was that a semi truck had been loaded with coffins." William turned to June. "Those are the transp—"

"She knows," Freya said.

"Oh, okay, um, so yeah, truck, coffins, possible survivors. We're working on tracking it."

Suddenly the mountain shook and cave-ins could be seen.

"It's finally caving in," William said, looking up at it. "Never thought I'd see the day."

He turned to June and held out his hand. "Come, you and I need to talk."

He then turned to Ken.

"Ken, head to landings, they're taking us to a military base. We'll meet you there soon."

Ken helped Freya up and gave her a hug. The group walked away while William and June stood together. William hugged June tightly and began to sob uncontrollably. June felt confused and unsure of what to do.

"Sorry, I'm sorry, I'm sorry! Ah, I didn't mean to, I just..." William cursed and fell to his knees. "She's gone. I've lost her twice and this time she's not coming back."

June put her hand on his shoulder and he glanced up at her. Her expression was cold.

"If you'd have left us alone, she'd still be with us."

June felt cruel saying this, but the anger inside of her was raging and she wanted to make someone pay. The tall man was first on her list. William was to blame for stalking them and making her live in fear her whole life. She didn't know how their relationship would be from here on out. Now, her new home ruined and her friends distraught, she knew William might have still loved Melody, but his mistakes, his choices, all of this, it was on him. June was not going to let him off the hook easily. Tears of anger ran down her face as she looked straight into William's eyes.

"I will never be like you. Your plan for me ended with her death, but I will stay with this useless organization until I kill the man responsible for killing Mom. You're lucky I don't kill you."

June never thought she was capable of saying these things but she didn't care. These past few days had taken a toll on her sanity and right now, the world was going to face her wrath. William stood up, wiped his face with his hands, and sighed.

"I wouldn't expect any less."

"Why?"

"You're your mom's daughter. A Romero. There's something in you that I feel will change the world. You've been through so much. You needed better guidance. Mel... She did so much to give you a normal life, but you're not meant for that. I know I sound like a dreamer, but I know you were meant for more."

June wanted to punch him. To silence him. June wanted the world to explode around her and take her with it. To feel nothing.

She took a deep breath and looked up at the mountain with tears filling her eyes.

"They were my family," said William, looking up at it too.

June glanced at him and turned back to the burning mountain.

"I saw so many grow, fight, and learn, and love... And now they're gone."

June felt her anger sway. She knew he must feel as angry and as helpless as her. But she still felt like this was his fault. If he hadn't found her, they would all be okay now. She noticed the tears running down his face.

"Describe him to me," he said through clenched teeth. June crossed her arms, stared at the floor, and told him what happened.

5

Moving Mountains

June glanced back at the smoke billowing from the mountain. The car ride was silent as the seven of them rode in a van across the desert. William had taken another vehicle, but June didn't care. The world felt more unsafe than ever. Her mom was gone. Her dad, who seemed like a nice guy, betrayed her. Maybe she was being hard on him, but she couldn't help it. Her anger made her want to implode. So much loss of life, people who were volunteering to work there because they knew a Brick who had to live there, people who were there as their job, trying to make the world a better place. It was not fair. June's head dropped back against the headrest, and she looked ahead at the rest of the team. Zoe, who sat next to June, leaned on her side and held herself. June could tell everyone was suffering immensely. Isaac seemed to be the only one whose demeanor didn't change much, but he always appeared angry and frustrated. It seemed like his anger and frustration had a focus. The large passenger van continued to drive for a way until they saw an army base off in the distance.

"Is that..." started Hector, leaning forward and peering

through the windshield.

"Seems like it," said Ken, surprised as well.

"Think we'll see some aliens or something?" Hector chuck-led dryly.

Ken only shrugged his shoulders. Soldiers opened the gate and let them through, only peeking in to look at the team. The mood was grim, and no one seemed in a talking mood. The car came to a stop as William waved them down. Ken clicked his tongue and exited the vehicle first. The others still stayed seated, unsure of what to do. June craned her neck to see what they were doing. Standing beside a military vehicle, William was trying to keep calm while talking to Ken; they seemed to both be trying to hide their devastation. Finally, she could tell that Ken didn't like what William said and stood with his fist over his mouth. William walked to the van and opened up the sliding door.

"Okay, team." He sighed. "This is a temporary residence until we can find a safe place. Please refrain from the alien jokes, though I know most of us aren't in a jovial mood. Sergeant Primrose has been assigned to help with any of our needs. Any questions should be directed toward her. There's a shelter underground where we will stay until the director decides our next course of action."

He looked over at everyone and lingered a little on June, who was trying to avoid eye contact.

"Okay, team. Grab your suits and meet me by the office."

The team quietly walked out of the van except for Jin, who turned around to thank Charlie for the ride. They all walked a ways toward the military office. Ken waved at them and opened the door to let everyone in. Once everyone was inside the lobby, a tall woman with broad shoulders and a fit frame walked in. With dirty blonde hair and robust features, Sergeant Primrose was about a foot taller than Ken.

"So these are them," she said with a voice much softer than June was expecting. "I'm sorry to hear what happened. In a moment, a shuttle will come and collect us and take you to your bunker. We're on high alert and keeping an eye out for any further attacks."

"When do we attack!?" asked Freya angrily but catching herself before she said anything else. Primrose seemed confused. "Uh, not sure, but you're welcome to join the army if you're interested."

The group scoffed, and the door opened behind the sergeant. William walked in and said, "Oh, you don't know. Long story short, Sergeant, these kids are specialized black ops agents. They, uh, they technically don't exist."

Sergeant Primrose laughed dryly and looked back at the group.

"Even the little one?" She eyed June.

June grimaced at the statement, but she shook her head softly and closed her eyes, trying to ignore it. William chuckled. "She just joined. Anyway, they should wait outside, Sergeant." He gave June a tight-lipped, apologetic expression before continuing.

"You and I have a lot to speak of."

Ken turned to the group and said, "You heard the man," then motioned for the others to follow him out of the office.

Everyone began to walk out before William called out, "June, you can stay."

She didn't acknowledge it, but she walked back and stood next to William with her arms crossed. June felt conflicted, but she figured hearing what William planned to tell this Sergeant would be better.

"These kids are special—er, invulnerable to many things. We did a mission in Colombia two nights ago, and it came to bite us in the ass," said William bluntly.

The sergeant just stood there, blinking, and raised an eyebrow.

"You might not believe me, but the director is on his way with files and paperwork for you to consider. These are good, well-trained soldiers with an ace up their sleeves. We guaranteed them seven years of service, keeping the world safe from others like them and..."

"Listen, I don't know what bullshit you're trying to sell me on, but super-powered teens are not on my list. I thought these were refugees, or something, that needed to be protected from terrorists. Not the goddamn *Power Rangers*."

June was growing impatient with the conversation and walked up to a desk and found a letter opener.

"Fine. Believe this." June wound up and plunged the knife into her hand.

"No!" said Primrose, reaching for her. The knife snapped and hit June in the face, but June didn't care if she looked silly now, she just wanted this to be over. Primrose turned to William, and he just gave her a sympathetic shrug.

"You, what..." She stared at June's hand. "Are you an alien?"

"She said it, not me," said June, holding her hand out in frustration. William gave a chuckle and took a step toward Sergeant Primrose.

"I told you they were people of interest. Our government's interest."

Just then, a honk could be heard outside. The team was

already piling into the twelve seat cart, Ken sitting in the front and waving June in.

"Thank you, June," said William. "She wouldn't have believed anything otherwise."

June shrugged and walked toward Ken. William sat in the back with Primrose, and they both began speaking, but June didn't care. She sat next to Ken, who put his arm around her. A bit forward, but she needed to feel protected, cared for, anything. Anything other than pain. She put her arm around Ken's back and held him tight as the cart began to drive past the gates and buildings.

***

The team was dropped off in front of a door guarded by two soldiers with dogs. They saluted Sergeant Primrose and continued to patrol. It appeared like a regular bunker, but the doors were heavy; this must be a bomb shelter. The team walked in and noticed it was huge inside, with bunk beds along the walls and bench tables in the middle.

"You'll all be safe here till the director comes," said William as he peered around.

"Will we?" said Jin, half joking. Jin hadn't said much throughout the trip and seemed to have had difficulty looking at June. He was the first to walk up to a bunk.

"Dibs." Jin claimed it by lying in it on his side and curling up.

William stood still as the team quietly followed Jin, and each took the bottom bunk of the beds. William turned and thanked Sergeant Primrose.

"I'll call you if we need anything. When is lunch?"

Sergeant Primrose nodded with confusion as she focused on the team.

"Soon, the cook was waiting for you to arrive, and they'll have something out soon. In the meantime, the sink is filtered, so feel free to drink, and bathrooms are toward the end."

William gave her a nod and thanked her again. She walked away, closing the door behind her with a loud clank.

"Okay, team, you..."

"We heard," said an agitated Freya. "I don't think any of us want to eat anything right now."

William glowered as the team all curled up into the beds. June glanced at William before looking around at the others.

"They've seen horrors before, but never this close to home. It's usually one megalomaniac who thinks he can do whatever he wants, or a cult that uses people to appease their leader, but this was personal. Violently personal." He sighed and walked away from the team to get a bunk on the opposite wall. He lay on his back and stared at the ceiling. June could see his chest rising sporadically. He seemed to be holding back his crying.

June only felt anger. Anger at the fact she was taken from her life and forced to serve before she could do what she wanted, and even then, only what they'd allow. To top it all off, she had to watch her mother die at the hands of some Goliath Neanderthal. The person who wasn't truly her mother but raised her nevertheless. She wanted revenge. June gripped the pillow and squeezed it. She wanted to tear it to pieces. Then she heard Jin sob, then Zoe and Ken cursed, and they all got up and just cried. June just stared at the foot of her bed. She couldn't imagine how it felt when living in this small community, where everyone knew each other and saw each other every day, suddenly vanished. Hundreds dead. *Hundreds*. June surveyed around at the team and couldn't imagine what was going through their heads. Probably the same feelings of helplessness and anger, a need for revenge, or maybe numbness. William got up out of bed and walked up to them.

"Clearly, we're not resting today." He sniffed and rubbed his nose with his sleeve. "We need a plan. When the director comes, he'll have some intel on the attack. He might have gotten footage from our security. What terrifies me is that they had access to our systems. Whoever led the attack was much smarter than the average drug kingpin and knew exactly what to do. We need to have a plan of attack. It's just us. We have to figure out how to get back at Cesar and stop him for good."

"You think it was Cesar, for sure, boss?" said Ken, rubbing his eyes dry.

"Clearly, we got a stand-in," replied William, humming pensively. "He had to have known someone was coming for him, whether us or some other government agency."

"Maybe someone leaked us the wrong info or set a trap?" Ken said, sitting back down on his bunk and crossing his arms pensively.

"Maybe, or maybe that was their fallback all along, but why target the base? They could have taken him back at any moment," William replied.

The team paced around and fell deep into thought.

"A mole, maybe?" said Freya, her lips pursed angrily at the thought.

"Plausible." William nodded. "He's too clean, set up a church in his thirties, no incidents, no arrest, no marriage, children... nothing. The man was a saint."

"Planted," said June. "They, uh, they might have planted him. Created a clean paper trail and pointed him to the place that would get him the most attention. Like, how do you attract the most attention by the people you want the most? Sell what they want. We want to take out Bricks, so dangle a rogue Brick in front of us. It's possible it could have been an inside job or just someone who knows of us."

Everyone stared at June, and she shrugged nervously.

"What? I listen to a lot of true crime podcasts."

The team chuckled softly, but William walked over to her with determination in his eyes.

"You might be right. I have phone calls to make."

The two of them stood outside the bunk as William fiddled with his cell phone. A moment later, Sergeant Primrose arrived in a small golf cart, and the three of them drove back toward the main office.

"You have new information?" she asked. "The director is on his way."

"Yeah," said William as he turned to June. "This might have been an inside job, and I think I know who it is."

The rest of the ride was quiet until they made it to the sergeant's office.

"Phone, please," William asked the front desk officer, who handed him the landline phone. He dialed and waited for an answer. While he waited, he nodded to June to have a seat, and the sergeant stood next to him with her arms crossed.

"Dr. Cassandra Glendale, please. Tell her it's Agent Saturnino. It's important."

He paused for a moment.

"Cassandra, oh, it's great to hear a familiar voice. ... Yes, everyone. They're all... Yeah." William's voice began to crack. "They got Melody, too. Seemed she was trying to take June again. ... I know, it was. I need everything you have on the Freeman case. This feels like it. Like, he's finally putting things into motion. ... There was nobody, it could still be him. ... Yes, I'll bring it up to see what he says, but yes. I'll put on the assistant, he can give you the best place to send the files. ... It was. ... It was nice hearing from you again. Bye."

William passed the phone to the assistant, who began to give Dr. Glendale an email address to send the info to. William walked up to June.

"The director is the guy that handles everything at B.R.I.C. Agency, approves missions, budgets, the works. Please don't give him a reason to stick you in a coffin. I know you're mad at me, but that stays with me. He's powerful, and his general is one of the best Bricks in the force. General Delany is a legend, so please be on your best behavior."

June nodded and felt it was unnecessary for him to talk down to her like that, but she figured she'd stay quiet and start "behaving" now.

Sergeant Primrose peered out the window.

"They're here."

June got up to look at the convoy of black SUVs that lined up in front of the office, and several agents dressed in black walked out and surveyed the area while one opened the vehicle's door, and a tall man in fatigues walked out. Fairly handsome and with a strong jawline, June assumed he was the general. His short brown hair and piercing brown eyes almost made it seem like he was staring straight through the building at everyone inside. Behind him was a tall, dark-skinned man who seemed much older with a shaved head and wrinkles on his face that showed he really did seem to have the weight of the world on his shoulders. He was equally tall but dressed in a more casual suit than the agents. He walked with a little bit of a limp. The two men walked in and saluted the sergeant, shook hands with William, and turned to introduce themselves to June.

"You must be June. I've heard a lot about you, miss. I'm—"

"Nick Fury?" said June before she could stop herself.

Delany let out a hearty laugh, while the director sighed deeply. William's eyes widened, and he gave June a desperate glance. June just smirked and walked up to the director to shake his hand.

"I'm Director Louis McAfee. Not such a cool name, but it's mine. Plus, I've got both eyes."

"Thanks to me," said Delany as he shook June's hand as well. His expression became heavy.

"General Bruce Delany. Nice to meet you. We heard what happened. I'm sorry for your loss."

June wasn't sure how to respond, so she just nodded and focused on the floor.

"Please, bring us up to date," said McAfee, trying to diffuse the awkwardness that encompassed the room.

William stood next to June.

"She brought up a point; this could have been an inside job, sir. I'm looking into the Freeman case. I requested the files. I theorize that if he survived, he might have gone undercover and might be recruiting Bricks to his cause."

"That was, like, twenty years ago, Will! We saw him fall into the Atlantic, he couldn't have survived," said the general. "I was there. I punched him off the boat. The two of you are alive, thanks to me."

"Yes, but who of us knows the inner workings of the Nevada base, let alone our procedures? Our weaknesses? Freeman was one of our first, and your partner, everyone else is up in the Midwest under surveillance. No one's made a move. They're all enjoying a quiet life, but he was the only one of us who wanted more; he wanted power, he thought Bricks could rule the world."

"I know, Will!" yelled the general. "I know." He said calmer, "Freeman had issues. He had ambition, and he had skill. But he's dead—has to be. No one could have swam from the middle of the Atlantic to shore without drowning."

"What's your theory then? Because it wasn't Melody. She died trying to rescue June. They would have taken her with them if she was one of them. But instead, they buried her along with the bunker and probably took our prisoners to recruit. God, just knowing Ryan is back out there, gentlemen, I am scared."

William stood there with his hands on the sides his head, and the others stood in silence, contemplating. Just then, Sergeant Primrose exited her office and handed William some papers. He thanked her and flipped through the pages until he found what he was searching for.

"This. This is why I think he might have made it." He handed the papers to the director who riffled through them and then turned to June.

"They, uh... A similar mutation?"

"Yes!" exclaimed William. We know it only deals with gasses and smoke and the like, but what if it can withstand water?"

General Delany let out a defeated sigh.

"It's a possibility. But why wait so many years for revenge?"

"It wasn't revenge!" William paced around. "It's his plot; we're just pawns in it. He's a megalomaniac who spoke of recruiting other megalomaniacs and followers and amassing a global army of what he believes is a unified Earth under the rule of superior beings. Cesar seemed to preach that same ideology." William grabbed his fist with his left hand. "We have to follow this lead."

The director handed him the papers back and turned to General Delany.

"Follow this, take one of Dewitt's analysts, and meet me back at HQ. William, I know you're proud of your team, but right now, lie low and go incognito. Gather them up and take one of the trucks back to the airport and meet us at HQ. I'm going to our Jersey base because there have been rumors of another group forming, and I want to speak to Agent Sousa on this one personally so we don't make the same mistake you made."

William's head dropped as he said, "Yes, sir. I'll get the team and head out now. June, you can wait here."

"What if they're waiting for us?" she asked. "Like, they know we're in here and don't attack despite knowing they can bring down an entire base with just a few Bricks, but what if they're just looking at us, waiting for us to take them back to base and give them an easy in?"

The director studied June and then turned back to William.

"Kid's brilliant, but we have this covered. Just like you learned in Colombia, we swap cars and play a bit of shuffle. These trucks are a dime a dozen in Vegas. We'll definitely lose them there, hopefully, and be able to keep an eye on whoever is tracking us."

The director gave June a pat on her shoulder.

"You got spunk, kid, and a bright mind. A shame we had to meet in these circumstances. Take care now." General Delany gave her a salute and a sad look before walking out. William, having finished asking Primrose to get someone to bring the team up, walked over to June.

"Well, he seemed to like you, so that's good. Everything else sucks, and we need to start getting ready. There are clothes in the trunk for each of you in backpacks, as well as your papers. Grab yours, and let's go change in the bunk before we take a car to the airport."

June followed as they made their way into the large vehicles that were a little less comfortable to get into than the vans she was used to.

***

A short while later, the team was all seated in the car. William rode in the front passenger seat while Isaac, Freya, and Hector sat in the middle, Jin, Zoe, and June sat in the back, and Ken sat in the trunk behind them.

"Is that safe?" asked June.

Ken let out a laugh.

"Right... Still, though..."

Ken put his hand on her shoulder, before saying, "We'll be fine, the dark tints and government plates mean we're not gonna get pulled over or have anyone looking in too closely."

William turned in his seat and asked if everyone was ready to go.

"Yes, Dad," they all said in unison.

June turned around to hold Ken's hand. He grabbed it and his eyes met hers. They both smiled at each other despite the sadness in their eyes.

"We should have taken a cart. At least there, we weren't so cramped," said Jin, causing Zoe to let out a snort.

Sergeant Primrose waved them goodbye, and they soon were out of the base following the convoy of vehicles. In a few hours, they were already near the Las Vegas area, where June could almost see the tall hotels from a distance. More similar vehicles came to join them, maneuvering around traffic. The vehicles split up after a while, as they had already driven past the Vegas Strip and were making their way to the airport, when June noticed one of the vehicles being followed by a large gray pickup truck. Suddenly, it rammed the back of the vehicle, causing it to lose control and swerve into another car on the road. It bounced back and hit the median.

"Keep it steady!" William yelled at the driver.

June turned back to see General Delany break through the rear window and face down the men who were driving the truck. As they kept driving, June couldn't see what was happening.

"He'll be fine," said William. "We need to get to the airport now."

"But..." Hector protested.

"Now. No time to waste. This is what we wanted. Luckily they hit one of our sleeper cars, so they'll have their hands full with backup."

They made it to the airport. June's adrenaline was still high after what she saw, but the team walked down the airport, and June noticed how different it was compared to when it was nighttime. The slot machines on the walls were a little more visible, thanks to fewer people being there, but she tried to keep an eye on everyone when she felt a tug. Ken held her hand again. He gave her a reassuring nod, and they both hurried behind the group.

"Any carry-on or luggage to check?" asked the attendant.

"No, just backpacks and checking in before the flight." William handed her all the tickets.

"Thank you," said the woman, handing him back the boarding passes.

William guided everyone to some seats, and they huddled nearby. Ken wrapped his arm around June, who decided the floor was probably comfier than the plastic seats.

"So, did anyone notice we were followed?" asked Freya.

Everyone shook their heads and glanced around.

"We lost them," said William.

"For our sake, I hope we lost them." Freya clicked her tongue. "I don't know about you guys, but we didn't even get to eat the lunch we were promised. I'm starved."

"Shit, you're right," said Isaac, "I'm gonna pass out. No sleep, no food. Being chased. This is messed up."

William put his hand on Isaac's back. "I know, this has been a 'messed-up' day, but you guys can eat whatever you want on the plane. It's a four-hour flight, so watch the in-flight movie too, if you want. We're going to D.C., try to stay low there. Our cover is a teacher with students on a field trip."

"In the middle of June?" said Jin, confused.

"Summer school, college—I don't know, pick—but we gotta figure out how to stay together until we hear back from the director, which means avoiding bases and contact with anyone we can compromise." William leaned back on his chair. "We got about an hour till, so just sit tight."

***

The flight was uneventful, but June had never seen anyone

scarf down what seemed like a small TV dinner so quickly. As they got off the plane and walked through the terminals, June turned to Ken. "Did you breathe?" He chuckled.

"We all scarfed that shit up," said Hector as he caught up to them.

"Man, I felt like I was gonna pass out if I didn't stuff my face soon," Isaac said, rubbing his stomach.

Eventually, the team made their way out of the airport and contemplated hailing a taxi.

"I don't see any vans. How are we gonna fit eight of us in a compact?" asked Hector.

"Fine," said William. "We split up into two groups. Freya, you, Jin, Zoe, and Hector, go meet up with us at the mall. Stick close and don't cause trouble."

"We never do, boss," said Freya coldly.

"Okay, the rest of you are with me. If we get lost or lose anyone, we wait by the Sears."

"Sears aren't around anymore," June explained.

"Oh, uh, you pick."

June felt a lot of pressure suddenly. "I don't know, I've never been to Virginia, let alone the Capitol."

"The Capitol!" exclaimed William. "Perfect. Meet us up there after you've done all your shopping. Here's a spare card. Meet up at, say..." He looked at his watch.

"Midnight?" asked Freya, feeling frustrated. "When are we gonna stop?"

"Soon," said William. "Once we get what we need, don't forget to see if you can get me a luggage tote or a bag. I'll get us some phones, so we can finally communicate, and grab some snacks. We might need them when we finally find a motel we can stay at." William clapped his hands and hailed a taxi. "See you guys in a few hours."

The taxi stopped, and William spoke to the driver while the others piled into the back seat. June sat in first and Ken after. Isaac sat at the other end, and William, as usual, rode up front.

"The nearest mall, please."

"Tourist," the driver scoffed, and he drove off. June turned back to see the rest getting into their own taxi. She would have liked to have stayed with Zoe, Jin, and Freya, but she had a feeling William just wanted to keep her close.

At the mall and near closing time, the group walked around and picked out new outfits and some spare clothes as quickly as they could. Isaac found a pair of fancy, expensive sneakers and convinced William they were necessary. Still in her roughed-up summer dress with polka dots, June had almost forgotten about the emerald William got her and looked at herself in a store's reflection. Her hair was messy, her skin was dry, and her lips were chapped. She looked terrible and felt it. She wanted to stuff her face with pizza again, but Isaac convinced them to try out a hot dog place that seemed to have opened recently in the mall.

"They fit perfectly in your hand," Isaac said as he grabbed a handful of mini dogs and shoved them into his mouth.

"Dude, these are delish!" Ken said with his mouth full.

June watched them eat. She wasn't hungry; though her body was, she didn't feel like eating, and she didn't even eat during the flight. The memory of holding her dead mother still lingered, and she found herself sitting closer to Ken. She heard footsteps approaching. William joined them after going to an electronics store.

"Oh, my God! I love these!" He grabbed a handful of the mini dogs. "Pigs in a blanket, we call these back where I'm from." Then he tossed a few into his mouth.

After a moment, he swallowed and took a drink from his water bottle.

"Here, got us some phones. Nothing fancy, prepaid, and disposable. We'll use these while we're here. Hopefully, we'll get new phones when we get picked up for transfer."

"What happened to your phone?" asked Ken as he finished drinking his soda.

"I had to chuck it. The base was compromised, all our info was stolen, and who knows what else, so to avoid being tracked, I threw it out in the desert."

They all nodded, still seemingly upset but continued eating.

"June, you like the clothes you found?" William asked, in a desperate attempt to talk with June.

"Yeah," she replied coldly.

I want to be mad at him, but... he's lost more than I have, she thought.

June peered up at him and her expression softened.

"I, er, I found some nice stuff. Nothing as cool as Isaac's new shoes, but they fit me."

"That's good, that's good... Good. Uh..." William trailed off, trying to think of something to say.

Ken spoke, "Well, this is awkward. I'm going to head to the bathroom. I'll keep in touch."

He grabbed a phone and a napkin with all the numbers written. Isaac nodded as he continued to shove more mini dogs into his mouth.

"I'm sorry, June. I'm sorry for all of this. It wasn't fair to bring you in like this, but you're special, and we were scared you'd be turned to the other side, or worse." William sighed. "And I couldn't bear the thought of having to fight you." William held her hand. "Kid, I saw you grow up. I was there for your first steps. I might not be your father, but I raised you, fed you, I..." He choked up a little. "I came home one day to an empty crib and a note from the two people in my life who I would die for."

June wanted to pull her hand away but felt sorry for him. This tough-as-nails secret agent was falling apart for his love and a random baby they found. June knew Melody was a wonderful person. She could see what he saw in her and started to notice what she saw in him. He was pleasant, and very genuinely kind. Though a little clingy and headstrong, but seeing the line of work they were in, it seemed understandable.

"It's okay," June said after a moment. "You love her— loved—uh, we... This has been a disaster, you know, and it sucks, it really does. I don't know about you, but I'm antsy. I want to get those who killed the people we cared about. I want them to suffer."

Isaac finished up the last of the mini hot dogs and leaned forward.

"Likewise. They have to pay. We do too much to help, just to have some psycho take everything from us."

"Vengeance only leads to pain. I've seen it happen. But there must be justice. So we'll organize. We're not going to sit idly by while the director takes charge and puts others in danger."

William leaned back in his chair as Ken joined them, taking a seat.

"The eight of us are going to destroy Cesar and whoever is pulling his strings."

Ken looked around, realizing the grim conversation he had

missed and asked, "So, we're going to Columbia again?"

***

The team met up at the Capitol building, standing outside the gates, and noticed the jaded passersby and tourists fighting, trying to make their way past each other.

"Okay, maybe this wasn't the best idea. Everyone grab a phone, the numbers are already saved within. I'll text you the address of the motel we're staying at." William handed out the phones to the team and hailed a taxi.

"If you get there before me, just wait. This is a safe house, so we'll be in touch with some law enforcement."

"Great," said Freya dryly. "We'll meet you there."

They all split up again and grabbed separate taxis. June could tell their moods weren't anywhere near how they used to be. The gloom hung over everyone, and jokey remarks weren't being said. The car ride was quiet until they managed to get to a motel several miles from the capital city, deeper into Virginia.

The motel was a little open balcony hole-in-the-wall that reminded June of some of the run-down apartments she would stay at with her mom.

"Okay, give me a minute with the front desk, and then I'll give you the signal to come over."

William gave the taxi driver money and told him to wait a bit longer, then got out of the car and walked into the motel lobby. The three of them just stared while the taxi driver sat there reading a magazine. After a moment, William stepped out of the motel and waved them down. The trio walked out, grabbed their bags, and the taxi drove away.

William shuffled through the keys and handed them out to Ken, Jin, and Zoe.

"We're all along the first floor toward the back end. Ken, you and Isaac take 1 L, Jin and Hector can have 1 K, and June and I will stay in 1 J, and 1 M for Zoe and Freya."

"Two keys for each room. Please don't lose these."

June turned to William. "How long are we gonna stay here for?"

"A while," replied William. "I'm getting intel on our situation, don't forget your IDs in the backpacks. An officer is coming to pick me up. You guys stay put."

William handed June a key to their room, not wanting to leave June's side. He gave her a sad look before walking away toward the motel lobby again. Isaac spun the key with his finger and let out a sigh.

"Bro, I'm hitting the sack."

"All right," said Ken. "Same."

Ken bounced the keys in his hand. He turned to June. She watched as Isaac was already heading inside and turned back to Ken.

"Maybe I could stay with you... Till William gets back?"

Ken rubbed the back of his neck nervously. June wasn't sure what to do. She had never been in a room alone with a guy, and her mouth moved before she could think of anything.

"I gotta shower, change out of this outfit, and I'm really tired, and you guys need to rest, and..." She trailed off.

"Okay, yeah, you're right, but..." Ken said, rubbing his neck and peering down. "If you need company, I'm just a few doors down."

June could have kicked herself, but she managed to compose herself.

"T-thanks, I'll probably just knock out soon. You know, it's really been... It's a lot to process, but thanks. Thanks for the offer."

She quickly turned around and tried to unlock the door.

"Good night." She glanced at Ken before shutting the door. The bag of clothes and the backpack felt heavy, and she didn't want to keep standing anymore, but she made it to the bathroom, where she pulled out her sleepwear and set up her outfit for tomorrow on top of the toilet. After grabbing the soap and shampoo, she turned the shower on and waited for it to warm up.

June was lost in thought. Her mom always had dinner ready when she'd get out of the shower after a long day at school. Then, homework would just be in the way of movie nights, and the two of them would discuss what they wanted to watch. *The Land Before Time* was one of June's earliest memories, and she remembered Melody tearing up and saying that she couldn't bear the thought of leaving June alone in the world. The movie felt a little boring, but after all these years, the emotional impact hit her hard. The memory of Melody reaching out for her in her last moment. June wanted to scream, to punch the wall, to kill that man. As she got up to shower, her knees buckled, and she found herself on the floor, where she finally cried.

***

A few hours later, June surfed through channels on her tiny twin bed in the motel room when she heard the door jiggle. She started panicking and was about to attack when William entered the room.

"Hey, kiddo, it's just me. You can put the controller down," he said, lifting one hand defensively while the other held a few bags. "I got us some snacks."

June nodded and thanked him.

"We'll take it easy tomorrow. If there's anything you wanna go do, let me know, but I feel the lot of us definitely need to take a breather."

June nodded again and got under the sheets. William's cheek twitched as he told her good night, and entered the bathroom.

"If you need to go, let me know. My showers are usually pretty quick, though."

June gave an acknowledging grunt, turned over, and tried to sleep. A tear escaped, but she managed to keep her emotions in control. She did manage to hear a sob come from the shower. William was trying to be brave for her sake, but she thought about how devastated he must be too. She remembered how he broke down as they left the base. He was in charge of all those people, and knew all of them by name. She thought she should be nicer to him. It was going to take work, but she would try.

June finally drifted into a deep, exhausted sleep.

***

The sunlight broke through the cheap curtains, and June woke up disoriented. It took her a moment to realize where she was before she put her head back on the pillow. William wasn't in his bed.

Was he out running another errand?

June didn't want to think. She didn't want to feel anything

anymore. Sleeping gave her the peace she had needed for a long time. Then she thought of Ken and how she wouldn't mind his company, but first, she had to eat something. She slowly rolled off the bed and landed on the floor with a thump. She had never felt this exhausted in her entire life. June managed to get to the bathroom and saw a note stuck to the mirror.

Gone to get intel. Stay at the motel. Left you my card for food.
  -WS

June just stared at the note while she brushed her teeth. She wished she could have gotten her creams for her skincare routine but wondered if it would make a difference since her skin was impenetrable. After getting dressed and feeling a slight cramp, she decided she needed to get sanitary products in case her cycle started. She walked out and went to Freya and Zoe's room. Zoe opened up, looking as disheveled as June did. Freya was still in bed, sprawled out.

"I need... woman... stuff."

Zoe shook herself awake, and the realization sunk in.

"Crap, we didn't get any at the mall. Too busy finding food and clothes."

Zoe walked up to Freya, put her hands on her shoulders, and shook her awake

"Wake up, bitch! We need tampons!"

Freya, trying to grasp what was going on, mumbled, "Wh... What? Oh, shit! I forgot!" Then she saw June standing at the door. "You got it?"

June shook her head. "Nah, just starting to feel the bloating and cramps. Nothing yet, so I figured it was better safe than..."

136

Freya got out of bed.

"William said we need to stay, but there has to be a mart around here somewhere."

Zoe, already dressed, walked out of the bathroom.

"I think I saw one on the way here."

After a moment, all three of them left the room, and Freya knocked on Ken's door.

"Yo! The ladies are heading out for womanly things. You guys need anything from the mart?"

Ken let out a laugh and yelled, "Some manly things! Tools! Beer! And condoms!"

Freya chuckled softly and replied, "Old car with a V8?!"

"Supercharged!" added Ken.

It was nice to hear everyone laugh again, thought June, but she knew everyone was still grieving in their own way. The women headed out past the enclosed parking lot and toward the lobby, when suddenly a police officer chased after them.

"Hey, hey, girls, please." They turned around to see a young man in uniform chasing them from the lobby. He was barely taller than Zoe and shorter than Freya, skinny, and the utility belt he wore seemed too big for his waist. "You girls need to stay here. Agent Saturnino gave me explicit instructions to protect you."

Freya and Zoe snorted in laughter.

"Listen, Officer..."

"Tobias."

"Officer Tobias," said Freya coldly. "If you know how to buy tampons and pads, be my guest, but we need to go to the market really quick. It'll be fast, and you won't even notice we left."

The young officer seemed to blush, his face turned red like

a tomato compared to his pale and pasty skin.

"Oh, okay, I can get you an escort..."

Freya put a hand up. "They'll take longer to get here than we would go and come back. Relax, that'll probably be the easiest job you've ever had to do."

June was impressed, almost a little intimidated by her commanding attitude.

"Come on, let's go before it gets later."

The trio walked out of the motel lot and walked up the sidewalk, seeing what looked like a pretty shady part of town at night. It seemed much more inviting during the day.

After a few minutes of walking down the street, Zoe exclaimed and pointed excitedly. "Ah! There it is! I knew I saw one!"

The three walked into the small market. June found the essential section first. "Here!" she yelled in the quiet store that almost seemed to echo her voice back. Freya and Zoe met up with her and started looking through the different types of pads and tampons. Once they grabbed a few packs of each, they approached the cashier, who seemed to have difficulty staying awake.

"That'll be all?" he asked, not paying much attention as he scanned the products and put them in a bag almost mechanically.

"Thanks," said June as she used her card to pay.

"Have a good day," the cashier said in a monotone voice.

"Thank you," said Freya, seemingly mocking him by sounding like a robot. The three giggled and walked out.

"Half tempted to get some moisturizer and some creams, but if we go on a plane again, it'll just delay us," said Zoe, frustrated.

"Ugh, I know. I miss..." They became quiet.

"Whatever, at least we got these, and thanks to June, we'll be ready."

June shrugged her shoulders in acknowledgment. As they walked back onto the sidewalk, they heard a voice from behind them that made Freya and Zoe freeze. June turned around to see the two of them give each other a look of dread.

"I'd love to see your blood," said the voice from behind them. "I was told you might be around here. Zoe. My lovely Freya. And I see you have a new friend. So petite, how cute."

June's eyes darted between the women and this tall, slender man. His dark, unkempt hair and piercing dark eyes stared directly at her and made her feel extremely uncomfortable. Dressed in a tight T-shirt and loose-fitting, oversized hoodie, he kept fiddling with something in the pockets of his jeans. He grinned wickedly at the three of them. Freya held her hand out and stood in front of Zoe and June.

"You monster. They let you out? Who took you? Why are you here? How did you find..." Freya was stopped by him placing his finger on his lips and shushing her.

"Tsk, tsk. So many questions. I've made peace with who I am. All that time in the bunker attached to machines in a half-awake, half-dream state. Do you know what that does to the mind?"

Freya shook her head and held June and Zoe closer behind her.

"I'm not here to start anything, my instructions were to let you know we're always watching. I especially like watching you."

"Who!?" said Freya angrily.

"Ah, ah, ah, I can't say. All I can say is that *he* sends his

139

regards. Also, that we are strong, we will not be stopped, and we will rule the world. Nature dictates it."

"Ryan, I swear to God…"

Ryan turned around and began to walk away. "I wouldn't swear to 'em, they seemed to have abandoned you."

Freya was about to leap when Zoe grabbed her and pulled her back.

"Not here. Not here, Queeny."

"Yeah, you wouldn't want to harm your precious sheep," Ryan said as he pulled out a key from the motel they were staying at. He walked away and turned the corner. The three women stood there, staring in his direction.

"Following him would be a trap," said June. Freya and Zoe nodded in agreement.

"We gotta tell the others!" Zoe exclaimed as she pulled Freya by the arm.

The three ran down the sidewalk toward the motel, up to Ken's door, and started knocking hard.

"Yo, yo! I get it, you're here…" Ken said as he opened the door before Freya and Zoe barged in.

"Yo, your time of the mon—"

"Shut up and listen," Freya demanded. "Ryan's here. He knows where we are, and he said they know where we are."

Ken was holding his hands up jokingly, but placed them on top of his head as dread overcame him. Isaac rushed out of the bathroom.

"He… no. He's here? Can't be."

Ken pulled out his phone.

"We have to warn William. Pick up, man, pick up…" He paced around the room.

Suddenly, the door opened up behind them. Jin and Hector

walked in.

"Hell's going on here?" Jin was fully dressed, meanwhile Hector seemed to have just gotten out of bed. Messy hair, shorts, and an A-shirt, but everyone started to snort and chuckle nervously when they noticed Jin was probably bored and put makeup on Hector while he slept.

Drowsy and confused, Hector was about to ask what was going on before Freya approached him and held his arms.

"Ryan Borden is here, and who knows who else, and how many, but they know we're here, and we're royally screwed."

"William!" said Ken on the phone. "William, we're in trouble here, big trouble."

A thump was heard at the window. Zoe opened up the curtain and yelled. Everyone turned and saw the blood splatter and what appeared like Officer Tobias's legs stretching out from the bottom of the window.

"We're totally screwed, Will..." Ken said as the group all peeked out of the window, trying to see if there was any movement.

June could hear the panic in William's voice as he shouted, "Stay put. I'm on my way, and I'm calling for backup."

They all kept peeking out the window. June had never seen them so scared. She remembered the story of Ryan and how it really shook all of them. Somehow dealing with a crazed cult leader seemed a little less dangerous.

A Brick and a Hard Place

June found herself in Ken's embrace. As the team seemed to just pace and take turns peeking out of the window.

"We're screwed, totally screwed."

Hector paced before noticing his face in the mirror.

"Bro, stop, worrying isn't helping. We need to make a plan," Isaac said as he looked out the window. Hector walked into the bathroom to wash his face. Jin and Zoe held hands sitting on the bed farthest from the window. Freya sat at the corner of the room, with her arms on her knees and her head tucked in them.

"We barely survived his last attack, but now we have no weapons, no backup, no masks, and no coffins. Now is the perfect time to worry!" Hector said, coming out of the bathroom wiping his face with a towel. "Came out pretty good this time, Jin."

"Thanks, helps you are such a heavy sleeper," Jin said as he and Zoe huddled together on the bed and he wrapped his arms around her. Ken let go of June and walked toward the door.

"I'll try to draw them out. You guys make your escape out the back."

"No, you're insane!" said Jin, leaping off the bed after him. "Bitch, they have us surrounded or, at the very least, thinking they have us surrounded."

June spoke up. "They might have our exits covered, but if they had gas, wouldn't they have used it by now, no?"

"You don't know Ryan," said Freya, still with her face buried in her arms.

"He likes to play games. In his mind, he already caught us. So, now he's toying with us like he does all his victims," Ken said. "That's why I'll be bait and you guys get out, and hopefully you can make it out while he's distracted by me."

Jin grabbed Ken by the arm. "I told you, bitch, we ain't going nowhere without you. Besides, William's coming with reinforcements, no sense getting ourselves killed before then."

June, still huddled on the floor at the foot of the bed, just glanced up at Ken and he gave a knowing nod.

"Fine, you're right. I just... I hate waiting."

He sat back down next to June and wrapped his arms around her.

"It's all right. It's all right," he told her as he held her tightly. She pressed herself against him and hoped this would all be over soon.

After what seemed like an eternity of waiting, sirens could be heard and the place was surrounded in a matter of seconds. The officers got out of their vehicles and formed a perimeter and a couple of SUVs parked behind them. William could be seen with another man that was pointing in several directions to people in the Brick suits.

"The cavalry is here!" exclaimed Jin as he peered out the window.

The agents scanned and checked the perimeter before William and another man walked toward their motel room and knocked. Ken opened the door and let them in.

"I'm so sorry, guys. I tried to get here as fast as I could."

"It's okay," said Freya, finally standing up from her corner. "We knew you wouldn't let us down... But how did they find us?"

"I wish I knew." The despair in his voice came through.

"Regardless, right now we have two dead bodies and problems near the Mexican border. I had hoped you guys got some rest before we had to fly again. We've been assigned to the Texas branch. We'll be following Agent Penn Quinn. We'll be folded over to his base, but you'll all still be together."

"What about you?" asked Jin.

"I'll be fine. I'll be working alongside Quinn as an advisor. Don't worry, the seven of you aren't getting separated." June turned to William, puzzled, and he gave her a knowing nod. Just then, an agent walked in and took off his mask.

"Perimeter clear, sir. We found an empty apartment space across from here with surveillance equipment abandoned, and this."

The man handed the motel key and a note that read:

There are a lot more of us than you know, William. Your little charade will come to an end. The director will pay and the world shall be remade with the blood of the weak.

"He writes threats like a child."

William then nodded at the agent and pointed with his chin at the door, motioning to everyone to get going. He stopped June and handed her an envelope.

"Happy early birthday, kiddo."

***

The team packed their belongings into their backpacks and followed William to the large SUV and they drove off toward the airport.

"It has to be someone who's still in the agency," said June to Zoe.

"You think? It's pretty obvious... But who's insane enough to go against it?"

"Someone in William's position or higher."

"It can't be one of us, can it?" Jin asked, leaning over Zoe.

"No," said June, thinking hard on that. "We're accounted for, at all times. You guys kept an eye on each other the entire way, and the four of us were together the whole time." June sighed. "It has to be someone with the power to know what our safe houses are, who we speak to, and what emergency plans we have in place."

"Charlie?" Jin guessed, scratching his chin.

"No, he's just a driver, he never really went into a base," Zoe said, shaking her head.

Freya turned around. "Plus, he only worked in Nevada, I spoke to him once and he seemed like a nice guy. His kid was a Brick, probably around Seb's age."

"Shit," said Jin. "No wonder he was so quiet."

They stayed quiet for a moment, then William spoke up from the front. "We're going on the plane to Houston, from there it's a three-hour drive to the base. So you guys get some rest." He leaned his chair back a little and closed his eyes. June noticed him give her a quick glance through the mirror

145

and gave her a wink. She looked to see if anyone noticed, but they were all staring out the windows.

She opened up her backpack and pulled out her birthday card.

***

At the airport, William led them to their terminal.

"Okay, long flight ahead of us, so use the time wisely."

June went to give him his credit card back but William just put his hand over it and shook his head. He turned around to speak to Ken. June put the card back into her pocket. She was lucky she managed to find a pair of jeans that actually had deep pockets, plus the large dark green T-shirt matched with her combat boots, so she felt comfortable in case chaos happened; she wouldn't be trapped in a sundress again. June sat next to Zoe and Jin and leaned toward them.

"We bolt when we arrive."

"We what?" said Jin, half paying attention.

"We. Need. To. Run," reiterated June as clearly as she could with Zoe and Jin leaning in closer, wearing matching faces of disbelief.

"After the flight, we need to go. It's our last chance to stop Cesar."

"And go where?" asked Zoe.

"Chihuahua."

"I'm so confused," said Jin.

"Listen," June started, looking around. "The seven of us are clear, right? We know it's not us. The agency is taking us to Texas, why? We'd be sitting ducks. William said there's a problem near the border. Aaaand, they know where we are as long as we're with the agency. On our own, they won't know what we're up to."

"So, didn't they find us at the safe house?"

"Yeah, Jin, because it's a known B.R.I.C. safe house. We're on our own. The card William gave me is his personal card, not the agency's. He wants us to hide out and try to see what we know on our own."

"Jeez," said Jin. "No wonder he wants you to replace him. You're just as methodical as he is."

Zoe chuckled. "Yeah, so let's get the others on board."

"Uh, we should split up and tell them one by one," June said, staring at them resolutely. They all nodded and got up to tell the others. June walked up to Ken as he peeked out of a window at the passing planes.

"Hey you," she said, sounding cuter than she wanted to. Ken turned around and smiled at her.

"Hey, how you holding up?"

June nodded. "I'll be okay. The shower and sleep helped, but right now there's something I have to tell you."

Ken cocked his head. "Is everything all right?"

June nodded again and held him by his arm and walked him toward a less crowded area.

"It's about our flight."

"Yeah, William told me to follow your lead on this. Kind of confused me, but hey, if he trus—"

"We're ditching as soon as the plane lands in Houston."

"What?"

"Yeah, we're all going to get to Colombia ourselves. William put all of our new passports and IDs in my birthday card."

Ken cursed under his breath and turned to June with wide eyes.

"Damn, Mighty Mouse. Hell of a drive."

June leaned on a leg and crossed her arms, staring at Ken with a raised eyebrow.

"Sorry," said Ken, looking a little embarrassed. "I should tell the others."

June shook her head, trying to ignore the nickname. "Zoe and Jin are letting them know."

"Oh, okay. Awesome."

"The flight boards in thirty minutes, guys." William waved and walked up to the others.

"Okay!" said Ken.

"We got everyone on board, what do we do when we get there?"

William made a slight motion with his hand to talk lower.

"Trust Isaac on this one. He's good at blending in and directions."

June gave a nod and got up to get her backpack. Hector, Isaac, and Freya walked up to her, all holding their bags and ready to go.

"We're doing this?" asked Freya "How do we..."

"You're on point," June said, pointing to Isaac.

He let out a low curse under his breath and pulled out his phone.

"Houston, right? I'll see what I can do." He walked away to pace back and forth.

Freya glanced back at June. "So, barely a week and you're in charge, huh?"

June shrugged her shoulders and seemed embarrassed.

"No, it's good," said Freya. "A fresh mind helps see things more clearly."

Hector leaned in between Freya and June. "Dudes, we need

to start boarding,"

Ken placed his hand on the small of June's back, making her blush a little.

"Yup," Freya agreed, handing him his backpack. Everyone gathered and William stood in front of them, holding all their flight tickets.

"I love you guys." He took a deep breath. "See you on the other side."

He turned to walk toward the ticket counter and the others followed.

***

June opened her eyes and was grateful the flight was uneventful. As the team exited, they didn't really speak much, they just gave each other worried glances. June turned to Isaac, who was sitting on the row on the opposite side, and he looked up from his phone and gave her a thumbs-up. Once they landed and walked to the baggage claim, they saw William walking up to a man who had a sign that read *House of the Rock Church*. June thought that was all but subtle, then turned to Isaac again.

"Okay, this is our chance, he's got them distracted."

Isaac gave her a nod.

"Follow me... now!"

He walked into a crowd of people walking past to go into the ticket counters while staring down at his phone.

"Freya, you three go."

He pointed at a group of women who were heading out from the baggage claim area. June, Freya, and Zoe broke from the group and walked out with the group of women heading

149

outside. June glanced around to see if anyone was looking at them, but everyone else seemed too busy with their phones or reading the terminal signage. Isaac and the others managed to hide behind a large group of tourists that had just disembarked from another flight, and the seven of them met outside behind a pillar. June could see other people surrounding William and talking into their wrist.

They found a taxi van and climbed inside. Isaac asked the driver in a different accent, "Where is, eh, car buying?"

The driver gave a confused grin. "A ways out, where y'all from?"

"Turks and Caicos," said Isaac.

The driver nodded. "Must be nice, but get in. I'll drop you off as close as I can. Should be 'bout a forty-five-minute drive. It's pretty early, traffic should be a bit lax getting out."

Isaac nodded and turned to the others and spoke in Creole. June understood some of it even though her French was pretty rusty and Creole was a little different.

"*Mési,*" Isaac said, and they all sat down. During the ride, he continued to speak in Creole.

"We're in a heavily Spanish and English place, figured a different language might throw them off. Anyone who understands is either following us or trying to impress a girl in college," he said dryly.

June gave a soft chuckle and tried to respond back. "We need to, eh, figure out a way to get past the border as soon as possible. Um..." She searched for the words. "Car, we need to get. Should be long drive, so something, uh..." She changed to English and forced an accent. "Economical?"

"Inexpensive," corrected Jin in a flawless accent. "But yes, we need to figure out a path to get there, but the thing is..."

Jin rubbed his chin. "What do we do once we get there? How do we know where the Zealots are?"

Freya turned in her seat. "All we know is he's amassed followers along the border."

"We find them, make them know," said Hector in a weaker accent than the rest.

"Bro, *konnen* means know, *pale* is talk," whispered Ken in English, then continued in Creole. "You should have paid more attention to Mrs. Brown..."

The group slumped and grew gloomy.

"Yeah," said Hector in English, then continued in Creole. "Sorry, it's hard to believe they're all gone." Everyone turned back into their seats, and the rest of the ride was quiet.

They finally made it and asked to be dropped off at the bus stop. The driver gave them walking instructions toward a used car dealership and Isaac thanked him. The group continued on foot toward the dealer, stopping at a fast-food restaurant along the way to eat.

"We got a long-ass drive, my dudes," Ken said, walking back from the restroom to the group as they ate and came up with a plan.

When the group was done with their meal, they got up from the table.

"Time to go," said Hector. "It's probably late, so now's the best time to go haggle, since the financiers are dying to go home. Let's see what we can get."

"A van or a truck. Ideally a hybrid but..."

Jin threw his head back with a frustrated sigh and put his hands on his hips.

"Depends on what they have. Remember, these shady places usually don't look too closely to background information, so we're at their mercy when it comes to selection."

The team agreed and June shrugged her shoulders. She had never had to buy a car before, so this was another new experience for her. They walked out after cleaning up after themselves, and continued walking toward the dealership.

***

They stood at the entrance of the car dealership that seemed just as cheesy as those commercials June watched on TV, right down to the silly inflatable tube men.

The group walked in and roamed around for a while, when Hector suddenly exclaimed, "We got one!" The group gathered around an old, rusty-looking van that had a window sign that read, *"$600, o down, low mileage!"*

Jin scoffed. "Low mileage? Like what, seven hundred thousand?"

Just then, a salesman showed up from behind another vehicle.

"Nah, two hundred, kind of surprising given the area, but I was told it was a one-owner and well taken care of." The group looked back at the dusty, rusted van. "All things considered."

Ken sighed and stared at Hector, who gave him a shrug and a nod.

"We'll take it."

Ken turned to June. She nodded and grabbed William's card. The two of them walked into the office and sat down to fill out paperwork. The salesman kept trying to ask questions and make small talk, but Ken just shrugged him off with short answers.

"Where you folks from?"

"Florida."

"What brings y'all way out here?"

"The housing market."

"Y'all planning on moving here?"

"Maybe."

"Sign here..." The salesman glanced between the two of them. "So, y'all looking at a place?"

"We have one in mind."

"A house for all y'all? Y'all some kind of cult or something?"

"Something like that."

The salesman chuckled at Ken's reply, but Ken never looked up at the man.

Eventually, the salesman decided it was too much of a hassle to keep talking and just kept moving paperwork and signing dotted lines.

"Y'all are now the proud owners of a 2006 Pontiac Montana. Ya interested in adding our GAP policy?"

"We have our own insurance. But we'll be looking around for something else, thanks."

He and Ken shook hands and June gave him a nod of thanks before they all walked out. The group was still gathered around the car, while Hector was under the engine checking for leaks or damage. Ken opened the doors with the electronic key fob.

"Thanks, y'all, come back if there's any—" Everyone closed the doors and they drove off.

"Here, stick this on the window," Ken said, handing the paper license plate down the van, and Jin grabbed it and jammed it on the side of the rear window so it was visible from the outside.

"Isaac..."

Isaac pulled out his phone.

"Grab the highway coming up and stay right. It's gonna be a drive, bruh. Probably 'bout eight hours."

Jin's head popped up front to the middle seats.

"We're stopping, though, right?! I need my beauty sleep!"

"Yeah, dude!" said Hector. "We need to sleep, I'm freaking feeling these days finally creeping up on me, man. I PASSED OUT ON A PLANE, MY GUY!"

Ken held up a hand. "Fine! Bro! Fine! Chill! We'll find a spot and chill. Let's just get some miles on this junker and we'll find a spot, gas looks like we probably got a hundred miles to go. So we'll fill up close to that, and then stop. I promise!"

"Hey, don't talk bad about Betsy. She seems to have had a rough go, but she's still in one piece." Hector patted the steering wheel.

Ken shrugged and rolled his eyes. "He tends to name random things."

June chuckled next to Ken in the passenger seat, gave him a smile, and turned to peer out the window at the wide-open areas of Texas. They had left the city behind and June felt small, smaller than usual. Texas seemed huge and the valleys seemed to go on for miles.

Isaac said, "Ken, take the ten basically all the way to San Antonio, 'kay?"

Ken gave an acknowledging "Uh-huh" and continued staring at the road.

Everyone seemed to have settled in their seats and got comfortable, preparing for the long drive. Ken glanced at June as she was taking in the sights.

"Been a while since you've traveled like this, huh?"

June nodded and turned to him. "It has been, but I used to

drive like this with my mom from state to state, city to city. It was nice just the two of us. Felt like the world was ours to discover. Though growing up and realizing we were running away constantly made it feel less magical."

"I'm sorry," Ken said, putting his hand on her shoulder. "Maybe when we retire, we can go cross-country on an actual vacation."

"That'd be nice. If they'd let us." June glanced back out the window and leaned the chair back a little. Heavy snoring was heard behind them and June and Ken looked at each other.

"Stay with me, please," Ken said, holding her hand. "It's a long drive..."

June nodded and shuffled in her seat to face him. "So, what were your parents like? How was life before all of... this?"

Ken let out a dry chuckle. "It was... pretty decent. Honestly, growing up, my parents never really noticed me. They just, uh..." He sighed. "They paid for my happiness. They both worked two or three jobs, and I'd stay home all day with my grandma. Then one day in first grade we played dodge ball and the ball hit my face so hard the teachers freaked out and thought I would bleed, but nothing happened. My parents never really found out, and if they did, they didn't care. It was business as usual in the Bennett house. Probably until a few years ago when I decided to try out for football, the guy who tried to tackle me broke his shoulder. I just stood there, dumbfounded. Somehow news got out and I felt like a freak, and everyone wanted to kick my ass. School was different then, until William showed up. He explained what I am, and made it all go away somehow.

"Next thing I know, I'm at the agency, Freya took pity on me, and we've been friends since."

155

June smiled and turned away. "Feels like I should tell you something embarrassing about myself."

"Yeah?" said Ken with a curious smirk.

"Yeah, it's only fair. Um, let's see..." she said, putting her thumb to her chin. "I pushed a boy across a classroom once. He was a bit of a bully, and his favorite pastime was slapping girls' bras. So when he had done it to the girl next to me and went to attempt it on me, I pushed him so hard he flew probably about eight feet, and thankfully landed on a couple of other kids that broke his fall. Mom... Melody pulled me out immediately and we moved about two states away. Changed my name to Heather then." Ken was about to ask, when June continued. "Yeah, a video game character that lived her life on the run too. Probably not the best game to play as a little kid, but I related hard."

Ken nodded and said, "My embarrassing story is that some kid broke his shoulder trying to tackle me... and yours is that some jerk kid was making people's lives insufferable and you stood up for yourself. Man, you and I are so different."

June smiled at him. "Yeah, sorry. I didn't have a normal life, just tried to lay low, you know? Besides, don't they say opposites attract?" June's eyes widened and she couldn't believe she just said that.

Ken just let out a soft chuckle. "Yeah, June, so I hear."

She wanted the car door to open up and drop her off right there. Maybe she should just jump out of the moving vehicle. June felt her face warm up and she knew she was blushing something fierce. Ken gave her a large smile.

"Guess you'll add this to your list of embarrassing moments." Ken smirked slyly.

June put her hands on her face. "Oh my God, stop!"

"Heh, it's all right. We got hours and everyone else seems to be out, so let's just talk whatever."

June nodded vigorously. "Movies?" June asked, to which Ken responded with a shrug.

"Hardly watched as much as you seem to have. Between sports and school, I didn't do much else. Did watch the occasional blockbuster."

June turned to him. "Yeah, I, uh, I would watch most things on TV. Kind of bummed that video stores started disappearing, and streaming was out of the question. Melody kept us off the grid. Besides a handful of classics on DVDs, we didn't have much. I still had a flip phone up until a few years ago, when she got me a touch screen, but she forbade me from signing up for anything."

Ken seemed saddened by this and wanted to say something but couldn't find the words.

"Yeah," June said. "Clothes, cups, plates, and utensils usually made it. A thirteen-inch emergency TV my mom would carry sometimes under her arm. And that was it. Till I got a little older and could carry my game system with me everywhere, and my books. Kind of sad that even that's gone now. My whole life is just buried under that mountain."

Ken let out a sad sigh. "Yeah, it sucks. All of our stuff was under there too, which is ironic. All of our past lives are buried there, and it's like we're meant to start over by force... again."

June pondered and gloom set in before she replied. "The start of a new life ended before it even started. I can't imagine you guys who were just getting used to this."

They both sat quietly for a moment, then Ken stared at her with determination.

"It's all right, though. As long as we've got each other, we can get through anything, 'kay?'"

He reached out for her hand and she looked at it, deciding this was it. Her life had come to this and they accept her. They were a family now and seemed to have her best interests at heart. And Ken, he seemed to genuinely like her. She held his hand and they both turned toward the road.

"How? What do we do after all of this?" she asked hesitantly. What she really wanted to ask was, *How does one start a relationship?* But she figured she'd wait and just focus on the impending doom they might be facing.

"I hope we can rebuild. Bricks need a safe haven. If we manage to do this right and keep this under wraps, then we can go back to living our quiet lives sheltered and away from society. You know, the status quo." He let out a defeated sigh and loosened his grip on her hand just a little.

"There has to be something we can do to change this," June mused, more to herself than to Ken.

Ken nodded his head and gave June a pensive glance. "There is. We should brainstorm. The seven of us... Founding fathers?" He chuckled dryly. "Who am I kidding? We'd be destroyed if society knew what we are. I really wish it wasn't like this."

June turned to look out the window. The sunset was beautiful over the horizon, it felt like it had been ages since she had seen one. Living in the city and, always trying to be home before dark, didn't let her experience one often. It felt like the sun was setting on her old life and rising in her new one. The future was absolutely unknown now and the existential dread was creeping up on her, but she knew they were all counting on her to call the shots.

William left her a little birthday card with a picture of a

chihuahua on it. It read:

If I don't see you again, I'm glad I got to see you. You were a bundle of joy that I knew for far too short a time. I regret the life I've thrust upon you, but you've grown to be a resilient and brilliant young woman. Any father would be proud. Now try not to get into too much trouble in Cali, but I wouldn't blame you if you stayed there.

—Love, WS.

Thankfully no one else saw it. She wasn't in the mood to be celebrating her birthday, let alone during a life-or-death mission to save the world. It was a few days until the fifteenth of June, and with everything going on, all she wanted was things to return to some semblance of normality. Ken noticed June pensively sighing.

"Penny for your thoughts?"

June just quirked her lips.

"We're gonna get through this. You'll see."

She nodded and sighed quietly.

"Together. We'll be all right, it's all right." Ken gave her hand an assertive shake and he let go of her to grab the wheel and give his other hand a break. All June could think of was how her mom was there, days before her birthday to rescue her. It was all so fast: the attack, the deaths, seeing her die in front of her, and being helpless to do anything about it.

June was angry, depressed, overwhelmed, but she liked the thought of having Ken and the rest of the team for company. He seemed confident. *At least I'm surrounded by capable bad asses*, she thought. She let out a chuckle under her breath.

"I hope you're right, Ken. I'd like to see what our future

brings."

"The future is what we make it, June." He gave her a genuine smile. "And I want to make it great."

***

The sun set and after driving for hours, they finally arrived at San Antonio.

"Let's find a spot to spend the night," Ken said after a big yawn. June yawned right after. She reached back and nudged Isaac awake. He rubbed his eyes and let out a big, yet silent, yawn as he stretched forward, trying not to move Freya and Hector, who were sitting on either side of him.

"Okay, get off.... Not this one but the next exit." Isaac pulled up his phone. "Should be a little hole-in-the-wall we can stop at for the night. A few blocks down."

He put his head in his hands and June could have sworn she heard him snore a little. He sat back up and shook his head. "We gotta take the thirty-fourth down. Should get us close enough to the border so we can cross it. It'll take us to Nuevo Laredo, from there we can probably make our way to wherever William said."

"Cali," said June, turning around toward Isaac. "But, it seems like they're amassing in Chihuahua."

Isaac pressed his palm on his face and looked up.

"We're gonna die."

June scoffed and turned to Ken who was focused on the exit signs.

"We're gonna be all right, dude. Just go back to sleep. We'll wake you up when we get there."

"You're gonna kill us," Isaac said, leaning back in his seat.

"Man, I just wanna get out of this hellhole in one piece."

The guys laughed and June saw Isaac close his eyes and pass out immediately.

"He's so gloomy," June said to Ken.

"He's been through it. We don't even know the half of it, but William said to go easy on him. He's had it rough since childhood. We're the best thing that's happened to him, and, well, we're not exactly ideal."

Ken let out a soft cheer as he saw the motel and turned in.

***

The group groaned and complained as they all grabbed their backpacks and got out of the van which had a bit of white smoke coming out of the hood.

"Radiator..." groaned Hector as he checked the engine bay.

"This is so ratchet," Jin said as he put his arm around Hector.

"It's what we got and this sunny palace is gonna have to be our castle for the night, so until we get this mission done and we save this ungrateful world, we're gonna be living like freaking rats."

Hector shook his head and sighed. He cleaned his hands on his shirt and closed the hood.

The group walked into the lobby and it was definitely a step up from the last place they stayed.

"Uh, hi," Ken said to the receptionist as she sat back on her office chair while watching TV.

"Room for seven?" The receptionist, who appeared to be in his seventies, turned and grabbed four keys.

"Four rooms, fifty a night."

"Just tonight's fine," replied Ken.

"All right. Two hundred then," said the old man. "Don't get much visitors around here, but if y'all are here for the lady in white, just try not to make noise, mkay?"

Ken stared at him, waiting to see if it was a joke, but the man just took the card and processed it.

"Here you go. Y'all have a wonderful night, now."

He went back to watching TV. Ken turned to the group and everyone just glanced at each other, puzzled. They made their way to the stairs, searching for their rooms.

"Seems like we're all on the same floor, thankfully," said Ken, riffling through the keys. "How..."

Freya grabbed a key from Ken's hand.

"Hector and Isaac, Jin and Zoe, You and June, and I'll take the last one. Would be nice to get some R and R by myself. Queen needs her beauty sleep."

No one protested, a silent understanding that sleep wasn't what she needed, and the team split into their assigned pairs. June could feel herself blushing, she had never stayed alone with a guy before. At least the first time she stayed with Zoe and Freya, it didn't feel so awkward. Now it was like her hormones were telling her one thing and her logic was trying to say another.

Ken's lips quirked and he cocked his head toward the door. "Uh, this is us," he said, turning the key. The room was quaint with soft, canary yellow walls and old, rustic mint-colored furniture. "This is... nice?" said Ken, trying to find the right words.

June just nodded and made her way to the bed farthest from the door. The floral pattern on the bed sheets almost made her laugh. The light blue with the pink flowers made it look like a pot of tea. June sighed. What she'd give for some lavender tea and one of her good books right now. Ken turned on the TV and sat on the other bed. He seemed nervous too, and that made June feel a little more comfortable. She watched as his hands fidgeted with the control.

"Hey, uh, wasn't this that show? The dude who tripped over—ah yeah, there it is. My dad loved this show so much..." He trailed off, appearing like a flood of thoughts overcame him. "I should really call it a night. Um, good night, June. We'll try to be up early so we can find a decent meal. Hopefully the van still works in the morning."

June gave an affirming sound and rolled over under the sheets, turning away from him. Her face felt warm but she just wanted to cocoon herself and feel safe. All the emotions were still running through her mind. Something inside her kept wanting to go snuggle up with him, to feel something like a warm embrace, feel something other than helpless and alone. To feel safe. She shook her head and curled up into the fetal position. Ken turned off the light and left the TV on with a very low volume. She heard him sigh and turn over in his bed.

June wanted this ordeal to be over with. Her mind raced as she wondered if, in different circumstances, she would have had a chance to be with a guy like Ken. He seemed much nicer than she originally thought. She was wrong about this group, and she was glad for that. Melody always taught her to look for the worst in people. June was happy to have been wrong this one time. She remembered the talks she had with Melody and the memory of June's last birthday together with her. Melody got her a first edition of the book she loved as a kid, and they sat and watched half a season of *Gilmore Girls* together over pizza and milkshakes. June sighed and shed a tear, then she closed her eyes and drifted into sleep.

***

The following morning, June felt a warm hand on her shoulder gently nudging her awake. It was Ken holding on to his backpack.

"Come on, sleepyhead, we've got a four-hour drive and we're going to go get breakfast."

June hadn't felt this comfortable in a bed in a long time. Getting up was hard but the promise of pancakes made her mouth water. It was hard to believe it had been ten days since she was taken by the agency. It felt like it had been months, and it had only been three days since she lost her mom. The rage still filled her, but she currently felt weak and hungry. She was physically and mentally tired, and emotionally drained, but she knew she had to keep going.

She needed to find Melody's killer and make him pay.

The team gathered into the van while Hector closed the hood. "That should do it," he said, and climbed in after everyone. He closed the sliding door. "Let 'er rip, Ken!"

Ken turned the engine on and started driving. June could barely see past the radiator smoke coming out of the engine when Ken started laughing and drove off.

"I'll find a mechanic," said Isaac, rolling his eyes and pulling out his phone.

Jin leaned over and poked Hector's back.

"Damn, bro. I thought you had this. You can fix an M 1 Abrams tank, but you can't fix a minivan?"

Ken glanced at June. "Story for another day."

"Dude, I did my best, I'm not around these types of engines all day. These cars are old, beat up, and they don't make them anymore."

They drove until Isaac tapped Ken's shoulder and pointed to a mechanic shop at the end of the street. Ken pulled into the lot parking in front of the opened garage. He got out and June followed him, while Hector made his way into the hood again, exposing a larger plume of smoke. The rest of the team laughed and exited the car.

"If this thing blows, I do not want to lose my stuff," said Jin jokingly as he shouldered his backpack.

Ken and June came back with the mechanic who glanced at the van and said, "Y'all be needing a new radiator. Thing looks like it blew something fierce. I'll tell you what."

Hector gave the guy a puzzled expression.

"Son, let me take a gander." The stocky man in mechanic overalls and a backward-facing baseball cap peered under the hood. "There—there's your problem. It's got a crack along the seam. Heh! Place that sold it to ya probably put some temp sealant to cover it up but after one too many potholes it tore open again. Tell you what, I've got a Chevy Van back there needin' some parts too. Probably 'bout a week till it arrives. I can swap out its radiator for yours and place the order to replace theirs if y'all don't mind. Should be a few hours' work, if my guys ain't too busy."

Ken turned to Hector who just shrugged his shoulders.

"All right, sir, if you can work a miracle, we'd be grateful. Our parents would be so happy we made the trek."

The man held up his hands. "Sure, sure! I'm always about helping the needy and if y'all missionary kids are out there doing the Lord's work, I'm down to help any way I can!"

165

The man walked back into the shop yelling for his coworkers. Jin turned to Ken and June. "Y'all are going to hell." The group burst into laughter.

"Listen, man, it was the best I could come up with. Dude's got all sorts of religious stuff in there and he made it seem like we were never gonna get our car fixed."

Jin looked at June, who nodded in agreement but felt bad about the lie too.

"All right, he said probably by noon, so we should grab a bite now," Ken said, looking around for anything nearby.

"There is a pancake house down the street a few blocks that way," pointed out Isaac.

"Man, I want a milkshake. Pancakes. Heck, even some sunny-side ups with some hash browns!" exclaimed Zoe.

"Oh my God, same!" Freya said, slouching in exhaustion.

The group grabbed their backpacks and headed up the street.

The diner seemed like it got a lot of traffic, with parking for semi-trucks and all sorts of characters coming in and out that the waitress didn't even question what a bunch of young people with backpacks were doing there. She just took their order and carried on with her day. The group glanced at each other, waiting for someone to say anything.

"Ugh, I can't take it!" said Freya. "You guys are killing me with the 'will they, won't they.' What is it then!?" She stared daggers at Ken who seemed visibly confused.

"What are you talking about?"

Freya looked at June then back at Ken. "WELL!?" She held her hands up, gesturing at both of them. The rest of the group, trying to contain themselves, seemed curious too.

"Nothing happened," said June. "I passed out while he watched TV."

Freya rolled her eyes. "Men."

Hector stared at Freya. "Hey!"

The group laughed together. Ken seemed like he was about to pop. His cheeks were red and he fidgeted in his seat.

"You can't rush a good thing!" said Jin as the waitress arrived, bringing their food.

"Like these eggs! Oh my gawd!"

The group fell silent as they devoured their breakfast. The rest of the restaurant continued to bustle with the sounds of people coming and going.

After the group had finished eating and relaxing at the diner, Ken looked at the time. "We should start heading out. We've been here for two hours."

Jin motioned around. "So have some of these other people..."

Ken pointed a fork at him. "We gotta pick up our van, or did you forget?"

Jin snickered. "It may or may not have slipped my mind while I enjoyed this greasy, salty, and absolutely delicious meal!" He winked at the waitress who just gave him a blank stare and continued walking.

Ken sighed and rolled his eyes. "We gotta go, guys."

Freya looked at him and then around the table. "This'll probably be the last time we're gonna get a peaceful meal for a long time."

Ken nodded and put his hand on June's back. "Ready?"

June nodded. "As ready as I'll ever be."

After paying for the meal, the team got up, grabbed their bags, and walked back to the mechanic. Zoe slowed down to walk with June as she trailed behind the group. "Sorry. About Freya, I mean. She can be really bold sometimes."

June just shook her head and shrugged her shoulders. "I..." She glanced at Ken leading the group. "He seems like a really great guy, but I don't know anything... about... well, dating. Plus, my mom, and with everything going on, is it even right? I don't want to say no, but now is not a good time for me."

Zoe gave June a sad look of understanding and placed her arm around her. "Lady, I know. I don't know what Freya was thinking. She's usually headstrong and means well, but wants things done fast. We call her Queen for a reason."

June laughed through her nose. "I... I like you guys, all of you. I've never really had a family and you guys have been nothing but helpful to me."

Zoe shook her head. "Same, June, we're trying to not die. Teamwork has kept us alive and friendships kept us from losing hope. We ultimately want different things for our future, but right now if we all want to make it, we gotta trust each other. You haven't failed us and I hope we don't fail you. We've already felt betrayal. And now we've got devastation in common. We all lost people."

June nodded and looked up at the rest of the team.

"We have to keep fighting," Zoe said, looking at them too. "So no one else feels our pain."

June turned to Zoe who had a tear running down her cheek. They both hugged for a moment and then sped up to catch up with the rest.

***

At the mechanic, Ken walked into the office with June following closely behind. She'd never seen the inside of a mechanic's shop outside of the usual TV appearance, but she never imagined it to be so colorful. Blue-and-yellow walls adorned with all sorts of posters, some not even car related, and the main office was decorated with all sorts of Catholic memorabilia. The door from the garage opened and the mechanic walked in.

"Hey, my boy, glad you're back! Got 'er good 'n' fixed!"

Ken thanked the man and made the payment. The team gathered next to the van. Ken walked out with the mechanic who was telling him every minor detail about the process.

"Thanks, sir, we'll be on our way," Ken said as he shook the man's hand.

"Y'all keep doing the Lord's work! Bless ya!" He walked away, back into his office, and the team climbed into the van. This time June decided to sit toward the back and let Isaac ride shotgun. She sat with Zoe as she was getting ready to take a nap.

"Hey," said June, "sorry for getting emotional."

"No," replied Zoe. "We've all gone through it, but this got us, and I know some of us still haven't realized what's happened. But rest, lady. We've got a heck of a drive."

Zoe glanced up quickly but June couldn't see who she was referring to. Then Zoe picked up her backpack and placed it by the window, laying her head on it and getting comfortable. "Let's go, Betsy!" Ken put the car into drive and they went on their way.

The drive to the border was quiet and the tension began to rise. They stopped for gas once and continued. Zoe, who slept for the first few hours, was now leaned forward on her seat and everyone was fidgeting in their own way.

"T minus thirty minutes, guys," Ken said, turning to Isaac who gave him an affirming nod. The tension was palpable.

"Gawd, we're breaking into another country and I didn't bring my camera," Jin scoffed, but no one laughed. June knew this was getting too real but it had to be done. William was counting on them, on her, to save the world from an outright war with Bricks. June clasped her hands and closed her eyes. She took a few deep breaths and opened them. This was it. She could see the border checkpoint. They were close to Laredo, and almost as if a director yelled *Action!* the group got into character.

"*Papeles, por favor.* Papers, please," the officer asked Ken.

In his most southern accent, he answered, "Why, sure, just a sec. Here we go."

He handed everyone's passports and the officer checked them. The dogs sniffed around the car but didn't notice anything. After a thorough inspection and Ken doubling down on his missionary group story, the officer gave him back the passports and they went on their way. June felt like that invisible director yelled *Cut!* because almost immediately everyone let out an exasperated sigh.

"Well, the easy part is over," Jin said but, again, no one said a word. Ken looked at Isaac who nodded and pointed at the highway signs.

"Should we..." Hector said nervously. "Should we stop somewhere and see if we can get any info?"

Ken peered at the mirror toward Freya as she contemplated the question.

"Quick bathroom break," said June assertively. "Quick stop at some food place, listen around, and meet back in twenty."

Freya smiled proudly and Ken reciprocated.

"There, food market and cafeteria. Could hear some stuff there," Isaac pointed past Ken.

Ken nodded. "Yep, sounds good." He pulled up to a parking spot and they got out.

"Okay, team, split up and see what you can find. Meet here in twenty."

Ken turned to June and nodded. She gave a shy grin.

"Let's go, we're killing daylight!" said Freya as she grabbed Hector and walked off.

The team split and tried to find a different crowded spot to listen to conversations. It didn't take long for June to hear someone say Cesar. She listened to a pair of elderly women talking over a barrel of limes and choosing the best ones. They spoke about how there was a man doing miracles in a town not far from there that has amassed a large following by giving the same powers to others who will believe in him and the old women crossed themselves calling it blasphemy. June, who seemed very interested in the lemons next to them, caught herself just staring at the fruit and walked away.

Meeting everyone at the van, some of whom actually took the opportunity to use the bathroom and grab some drinks, she sat in the car.

"So..." said Freya, waiting for anyone to answer.

"I heard some lady say she was watching TV and that Cesar guy showed up. Long story short, her son broke through her wall and is probably already a cult member," said Jin.

June let out a sigh. "Yeah, heard some ladies talking about how he's on TV and trying to perform miracles and getting people to join by 'giving them gifts' or something."

Hector nodded. "Yeah, same."

Isaac spoke up. "Still, though, seems like some of them are thinking it's all bull, so we might still have a chance and his army might not be as big as we thought it'd be."

Jin, with his hands on his temples, clicked his tongue and let out a long sigh. "Your lips to heaven's ears, my man."

Ken nodded and said, "I didn't get anything, anyone else?"

Freya and Zoe shook their heads.

"All right. Let's go meet this miracle maker."

Ken put the car in drive and they drove off.

After a few hours and a quick pit stop, the team reached the city of Chihuahua. Everything seemed calm and normal.

"See anything?" asked Ken, looking around.

"Nothing out of the usual," said Freya, craning her neck from the middle seat all around.

"All right, let's see what we can find out. I'll stop for gas here. You guys split up and see what we can get." Ken pulled up into a service station.

"Let's do this," he said, rubbing the back of his head with a worried expression on his face.

The team exited the van and they all walked separate directions. The sun was coming down and June noticed a neon cross light up down the block. She tugged on Jin's arm while he was talking to Zoe, and she pointed with her chin toward the sign.

"Doesn't hurt to check it out, but if they try to burn me at the stake, I'm sending them to meet their maker."

Zoe and June let out a soft chuckle and the trio walked toward the church.

Zoe walked in first. The heavy catholic symbolism adorned the entrance lobby and she could hear the service already in progression inside. The three looked at each other and listened in on what the pastor was saying.

"The blasphemers, these demons who claimed power and are using it for personal gain, their day of reckoning is coming."

Jin chuckled. "They have no idea."

The girls laughed through their noses and kept listening to the priest continue about how they had come from all over South America and their crusade for injustice would be judged by a greater authority. And their so-called church, an old ranch toward the north of the city, was their haven, but it wouldn't be for long, as God himself was going to judge the demons and smite them.

The trio almost broke into a laughing fit, then they walked out of the church.

"Time to catch some demons." Quipped Jin.

***

Back at the van, the team met up, climbing into their usual seats and buckling in.

"North ranches were all we managed to get," said June, shrugging her shoulders and hoping Isaac would know what that meant. He just shook his head.

"There're hundreds of them scattered all over the place. We need someone to point it out." Jin scratched his chin. "Maybe the TV commercials mention something?"

The team shrugged it off, when suddenly they noticed a TV playing football at a bar where several people had already passed out from the drinks. They climbed back out and made their way to sit and watch the TV. The bartender asked them if they wanted drinks and they all ordered soda simultaneously. The bartender seemed confused at their unison, but carried on.

"All right, so, we just wait here till the news plays?" asked

Ken.

"Ideally," said Freya.

"This could take a while, I should order chips," said Jin.

The football game stopped for a commercial break.

Several pointless commercials played. Before a news bulletin came on. "Shh, shh," Freya said, motioning for the others to quiet down.

"Something big is happening in Rancho El Cáñamo. Helicopters are circling. Loud explosions can be heard for miles, but no one knows why. I'll do my best to keep you informed. This is Graciela Fuentes and we'll see you later tonight for—"

Freya turned to the team. "So, explosions at Rancho El Cáñamo, and they don't know why, so now we have a place and we have a distraction. Isaac?"

Isaac had already pulled out his phone. "Twenty minutes." They ran toward the van and hurried in. Ken accelerated so hard the van's tires squealed.

***

They drove toward the ranch and eventually saw the helicopters circling.

"William?" asked Jin.

"Doubtful," said Freya, "that looks local. I don't see agency vehicles."

Just then, a shiny object could be seen launching from the ground and hitting a helicopter, and the damaged helicopter flew away and the others followed suit.

"Great. They couldn't give us ten minutes?" Jin said, defeated.

They heard tanks coming from the hills.

"Thank you, universe," Jin said, lifting his palms.

"All right, we don't have a lot of info, so be extra careful. Meet here in an hour with or without Cesar."

The team exited the van and tried to encircle the ranch, keeping low to the ground. The chaos occurring between Mexico's military and officers against just a handful of Bricks was explosive. They lit up the night with explosions and gunfire.

Ken and June made it around the back to a tall wall and saw an armed guard patrolling the balcony, aiming up at the helicopters that were coming back. "Brick?" asked June. Ken just shrugged his shoulders. Another Zealot came out through the balcony door and yelled something at the man and they both went inside.

"Crap, you think they know we're here? He has to have cameras, right?"

Ken shrugged again and said, "That's what I was hoping for. We're the distraction—we bust this wall and get everyone to chase us while the team grabs Cesar."

June grimaced at him. "Since when? That is a dumb plan. When were you going to tell me?"

"I just did," he said with a cocky smile. Ken stood up and took a few steps back. "You're gonna want to watch my back. I'm going in!"

June yelled, "No, you idiot!"

Ken smashed through the wall, the glass double doors, and a few walls before landing in the kitchen.

"Sup, I heard there was a party here," Ken said as two of the five people standing there holding what was left of their meals rushed him.

"Now it's a party!" Ken sidestepped the guy rushing at him

from the right, then grabbed and threw him into another guy, and they both tumbled, cracking the floor beneath them.

"That's two. Come on, we're doing this!" Ken said mockingly to the others who were very confused by what just happened.

"I'm the chosen one!" yelled one man in Spanish, before he rushed at him with a closed fist which Ken easily dodged, slapping his arm away. The crunch verified it.

"Not so chosen, are we?" Ken chuckled as he blanched at the guy writhing in pain with a broken arm. The other two men who were on the floor were put into sleeper holds by Jin and Zoe who walked in from a door past the dining room. June gave them a small wave and they just shook their heads and rolled their eyes. Jin then walked up to June without being noticed by the group in the kitchen.

"He does this. All hell breaks loose, so he goes all Cáñamo Jenkins. It's a little annoying."

June raised an eyebrow and was about to ask, but Zoe interrupted, "Little!?"

"Eh, just get ready to knock out another fool."

Just then the woman and man who were left in the kitchen decided to throw everything they could grab at Ken and he just laughed it off. "Guys, come on. Seriously!?" The woman grabbed a knife from the kitchen counter and charged at Ken.

"He seems to enjoy this a bit too much." June raised an eyebrow.

Ken raised his head and pushed out his neck. "Lady, this is the only shirt I have. Please aim for the arms or neck." He lifted his arms to stop her but she managed to stab him right in the sternum, tearing a hole in the shirt. "Damn it! Now I'm pissed." The other guy came from the side with a fork and tore Ken's sleeve. "Oh well, now you guys are just trying to get on my nerves." He grabbed both of them by the neck and threw them across the kitchen into the dining table. More explosions could be heard outside and the team regrouped by the fridge, which somehow was still standing.

"Oh, hey, pineapple soda," Jin said, rummaging through the fridge.

"Okay, so my fear is true, we're looking at normies and Bricks all in the same place. We have to tread carefully if we don't want to kill anyone. Remember, this is unsanctioned and we are vigilantes in this, so if we all don't want to end up in a Mexican bunker, I suggest we engage minimally."

The others raised an eyebrow at Ken.

"My guy, seriously?" said Zoe, shaking her head slowly.

"I needed to know. Back of the house felt like the place where there would be the weakest of the bunch." Ken shrugged.

"Okay, so now what?" Jin asked as he took a handful of some pork rinds he found in a cabinet.

"Now, I was hoping a door would open, telling me where they were all coming from but..."

"It's a trap," said June. "The rumors to get us here. They figured the Texas branch would have sent us, or at the very least we'd be here one way or another. Cesar's not here, just disposable Zealots, while the rumors spread. We have to go. Now!" June urged the team as she turned toward the door.

"No," said Ken. "They might be a distraction, or a trap, but they need to be stopped. Our guys are out there and I think there might be hostages or something else here. We stop the Bricks, gather the normies, and meet up with the agency."

"So, all of this was for nothing," Zoe groaned. "We ran,

came here, and—"

The house shook from an explosion.

Zoe sighed. "We're just gonna turn ourselves back in?"

June grabbed Ken by the arm when he was about to run out. "Stop trying to be a hero. Cesar's not here. We need to regroup and get the hell out of here."

Ken scowled at her, then turned to the team and his shoulders lowered. "Fine..."

Jin and June pulled him by his arms and threw him on the grass. The guy with a broken arm looked up at Zoe and she just flicked his jaw with her foot, knocking him out instantly. They got in the van and waited for the others to show, watching the explosions in the distance.

"I hope they're okay," said Jin, still eating from the bag of pork rinds.

"They're okay. Freya's gotten out of worse situations..." Zoe said, squeezing his hand.

Jin glowered.

"...doesn't mean I don't still get nervous."

June leaned forward from the rear seat and pointed at some shadows coming toward them. "Is that them?"

Ken's eyes widened and he let out a gasp. "Hide!" Everyone ducked in their seats and they heard people running past and talking to themselves.

"They've lost faith," said Jin with a dry chuckle.

"Yeah, unfulfilled promises have a tendency to kill dreams," said Ken, sitting back up in the driver's seat. Just then, a bang on the sliding door window startled them. It was Isaac and Hector as they climbed in, out of breath.

"Bro, this freaking place was a maze. I think I walked into the same bathroom, like, five times." Isaac chuckled dryly.

"I kept finding stairs that led to bedrooms with more stairs, then eventually a basement with wine..."

"Bruh," Isaac interjected, "swear to you, it looked like a whole city of wine. We were there forever."

June glanced up at Ken and back at Isaac and Hector.

"Where's Freya?"

"Queen?" asked Hector, turning to Isaac. "She's gonna take that whole place down into another world. She found out Cesar's not there and she's going full commando on them. Told us we'd hold her back."

Ken put up his hands at them. "Whoa, no, you mean to say she's in there. By herself. She ain't killing peeps in there, is she?"

Isaac and Hector shook their heads. "Nah, fam. She's like something out of a Splinter Cell game. When I walked out of the bathroom for, like, the fourth time, there was a Brick there and she straight-up dropped from the roof and knocked him out. So chill, she knows what she's doing," Isaac said as he leaned forward to look out the front window. The place seemed to be getting surrounded by more and more black SUVs and military vehicles. Suddenly the roof of the van made a loud thud and caved in a little.

The team gasped and were about to run outside when Freya waved from the front window, leaning in from the roof. "Miss me?" The team let out a sigh of relief and opened the van door for her. Ken started the van and began driving. Freya panted as she finished clicking her seat belt and peered up ahead at Ken and Jin sitting in the front. "Did you guys figure out Cesar wasn't there?"

Ken shook his head. "June figured out it was a distraction."

"Yup, those agents showing up now would probably try to

take us in if they saw us."

"Yeah. This whole thing is sus, someone's out to expose the agency." Freya crossed her arms and breathed through her nose. "But, I got something."

She held her stomach and looked uncomfortable.

"I met someone..."

***

Freya was sneaking around the house after running into Isaac and Hector. Freya was checking the closets of each of the mansion's rooms and tried to avoid falling through the roof with every explosion. One of the rooms she came across had a pulley hanging from the ceiling. Freya smirked and pulled down the attic ladder. She made her way up, only to be met with a gun pointed at her head. She put her hands up and climbed up the rest of the way. The shaking hand pointed it toward her head and slowly walked backward.

"Who are you?" the man said with a heavy accent.

"Jane. Jane Doe. I'm with the American CIA, here to investigate Cesar Villalobos. You wouldn't happen to know where he's at, would you?" Freya asked in English. The man stuttered and waved the gun at her.

"You're messing with me!"

"Tell you what," replied Freya. "Drop the fake accent and I'll tell you who I am."

"You can tell?"

Freya cocked her head at him.

"Fine," the man said in an American accent. "Your turn."

Freya sighed and turned around. "See, that wasn't so hard. Now, Cesar. Where?"

The man's hand began shaking a little more.

"I'm not going to ask again."

"I... You're here?"

"You know me?"

"You're Team Alpha. I was told you'd be here."

"Really? Now, where. Is. Cesar?" Freya walked up to the nervous man slowly and put her hands on his gun.

"Please," he begged, putting his gun down.

"Listen, you seem like a nice guy. I'd hate to kill you."

"You seem like a nice girl. I'd hate to die."

Freya smirked at the reference. "You're American, from where?"

"Reno."

"Well, Reno. You know who I am, you know what we're capable of. What does Cesar offer that makes you follow him so blindly, and how did he pull off the destruction of my base?"

"I... No, he..." The man looked confused.

"He's a murderer. Where is he?"

"He's promised sanctuary from the coming war to all the weak people that follow him. He's in his compound near the border—" The man stopped himself before talking any more.

"He's what?" Freya asked impatiently. "What war? Does he have people on the inside?"

"Inside of what?"

Freya raised an eyebrow and angrily walked toward the man, so she could see his face better in the dimly lit attic. He seemed young, probably in his mid to late twenties. Tan skin and brown eyes, he trembled as Freya's face got closer to his.

"Who's the mole? Who's funding him? I want answers." Freya lifted the man by his collar and he began babbling. "I'm going to need you to form actual words now." Freya held him above her head.

"Cesar takes care of us. He wants to protect his people. All those who follow him shall be saved, and those with the strength to fight are our front lines. Someone tipped the government off here and now we're fighting for our lives, but we didn't expect Team Alpha to come here. We...we... I just want to go home to my family! I must keep them safe."

Freya dropped the man and rolled her eyes. He laid on the floor in the fetal position, crying.

"I don't want my family to die!"

"Get up, wuss. Where's your family?"

"The basement."

"There's a basement here?"

"Yes, through the kitchen behind the fridge. There's a small pantry door. It leads to the basement."

"This place, man..." Freya sighed and followed the man downstairs. They made their way through the crumbling building. The explosions seemed to have stopped. Freya peered out a window toward the main road and saw it still had military vehicles and helicopters forming a blockade.

"Getting out's gonna be fun."

"Listen, and listen good..." Freya stared at the man as he stood looking out the other window.

"Oh, uh, sorry, Jaime."

"Jaime, they'll come inside. Tell them you're normal. Just let them take you and process you. With any luck, they'll keep you safe in their base and you and your family can start over. Cesar is a murdering monster who's trying to bring the world down with him. He even took over a drug lord's empire in Colombia when we found him."

"He wouldn't do that. He'd stop the drug dealer, but not

take over. Cesar cares for his people, he will only kill if we are in danger."

"But why would he use a look-alike and make a trap if all he wants is to be left alone? I know he plans on expanding, that's what this place is, no?"

"No, this place was a sanctuary. He'd take people coming from America and hold them here until they can go to Colombia."

The two of them walked until they made it to the kitchen. Freya shook her head and examined the damage Ken had left.

"Oh my God! They're dead!"

Freya leaned over and started checking for pulses. "Nah, knocked out. They'll be okay... This guy's arm, though. Ouch." Freya grabbed the arm that was bent as if made of gelatin.

Jaime began panicking.

"Breathe, Jaime. We were given intel that Cesar was making plans here to invade America, and especially after we were attacked by people claiming to be his followers, we came here with a vengeance."

"I'm sorry, either they're lying to you, or they're lying to me." Jaime knelt down next to a woman who had a broken knife beside her. "Jane Doe, I... I don't know what to believe anymore. They told me the government's here to kill us or take us away, because the strong ones aren't allowed to exist."

"Seems like we're both being played. Also, I never did tell you. My name's Freya."

"Nice to meet you, Freya."

Freya's cheek twitched.

"Explain that you're an American and would like to speak to William of B.R.I.C. Agency. Give them the code 0820. He'll know what it means."

"Thank you."

"Stay safe."

Jaime opened up the pantry door and made his way toward the basement. Freya peeked in to see the man hug a small child that ran into his arms and they held each other tightly. Freya then walked over the unconscious body of a man near the fridge, leaving through the large hole in the wall and running in the dark toward the van.

"You sure he didn't know who the mole was? It could be anyone," Ken said as he leaned forward and put his elbows on his knees.

"Who could it be?" said Jin mockingly. "We have such few enemies."

Freya sighed. "There's a mole, he's working with Cesar or against him. He literally knows our playbook. This is major sus. Like, we're dead if we don't figure it out soon." Freya scratched her head and the team grew silent as they became lost in thought.

"Might not even be one person," said June. "Like, how messed up would it be if there's a network of moles working in the agency. This could be a lot bigger than we thought."

Freya froze. "The letter. 'There are a lot more of us than you know.' R-Ryan's letter. He was mocking William. But we all thought he meant the followers, these Zealots, but it could be traitors. People in the agency..."

Freya stopped talking and peered out the window. "Or the war? What if Cesar is the trap?" she said after a moment.

"A red herring?" said June.

"Not necessarily," replied Freya. "More like a convenient distraction. Think about it. Kind of suspicious that as soon as the decoy gets brought in, the place is destroyed. Overrun and overwhelmed. They were waiting. Not only because they followed the decoy's tracker, but had help from the inside that day. And they covered their tracks by blowing the place up with the decoy."

Freya rubbed her hands over her head then slapped them on her knees.

"Data logs!? We need access to them, to see who came in moments before or after the decoy was brought in."

"You'd need director-level clearance for that," said Ken.

"Ugh, yeah, so that means somebody up there. Who has access to all of that and can hide and change data from there?"

"The general?" said Hector, unsure.

"Yeah," said Ken. "But dude wasn't even there that day. He was flying in with the director a few hours after it all went down."

The team grew silent again for a moment.

"Regardless, we need to contact William," said Ken. "We don't have a clue. We're running blind, nowhere to go, and our one clue turned out to be a cluster, and we're nowhere nearer to catching this guy than we were at the beginning."

Ken smacked the steering wheel, causing the lights to flicker.

"Bro, chillax," said Jin.

"Yeah, go easy on Betsy," yelled Hector from the back.

"This is messed up," continued Jin, "but it'll be more messed up if we need to hoof it back to the States."

Ken nodded, realizing he was losing his composure, and let out a loud sigh.

"Colombia?" said Isaac. "It all started in Colombia. Colombia was the one place where Cesar had his double and was often seen. Which means he's probably still there."

"Especially with what that guy told Freya." Isaac rubbed his head.

"You want us to get to Colombia in Betsy?" asked Ken, a panicked expression on his face.

Jin turned back slowly, waiting for an answer he knew he would hate.

"Yeah, doofus. This shitbox has to take us as far as it can," Freya said in a matter-of-fact tone, rolling her eyes.

Jin and Ken threw their heads back, groaning in protest.

"Suddenly hoofing it back to the States doesn't seem so bad," said Jin.

Ken glanced back at Isaac and said, "Well, point the way, my guy."

Isaac was already looking at his phone. "Motel down that way. We'll spend the night. Gas in the morning... And then, about a thirty-four-hour drive."

The team groaned, cursed, and shifted in their seats. June blanched at Zoe and she returned a worried look. "Lady, this is gonna take a helluva lot longer than we thought."

June nodded and leaned back in her chair. "This sucks," June said as she crossed her arms and tried to close her eyes.

Zoe put her hand on June's shoulder. "Yeah, but at least we got each other." They both laughed.

"That was cringe," June said, smiling.

"Yeah, sometimes cringe is what we need."

They both leaned back and closed their eyes. It was going to be a long drive toward a motel. June couldn't wait to shower and get some sleep. All of this still felt like a dream to her. She kept imagining waking up and Melody would be there making her breakfast. June sniffed, turned over, and stared out the window at the night sky. The stars were much more visible than she had ever seen. She looked up at Ken who rubbed his eyes and yawned. How peaceful a life with someone in a cabin in the woods would be, June thought. She just wanted peace, but that dream seemed farther than their current drive.

Freya let out a curse. "Guys, we need to stop."

Ken turned around. "What happened?"

Freya just stared at him with gritted teeth. Ken let out a low curse and started driving off the road. Freya apologized and started reaching in her bag.

June glanced at Zoe who seemed confused for a moment before realizing what was happening and both their eyes widened.

7

Time Over Mind

Freya apologized from behind the van as she squatted there. Zoe and June stood guard and the men all paced around the front of the van, making sure not to look in that direction.

"How're you feeling?" asked June.

"My cramps aren't usually bad but they hurt like hell today."

Freya held out a hand and Zoe handed her a tampon. "Stress?" asked June.

"Thankfully, I caught it before it hit my pants but, damn, it sucks. I just got these undies, too. They were cute."

Freya held her hand out again and June handed her cleaning wipes, then she let out a low curse and threw the underwear into the bushes.

"Okay. I'm golden. Let's freaking go."

The guys hesitated except for Jin who turned around and sighed, "Boys," while rolling his eyes. He hopped into the middle bench after Hector and Isaac took the back seat, leaving Freya to sit in the middle and Zoe next to her. June was back in the front passenger seat. Unsure where her relationship was with Ken and still trying to organize her feelings, she still found him attractive and despite being a little hotheaded, he was definitely passionate. That kind of attracted her to him more. She'd never met anyone so passionate about other people while being so heroic. It was like he was a movie hero or something. June quickly realized she was staring at him and quickly turned away toward the window. Ken glanced at her, put the car in drive, and they were off.

The team finally made it to the motel and Zoe jumped out quickly as Freya ran straight into the lobby and searched for a bathroom. Ken turned back, startled.

"Sorry, this is new to me. We're usually a little more prepared and she's never had, you know, that I know of, unprepared." Zoe shook her head and grabbed her backpack from the van. June nodded and they walked together toward the lobby. "Honestly, with all the stress and the fact it feels like all of this is just one long day, none of us are prepared. Heck, we haven't eaten since the bar... And pretzels and soda are so not a meal."

The place was surprisingly nice compared to many of the others they'd been too. June noticed it seemed like an old colonial house converted into a hotel and kept in pristine condition. They grabbed their keys and made their way to the rooms. This time the rooms were big enough for four in a room. Two giant queen-size beds in white rooms with a small tube TV hanging from the wall and wooden floors.

They decided to split up into two groups. The girls in one room and the guys in the other. In the room, June could hear Freya gagging in the bathroom. Zoe walked out and trifled in her bag for some painkillers. She gave June a look that said *this is bad* without opening her mouth.

June laid down in bed and used the old control to flip through the channels, stopping on a show where the guy would wear a green hat and barrel attached to suspenders and everyone just screamed at each other. She watched it sometimes as a kid. Melody told her about how she grew up on it and she would watch it every morning before school. June grimaced. She didn't even graduate. She had one more year of school before she was free to pursue college.

She let out a sigh and turned over, hugging a pillow. June's whole life was unpredictable, what she would give to have a normal one. She craved adventure and seeing places when she was younger. Tired of going from apartment to apartment, and only seeing grassy weeds in shady-looking playgrounds, but June didn't mean for it to be like this.

***

The next morning, the team headed out. Freya was groggy and craving pickles, so they stopped at a market before heading back on the highway. This was going to be a long drive. The van kept making random sputters as they drove along.

"Betsy's fine. We'll stop if smoke comes out again," assured Hector.

June kept wondering what would happen if they arrived in Colombia and ran into Director Gutierrez and Agent Zoila again. It would probably be best if they didn't, but June felt safer with Zoila around. The team ate snacks and took naps as the hours and miles passed. Eventually everyone took turns driving except for Freya and June; June never really got around to learning how to drive and Freya just grimaced at Ken with a raised eyebrow when he asked. They made it past customs by eating their entire supply of meals before each checkpoint and keeping the van as free from clutter as possible to make inspections quicker. It helped that they didn't have their suits, though they knew they'd need them eventually.

***

Reaching the Darien gap in Panama, the team set out to see what supplies they could gather before the ferry carried them over. It was a wait before the boat arrived, so the team decided to stretch their legs and walk around. June stood by a tree trunk people were using as a bench when Ken walked up to her.

"It's gonna be about thirty minutes before the ferry comes to pick us up. It's gonna take us to Buenaventura." Ken stayed, contemplating June. "What's up, Mouse?" he asked as he sat next to her.

June sighed and rolled her eyes.

"Sorry. I... What's on your mind?" he said, fumbling over the words.

June lowered her head and tightened her fist. "I want..." She sighed again and took a breath. "I want revenge." June locked eyes with Ken. "I want to beat his eyes out with my bare hands. I want him to beg me to spare his life. I want to do violent things I never thought I would in my entire life. I want his corpse thrown into the deepest crevice, never to be found again. I... I... I want my mom back," she finally said through gritted teeth and watery eyes.

Ken glanced around to see everyone still going about their day and back down to June who was beginning to shake. They sat down on the tree log, and Ken said as he put his arm around her, "Hey, I feel you, 'kay? He and all those nuts took everything from us."

June put her head on his chest and wrapped her arms around him.

"It's all right." He said as he stroked her hair. "It's all right. We'll get them. We'll make them pay. No one messes with us and gets away with it."

Ken held her until she backed away and wiped her face with her sleeve.

"Thanks." She sniffled. "Nothing's ever going to be the same for me. I know you lost people you knew, but your family is still out there. You're hopefully going to go back to them. Melody was all I ever knew... And she's gone, and out there is a behemoth of a man probably tearing more families apart and enjoying it." She clenched her fist again.

And I want him to stop existing."

Ken sighed and pulled his arm back and leaned closer to her. "You gotta control this. I know it's easier said than done. It's been a few days and you've had time to replay that event a million times in your head. Same. I should have been there, we should have had different teams, we shouldn't have gone in. June, I'm sorry. I've felt guilty. My team led these monsters to our home and we lost... everyone."

Ken stood and faced the jungle behind them.

"I believed we'd be safe. If we stuck to our own, and not bothered anyone, we'd... No one was supposed to get hurt. Innocent people were not supposed to get hurt. I've seen some shit out there but..." Ken turned around and looked at the people passing by, then back down at June. "June, I—we've..." He knelt down next to her. "I've seen horrors.

192

Bricks that used kids for their entertainment in gladiatorial battles. Whole groups of people were made to slave away at their whim because they thought they were unstoppable. June, the thing that happened with Ryan Borden, Freya's not over it and probably never will be. She didn't tell you the whole story. But while she was knocked out, he ... he did things to her. She's his 'one that got away.' He'll stop at nothing for her. And, in a way, neither will she."

June grimaced at Ken.

"Yeah. The bodies we found at his last place... they're not something you forget."

June rubbed her eyes.

"Then let's get going. First we find Cesar. Make him pay for what he's done. Then the Neanderthal and Ryan. We'll make them all pay. No one messes with us, right?"

She stood up as the boat horn blared in the distance and Ken blanched.

"Right."

***

The team gathered inside the van and made the line to drive onto the ferry. "We got some time to kill," said Ken, leaning his chair back. Once parked, the team all found comfortable positions and stayed quiet, pensively.

The boat ride finally came to a stop a few moments later and they boarded off, driving toward the capital. Ken turned to Isaac, who already had his phone out. "Take that left and it should take us down a main road and from there just follow the signs, bruh. It's probably another few hours before we get there."

Ken nodded and turned back to the others. "Anybody need to stop before we go on a wild-goose chase?"

Jin lifted his head. "I need some pork rinds!"

Zoe nudged him. "You're gonna have a heart attack, you keep eating that shit."

Jin laughed, saying, "Girl, how much longer are we living, anyways? I want what I want!" Ken chuckled, while Zoe glared. "Fine. But pork rinds after." Zoe rolled her eyes and laid back in her seat.

"I think we're good," replied Freya. "Just go, I'll let you know if I get bad."

Reaching Bogota, the team stopped at a gas station to fill up the van and restock on supplies. "Okay, we gotta split up. You know the drill, keep your ears open, and do not engage. Keep phones handy and call if you find anything."

"Roger," said Freya, cocking her head for everyone to exit the van, and they proceeded to walk in different directions.

June decided to go with Zoe. "Sorry, I just..."

Zoe nodded. "I know, it's okay, you've only done this once and you're new to all of this."

June nodded, looking at the floor. "I wish I had your training."

"You're not bad, June, you just... need time. We all started out like you. William and everyone else, they made sure we got the training we needed. You just came at a really, *really* bad time, is all."

The two walked down the street toward a strip mall. They started going into the different stores, making it seem like they were just window-shopping, until they saw a group gathered around toward the far end of the mall. The man standing on a milk crate began to talk louder and louder.

"The hell is he talking about?" asked Zoe. June shrugged. They both got closer and heard the man rambling about the end of times. How the gods have summoned demons to this world, demons who cannot be destroyed. Zoe and June gave each other a look. The man continued yelling about how the world will be remade for these demons and humanity would be lost. Those in league with the demons shall be punished and find an eternal damnation waiting for them after death.

Zoe grabbed June by the hand and they gathered closer, surveying the crowd to see if they saw anyone familiar. June swore someone in the crowd appeared like the guy that was with the large man that killed Melody, but she couldn't make him out in the crowd. She turned to Zoe to ask her but was met with a large chest, and suddenly her eyes grew heavy and she felt the world fly upward.

***

June found herself in the back of a van tied up along with Zoe. It was dark and the mask over their heads couldn't let them see. She felt something was off, as if the van was on its side. "We're sliding!?" She broke the chains apart and screamed for Zoe. Zoe gained consciousness and June helped her with the chains and mask. "What the hell?" The van suddenly stopped after hitting something. They heard glass smashing and people yelling. The doors behind them opened and they heard a familiar voice.

"Oye! Come with me!" Zoila was holding the door of the van up and reached out for their hands.

"Our phones!?" asked Zoe as she patted her pockets.

Zoila shrugged and yelled at them to get going in Spanish.

She turned to see the two men who had been ejected from the van walking toward them. Zoila cursed in Spanish before pulling June by the arm out of the overturned van. That's when June saw them, the men who killed Melody. Rage filled up inside of her and she pushed Zoila away and charged at them. Zoe reached around June's waist and lifted her up.

"No, June! Not here! We gotta go!"

June didn't want to listen. She wanted revenge. Seeing him again. Walking. It was an affront to her.

How dare they still breathe.

All she wanted was their deaths. Especially the tall one's. Zoe pulled June as Zoila ran back and started her black SUV. The large men stood, disoriented, staring at the women behind the wreckage.

"We need to go, now!"

June began to think rationally again and looked at Zoe, gave her a nod, and they both jumped in the back of the SUV. The two men, realizing what was happening and trying to see past the smoke, began running at them but suddenly the van exploded and blocked their view. Zoila, holding a detonator, threw it toward the back seat next to June. Zoe, in the passenger seat, turned back to June.

"We good?"

June nodded, feeling defeated.

Zoe held out her hand and took June's. "We're gonna find them. We'll make them pay, but not by taking down an entire city block."

Zoila glanced back at June with a half-hearted quirk of her lips.

"*Mi hija*, you almost got us all killed. Next time you want to fight, try to do it away from us normies, okay?"

June went to apologize but Zoila held up a hand.

"It's okay. You're going through a lot. We heard here about what happened in America. That's crazy. I'm glad you two made it. Who else is alive? Is William okay?"

"He's fine. 'Sides the rest of Team Alpha, I don't think anyone else made it."

Zoila gasped and covered her mouth. She swallowed hard and turned back to see if they were being followed.

"*Dios mió.*"

Zoila stopped the vehicle in a large parking lot and crossed herself.

"*Qué*... what are you guys doing here? Where's William? Why wasn't I told about this?"

Zoila darted back and forth between Zoe and June. They gave each other a look and nodded.

"There might be a mole," said Zoe. "Someone on our end, we think, who knew what we were doing, how we work, and how to take us down."

Zoila cursed in Spanish.

"William sent us to México thinking that there was an army amassing there, but they just... It was a ruse, probably set up to lure us out," said June, slouching her shoulders.

Zoila leaned over the steering wheel with her hand over her mouth and she cursed again. "So, you decided to come here? After that?"

June nodded. "Yeah, we thought that if Cesar was pulling the strings with someone from our side, we'd have to come here to find more clues and figure out if Cesar is even real."

Zoila nodded and turned back to the girls. "*Niñas*, I have to bring you in. And we have to tell the director. And..." Zoila had a million thoughts going through her head but she stopped and eyed both of them. "Or... I take you back to your team and give you all the information I can on Villalobos, risk life in prison, and possibly get killed helping you." Zoila let out a dry laugh and leaned back in her chair. "Where can we find the others?"

June shrugged, as Zoe replied, "We were gonna meet back at Betsy near the gas station."

Zoila's face contorted "Who..."

"Our van," said Zoe quickly, "Hector named it."

"Oh..." Zoila nodded and put the car in reverse. "Let's go to Betsy, then..."

***

They drove up to the gas station where they saw Betsy parked at the convenience store and Jin pacing behind it. Zoila pulled up behind him and lowered Zoe's window.

"Hey stranger? Come here often?" Zoe said to a shocked Jin.

Jin ran up to the window and held Zoe by the back of the neck and gave her a long kiss on her head.

"Bitch, don't ever disappear like that."

Zoe laughed.

"I won't, bitch. I missed you too. We had an encounter but we found help."

She pointed at Zoila with her thumb. Jin gave Zoila a quick smile and eyed Zoe with a serious face.

"She knows and she's going to help."

Jin sighed heavily in relief. "Good. We could use some help. There's only so much we can do on our own. And our fearless leader is having a bit of a tantrum. Freya's tried to calm him down but now he's all 'dark vigilante' jumping on rooftops and searching for you two."

June felt a sudden respect for Ken. He was so loyal to them he'd go superhero to find them. June's crush felt a little stronger for Ken and she looked up at Jin.

"We have to contact him, we lost our phones. We got captured by Zealots. Zoila saved us, but we couldn't find our phones.

"Shit," said Jin. "We might be compromised then."

Zoe agreed.

"I'll code it. Let me send a mass text message and hope they understand." He stepped away and began texting on his phone.

Zoe and June thanked Zoila.

"We'll meet here again. Give me eight hours to get you the information you need. You think if I reach out to William, he'd understand?"

Zoe shrugged and nodded.

"I'll figure something out but, with his request, I could pull out some files and give you copies."

Zoe hugged Zoila before they got out of the vehicle.

Zoila waved at the group and drove away.

Zoe and June looked around to see if anyone was staring at them.

"Clear, but we can't be too sure. Let's get inside."

The two tried opening the doors to the van but it was locked. Jin held up a finger and pulled out the car key to unlock it, when suddenly there was a loud crash behind the store. The three got ready to fight when Ken emerged from the alley behind. He ran up to June and Zoe and gave them a big hug.

"I thought I lost you guys for good."

Zoe pushed him gently. "You ain't getting rid of us that easily, super boy."

Ken rubbed the back of his neck. "Jin told you."

Jin leaned against the van and glowered at him with a raised eyebrow. "Of course. You were so heroic running off and leaping from rooftop to rooftop. You're lucky it's dark and hopefully no one saw."

Ken apologized sheepishly. "I'm sorry... I..." He searched for the words and then turned to June. He and June stared at each other for a long moment, almost feeling like nothing else mattered.

"Where's everyone else?" Ken said as if the world popped back into existence.

Jin closed his phone. "On their way. We should find a place to stay. Eight hours before we meet with Zoila here. She's getting us info that might help us. In the meantime, you probably need to take a dump, I need a drink, and these girls need some R and R."

Jin walked to the convenience store after asking Ken for the credit card. Ken chuckled nervously at June and walked around to open the van, but realized that Jin hadn't unlocked it yet, so he just smiled at June through the windows. June moved her hair behind her ear and smiled back. Zoe leaned against the car next to her.

"You should ride shotgun," she said knowingly.

"I, we—well..." June looked up at Ken as he was walking toward the store, she assumed to get the keys from Jin, and turned to Zoe. "I... don't know."

Zoe sniffed. "If not now, when, lady?"

June pursed her lips as she contemplated. "I have a lot of emotions to sort through."

Zoe nodded. "I get it. But don't lose happiness in pursuit of revenge."

June bobbed her head. "What about you? Do you have anyone?"

Zoe shook her head. "Nah, a couple of people I thought were cute are..." Zoe's face grew somber. "They're gone now... I lost my chance."

June felt terrible for asking. "I'm so sorry... I—"

Zoe lifted her hand and shook her head. "Lady, I barely knew anyone. Jin and the others, we're really close. I was never good at developing close relationships. Growing up in an orphanage was... I just never had the chance."

June, still feeling guilty, didn't know what to say. Just then the door locks opened, and Ken walked out of the gas station waving at them and holding a few bags of chips.

"We're good, June, and I want you to be good too, 'kay?" Zoe continued, "He's a good guy. He hasn't let us down yet. Give him a chance. Sometimes a relationship can help you heal other wounds."

June forced her cheeks upward and nodded. "Thanks."

She sat in the front, and Zoe slid into the middle bench behind her and gave June's shoulder a squeeze. June put her hand on hers before they both leaned back in their seats. Ken sat in the driver's seat and placed the bags of chips in the center.

Jin walked out of the store a moment later carrying two full bags of food. Zoe opened the door for him, and he climbed in shoving the bags between his legs.

"Did you guys want anything?" he said, making June turn around with a puzzled face, and he laughed.

"Girl, I got you. You can grab anything in the bag. I'm just kidding."

Ken grinned at June, then he turned to Jin, perturbed. Jin realized now was not the best time to joke around. June felt like blushing a little, but the fact that she was kidnapped, had the man who killed Melody right in front of her, and her blood-lust almost leveled a city, made wanting a relationship with him too difficult to think about. She wanted it, Zoe's words kept ringing in her head. She thought she'd be safe in his arms, and a peaceful life settling down in one place would be a dream come true.

June crossed her arms and stared out the window, listening to the others banter.

"Stop hogging the pork rinds."

"No!"

A few moments later, Freya, Hector, and Isaac walked up to the van and lit up as they spotted Zoe and June.

"Took you guys long enough," said Jin, opening up the middle bench so Hector and Isaac could sit in the back.

"I'm glad you two are okay..." Freya said nervously, and the others agreed.

"All right, let's regroup at a hotel and you two can fill us in on what happened."

At the hotel, it was the usual routine. Inspect the lobby, make sure they weren't followed, assign rooms amongst themselves, and try to sleep. Though with today's stressful situation, sleep was harder than usual. Freya, Zoe, Jin, and June were sitting in a circle in their room.

"Tell me everything," Freya said with a concerned look on her face.

Zoe gave June a worried glance, and they both nodded. Zoe started first. "We found this preacher talking at a street corner

about Cesar. He was surrounded by a crowd when, all of a sudden, I saw a big hand reach around my face, and I lost consciousness." Zoe then turned to June.

"And I went a little ahead," continued June, "and spotted one of the guys that attacked us at the base. The smaller of the two guys, and when I turned around to tell Zoe, I was met with a big shadow and knocked out."

June and Zoe then went quiet for a moment.

"Damn." Freya crossed her arms.

"Yup, next thing I know, I'm waking up, the van's on its side, sliding at who knows how fast, and crashes into a pole. Zoila hit it with her truck and got us out."

"What was she doing there?" Jin asked as he tapped his fingers on his chin.

Zoe and June gave each other a puzzled expression.

"We... we didn't ask. Kind of grateful for the rescue and adrenaline pumping, didn't ask what she was doing there outside of maybe she was tailing the two big guys."

"She said she heard of what happened to us but didn't know many details. She's more in the dark than us."

Freya and Jin looked at each other.

"I trust Zoila," said Freya. "Mostly because William trusts her. So, we'll just ask her later what she was doing there." She took a breath. "When we see her, she better have answers."

Freya laid back on the bed and stared at the ceiling. Jin turned and glared at June and Zoe.

"We are in the middle of quite the shit storm... And to top it all off, you lost your phones, which means we had to nix ours, and to top that off, *they* know we're here."

The four of them laid down on the beds. The two queen-size beds made up with brown covers and light wood furniture gave

the room a soft glow that almost felt like candlelight. June felt like she could fall asleep then and there. Reflecting, June tried to make sense of her feelings, but all she could feel was an overwhelming anger. Eventually, the exhaustion kicked in. She closed her eyes and drifted off.

***

It was nine p.m. and the team gathered around the van and worked out a plan to keep themselves covered when they met up with Zoila.

Isaac drew out a map of the gas station. "A'ight, there's a spot up here, here, and here," he said, pointing at the tallest buildings around the station.

"Those would be ambush spots so keep an eye out. Ken, Hector, and I will be lookout. Zoila expects you two as contacts, Freya will be here." He pointed at the building behind the station. "There's a bus stop there. You're going incognito, and just wait there. Zoe, you know the signal. If all goes south, we run and meet back here."

Isaac folded up the paper and stuffed it in his pocket.

"You heard the man, let's go," Ken said, and everyone climbed into the van.

"All right, Betsy, let's go."

The engine sputtered as Hector turned the key.

"Betsy... now, Betsy."

The engine finally turned over and he gave a nervous grin to the team before they drove off. Just before they turned into the street of the gas station, Ken parked the car at another strip mall farther up the road. It was overcast and sprinkling rain when they arrived.

"Perfect lookout weather," said Hector with a shrug.

"We'll do what we can," said Ken, patting Hector in the back. "We're not losing anyone else. All right, break!"

Ken, Hector, and Isaac ran and found ways to the top of the buildings. Freya grimaced at Zoe and June. "Good luck." Then she turned to Jin. "Take care."

Jin laughed nervously. Freya walked away, pulling her hoodie over her head.

"Let's go, ladies."

Jin got in the driver's seat while June sat back in the front passenger seat with Zoe in the middle behind them.

"Let's see if we can still trust someone," Jin said as he put the car in drive and made their way to the gas station.

Jin drove in and parked in front of the convenience store almost in the same spot as yesterday. It was a cold evening and the rain was clearing up.

"The height of this place makes it seem like winter some-times," Jin said, trying to find Freya.

"Yep, the snow cap on the mountains reminds me of when I lived in Colorado once," said June, lost in nostalgia for a moment.

Zoe turned around in her seat. "All right, eyes open, this could be an ambush, or someone could be tracking Zoila, regardless. Eyes wide, June. Anything off, you let us know, got it?"

June noticed a familiar face coming from inside the store. It was Zoila. June tugged on Jin's shirt and pointed at the door. Jin cursed and knocked on his window. Zoila bit inter her *tequeño* and took a sip of her coffee before grinning at them.

She put up her hand, telling them to wait, and made her way

to a small blue hatchback that seemed like it was from the late eighties. Zoila left the snack but came with the coffee and her purse in one hand and a pink children's lunch box with unicorns on it in the other.

"*Hola, niñas,* this is what I could find. Everything should be in here, okay?" She peeked into the van and waved at June and Zoe. Zoila took a sip of her coffee. "I got you new phones too. They have my number programmed in there. Also, I spoke to William. In his way, he says he's very proud of you guys and can't wait to see you again. He's trapped behind a lot of red tape. The American government won't allow for any further sanctioned assistance until it's discovered who led the attack on your base. So you guys are here on vacation. William said you guys need to relax and maybe hit the beach or something, I don't know why, but anyways," she took another sip of her coffee, "I got you this too."

She reached in her purse and pulled out a coloring book. Jin handed it to June who felt it was heavier than a normal coloring book, as if something metal and large was inside of it. "That should hold you over so you're not driving with gringo plates."

Jin thanked her and Zoe leaned in. "Hey, I have to ask. How did you find us yesterday?"

Zoila took another sip of her coffee and leaned in closer. "*El loco ése*, that nut that was spewing apocalyptic crazy stuff. He was a Zealot member, but he left and has been yelling at anyone who will listen. So I heard about it and came, because it was weird he kept bringing up Cesar, and I wondered how long until they tried to silence him. Poor guy, he wasn't so lucky. The tall one we know as..." She looked around and lowered her voice. "Rafael Bovo, and his partner, Tomas Enrique, grabbed the man by his arms and threw him out a window on the fourth floor on the other side of the street. He... he didn't survive, and I couldn't interfere because you two were just being carried away. The group of people started panicking, so I grabbed my truck and saw that they had thrown you in that van. I followed until I could make the car crash and rescue you."

Zoe's head dropped and she apologized.

"It's okay, it was just me. I shouldn't have been there by myself, but I was just doing some recon." Zoila finished her coffee and her expression became sad. "You guys have always been good to me and have done great work. I'll do what I can to help. Director Gutierrez also sends his support..." She smirked knowingly. "On your holiday, of course." She tapped the door frame twice and wished them farewell as she walked back to the car.

"Give the others my best, okay!"

Zoila walked back to her small car and she drove off, enjoying her snack.

Jin started the van and drove back to the strip mall.

***

After a while the team regrouped and gathered inside the van. Jin grabbed the coloring book and pulled out the license plate.

"All right, who has a screwdriver?" asked Jin, and Hector raised his hand, staring at him with a raised eyebrow.

"She's on our side." Zoe nodded her head.

"She's as chaotic as we are," Jin replied with a dry chuckle. "But she means well."

"Beach?" pondered June aloud. The others looked back at her, puzzled.

"I should have asked what beach," June said, grabbing a phone out of the lunch box. She opened it up to see only one contact, 'Mama'. She chuckled and started writing a message.

*Wht *palm tree emoji* u recommend?*

She sent the message hoping Zoila would understand. Everyone leaned in, paying attention to June. The phone went off after a moment and she saw the reply from Zoila.

Papa recommended you go to Cartagena. Something about a spiritual experience. I luv u, bye. And she signed it off with a kissy face emoji.

"Cartagena it is," said June, grinning nervously at Isaac.

"You serious?! That's far from here. We should have taken the other ferry!" Isaac let out a frustrated sigh. "Lemme see something." He checked his phone and rubbed his head; he was no longer sporting a buzz cut as his hair started growing out. Isaac let out a low curse. "By car, we're looking at seventeen, eighteen hours, more'less."

The group groaned. Jin put his hands up. "I ain't driving that, you guys take the wheel, eff that."

Ken sighed. "Let's go back to the hotel, regroup, eat, and then head out. If we leave at six in the morning, we should be there by midnight. We'll use the cover of night to see what we can discover."

"We don't even know what we're looking for!?" exclaimed Jin.

"A church," said June. "William still thinks Cesar is in a church."

Isaac turned to Ken and they both nodded. "Isaac and I will look up what churches there are. See if anything new has popped up. Freya, you and Zoe go through all of these files." Ken handed her the folded paper pile. "And see if it says anything about Cartagena. June, you and Jin get us some more food and supplies. I'll make you guys a list."

Jin nodded. "Got it, boss."

June gave him a nod.

"All right, Hector, put on the new tag and let's head out."

Hector started to drive back toward the hotel. Ken, who was sitting in the seat behind June, put his hand on her shoulder.

"You're a natural at this."

June felt her face get warm. "Thanks. I... I was always taught cryptic codes and stuff by Melody. She always tried to keep me safe."

Ken squeezed a little tighter. "We'll keep you safe now." He leaned back into his seat.

June brushed the hair out of her face as she turned to peer out the window. She wanted all of this to be over with. Her life was a roller coaster, but his hand on her shoulder and the support of the others filled June with a sense of belonging and purpose. She was gonna do everything she could to help them like they were doing for her. She closed her eyes and held Ken's hand on her shoulder.

***

Back at the hotel, the team freshened up and did their research while June and Jin walked to the bodega down the street to get the supplies they needed. She also knew her time of the month was coming soon as well, so she grabbed some more pads and supplies for Freya and herself. Jin stared at her as she filled the basket.

"We never really get to talk one-on-one, do we?"

June shook her head. Jin was glancing at some makeup

items they had but saw nothing he liked.

"I... I know I come off as flamboyant."

June interrupted him. "Deflective," she said abruptly.

Jin stopped looking at the makeup products and faced her.

"Deflective—you seem like there's something you don't want to talk about, so you make over-the-top comments."

Jin bared his teeth and let out a low curse.

"Yeah, creepy, but yeah. I, er, I have a family that hates me for, you know... me," he said, pointing his fingers at himself. "They couldn't stand that I didn't want to be a lawyer like Dad, or want kids. My younger sister got all the praise because she graduated summa cum laude, the little shit, two years before she should have, too. Which means a year before me. That year was a nightmare. My folks just rode my ass, forcing me to find a good wife that can cook and clean and bear children. Like, bitch, hold up."

June walked closer to him after putting some painkillers in her basket.

"Sorry for unloading but if anything happens, I just want you to know, you know, my story and why I'm the way I am. Maybe we could share our messed-up family traumas when we get out of this. I know all about yours, seems only fair."

June gave him a soft pat on the shoulder. Jin crossed his arms and leaned on the shelf.

"I hated myself as a kid, you know. You've heard the stories. Sexually confused kid tries to end his life." Jin sighed. "I-I wasn't an active kid. Video games were the closest I got to an activity, but makeup was my passion. My dream was to be a makeup artist for big-time celebrities. See my designs on the red carpet. Live in Hollywood and have people line up for my beauty techniques. That... That's my dream. Until

I couldn't take it anymore one day and I grabbed my dad's old-school razor. Like Sweeney Todd old-school—man's living in the eighteenth century..." Jin's face scrunched and he dropped his head a little. "Long story short, I had to both look up where to find the old fart's razor and why I have indestructible skin." Jin let out a dry chuckle and June looked at him sympathetically. He shook his head.

"I don't need your sympathy. Just want you to know, everyone knows; figured you deserved to, too. You're family now. 'Sides, I guess the agency has trigger words that alert them, 'cause next thing I know I'm being followed and one day in school a ball gets beamed at my shoulder by some kid who runs at me saying, 'Sorry, sorry. I didn't mean to.' I felt it odd, but the ball didn't hurt much, and I realized I'd never really been hurt before. And then tall, dark, and old stands in front of me. Will's there, all like, 'You're different and I'm here to help you, come with me, let's talk.' I... I went with him because I didn't have anywhere else to go. I figured best case, I become a guinea pig. Worst-case scenario, they find a way to kill me. Win-win. I didn't care what happened to me. My life was a joke. I would never amount to anything. I didn't know what I was, why I was the way I was, my family would disown me, gah, all the drama."

June's expression turned to one of concern. Jin turned away and nodded. "William took me in and sat me down. And for the first time, someone talked to me like an adult. He asked me how I was, what were my dreams, fears, aspirations, and likes. And... I. Just. Lost it. I told him everything. Girl, it was word vomit. He came up with the idea that I was recruited by medical school and I was going to move away for seven years to become a professional doctor and that after he'd help me open up my own beauty salon, as ratchet as it might be, it'd be mine. I wouldn't be doing it for the stars, but the people I'd work on would feel like stars. That's how he got me to join. Mind you, being the only gay guy in a bunker of a hundred or so people suuuucked." He chuckled. "There might have been a few in the closet, but who am I to make them find their truth? I guess it doesn't matter now."

Jin looked somber.

"Anyways, girl, I've chewed your ear enough. You're probably getting tired of listening to m—"

"No!" said June, reaching out to grab his arm. "I'm sorry. Life is hard. It's like Ken says, horrifyingly beautiful. The world sucks, life sucks, but we find these moments, these memories that, you know, we can hold on to, that give us the drive to make more memories. I... I hate what's happened to us, but I don't hate that I've met all of you."

"Give it time." He chuckled. "But also, go easy on William. He means well and is probably one of the good ones. Anyway, you ready?" he said, grabbing some eyeliner from the shelf and putting a few items in the basket June was holding.

"Yeah. We should head back," June said, peering into the basket full of items.

"I'm sure Hector really needs his hair gel." She raised an eyebrow.

Jin laughed. "I got him into that. He has the hair type. And that one without the scent is far better for his hair. Oh, speaking of!" Jin said suddenly and walked off into the next aisle. June followed and saw him grabbing a pack of razors.

"For Isaac, I noticed his hair growing. He likes it shaved." June nodded as Jin smiled and put it in the basket.

"I think we're good."

June looked up at him. "Golden."

The pair walked to the cashier and paid for the items.

A moment later they were outside in the damp streets walking back, carrying the bags.

"Thanks for listening and not judging," said Jin.

June nodded. "Hey, we're pretty much family now. We watch out for each other."

Jin smiled and turned to June. "Can I be honest with you?"

June became worried. "Of course."

They stopped walking under a streetlamp.

"I'm terrified. I know you lost your mom, and you guys were close, but after losing everyone at the base and the fear of losing you and Zoe yesterday, I didn't know what I'd do with myself. Half of me wanted to join Ken in his crusade of chivalry, but I froze. We were torn apart, and no one knew what to do when we hadn't heard back from you two." Jin's chest quivered. "I don't want to lose any more. I want to grab a plane and go to Tierra del Fuego with you guys and live the rest of our lives with penguins."

June gave him a tight hug. "I was scared, confused, and I didn't want to lose you guys either. This is hard on all of us..." June met Jin's watery eyes. "But, as long as we stick together, we'll be okay."

Jin fought to smile and gave her a hug. "Thanks, girl. You always seem to know the right thing to say."

June hugged him back and spoke softly. "Okay, let's get back before you get really emotional." June held him by the shoulders.

Jin laughed. "That would be intense."

Back at the hotel, Jin and June walked in, placing the groceries on the bed since Ken and Isaac had maps and papers all over the table. Freya, Hector, and Zoe were all knelt beside the other bed that had all of the other paperwork and a map of Columbia on it.

"Okay..." said Freya while reaching back and making grabby hands at Jin without looking at him.

He handed her a Colombian soda and she twisted the cap and began to chug. Hector just stared at her in amazement. Freya finished the bottle within seconds and let out a satisfied burp.

Zoe gave Jin and June a half smile.

"What she was saying is, we narrowed it down to a few places. Seven, to be exact."

Zoe sighed and Freya set the empty bottle on the nightstand. Hector was still watching her with a mix of confusion and awe before Freya let out another loud burp, and he glanced back down to the map.

"Seven, and here's the weird bit. They each have a name that starts with the first letter of our names."

Hector shook his head and turned to them.

"It's nuts, dude, check it out." He got up and showed them pictures. "Kiosco de Salvación, Jarabe del Alma, Hacienda de la Roca, Jarrón de Vida, Isla del Poder, Fuerza del Padre, and Zafiro Del Desierto. Basically, um... Salvation Kiosk, Soul Medicine, House on the Rock, or of? Anyways, um, Jar of Life, Isle of Power, Strength of the Father, and Desert Sapphire," Hector said, scratching his head. "Like, the only thing we saw in common is that it has our first letters on 'em. Which is a little weird... And they are scattered all over the city."

"So either..." Zoe continued. "We check 'em out one at a time, or we split up and hit 'em all at the same time," she said, looking down at the papers.

Ken and Isaac, who were both practically laying down on the table, sat up and turned to June and Jin.

"This is nuts. They all popped up in the last few days, Jarrón de Vida being the latest that opened up, literally, two days ago."

Ken scratched his head.

"Dude's got us numbered, or tagged, or maybe we're reading too much into this and we've all become paranoid."

Isaac had his head in his hands and Jin pulled out the razors from the bag and gave it to him. Isaac nodded in appreciation, then Jin walked toward the door and turned around. "Okay, ladies, here's what we're going to do for the next hour or so." He clasped his hands. "We are NOT going to lose our minds, we ARE going to take some me time, and you guys are gonna freshen up, and meet back here in two hours. Where I am going to be in a food coma, and we will brainstorm then. 'Kay?"

Ken sat up, shaking his head and staring at the maps. "Yeah, I'm not gonna argue with that. Come on, let's go." He got up and made eye contact with June. "Did you, um, find everything okay?"

June found his nervousness endearing and replied, "Yeah, I found what I needed, now go! We need to recharge our brains." She pushed him out of the door with a bag filled with the items he needed. She turned to Jin as he was helping Freya stand up.

"We definitely need a spa day after this is all over," he said.

Zoe concurred. Hector grabbed the paper with all the names on it and placed it by the map. June studied it and saw the little X's drawn on where each place was located. It formed a sort of Star of David. She turned to Freya.

"It's the Star of David, the Jewish symbol..."

"Yeah, we know, but, like, why?" said Freya, dragging her feet as she headed to the bathroom.

"Because in the center there is a space. Probably large enough for a compound. Each church is about the same distance, give or take mountain roads, but... what if?"

Isaac peeked around the door as he was about to leave, listening to what June was saying.

"What if it's a jungle base?" he added.

June nodded.

"He's setting a trap, doesn't matter how many of us go where, because he can send out a team quickly from the center in any direction. He probably has aerial support. All of these massive leaders and drug dealers have means for this." Jin turned to Isaac who shrugged his shoulders. "She was talking maps. Maps are my thing, bruh."

Jin smiled. "I know." And he walked away as Isaac walked back into the room.

Freya, who was standing in the threshold of the bathroom, pressed her hands on her face. "Okay, this is great, but can we, like, shower first? Maybe eat something?"

June nodded apologetically. "Yeah, sorry, you do... your thing, we'll..."

Freya didn't say a word, she just closed the door and turned on the shower. Zoe was already asleep on the bed and Isaac scratched his head as he studied the map one more time.

"...I'll be here looking at this, you guys freshen up and rest."

"We got a few hours to eat, sleep, and get on the road," Jin said, trying to get Isaac's attention.

"It's gotta be..." Isaac stared at the map. "We'll talk more, later." He got up and nodded at June. June nodded back and Isaac walked out, carrying his pack of razors, and he closed the door behind him.

June sat in the chair and embraced the quietness for the first time in a long time. It was an uneasy peace, but she tried to revel in the tranquility. She was positive Cesar would have a spot there in the middle of the jungle, but she knew it could be a trap too, or at the very least, heavily guarded. They'd have to be very careful. June scrunched her eyebrows and pulled out her phone. She messaged Zoila.

Mama, 7 places 2 go 2. But the place in the middle seems good, let Papa know, if u can, that we'll be taking a scenic route 2 get there, the other 7 spots seem like a waste of time. So much beach, but not enough fun. Hopefully, we'll meet the bartender. Miss u.

She sent the message, hoping Zoila would understand. June closed her eyes and laid her head back on the chair. A moment later the phone buzzed, and she received a reply.

K, thx. Luv u, with heart emojis.

June leaned back in the chair. With any luck, they'd have support from the Colombian branch, but she doubted it.

They'd have to scope out the place first and make sure Cesar was really there before they could send out a team. June scratched her head and looked back at the map, hoping her idea would work. Cesar seemed like the religious type, so why wouldn't he have made something religious-looking? Cesar came across as a simple man who liked fine luxuries and power. This spot seemed like it. Whatever they were going to decide, they had to decide soon.

***

The next morning, the group reconvened back around the map and waited for June to walk out of the shower. June opened the door to see everyone staring at her.

"Um, hi," she said, taken aback a little and embarrassed she was just in a towel.

"Sorry, June, we're just anxious," said Zoe, crossing her arms and leaning against the wall. Suddenly, there was a knock on the door. The team freaked out and began to hide papers when they heard a familiar voice.

"It's Mama!"

The team sighed in relief.

"You didn't think I'd leave you alone without knowing where you're at, would you?"

Ken held up his phone and pointed it at Jin with a raised eyebrow, and everyone nodded in acknowledgment. Jin rolled his eyes and opened the door to let her in.

"Hi, my babies! I'm glad to see you're all okay. June, hurry and get dressed, anyways... Okay, I sent your message to William and he sent me back this."

Zoila opened her large purse and pulled out a lidar image of the jungle area June sent her earlier and set it on the table. It seemed like an air base with a hangar on the side of a cliff. The team nodded at each other, certain that this was definitely Cesar's main place of operations.

"How freaking deep does that go?" asked Ken, leaning in closer to the image.

"Probably five or six stories down, plus three or four stories up. That part looks like a helipad. And these look like turrets on, well, the turrets. He's armed to the teeth and any attempt would get a normal person killed and Bricks captured."

"Not if there's just a small group that goes in," said Freya confidently over the map. "Seems like there are tunnels that run from church to castle. Probably about a mile in each direction. We each sneak in and converge in the middle, taking out the turrets and any security along the way." She paused, studying the map and thinking deeply.

"That's how we all get caught and killed," said Jin. "We need to go in as a group and to do that, it has to be together."

Freya wanted to protest, but couldn't find the words or strength.

"Jin's right," said Ken. "We can't just leave June alone. She doesn't know how to bypass security systems, let alone sneak into a base."

Everyone turned to June as she was grabbing clothes from her bag, and she felt her face blush.

"Sorry, but it's true," said Ken, feeling a little guilty for calling June out like that.

"But we need to be ready. They almost got two of us out of nowhere. I'm not losing anyone else to these maniacs." Ken slammed the table as softly as he could, but still caused a small crack. "I'm not losing any of you."

The group grew quiet for a moment until Zoila had a suggestion. "What if there's a way to get you all in and distract the church bases?"

"I'm sorry, what?" asked Jin.

Zoila pondered the question and drew a line with her finger from the center point to a nearby airstrip.

"Two hours and you guys can drop in like before, and my people will have the churches surrounded."

"Not a good look seeing heavily armed soldiers raiding churches. It'll cause more people to join Cesar's cause, although..." Ken continued thinking. "Plus, we don't want to put any of yours in harm's way."

"Drop us off here." Isaac pointed to a swampy area on the

map. "It looks like heavy mangrove, so it should cover our drop without alerting anyone."

Jin sighed. "And I doubt many people live there."

The team turned to each other, nodding in agreement. Zoila agreed and focused on the crack on the table, running her finger along it. "You have to be careful. There's no extraction point," she said, glaring at Ken and then glancing at June. "And no backup."

Ken took a deep breath as June walked around the group to sit down at the other bed.

"We'll be careful. We just need to figure..."

Zoila held up a finger and pulled out her phone. She sent a text and received a response almost immediately. "Your supplies are ready."

Ken and the others were taken by surprise.

"What? I wasn't gonna have the legendary Team Alpha fly solo without at least some protection. There should be a package..."

Suddenly the room's landline phone rang and a confused June, who sat on the bed next to the phone, answered. She thanked the caller and told them she'll be right down in Spanish and hung up the phone.

"I, um, I guess there's a package waiting for us at the lobby."

Zoila smiled. "It's for you. I wasn't going to let you go in completely unprepared."

The team thanked her, and Hector and Jin went to go get the package while Ken and the others continued to strategize and choose the best time to make the drop, allowing June to sneak by and get dressed in the bathroom.

"Midnight then," said Freya, staring down at the map solemnly.

Zoe asked if planes normally fly over at that time, and Zoila responded in a matter-of-fact tone, "Yes, it's a tourist area."

Zoe nodded and went to sit down with June who had just come out of the bathroom and was putting on her boots.

"You okay?" she asked as she sat next to her on the bed.

"I... What if there're prisoners there? I know we have to stop him, but what if he's got innocent people locked up in that place? We're going to do the same thing to him. Right?"

Zoe shook her head. "Nah, lady, we're going in there to stop killers. Any innocents we find along the way, we'll rescue, but, June, you can't do this to yourself. I know you're locked on revenge but those contradicting voices in your head..."

June glowered at her and her voice quivered as she crossed her arms. "I don't know what I want or if I can even go through with it. What if he's there and I mess this up for everyone and end up putting people in harm's way again?"

Zoe shook her head. "That's why we're gonna be there for you, with you, lady. We got your back."

They hugged and looked at the team gathered around the table, when Hector and Jin walked in carrying two large brown boxes.

"Merry Christmas!" said Zoila, smiling and pulling out her keys from her purse to cut open the boxes. They all gathered around her as she opened the boxes on the table.

"Okay, these are all labeled with your initials, spares William kept at the agency, just in case."

She started handing out small opaque packages with initials marked with a magic marker. "This one is for you, June. William made it especially for you."

June grabbed the package and opened it to see the black pleather-looking outfit. She then saw the team checking out their jumpsuits. All black with harnesses and pouches along the waist. Balaclavas to cover their faces, and the gas masks and goggles seemed menacingly tactical.

***

June turned to see everyone in gear and put on her own mask. The goggles had electronics in them with visual options for night vision and infrared. "Cool," she said a little louder than she wanted.

Zoila smiled and explained, "Upgrades they were working on, William got you the latest version."

The team cheered softly and Ken turned to June. "Welcome to Alpha."

The words swelled up in June and she didn't know if she wanted to cheer or cry, but it was a strong emotion. The team then focused on the other box.

"Gas cans, launcher, electroshock weapons, and seven nine-millimeter pistols."

June raised an eyebrow. "I've never shot a gun before."

"It's okay." Jin chuckled. "They're mostly for show. In case normies try anything on us. Usually a last resort to spot Bricks." He checked his ammo and placed it in the holster.

"Okay," said Zoila, putting the papers in her purse and grabbing the empty boxes.

"Twenty minutes. You run to the lobby and get in the van. I'll be on the way to the airfield, prepping everything for you. Good luck, *mi hijitos*, I'll see you soon."

She walked out as the team sat in different parts of the room.

"Okay, this might be it, but I'm not getting my hopes up. This really seems like we're finally going to face Cesar and his close army of Zealots," said Ken, holding his mask.

"June, it's up to you if you want to come or not," Freya,

putting gas canisters in her backpack, said without looking up.

"I know you've only been with us a few days, but..."

June stood and walked up to Freya. "I'll be okay, you guys are all I've got now. In these past couple of days we've been through more than any actual family might have in their whole lives. So, I'm in. We're gonna mess up these nuts and put a stop to their crazy jungle cult and save anyone we can."

Freya gave June a smile and put a hand on her shoulder. "You're gonna be a great leader."

Jin cleared his throat. "Fifteen minutes, ladies."

The team grabbed their backpacks and headed toward the lobby. They climbed into the black van that was waiting for them.

"A paddy wagon?" asked Hector.

The driver just shrugged with his hands up and drove off. The team sat along the benches, making themselves comfortable.

Jin faced the others. "Zoila said it'll be about an hour until we arrive at the airstrip, you guys think they'll let us grab some food along the way?"

8

Jungle Ghosts

At the airport the team gathered around a small two-propeller plane, and Zoila was there handing them out their new phones.

"These are satellite phones. William sent them to me along with these." She handed them granola bars. "In case you get hungry during the flight."

Jin reached out and snatched one from her hand and started eating it immediately. Zoila smiled and bid them farewell.

After preparations and one last look at the maps, the team climbed into the plane and Zoila waved at them from the ground.

"Hello, *muchachos*," said a gruff voice from the cockpit as the team put on their headsets. "It's been a while."

It was Director Gutierrez. The team glanced at each other in confusion.

"I have a meeting with the Mexican director and have to make a trip to see him in person. I have received new information that may lead to the arrest of Cesar Villalobos and his followers. My flight happens to go over a certain part of the coast." He turned to the team and gave them a wink. "Good luck. You guys are going to be on your own once you exit the plane." The team nodded and quietly buckled in, and soon the plane took off. Ken put on his headset and the rest of the team did the same.

June sat, fidgeting with her hands, unsure if she could go through with all of this, and then she felt a warm hand holding hers. Zoe nodded and pointed to June's chest.

"You've got heart, and especially skill, and we all know it. You're gonna be great. You know what we need to do, so be the halfheartedly we know you are."

June smiled and settled in her seat.

The flight was calm and the team was quiet, most with eyes closed and heads leaned back, but June was still nervous. Their last attempt at storming a place almost led to a trap, she was almost captured by just walking down the street, and now she was going headfirst into a drop zone, literally. Her eyes widened as the thought of getting pushed off a plane and landing miles below at terminal velocity put butterflies in her stomach. June started to breathe heavily and Zoe noticed. "June, breathe. You're gonna be okay."

Isaac glanced at her and nudged Ken. "She's gonna have a heart attack, fam."

Ken seemed worried and talked to her over the radio. "June, breathe. You're gonna be okay. Once we're on the ground you'll see how strong you really are. You're gonna be fine. ZOE!"

Zoe nodded and reached overhead for an oxygen mask and placed it over June's head. June felt herself breathing softer but her head felt dizzy. She turned to everyone and gave them an apologetic look. Freya got up out of her seat once the pilot said they reached cruising altitude and walked toward June. She was hunched over and hugging her legs.

"This part sucks. I'm glad I had a team before that let me worry and gather myself up before each mission, but you're in a sitch that didn't allow for that, but we got you, 'kay?"

Freya put her hands on June's knees.

"Mama bear's gonna take care of you, but I need to know if you're ready to do this. Can't have you having a panic attack mid-mission. You've been great so far, and yeah we've had setbacks, but we've managed to get out of everything so far."

June wiped a tear from her face and gave Freya a soft smile and nodded her head with affirmation. June closed her eyes and took a deep breath then opened her eyes and stared at Freya with determination.

"Let's make these assholes pay."

Freya smiled and put her hand on top of June's. "That's what I like to hear."

June still worried, but she figured there'd be time for that later. Right then she had to follow everyone's lead and try to fall where they fall.

"ETA, ten minutes!" said the pilot over the headphones. Freya hurried back into her seat and put on her mask. Ken was the first to unbuckle and stand up before he made his way to the door. He peeked at the cockpit window. Director Gutierrez gave a thumbs-up and Ken opened the door. Everyone else lined up behind him. Zoe gave June a nudge and Hector and Isaac held her with one hand on each of her shoulders. Hector gave her a wink. They gave June a nudge to walk forward and Ken jumped out first. Freya stood at the door and motioned for them to walk toward her. Jin glanced back at June and gave her a thumbs-up before swan diving out of the door. Hector held June's left hand and Isaac her right, and in one motion they dove out of the plane.

The feeling was incredible. June felt like she should be scared but she noticed Hector and Isaac who were still holding her hands with their other arm outstretched. The night sky made the ground look like an empty abyss, but June could see in the distance village and city lights along the coast, seeming almost parallel with the mountaintops. She barely noticed the wind rushing past her, if not for the fact she couldn't hear anything but. The mask's oxygen cycling system made it easier to breathe at such heights and the goggles helped keep her eyes open. She wondered how it'd be to actually skydive, but before she could finish that thought the ground was zooming in quickly. Hector and Isaac pulled her closer and they all hugged and tucked their heads in, trying to land on their backs. The water broke their fall and June now knew why the outfits had heavier padding on the torso.

With the sound of breaking branches and a loud splash, the three finally landed in the mangrove. Hector asked June if she was okay and she nodded. Isaac then pulled out his phone and checked the map. He walked around in a circle until he got his bearings and knew which way to walk. A ways ahead, June heard another loud thump and splash. They began walking in the dark jungle until June realized she had night vision in her goggles. She turned it on like Zoe taught her and followed the guys making their way up the side of a slope. They reached the top and were met with a helping hand. It was Zoe and Freya.

"So, who hit the ground this time?" asked Hector, knowing what the answer was going to be.

"Who do you think?" said Zoe, annoyed.

June could almost make out a few tears in the back of

Zoe's armor and felt glad her mask hid her smirk. The group continued walking through the jungle, following Isaac. He pointed them toward a spotlight coming from a wooden tower.

"This is it. Where's Ken and Jin?" said Freya, surveying the area.

Suddenly the light stopped moving for a moment, then continued in its path of surveying the area. A buzz was heard coming from Freya's pocket. She pulled out her phone and said, "Huh, someone's coming in clutch." Freya turned to the team and motioned them to follow her. "Jin and Ken took that tower. Stay hidden and avoid the path of the light, there might still be some guards around."

June was glad she had the mask on because she couldn't help but smile. When all this was over she really wanted to get to know Ken. But that was gonna have to wait. Right now she needed to find Cesar and Bovo and not mess up this mission. She followed the team's lead and ducked into the bushes whenever the light passed over them. They finally made it to the tower where Jin was waiting for them.

"'Bout time, bitches, I could have had a whole meal by the time y'all got here."

Zoe giggled and gave him a hug. "All right, dork, now what?"

Jin nodded and hugged her back. "Ken's buying us some time, but they will check in on him soon, so he's got to check in and hope the ruse works long enough for him to catch up to us before the alarms set off." Jin crossed his arms. "The fun part now is that door."

The group turned to where Jin pointed and it was a barely visible gray bunker door hidden under jungle thicket on the side of the mountain base. It seemed about twenty feet tall and thirty feet wide.

"An overhead or sliding…" started Hector, crossing his arms and scratching his chin. "Gimme a minute."

Hector ran toward it and the group glanced at each other, confused, before following him. At the door, June heard Hector let out a few Spanish curse words softly.

"Finally!" he said in a whispered yell. "*Dalé!* Let's go!" he said as he motioned to the others and walked away from the large door.

"Where—" June started before Hector interrupted.

"There's a side door that is also controlled by that panel. Through here!" Behind the walls of heavy leaves and plants was a door that seemed seldom used. "This seems like a service entrance in case the big bunker door doesn't open."

June assumed he was giddy because something he did actually worked and she smiled to herself.

Once inside, Ken caught up with the group and stood in front of them, removing his mask. "I'll take point. Queen, rear. Mouse, stay in the middle, and everybody keep your eyes open."

June turned off her night vision goggles and followed behind Isaac, turning back to see Jin, who gave her a reassuring nod. She could feel her heartbeat pounding from the anxiety. They walked down the dimly lit and tight corridor that led to the large hangar door and saw military tanks and vehicles. There were a few heavily armed guards walking past and Ken rolled out a gas canister that knocked them out. Another guard came in to investigate the loud thump but Jin had already set up an ambush that choked the man out. The rest of the team regrouped and went in the direction the last guard had come from. It led to a large corridor. The team followed the corridor down and it seemed to lead farther and farther underground. Ken stopped the group. June could hear a loud voice coming from around a corner. The team peeked around and saw a large gathering of soldiers with Cesar standing in front of them all at the tail opening of a large cargo plane. The team quietly got closer to investigate and June could finally make out what he was saying in Spanish.

"...Brothers. Some of you are chosen and some of you fight for us! With luck and devotion, perhaps all who come back shall be made whole and perfect like me! We will find them! We will make them pay! And the world!? The world will bow to us! Worship us! We are chosen and selected to carry out a mission of righteousness and the will of God!"

June shook her head and whispered, "These people buy that?" Isaac turned to her and shrugged his shoulders. June rolled her eyes, knowing people believe anything if someone's charismatic enough.

Then, as Cesar continued to monologue, Ken told the team to split up. "Okay, they have a cache of weapons along that wall over there, behind the old-school fighter planes. Try to find explosives and pop them off. Me and you three," he pointed to Hector, Isaac, and Zoe, "ready the gasses and be prepared to freaking run. After the explosions, throw the gas and all of us are gonna get the hell out of here, hopefully by causing this mayhem. It'll slow them down since apparently they're ready to invade."

"They're here!" they heard Cesar say and the team froze in place. "They're in this country trying to stop us, my brothers and sisters. But we won't let them! They may find out soon where we are, but our contacts in their secular government say they have fed them the wrong information and they're all still trying to find their heads. But we know some are here. Our brothers Rafael and Enrique both bravely tried to stop them but were attacked and forced to run. Our own government has us oppressed and will stop at nothing to stop us! They experiment on us! They think we are a mistake to be studied without knowing that we are chosen!"

Ken and the rest sighed in relief. "Dude really likes to hear himself talk, huh?" Ken said and gestured to the team to move out. June followed Freya and Jin past the planes and found storage crates filled with packing hay and what seemed like grenades, rocket launchers, and heavy machine guns.

"How big is this army?" asked Freya as she grabbed a couple of grenades and handed them out.

"Regardless. It's time to put a stop to them," Jin said, examining the grenades.

Freya pointed back up the corridor. "I saw a large refueling station down that way. Place, like, two of these there and toss another one at a big head's big plane."

June nodded and glanced at the grenades.

"Like the movies, grip this lever and pull the pin. But not with your teeth, that doesn't work, and it feels weird. Also make sure you're far away, you don't want to damage your suit and blow open your own gas canisters."

June nodded more assuredly this time, even though now she was even more nervous. Jin grabbed his grenades and nodded at Freya, then left in another direction. June knew once she tossed the grenades, she had to make her way back through the corridors and out the side of the mountain entrance, yet the nerves kept creeping up on her and self-doubt loomed over her, but she still pushed herself to get to the gasoline tanker.

Zoe, following Ken's lead, had found a spot to hide behind a military truck and eyed the way she came back from, making sure they couldn't get surrounded. The four of them patiently waited to hear the explosions begin.

Zoe turned to Ken. "Why are they taking so long? I hope everything's okay. They're in no position to mess up now. We're seriously outnumbered and getting caught here would mean Cesar's got the upper hand again."

Ken swallowed. "Queen's got this, she's never let us down. Plus, Mouse is a tiny halfheartedly."

***

June recognized the silhouette. The tall, menacing man. She couldn't move as he was standing right in front of the gasoline tanker and he almost caught her as he patrolled around it. June didn't know what to do, her logic kept battling with her rage and she was frozen, hiding behind a plane. She hoped that Jin or Freya would distract him with an explosion, unless they were waiting for her to start. June was going to risk it and pulled a grenade from her pouch. She was about to pull the pin when a familiar voice came from behind her.

"What do we have here?"

June tried to run but was caught from behind by Enrique. Rafael then walked up to her and grabbed her by the throat and lifted her up. June felt a squeeze and her breath became harder to catch. The rage she felt inside was enough to make her stop squirming and take off her mask. "Hey... Bobo," June said defiantly.

Rafael's face became red with anger and he squeezed harder and yelled at her. "You think you're the first to make fun of my name!? I've made everyone pay for insulting me."

June let out a laugh through her choked breath. "I can see where your deep-rooted anger comes from." She strained to let out the words as she held on to Rafael's arms. June tucked in her mask inside her chest plate and pulled out a grenade. "Let's explore that."

She pulled the pin and tossed the grenade at the gasoline tanker. Rafael and Enrique tried to run. He dropped June and she landed on her knees, facing the explosion. She covered her face with her hands but was thrown against a plane and an engine fell next to her. June felt disoriented but managed to get on her feet. She heard the other explosions go off and ran toward them, knowing the corridor was past them. She put on her mask again as the lights began to turn off and emergency lights began to illuminate the way. She heard screaming and gunfire but couldn't tell what was going on.

Suddenly an arm reached around a truck and grabbed her by the wrist. "Thank God you're okay! Let's go!" June followed Freya and caught up with Jin as they made their way through the large corridor and saw that the doors were open, the entrance blocked off by a tank and several soldiers. They had June, Freya, and Jin blocked off and behind them the smoke of explosions was getting closer. The team stopped in their tracks as the soldiers got closer. Then the tank started turning its canon, pointing past June, and kept turning toward the soldiers. They panicked and ran back toward the smoke but the tank shot and blocked them off. It then turned again and shot at the roof behind it, causing a cave-in. Hector opened the tank's hatch, celebrating.

"Hell yeah! Suck it, suckers!"

"Bruh, we gotta work on your smack talk, now let's go."

Isaac pushed him out of the way. Zoe and Ken came out from under the tank, lobbed gas cans in the direction of the smoke and fire, and met up with the others at the side door.

"All right, we gotta go," Ken said, getting everyone to go through the hallway first. "Let's find a ride and get the hell out of here!"

They ran out and noticed the dimly lit airstrip. "Over there!" Hector pointed at a truck and the team gathered in.

"Okay! Let's go! Go! Go!" Ken yelled as he waved his arms for everyone to follow. Hector started the truck as they climbed in and he drove through a thickly canvassed jungle road that eventually led past a farmer's house. The owner seemed very confused at the seven people dressed all in black, sitting in an open-top, six-wheeled military truck. Ken pulled out his satellite phone from his pouch.

"King to Grand-master. It's done."

"So they're going to come?" asked June as she took off her mask.

"Hell yeah!" said Hector enthusiastically. "Once the explosions went off it was enough to investigate and bring the army!"

The team cheered and Ken drove the truck to a road where he parked on the side of the street.

"All right, team. We split here." Ken turned to the others. "Grab a taxi and make your way to a hotel. We cannot be seen here when the army comes," he emphasized as he pulled off his mask and smiled softly at June. They agreed and split into two groups, removing the tactical vests and pouch belts, along with their masks, and shoving them into a duffle bag that was in the truck. June, Ken, Hector, and Isaac found a taxi that would take them to their hotel. Freya, Jin, and Zoe ended up having to take a bus. Worried, but still glad they made it out, June found herself taking deep breaths.

"Not a bad first mission," Ken said with a wink as he turned from the front passenger seat. June's eyes widened and darted from the driver to Ken. Ken smiled and shook his head. Then in his heavy southern accent said, "I'm just saying, as far as saved souls, y'all did great. Bless your hearts. The holy spirit shall be coming and snatching these souls up!" He chuckled and turned around, facing forward again. The driver glanced at Ken and just shook his head. June turned to Hector and Isaac, sitting to her right, and they just laid their heads back on the headrest.

June's stomach growled and everyone noticed. She felt a little embarrassed but then Isaac's stomach growled too. The group chuckled before they all reached into their side pouches and pulled out the granola bars Zoila had given them. "To victory!" Ken lifted his bar at the group in the back seat and they all let out a small cheer. June opened hers and sighed when she saw it was flattened. The rest of the car ride was just the sounds of chewing and soft classical music playing from the car radio.

Once at the hotel, Ken paid the taxi driver and waited for the others to arrive at the nearest bus stop. The trio stood there dressed in black, waiting while Ken held the duffle bag with the team's tactical equipment.

"So, now what?" asked June and Ken gave her an unsure shrug.

"Finally!" Hector exclaimed and pointed down the road. The bus arrived and the rest of the team got off. Meeting up again with Jin complaining about how smelly the ride was, they began walking back toward the hotel.

"Thankfully Zoila lined up the new suits with enough money for us to get by," said Zoe. "Now let's go check in at the hotel and update her."

June nodded and wondered if her suit had money too as they continued walking down the street.

The sun seemed to be coming up. How long had it been? June remembered it was almost midnight when they jumped out of the plane and arrived at the fortress. She hoped it was over and that Cesar, Bovo, and the rest of these monsters would finally be caught and put away. She let out a contented sigh. Things seemed to finally be going in their favor.

The group finally made it to the hotel and the sun was breaking over the mountain peaks. June looked past the tall buildings to the beautiful sunrise and sighed in relief.

"All right, team, quick shower, shut-eye, and let's go home," Ken said as enthusiastically as he could, but his fatigue was starting to show. June's own eyes were heavy and she found herself lost in thought. Realizing she was already in the bed she was sharing with Zoe, June didn't even bother taking off her boots. Her eyes closed and she drifted off.

***

The next morning, after having slept the whole day, June could hear the shower running and Zoe banging on the door.

"Stop being a hog, you've been in there for an hour!" Zoe said in an exhausted tone.

Through the door June could make out a muffled Freya replying, "Your queen requires TLC!"

June chuckled and Zoe turned around, letting out a grumble. "Ah, you're up," Zoe said, fighting a smile. "The guys got breakfast. Hope you like arepas and hot chocolate."

June nodded softly and rolled out of bed. "And you guys do this often?" asked June as she found her backpack and pulled out her traveling toothbrush.

"We usually get more rest and prep time. Also, Zoila dropped off some stuff," Zoe said as she put her clothes on the table and took a seat. "Man, things are never going to be the same," she sighed.

June couldn't make out in the dimly lit room if she was crying but it seemed like a tear rolled down her face.

"Everyone we usually went back to, every familiar face, our teachers... gone." Zoe seemed to be talking more to herself than to June. "Sorry, I know that it's finally over. I can't imagine how painful it's gonna be for us not having our base. With any luck, they'll just release us early and we can have a somewhat normal life." Zoe leaned forward on her chair. "Maybe we'll be free." She became quiet and June didn't know what to say. She searched for the words because the awkward silence was becoming unbearable.

June walked up to Zoe and put her arm around her. "I... I hope so. I hope you get to live the life you wanted."

Zoe rose from the chair and took a step back, holding on to June's hands. "Thanks, lady." The two shared a quiet moment before Freya walked out of the bathroom.

"The queen is ready and hungry. I'll be next door stuffing my face whenever you guys wanna come over."

She glanced at the clock on the wall and cursed under her breath. "Five a.m., we slept the whole day. June fourteenth disappeared in a blink." Freya sighed. "Hope we can just stay flopped until we get our internal clocks aligned again. In the meantime, Imma have me some delicious hot chocolate."

June closed her eyes, realizing it's her birthday.

"You okay? You look sad." Zoe stood in the bathroom doorway, holding a bundle of clothes and bottles.

June shook her head. "Just tired. I'm just gonna lay down till you finish."

"You do you." Zoe, who was already inside the bathroom, peeked out and spoke to Freya. "Save some for us, you know how the guys get."

Freya chuckled dryly. "Yeah, there'll be hell to pay if they eat it all." Freya turned to June. "You did good last night, I'm proud of you. I'll try to save you the best arepa. You ever have one?" June shook her head. "It's a thick corn tortilla with cheese, and it's glorious. Come by when you're ready."

June forced a smile while Freya lingered, seemingly analyzing June. She then walked off to the other room without saying a word. June laid in bed enjoying the quiet room and just listened to the running water with her eyes closed. June kept reliving that moment. He was right in front of her and she froze. She didn't know what to do but she should have done something else, something braver. She hugged herself as she curled up in bed, feeling guilty. It was her against a mountain of a man and an army of indestructible Zealots. The way she heard them cheer as their leader spewed supremacy nonsense. June sighed and opened her eyes, staring off into the ceiling.

A long moment later, Zoe peeked out of the bathroom door. "You okay there?" June made an acknowledging grunting sound and Zoe pushed the door open and began to blow-dry her hair. June hugged herself and rolled on the bed, facing the window.

"'Kay, done." Zoe came out of the bathroom dressed in

one of her usually sporty outfits. A purple tube top and dark blue yoga pants. She sat and put on her lace-up sandals. June wished she could pull off an outfit like that, but her petite frame made her self-conscious and she avoided dressing in tight-fitting clothes.

"I'll make sure the boys leave you something."

"Awesome, I'll meet you there," June said, grabbing the toothbrush from the nightstand and making her way to the bathroom.

Zoe nodded and put her stuff away in her bag. "Hey, for what it's worth, I'm glad you're with us..." Zoe gleamed, peering into her bag, and June noticed she seemed preoccupied for a moment. "...otherwise," Zoe chuckled, "it's a sausage fest. Freya and I have to hear about dumps, farts, and nuts all the time. It's nice to have another girl to talk to." She forced a laugh. June sighed empathically, but she knew this wasn't why Zoe was really grateful. June nodded and Zoe walked away to meet up with the others.

Alone in the room, June grabbed the clothes she left on the table and walked into the bathroom. Small but still roomy enough to move around, June brushed her teeth with what was left of the complimentary paste and rinsed it with the adorably small mouthwash bottle. She made sure the door was locked before she undressed and turned on the water, trying to fine-tune it to where it was just hot enough to not burn her skin. She stood under the spray and felt like a million thoughts had lifted from her head. Her shoulders dropped as she let the water run down her hair and back, taking a moment before she washed off the smell of the jungle.

After what seemed like an hour, June walked out and wrapped a towel over her head and another around her body.

She plugged in the blow-dryer but decided to just sit on the toilet for a moment. She enjoyed having her mind clear of most thoughts and took a few deep breaths. She unwrapped the towel from her head, leaned her head back, and let her hair swing behind her ears. The memory of Melody reaching out to her flashed in her mind and she sat upright, breathing heavily. June shook her head, grabbed the blow-dryer, and turned it on. She realized she forgot the hairbrush in her bag and went to fetch it.

She could hear everyone laughing in the other room. She wanted to join them, but didn't feel emotionally ready yet. She took her time grabbing the brush and noticed her necklace. She smiled softly as she put it on before going back into the bathroom to dry her hair. She sat on the toilet again, whipped her hair forward, and began to brush. The image of Melody's still body in her arms was still branded in her mind. June took another deep breath and kept brushing and drying her hair. As she turned off the blow-dryer, her stomach growled loudly. She remembered that a granola bar was all she had yesterday.

"Some Colombian food should do me good, right?" she asked herself in the mirror. She finished brushing her hair and noticed the bags under her eyes were becoming visible. She grinned weakly, held her necklace, and closed her eyes. "It's all right," she said in affirmation. "It's going to be all right." She took one deep breath and continued to get ready. Putting on the outfit she bought for herself, a graphic tee that had a picture of a cat with sunglasses that made her snicker and a red plaid shirt on top. She put on her black cargo pants but, as soon as she tightened her belt, June felt a small cramp. "Crap."

She finished putting on her favorite boots, sighed to herself, and went to grab a pad from her backpack but noticed a shadow pass by the window. She hurried and went to the bathroom to call Freya on the cellphone.

"June?" Freya asked worriedly.

"I think there's someone outside the window," June said quietly.

"Window?" repeated Freya in a hushed voice. June walked out the bathroom and headed toward the backpack again. She wished they had left the duffle bag with her or at least her suit. Suddenly the window crashed open and smoke filled the room. June tried to run but the gas was overwhelming.

***

In the other room, Freya and the team had all put on their suits and heard the commotion coming from the room June was in. The fire alarm blared and as the team went out into the hallway, it was filling up with guests who were panicking and rushing out of the building.

"June?!" yelled Ken as they all made their way into the room, but inside all that was left was shards of broken glass and no signs of struggle. Ken ran to the window and looked around for any sign of where they may have gone. Freya grabbed Hector and Jin and motioned back at the door, and the three ran out into the hall searching for the stairs. Ken jumped out the window onto the other building and lunged back, trying to make it to the roof, but missed and grabbed onto the ledge of a window. Over the edge of the roof stood a large shadow that Ken couldn't make out against the sunlight.

"*Adios,*" said a gruff voice.

Ken heard a click and saw a flash of light. He felt an

electrically charged thud hit his chest. The shock made him lose control of his body and he plummeted toward the ground. Zoe and Isaac bounded down and checked on Ken. He was having a hard time breathing. Zoe pulled off his mask.

"Bro, talk to me, what the heck happened?" She tried to shake him and slapped his face. "Ken, what happened?!"

Isaac was pacing, glancing upward and trying to see if he could make anything out along the rooftops. "I don't see anything!" He then knelt beside them and put his hands under Ken's body. "We need to go!"

Zoe protested. "But our stuff, passports, everything!?"

Isaac hesitated before turning to Zoe and taking off his mask. "I'll take him to the van. Grab what you can. Meet me there."

Zoe nodded and Isaac grabbed her by the arms and spun her around before launching her toward the window they came out from. Isaac then picked up Ken and ran around the building to join the group of tourists who were panicking and making it to their cars. No one noticed them as he leaned Ken against the van. "Bruh, you're heavier than you look."

Ken breathed through his nose and weakly said, "Bro... you even lift?" They chuckled and Isaac gave him a pat on the shoulder. "Sit tight. Zoe should be back soon. Any sign of trouble, you run."

Ken nodded. "I'll try but..." He coughed "What about..."

Isaac put his hands on Ken's shoulders. "We'll find her." He ran back into the building as there were still people trying to exit it as the fire alarm still blared and the ambulance began to show up. He made his way upstairs where Zoe was examining the room.

"Her phone isn't here..." She lifted up June's bag. "Clever girl," Zoe said with a sad grin.

"We can't waste any more time," said Isaac as Zoe tossed him the duffle bag and a couple of backpacks. Zoe carried the rest of their belongings and the two of them made their way back down the stairs as firemen came up and started to yell at them to get out. They agreed and hurried out of the building. Zoe and Isaac made it to the van but Ken wasn't there.

"What did you do with him?" Zoe asked Isaac with wide eyes.

"I left his ass right here. What the hell did he do?"

Just then, Freya, Hector, and Jin appeared behind them.

"Anything? Where's Ken?"

Zoe gave Freya an exasperated glare. "I don't know what the hell is going on. Did you find anything?"

Freya locked her fingers over her head and frowned. "We came out here and looked around. We split up; I took to the rooftops, Hector checked the alley, and Jin checked the streets. I ran into someone, but they didn't have her. They threw a smoke bomb and I lost them. They... they had a suit."

Zoe blanched. "Suit?"

Freya nodded. "Yeah, our mole problem is a lot deeper than we thought."

Zoe and Isaac cursed under their breaths. Hector clicked his tongue and reached into Ken's bag to pull out the keys. "So, now what?"

Freya turned to him. "We take Betsy, find Zoila, and use Ken's phone to track his ass. No time to lose, guys, let's freaking go!"

243

9

No Shelter Here

Hector struggled to keep calm and drove erratically, yelling at the traffic around him. Freya put her hand on his thigh and took a deep breath. Hector nodded and did the same.

"Not gonna help them if we burst into flames."

"You're right."

Freya then reached into her backpack and pulled out her phone. "I need to call Zoila, maybe she'll know what to do." Freya turned back to the others and noticed their concerned faces. She dialed and immediately Zoila answered. "Hey, we got hit! We lost people. Zoila, we need... Yeah, yes, now. Please. ... As soon as possible. Thanks." Freya hung up the phone and leaned forward in her seat, putting her hands on her head. "They, uh, the Zealots, um, some of them got away after our attack. Cesar among them."

Jin let out a loud curse and questioned Freya. Freya replied angrily, "They had an escape plan that we didn't notice! The churches were hit, but... despite all of the ones arrested, he got away through some secret tunnels or something. Zoila wasn't sure, she didn't give me all the details, what with our teammates missing and all."

Jin sighed, cursed under his breath, and sunk more into his seat.

"What do we do?" asked Hector.

"We wait for Zoila. It's all we can do now." Freya peered out the window. "Wherever they are, I hope they're okay."

Isaac leaned forward between Freya and Hector. "We need to be safe too. If they find us, what's to say they don't know where else we could go? We might need to mix it up. Jungle, maybe? Leave the city?"

Freya nodded. "Jungle might be the safest."

Hector squinted at both of them. "You know this ain't really an off-roader, right?" he said with concern etched on his face.

"It's 'bout to be." Isaac leaned back into his chair with a smirk then focused on the map on his phone.

"...And me without my mud boots," Jin said sarcastically from the rear bench.

The team made it out of the city and started driving past farmland. "Should have filled 'er up back there," Hector said, tapping his fingers on the steering wheel nervously.

Isaac shook his head. "And risk getting seen. Nah, fam. We gotta go Stone Age and try to avoid CCTV as much as possible. 'Bout a few more miles south and past those mountains, I think, should be good. We'll find some cover in the jungle and wait in here till we get word from Zoila."

Hector begrudgingly agreed. Zoe was pensive, staring through the window when Jin reached from behind to put his hand on her shoulder. "We're gonna find them. We're not losing anyone else."

Zoe held his hand tight and nodded. "I know. We're all we've got left."

Jin quirked his cheek sadly and leaned back into his seat.

"'Sides, when we find them," Freya said, gritting her teeth. "We're not leaving a single one of those nuts alive. We did it the right way once, now we do it my way... They're about to see what my vengeance looks like."

Isaac and Zoe turned to face each other with matching expressions of fear. Isaac peered ahead on the dirt road and saw a path.

"There, bruh, on the left. Horse trail."

Hector nodded and turned the car. The road was very bumpy and seemed seldom used. "Huh... This thing surprisingly has good ground clearance." He sounded surprised.

"There—stop there," Isaac said as he pointed at the clearing near a lake. "This seems like open land, so if anyone asks, we're just fishin'," he said with a weak smile.

The team walked out and stretched their legs. Jin and Zoe sat at the water's edge and looked out into the lake. Jin held Zoe's hand.

"I don't know what to make of all of this and it's driving me nuts," Jin said as he squeezed her hand a little harder.

"Same," replied Zoe. "We're so far out of our element. Shit, a few years ago, I was trying to figure out how the heck I was gonna pay for my own place, a car, and school. Now we're tryna figure out if we're gonna live to see tomorrow. If we're gonna see our friends again. And, bitch, I haven't even processed what happened at base. Like, life is crazy, but this is on a whole 'nother level. And June..."

Jin hugged Zoe. "She's a fighter. Wherever she's at now I'm sure she'll be okay. Our little trooper's gonna be fine. You'll see. Helluva way to get dropped into our world. I know Ken'll be fine too... you'll see."

Zoe sighed. "I hope you're right. She didn't deserve what happened to her. None of us did... You think that's why they picked us for Alpha? Heh, now that no one is listening to us, why do you think we were chosen?" Zoe asked Jin, and he contemplated her questions.

"Shit, I can't remember the last time someone wasn't listening to us. Hmm, I think it's because of how limited we all were to the world. Some of us don't have families and the ones that do are estranged."

"Yeah, you're right, I don't even talk to my own family."

"Yep, Ken is basically gas-lighting his parents. Heck, I am too, technically, but they'd disown me in a heartbeat if they knew the real me, anyway. I think that's the knot that ties us all together. Our desire to be accepted by a family unit. You know, on top of our problem-solving skills, dexterity, smarts, and teamwork."

Zoe giggled and the two of them sighed deeply and gazed back out at the lake. The moonlight began shimmering on its surface as the sun set.

"I'm sure June would have a better psychological answer, though."

"You ain't wrong." Zoe put her head on Jin's shoulder, closed her eyes, and asked him, "Do you ever dream of them? Your family?"

Jin Scoffed. "In my nightmares." He let out a defeated sigh. "I do, I miss them, homophobic, high standard, holier-than-thou as they are..." He breathed in. "I do."

Zoe chuckled dryly. "Same."

Freya paced behind the van. "She should have called by now, are you sure we can get a signal here? It shouldn't take this long."

Isaac sighed and got up from leaning against the van. "Queen, chill. It'll be a'ight, Zoila's gonna call and we're gonna bust some heads, 'kay?"

Freya stopped pacing and faced up into the sky, closing her eyes and taking a deep breath. "Fine." She dropped onto the floor with a loud thump that shook the van, and laid in the grass.

"It just shouldn't take this long."

Hector, who was pacing farther away by the road, kept trying to call Ken, but got no answer. "Why is it that waiting is always so freaking painful?!"

"We just gotta, bruh." Isaac scratched his head. He got up and started walking around to the side of the van.

"What are you gonna do?" asked Freya.

"Lay down comfortably, hippy."

Freya ran her fingers through the grass around her and scoffed. "Fair enough."

Hector was about to pull out his phone again when Freya's phone rang and he ran toward her.

"Hello!? Hello?!" She stood up nervously. "Where? What? What about... In the city? Oh, ah, well, damn. ... Yeah, okay. I'll let them know. ... We'll find him first, yes. And go off of that. ... Okay, thank you, Zoila. ... We're... doing okay, I guess. ... We'll get right to it. Any— Does he know? I'm sure he'll bring hell with him when he can." Freya nodded and, with a sad expression, thanked Zoila again. She hung up and stood to see the team gathered around her, waiting for her to speak. Freya swallowed and straightened up.

"Ken's fine. Some well-meaning normie carried him to the hospital, and that set off red flags with the agency. Dr. Glendale picked him up and he's at the agency now."

"What about June, who took her?" interrupted Jin.

"June's more complicated. Satellite ping and cellular triangulation last spotted her on the southeast end of the city along the mountains, but the signal went dead." Freya swallowed, closing her eyes. "They have trackers and are gonna come out with a canine unit from the local law enforcement. So we gotta meet up with them and bring June's stuff so they can grab her scent." Freya stood for a moment, pondering, as the others waited for her to say something else.

Jin eventually clapped his hands. "What the hell are we waiting for then?! Get back on the bus, bitches!"

Freya snapped out of it and motioned for everyone to get in the van. Jin ushered everyone in. Freya put her hand on his back. "Thanks, felt a little off back there."

Jin held up a hand. "Queen, with all this crap going down, I'm amazed we can still walk and talk. Now go, we're wasting time."

Freya nodded and got into the front seat. Hector put the car in drive and drove hard through the jungle trail, finally making it to the dirt road, and traveled back toward the city as fast as they could while the van sputtered and creaked.

"Come on, Betsy, you've made it this far," Hector said, rubbing the dashboard. "You're one of us now, and you're not gonna let us down, are you?"

Making it to the outskirts of the city, Hector drove as fast as he could and everyone else held on to anything they could as the team kept their eyes on the road ahead. Hector cursed every time a red light would stop him, but he kept pushing the van to its limits. "Come on, Betsy, let's freaking go!"

Isaac, checking the map on his phone, pointed from the middle seat. "Left up ahead. Follow the curve and the station should be about fifteen minutes out—" A loud crash caused the van to roll over and embed itself into the side of a building. Sounds of screaming and metal smashing filled the night on the quiet street.

***

The team came to and shook their heads. They groaned and called for each other. "What the hell?" Isaac grumbled, trying to reach for his phone that was lying on the sliding door. Then he realized the van was sideways, crushed in the middle, with his seat facing the driver's side door.

Zoe, who was sitting next to him originally, was laying on the ground. She looked up and tried to reach for Jin. He was holding on to his seat belt, staring at the ground with wide eyes. Freya was dangling from the passenger seat and slowly gaining consciousness. She reached for Hector, who seemed disoriented. Isaac managed to unbuckle himself and drop down. He broke the passenger side sliding door by pushing it upward and peeked to look at what hit them. The large truck had white smoke coming from the front and men were gathering around, carrying large weapons. In the middle stood Rafael Bovo as he crossed his arms and laughed.

"That dude ain't right," Isaac said, climbing back down and helping Freya unbuckle her seat belt while holding her up.

The team all knelt down and gathered their things then turned to Freya for orders.

"We need to get that scent to the police."

Isaac shook his head. "There's, like, twenty guys out there. Bovo's leading them, plus they might have that weapon that they used on Ken."

250

Freya's brow furrowed as she pursed her lips in thought. "Zoe, you grab June's bag and run to the station..."

"Why?" Zoe protested.

Freya grimaced. "You're the quickest of us. If any of us can get there, it's you. Now let's bust out of here. We'll hold them off."

Zoe nodded and everyone turned to Hector as he was the closest to the roof.

"Man, I'm sorry, Betsy," Hector said as he wound up and shoulder-rammed the roof, making the van roll over and more of the building collapse around them.

"Crap," said Freya, turning back to notice the van had broken through an apartment complex. "Jin, look for injured people or survivors and get everyone you can as far away from here as possible. Zoe, out the back. The rest of us..." She took a deep breath. "Let's show them why we're Team Alpha."

Jin and Zoe ran out toward the building, and the rest rushed out of the van toward the Zealots. Freya put on her mask. "This is going to be fun."

Hector and Isaac blanched nervously. Freya charged at the truck, holding the van door as a shield while Isaac and Hector followed close behind. They pushed forward, smashing into a few men, some of which were not Bricks and therefore sending them flying into the air. Freya heard the screams and a few bones crunch as they landed. "Ew..." she said in disgust. Bovo, who had managed to dive out of the way, got up and dusted off his shirt, towering over the other men. Freya noticed Bovo's black leather jacket over a white shirt that seemed to fit too tightly. "Skinny jeans? Really?" Freya said and sighed. "I've been hanging around Jin too long..." She shook her head and got into a fighting stance. "Where's June?"

"I'd ask you the same thing," Bovo said, taking Freya by surprise. Then he charged at her before she could say anything else. Freya dropped with a feint and dodged his punch toward her left. She grappled him and used a hip throw that allowed her to grab a weapon, while everyone glanced quickly to see what happened.

Isaac grabbed Hector by the arms and flung him around, causing the other men to duck down or leap back. Isaac then threw Hector at another guy that was about to shoot, causing them to tumble. "Warn me next time!" yelled Hector as he began attacking the men. Isaac shot him a wicked grin. Freya shot at a couple of guys with the heavy assault rifle while running to take cover behind the truck. Hector tussled with the man on the ground and punched him until his head broke through the floor before being tackled by two other guys.

Meanwhile, Isaac was fighting another three guys. He twirled behind one, causing them to lose their balance, and used his hip to push them to the ground, leaving another guy open for a clothesline take down. Isaac then spun and ducked down to grab the weapon that the guy he pushed down first dropped and fired it at the third guy who stayed back and attempted to aim at him. Isaac noticed that it shot high-powered arcing bolas that release sparks on contact. "Don't get shot!" he yelled at the others. Freya was using her weapon to block other attacks and grunted in agreement.

Hector, while getting pinned by the two guys, was about to get shot by the man he punched through the floor until Isaac fired at them with a machine gun, causing the men to flinch. Hector then twisted and kicked his legs, sending one of the men off of him. He then punched the other and kip-upped to tackle the last guy, but Isaac shot him with an electric blast before he could. Hector stepped back, noticing the sparks coming off of him. "The heck is this?" he asked before he noticed Bovo was pushing more men toward them.

"Incoming!" yelled Freya. The remaining six men started firing. The weapons seemed like a one-time shot. Freya noticed this as she timed her moves and used the men she was fighting as a cover. Isaac grabbed a man and held him over his head before throwing him at the Zealots.

The team noticed the remaining men weren't Bricks as they dodged out of the way and hurt themselves. Suddenly Betsy came barreling through the air and Bovo looked up to see it flying toward him. He put his arms up as the car crashed against him, pinning his body to the front of the truck.

Jin stood in the rubble of the building, breathing heavily. The remaining Zealots scattered and Jin ran and grabbed one of them by the collar. Infuriated and shaking the man in the air, Jin asked him in Spanish, "Where is the girl?!" The man, panicking and praying in Spanish, could only flail as Jin held him almost a foot off the ground. "Where is the girl?! I will not ask again!" Freya and the others stood there, staring at Jin who didn't have his suit on. The man started crying. "Wrong answer." Jin put a fist in front of the crying Zealot and flicked his jaw, causing the man to go unconscious.

Jin dropped him and searched the ground for another man. There was another Zealot that was crawling away toward the flaming semi truck. Jin grabbed him by the leg and lifted him up.

"Same question. Same answer. Same result."

The man started breathing heavily and said, "He'll kill us, our families, everyone we know. You might as well kill me now."

253

Jin grimaced at the man. "As you wish." Jin dropped him on his head and as the man tried to get up, Jin flicked his foot against the man's jaw, knocking him out cold. Freya, Hector, and Isaac just stared at Jin.

"What? I cleared as much of this place as I could, and gave the police a warning not to come until I returned. The Zealots here are pretty well-known and the police are terrified of them."

Freya gave him a nod. "'Kay, there's still one person who might talk. But it's gonna take all of us. So let's go."

Rafael Bovo, while breaking his way out of the remains of Betsy, coughed and tried to get out of the thick smoke. The truck was starting to explode and the flames were singeing his pants and shoes. He cursed in Spanish as he put out the flames and got up. The four of them gathered around him, each holding the electric weapons.

"*Habla, cabrón,*" said Hector. "Talk!"

Bovo laughed and replied in Spanish, "You idiots. All you had to do was die. They control the world."

Freya roared and kicked him, making him stumble and fall down. "You nuts think you can own the world by believing in some guy who's not even different than you?"

Bovo laughed hard. "No, *señorita.*" Bovo replied to her in English, "I don't believe what he says. I believe in superiority. We have the strength, power, and will to change what they messed up. Cesar is just a pawn to something much bigger, and you kids are too stupid to realize that the future is unstoppable."

Jin shook his head. "What future? What's bigger? Where is June!?"

He pointed the gun aggressively at Bovo, while Bovo wiped

the dirt on his jacket from where Freya kicked him and looked up confidently at the four.

"Questions, so many questions. Yet, so sure about what you're fighting for." Bovo leaned back on an arm and glared at them. "Tell me, when the time comes, who will you really fight for? Those like you, or those who want to destroy you?" Bovo let out a wicked snarl. "Who do you think made such a weapon?"

The truck was still causing explosions and the fire grew wilder.

"We need to end this now," said Isaac, looking around at all the bodies surrounding them.

"You—you seem like you know what I'm talking about," Bovo said after hearing Isaac's voice.

"You don't know shit, asshole."

"Of course. So what will you do to me now, children? Put me in a box? Kill me?"

Freya grabbed him by the arm and pulled him up. "Box, you chatty gorilla." With that, she walked him toward the other side of the burning truck.

"You will let these innocent men burn?" Bovo said, pointing to the ground at the knocked-out bodies of the Zealots.

"I'm on it," Jin said as he tucked the weapon under his arm and began piling them up. Isaac joined as well and they started to carry them three or four at a time.

Hector and Freya still had their weapons pointed at Bovo. They carried everyone as far as they could before the truck let out one last large explosion before being encompassed in flames. The team flinched but that was all the time Bovo needed to punch Freya, causing her to fly off her feet and on top of Hector. The others ran as fast as they could and tried shooting at Bovo, but he had already jumped onto the second-story window and smashed inside. Freya chased him, yelling at the others to keep an eye on the rest of the Zealots. Jin agreed, but said he had to get word to the police and let Zoila know what was happening. Hector nodded and pulled out his phone. Isaac readied his gas grenades in case they woke up.

Freya followed the trail of holes through the walls between all of the apartments, chasing Bovo. The images of the destroyed base flashed across her mind. She gritted her teeth as she ran as fast as she could. Faster and faster, breaking through chunks of wall and debris that Bovo left in his wake as he jumped from building to building.

"Stop. Destroying. EVERYTHING!" Freya screamed at Bovo. The tears formed in her eyes from anger made it hard to see past the smoke and dust. She lost his trail at the end of the block and stood at a hole on the side of a building, looking around to see people running in panic in every direction, but there was no sign of him.

"How do you lose sight of someone so tall, distinctly dressed, and covered in concrete?" Freya yelled. She hated herself. She knew she failed—she failed her family, again. She took off her mask and dropped down to the street as pedestrians ran. She heard the civilians screaming, "Terrorist!" as they all continued to gather together and run away. Freya saw the chaos and her shoulders slumped as she walked back toward the others.

***

At the police station, Zoe ran in, out of breath and panting heavily. She walked into the station where the officers stared at her with suspicious glances. Zoe walked up and asked the front desk, "Zoila sent me here. Is she here? Zoila De Armas?"

The officer cocked his head in confusion and then their eyebrows lifted. "Ah! Zoila! The missing girl!" The officer turned and whistled loudly at his colleagues. "The missing girl case, she has what we need!" They yelled in Spanish. "Have a seat. Have a seat, please!" He motioned with his hand at the waiting area near the entrance. Zoe nodded in agreement and took a seat. After a minute, she heard a familiar voice.

"*Mi hijita!*" Zoila said, walking through the door, opening up her arms and giving Zoe a big hug. Zoe closed her eyes and hugged her back.

"It's nice seeing someone who isn't trying to kill me." Zoe turned around and opened the backpack. "Here's June's stuff. I hope it helps."

Zoila grabbed the backpack. "Yes, *mi vida*, it'll be most helpful... Something's happening, where..." Zoila became distracted by the chaos erupting around her in the station. The police station began to fill up with phone calls and police officers began running out.

"We were attacked. Everyone else stayed back. They told me to bring this to you."

"Aye, okay, okay, follow me."

Zoe grabbed her bag and followed Zoila and they hurried up the stairs into an office. "Jefé, we got big trouble!"

The chief hung up the phone, cursed in Spanish, and looked up at Zoila. "You're telling me?! We have super people destroying a part of the city and none of my officers want to go in, saying that there's another Chinese Brick out there thinking he's Bruce Lee and is going to fight them all after he threw a car?!"

"Japanese," Zoe corrected him.

The police chief blinked at her, confused.

"She's part of the team, Jefé, the one I told you that are here to stop them. He is one too. If he says don't interfere, it's best for the officers to not go in."

The chief cursed again and begrudgingly agreed. He radioed orders to his officers. "What do we do?" he asked Zoila, getting up from his chair and walking toward her.

"*You,*" Zoila handed him the bag, "find the girl. She and I are going to bring the agency to pick up the mess."

The chief nodded solemnly. "Go. Save my city."

"We will," Zoe said confidently. "Just find my friend."

The chief nodded and walked out of the office. Zoila pulled out her phone and spoke in Spanish. "They're on their way. Give them half an hour. Let's go back to your friends."

Zoe nodded and walked out with Zoila. The two made their way to the precinct's garage and Zoila got into a red sedan.

"We'll find her, don't worry. I'm sure she'll be okay," Zoila said, barely believing her own words. Zoe nodded and faced the window after buckling in.

***

Later, Zoe and Zoila arrived at what seemed like a war zone. Holes in buildings, vehicles on fire, and bodies on the ground with only Jin, Hector, and Isaac standing.

"What happened here?" Zoila asked with wide eyes.

Isaac tossed her a weapon. "Explain."

"What is this?"

Isaac put his hands on his hips. "This is what they're using on us now. Agency tech?"

Zoila shook her head and turned to Isaac with a puzzled expression. "I've never seen this before. What is it?"

Jin aimed at the flaming truck and shot. The sparks disappeared in the fire but the metal clank and electrical sparks of the bolas could still be heard.

"A very large bug zapper," Jin said dryly. Zoila gasped and looked back down at the weapon. "This is... advanced, I've never seen anything like this in the agency."

Hector addressed Jin. "American, maybe?"

"Antarctic, as far as I care. I just need to know how we can defend ourselves from it. This is way worse than gas," Jin said, crossing his arms.

The team heard helicopters in the distance.

"Are we good to go?" asked Zoe.

"Waiting on Freya," Hector said.

"Oh, okay, where..."

Hector pointed at the hole in the second story of the building.

"What..."

Jin let out a sigh. "Bovo escaped. She went to find him. But we needed to stay 'cause of all these shitheads."

Zoila groaned and nodded as she noticed all the people on the ground.

"You four took on all of these guys together?"

"For the most part..." started Isaac.

"I had to evacuate and stop law enforcement from coming," Jin finished.

"Oh!" said Zoila in amazement. "You guys really are the best."

The group couldn't find the strength to smile. They noticed

Freya turn the corner.

"Zoila!" Freya yelled as she ran toward the group and gave her a hug. "You're here! I... I lost Bovo." She slumped in defeat. Zoila put her hand on her shoulder.

"It's okay, *mi hijita*, we'll catch him the next time he shows his ugly face." Freya gave a sad half-hearted smirk and nodded. "Okay, now can we go?" asked Zoila. The team agreed and walked away toward her car. Zoila called the police chief to give him the all clear and they all drove back to the police station.

***

Back at the precinct, Zoila was on the phone while the team hung out at the cafeteria.

"She never got her arepa. She must be starving," Freya said, staring down at the bag of chips she was eating.

"Don't do this to yourself. We'll find her and make them pay, 'kay?" Zoe said, putting her arm around Freya's shoulders.

"Yeah, I need to focus. We need to figure out what Cesar's next move will be."

Zoe hugged her tightly. "That's my queeny." Zoe got up and started to make herself some coffee when Zoila hung up the phone.

"We have a location. It's not ideal, but we're looking into it. The dogs found as much as they could before hitting a river. From there it's more difficult to tell. It seems like they may have put her in a boat or..." Zoila's voice trembled. "We need to keep looking. Her phone sent out a ping so it's probably still active somewhere near the jungle, heading south toward the coast. If... if she's... When we find her, it should lead us to

Cesar's base of operation. Hopefully."

Zoila made her way next to Zoe who had just finished making her coffee, and she started making one for herself.

"The men you hit with the electricity, they're okay, but barely."

The team perked up in astonishment.

"Like, how barely?" asked Freya with a raised eyebrow.

Zoila shook her head. "Internal bleeding, I guess from overloading. These electric guns are very powerful. Doctor says they'll be okay eventually, but they need to monitor them," Zoila said, shaking her head as she poured sugar into her cup. "*Dios mio...*"

She set the coffee machine and turned to the team. "This is bad. The director and I have never seen anything like this. He's flying back later today." Zoila glanced up at the time. It was half past three in the morning and she cursed softly. "You guys need to sleep..."

"No, we need to find June!" Freya protested.

Zoila held up a hand. "Sleep. I have a team looking for her. This is my jurisdiction, you have done enough. Sleep, then go meet Ken, he might have been hit with one of these electric weapons, and when the general gets back I hope to have better news for you."

Freya let out a disagreeing grunt but nodded her head in agreement.

Zoila finished her coffee. "You should go."

"Where?" Freya protested again. "Where can we go that's safe? Everywhere we go ends in losing people and destruction." Freya was about to break down crying when Jin and Zoe hugged her on each side, and she started sobbing. "We keep losing people!" Freya dropped to her knees. "I

261

wasn't fast or strong enough and they're dead! Tabby and Seb!"

Hector and Isaac got closer to them and hugged her too. The four of them held Freya as she continued to sob. Zoila stood there, holding her coffee. She didn't want to move. Zoila knew Freya needed to let this out; they all did. The team huddled on the floor and Zoila quietly left the room and stood outside, making sure no one came in. The sobs could be heard behind the door. Zoila closed her eyes and leaned her back against the wall. She'd have to stay with them for as long as it takes.

***

Zoila, having fallen asleep on the floor leaning against the wall, woke up to her phone ringing. *"Bueno?"* she answered. The person on the other end told Zoila that June's phone let out one last ping and the dogs managed to find a location at the far end of the Magdalena River. Zoila thanked them and walked into the cafeteria and saw officers quietly trying to make coffee as the team was huddled, holding each other on the couch. Zoila looked at them sadly and went to wake them up.

"Dalé, it's six in the morning. Let's go, sleepyheads." The team woke up groggy and rubbing their eyes. "Let's go, we need to find Ken and I got a lead on June. We need to take a trip toward Cali."

The team shot up and began to fix themselves up. "What lead? Did you hear anything from her?" asked Zoe.

Zoila shook her head. "No, no, but we know where her phone was last spotted and dogs followed her smell into a deep jungle. I have my team looking into it. If she's alive, they'll find her."

The door opened and a familiar voice spoke. "Or, they're walking into a trap." William walked in, followed by Director Gutierrez.

"Zoila, *mi amor!*" The director walked up to her and gave her a hug. "I missed you, the team sends their regards."

"Well, what happened? What is happening?" Freya asked dryly.

"It's nice to see you too," William said softly. "The director here helped me get access from the U.S. to supervise you guys as long as he oversees everything. They feel like it was someone in our agency that let the ball slip and it's been a mess since."

Gutierrez nodded and faced Freya with concern. "It seems someone from the U.S. is pulling the strings," Gutierrez said, making his way to the coffee machine. "Or, at least using someone in the U.S. This whole thing is a mess. Also, I'm very sorry for your loss." The director bowed his head at the team. Freya wiped a tear from her cheek and turned to William.

"What about the fanatics in Mexico?"

William and Gutierrez looked at each other and back at Zoila.

"A ruse to take away our attention," William replied. "They sent a few expendable Zealots and some hostages to fight." His gaze was stern.

Zoila cursed under her breath.

"That's messed up," replied Freya, clenching her fist. "They need to be stopped. They're out there breaking families and feeding bullshit to people who don't know any better." William agreed as he stirred his coffee. "So, what do we do?!" Freya asked curtly.

William took a sip of his coffee and turned to her. "We

kick their goddamned asses." Freya gave him a wicked smile. "Zoila, tell your team to hold and stay in position. We are going to go check up on Ken, get you all cleaned up, fed, and suited up..."

Director Gutierrez interrupted. "And I will handle the red tape and keep an eye on anything suspicious."

William smiled. "Thank you."

Gutierrez waved his hand. "You helped me take care of the Bricks here; I help you now take care of yours." The men nodded and William turned to his team.

"Well, what are we waiting for?!"

***

As the sun rose over the mountains in the small town, the team loaded up into a large black SUV and William took the wheel. He put on his dark aviator glasses and turned back to the group buckling in. "All right, team, I'm not gonna lie to you or even sugarcoat this," he started as he shifted the car into gear. "First, you all smell like trash, so in the back there're new clean suits, equipment, toothbrushes, and a change of civvies."

They smelled themselves and leaned back into their seats, giving each other shrugs. Freya turned to William. "Are you okay?" William glowered. He shook his head and gave Freya a look that told her everything she needed to know. Freya nodded and turned to face the window.

Half an hour later the black SUV pulled into a motel in the city. "We're here. Grab your stuff. I called ahead, so just give them my name and they'll give you a key."

"Where are you going?" Freya asked as she unbuckled her

seat belt.

William put the car in park and turned to Freya. "You are all going to take a shower and eat something. There should be room service here. I paid good money for this place, meanwhile I am going to go pick up Ken. He's finally been discharged and is waiting for me at the hospital." Freya grimaced. "You'll be fine," he said, noticing her expression, "We need to hurry. I'll be back—twenty, thirty minutes, tops."

Freya nodded, replied, "You better," and followed the team as they made their way out of the car and into the entrance of the motel. They glanced back briefly to see William drive aggressively through traffic and then made their way into the lobby. Jin walked up to the receptionist and told them William's name. The receptionist just nodded and gave Jin two keys for rooms across from each other.

Once in the rooms, they pulled out individual backpacks from the large duffle bag, filled with clothes catered to each of their styles. Despite that, the team couldn't get comfortable.

"This is hell. We should have gone with him. I can't eat anything," Freya said as she went to brush her teeth but couldn't find the toothpaste. Jin opened the nightstand drawer and pulled out the toothpaste, taking it to her. "I know, girl. This is messed up, but we can't go another twenty-four hours on just arepas and hot chocolate. I don't know about you but I need some pork rinds and a mammoth steak!"

Freya shook her head, forcing a smile. "I wish I could, but..."

"Queeny," Zoe walked up to her after looking out the window, "we're busting our whole selves saving the world. I know you're worried about June, we all are, but we ain't no good to her if we ain't got no energy to help. Imma order you some scrambled eggs and coffee."

265

Freya grimaced but nodded in agreement.

"This blows." Hector walked into the room after his shower. "Are you guys gonna eat anything?"

Jin, who was already placing an order over the phone, nodded his head and mouthed to him, "What do you want?"

Hector shrugged and pointed at Freya brushing her hair. "Whatever she's having." Then he lay down next to Jin. Jin nodded and turned to Zoe, motioning his head in inquiry.

Zoe thought for a moment. "Fried eggs and an empanada, oh, and chocolate milk."

Jin gave her a thumbs-up. "What about Isaac?" he asked, tapping Hector's foot.

Hector sat up, "Oh, right, his usual. The paisa platter with *platano* temptation, and, er, some *pan de bono*, with a Colombian soda on the side."

Jin gave another thumbs-up and finished placing the order. "Hope it gets here soon. Should I have ordered for Ken and William too?" The others shrugged and continued to freshen up.

***

William arrived at the hospital where Ken was waiting outside next to a female doctor. "Cassandra!" he yelled from the window. Dr. Glendale and Ken waved and walked up to the SUV. She helped Ken carefully climb into the back seat.

"Hey, bud, how'd the doctor treat you?"

Ken chuckled softly as he struggled to buckle in.

"William, he's lucky to be alive. If not for the suit taking the brunt of the shock, he could have bled to death."

William sighed and turned back to Ken with concern.

"Dr. Glendale says if it would have hit directly, it might have popped my heart. I'm lucky to be here."

William glanced at Dr. Glendale as she sat in the passenger seat. "You look like you haven't aged a day."

"Please, the crow's feet and obvious hair dye give it away. All your fault, by the way. Every time I think you guys are okay, you go and find new ways of harming each other."

"What can I say, it's the job." William motioned to his receding hairline before his expression became heavy. "Doc, this, um, new weapon. It's like nothing I've ever seen before."

Dr. Glendale addressed him. "So, it's a weapon?" She glanced back at Ken. "I thought they hit you with a power line or something." She turned back to William.

"The rest of the team faced it. They say it shoots out highly charged bolas that create an electrically charged arc that disperses on impact."

She shook her head. "Jesus."

"Yep. I took the ones my team recovered and sent them to your lab. Perhaps you can figure out a defense, or where it came from..." William trailed off, eyes narrowing as he thought about it.

"My God, imagine this on a larger scale. Whole armies equipped with these and gas grenade launchers."

"Shit." William's eyes widened.

"They'd rule the world," said Cassandra.

Ken leaned forward. "I know this is a bad time, but any news on June?"

William nodded his head. "We have a location. I just need to know if you're ready to kick some ass."

Ken bared his teeth as he crossed his arms. "All the ass, sir."

William dipped his head at Dr. Glendale. She smiled wearily at him and he drove away.

***

Back at the motel, William stopped at the lobby entrance and turned to Ken. "This is where we part. The team's waiting for you in room three o' four. Order something to eat, freshen up, and catch up with everyone. I'm sure you guys have a lot to talk about. I'm going to drop Dr. Glendale back at the Bogota base with the weapon and I'll send a shuttle to pick you guys up. You'll be heading southwest toward Cali, where you'll find a farm base that has a helipad waiting for you guys. Good luck, Ken, and give the team my best." He leaned closer to Ken and gave him a hug. "And please bring back my daughter," he added in a trembling voice. William stepped back from Ken and gave him a nod. Ken nodded back and turned toward the elevators while William and the doctor walked back toward the entrance.

Ken knocked at the door and Freya cautiously opened it. Her eyes widened and watered before she lunged at him, tightly hugging him.

"Whoa, easy now, I'm good, but don't break me again," Ken said as he hugged her back.

"Dude! You're back!" Hector said with excitement.

"Bruh, what happened? What'd the doc say?" Isaac asked after swallowing his food.

Ken put his hands up. "Nice to see you guys too. I, uh, okay, first off, someone get me some food, there's only so much pudding I can take. And second, it was rough. Dr. Glendale said whatever hit me caused an arc of electricity that fried my

268

insides and caused some lacerations in the lining of my organs, and that if it wasn't for the padding on my chest, it might have been my heart instead of my stomach that ruptured. I had a bit of internal bleeding but she managed to keep an eye on it and thankfully, it healed pretty quickly."

"So, you're alive because of chance?!" Freya exclaimed.

Ken nodded and shrugged his shoulders.

"You lucky bastard," Zoe said, and they all went in to give Ken a group hug.

"I missed you all too, but still, guys, I'm pretty hungry."

10

The Shackles That Bind Us

June woke up feeling herself dangling from a ceiling. Disoriented and with a headache, she was having trouble breathing and even more trouble moving. When she looked around, she noticed she was completely chained up with heavy thick links completely covering her from neck to feet. She glanced up to see she was attached from the roof of what seemed to be an abandoned farmhouse. She could make out the sounds of the rain forest from where she was, but at about three feet off the ground she couldn't get enough momentum to shake off the chains or swing hard enough to break away from the roof. June heard men talking outside, but she couldn't make out what they were saying. She closed her eyes and dreaded what fate awaited her, but more than that, the hate that was filling inside of her. She felt like she failed. She hoped the others managed to get away, but her vengeance, her need to make the men who ruined her life pay, was probably not going to go as she had hoped.

She opened her eyes as the door behind her opened. "Are you awake, my dear?" uttered a gravelly voice. June turned but the chains made it difficult to see past her hair. "Look at you, so strong, yet tied up here like a caterpillar in its cocoon. You are probably wondering why you're still live, when I have taken out so many of your friends. It's simple, yet... complicated."

June gritted her teeth. "When I get out, you are going to die!"

Cesar chuckled. "Of course. That is why I don't want you getting out, but first I need to know something." He scratched his chin as he walked behind June. "Do you know why you are special?"

June felt confused. "I'm not special. The only special thing about me is how I'm going to mess you up."

Cesar let out a belly laugh. "My dear, they never told you. In fact, I'm willing to bet that they've been keeping a close eye on you your whole life."

June rolled her eyes and scoffed. "I had, like, two days. I was barely there before you killed all those people."

Cesar snarled. "Two days, hmm. Seems my info may be wrong... Or perhaps yours. You must know, I didn't kill all those people." June's eyes squinted. "Perhaps, June, we are both being lied to." Cesar walked away to grab a folding chair leaning against a support beam. He dragged it over the overgrown floor and opened it in front of June. "Perhaps, Miss Romero. The ones who seek to help us, are, in fact, manipulating us."

Cesar pulled out the necklace that William gave her from his pocket and rubbed the heart gem with his thumb. "Such beautiful, fragile things these are. All living things are made... of glass hearts."

Cesar crushed the gem with his hand. June stifled a gasp and her eyes widened. She glared at Cesar; the man was well into his sixties, wrinkles around his eyes, and with unkempt wavy hair that flowed into a long scrappy beard. He was dressed in a linen robe and open-toe sandals. He dropped the chain and shards of the gem on the ground next to him and stared at her intensely.

"Except for you, June. You have been lied to by the same agency that lied to me."

June shook her head in frustration. "Lied about what? Jesus, you like to talk."

Cesar shook his head and hands.

"No blaspheming, please. And I will tell you. You see, I was given information by someone in your agency. Certain ways to kill Bricks, useful information that will protect us from the agency, and resources to change the world for the better."

June let out a loud fake laugh. "Ha! For the better? Better for who? You? You're committing genocide. I can list off the list of leaders that thought that was a good idea and how great it ended for them."

Cesar shook his head. "No, not genocide. A paradise, where we can all live together. But first, humanity must repent for their sins. We, our people, have been given a gift. A purpose. We are here to change the world. I know that now. I wasted my life hiding who I was until the man from your agency came to me and told me what amazing things I could do. Imagine, one minute I'm going for a doctor's visit, probably the first in my life because my churchgoers said I should get a prostate exam at my age, and next thing I know, I am chosen!"

"What happened? Doctor lost a finger checking you?" June said sarcastically, causing Cesar to laugh through his nose.

"No, the needle, it..." he reminisced. "It, broke right on my

skin. Twice, before the doctor went to go look for answers."
Cesar leaned back and shook his head. He glanced up at June.
"*I am a miracle.*"

June snarled at his blatant self-grandeur.

"I was chosen, and the doctor couldn't believe it. He said I
must be some kind of mutation." Cesar let out a belly laugh.
"A mutation?! Like some common evolution. Smart doctor
with a dumb answer. I knew I was meant for greatness. The
doctor insulted me, told me I should be studied like some
animal. I meant to just punch him, but not like... The next
thing I know, my hand felt wet and I was holding his heart.
I knew then, God judged that man." He pointed at his chest.
"Through me." Cesar leaned back on the chair and stared at
June pensively. "And it seems he chose you, too." Cesar got
up and pointed at June from top to bottom and back to her
face before getting closer to her. "You cannot die."

***

On a small police boat heading down the river, the team was
pacing and making preparations. Putting on suits and stuffing
backpacks with their clothes and supplies.

"Okay, we're three clicks from where her phone last pinged.
We'll meet up with a law enforcement canine unit and follow
them to where her scent was last detected," Ken said more to
himself than the team.

"Yeah, bro, chill. We'll find her." Hector patted Ken on the
back. Ken turned to him and nodded with a furrowed brow.
The sunset was breaking over the mountains and the jungle
looked eerie with the foggy mist becoming thick.

"It's all right... It's all right..." Ken repeated to himself.

"We got this, we got this. Coms check," Freya said, reaching out and holding Ken's hand to comfort him.

"Gambit in position. And reading you loud and clear. Over," William replied and gave them a thumbs-up from inside the boat's cabin.

Ken replied, "Copy that. Over."

The team finished preparing their gear and sat on the starboard side of the boat and got ready to dive into the water.

"Clear!" said William, and the team dove backward into the marshy waters. The boat kept going quietly and the team made their way onto the shore.

"I never thought I'd miss the city so much," said Jin, turning on his night vision goggles.

"Feels like we're in a different jungle every other day now." Hector sighed. "Heading?"

"Sorry, um..." Isaac pulled out a radar from his bag. "They're about a click west."

Ken nodded and they continued walking through the thick jungle until they found a clearing. An officer waved at them and called them over. They removed their masks and met with the officer and the other team inside. "¡Hola, muchachos!" said the gruff-looking police officer holding back a very curious German shepherd. The team greeted the man. The farmhouse seemed abandoned.

"Times have been tough around here. A lot of farmers have lost their homes."

"And their lives," said the Colombian Brick team leader.

"Hi, I'm Edwin, this is my team." He motioned to them and the others gave a half-hearted wave back. "Don't mind them, they're extremely tired and we're hungry, but they told us to wait for you."

Ken shook his head. "I'm sorry, I didn't..."

"It's okay," said Edwin. "We're used to this. We're the only team in this country. The five of us get put in a lot of bad situations." Ken didn't know what to say to that and gave him a sympathetic smile. "Anyway," continued Edwin, "this is Marisol, Ricardo, Herman, and Juan." He motioned to the officer. "And you already met Officer Manuel and Furia."

Manuel was sitting on a chair as he pet the excited dog. Ken and the group nodded, and he pointed with his thumb behind him. "Uh, Jin, Hector, Isaac, Zoe, Freya, and I'm Ken."

The officer got up once the excited dog laid calmly by the chair and met with Edwin at the table. He unrolled a map that had a red circle drawn on it.

"*Aquí...*" He pointed. "Two miles west. There's a farmhouse, but it's heavily covered by jungle. It's too thick to clear, at least for my men..." The officer looked up and Edwin nodded. "And we were told to stay back in case it was a trap."

Ken nodded at him and crossed his arms. "Yeah. They have advanced weapons that can take us down now."

Edwin squinted at him skeptically and replied, "We can handle anything."

Ken shook his head. "I got shot with one of their new guns and... I almost died."

Hector spoke up. "High-powered electrically-charged bolas that cause an arcing reaction that pretty much fries our organs if we don't have any protection."

Edwin and his team stifled a chuckle at the mention of bolas.

Freya agreed and added, "Yeah, and we don't know if this place is surrounded by stuff like that or even worse."

Edwin's eyebrows raised in disbelief and he looked back at his team that were sitting up attentively with concerned glances. He turned back to Ken.

"So you're saying they can shoot us and kill us immediately now, instead of gassing us?"

Ken nodded and Officer Manuel shook his head in disbelief. "I'm going to go. You have your location. And all the information I could give. I don't want to be a part of this. I have a family to take care of and my partner is getting hungry."

Ken nodded and Edwin said farewell to Officer Manuel, gave Furia a pet on the head and a tug on her chain, and the two walked out toward his off-road police cruiser.

"Now what?" asked Edwin.

Ken shook his head and stared at the map. "We'll definitely have to work together on this."

"There's eleven of us, but we don't have any backup. Surrounding the place might prove difficult. Damn, man. I just want to rush in there..." Hector said, peeking at the map.

Ken finger-combed his hair back, interlocking his fingers behind his head, and let out an exasperated sigh. The other team gave each other worried glances. "We'll find her," Freya said softly as she put a hand on Ken's back. He turned to the others and they all nodded sympathetically.

Edwin shook his head. "We were going to keep to the jungle and try to make our way carefully inside." Isaac cleared his throat and pointed at the map.

"There's a problem, though, once inside, there's about forty square acres of flat land. It's the summer and being at ground level, we'd stick out like flies in milk. Even in the dark." Edwin looked back at his team and shrugged. Zoe turned to Jin. His face scrunched up in thought.

"Jin... what are you thinking?" Zoe asked Jin while leaning

closer to the map.

"Girl, nothing good," he said, glancing up to Isaac.

"How far can you throw us?"

Isaac straightened up and shook his head. "Nah, nah, fam, nah..."

Ken shook his head and added, "What choice do we have? We'd be lucky to find a plane by tomorrow, and by then it might be too late..." He stared at the map and then looked up at Isaac. "Sixty feet, right?"

Isaac kept shaking his head. "Y'all are nuts. What if I miss and y'all end up back in the river. Nah, fam..."

Jin walked up to him and held him by the arms. "You can do this. You did it in the training room. You threw us at the missiles, you can throw us into a big-ass farmhouse."

Isaac continued to protest. "That's different, bruh, all I had to do was fling you up. This is up and over..." He blanched. "...and into the enemy's mouth, bruh."

Ken stared at him. "It's no longer a request."

Isaac's jaw tightened. "Yes, sir."

Edwin looked at his team and the five of them turned back to Ken. "What are we doing?"

An aloof grin appeared on Ken's face. "We are going flying."

***

The teams met up at the edge of a thick jungle. They tightened their backpacks and made sure their canisters of gas were secured within the padded pockets of their suits.

"Okay," said Edwin. "We've got about a few yards of thick jungle past here—"

"Thicker than what we just went through?" Jin interrupted.

"I thought we were already in it?!" Both teams paused to glance at him, then they continued walking.

"We can go from here, this is the closest to the farm." Edwin pointed.

Ken nodded and faced Isaac. "You know what to do. You and Marisol will stay here if things go fubar. The two of you return to William, got it?" Isaac nodded hesitantly but Ken stared at him with determination. "Y'all better come back with her and Cesar's head on a goddamned spike." Ken breathed through his nose and patted Isaac on the shoulder.

"You got it, man."

Ken turned to the rest of the group. "Okay, this is gonna be weird for anyone who hasn't done it before. Isaac's gonna grab you by the arm; you need to tense up and once you're in the air, go straight like a superhero. You're gonna feel a sensation in your stomach like you're about to fall, that's when you open up and try to fall by tucking in and landing on your back."

Edwin glanced back at his team. Ricardo stared at him and cursed in Spanish. Edwin turned back toward Ken. "No wonder they hold you guys in high regard. You're all crazy."

Ken chuckled dryly. "Yeah, but we get shit done." He immediately regretted saying that, so before the other team could protest, he added, "All right, now let's get these bastards and save June. Freya, you're up first."

One by one, Isaac flung them into the air and they all landed separate from each other by a few yards. Ken was the last to land and spoke over the radio. "Okay, we're all here! Go! Go! Go!"

They all rushed into the farmhouse, but it was empty. "Uh..." Edwin looked around and changed his goggle's setting. "No visual, or heat, there hasn't been anyone here for quite some time, even though some of the lights are on..."

Ken cursed loudly and kicked an abandoned can that was on the floor.

"So who kept the grass?" asked Jin.

Edwin and the others shrugged and began to search the area. Juan walked outside and looked at the area opposite of where they came from. "This is weird." He called the others to join him. On the side of the building was an abandoned barn.

"That wasn't on the map," said Isaac.

Ken put his hand on Edwin's shoulder. "You and I will stay back, and Ricardo and Juan should join Freya and Hector and head toward the barn. Herman, Zoe, and Jin flank." They all nodded and moved out. Hector, Freya, and the two men from the Colombian team made their way cautiously to the barn. With two on each side of the large doors and waiting for Jin and Zoe to get into position, they stood there in the dark.

"Breech!" yelled Ken over the coms, and Freya and Hector kicked the doors open with guns in hand. In the middle of the empty barn stood a cow.

"What the..."

Freya noticed the others who were staring at the cow.

"I'll go check it out. You guys cover me."

Freya walked toward the cow while Zoe and Jin made their way inside from the door in the back.

"It's fake?" Freya said as she reached out to touch the plastic cow. She noticed the mask on the cow. "Is that June's?" The cow tipped over as its legs seemed to be held by tension and it mooed as it did. Freya's eyes widened. "Get out of here!" The cow had triggered a pulley system that made a generator turn on. "Get ou—" There was a flash and the whole building

279

exploded in white light. Then a gas released from behind the pens.

Zoe felt tingles all over her body and tried to get up. She had made it a few feet past the door and glanced over to see Jin struggling to stand.

"What the heck just happened?" Jin asked as he staggered while getting up. Zoe shook her head and turned around. The barn was covered in gray smoke, barely visible in the night sky.

"Shit!" She got up and checked her mask. The goggles weren't working but the gas mask seemed to be. She made her way into the barn where she saw four bodies on the ground but what seemed to be two figures moving over them. "Who the hell are you?!" she yelled at the men.

Startled by her, the men reached down quickly and tried to remove the group's masks, but then Ken and Edwin showed up behind them and pushed them to the floor.

Edwin began questioning them. "Who are you?!" He kicked one of them in the leg and Zoe heard a loud crack. The man started screaming. The other man began pleading with them in Spanish.

"Please! No! Don't hurt my brother! They told us to prepare this place for you or they will kill my family!"

"What now?" Edwin asked Ken as he was checking on Freya.

"Bring them with us. He's gonna need medical attention too."

Freya shook herself awake and Hector groaned as he struggled to get up. Ken helped both of them up and turned to Edwin. "Let's regroup at the farmhouse. Zoe, Jin, see what you can find out about the traps here. Ricardo, bring Juan with us."

They agreed and spread out. Edwin carried Herman on one shoulder and the man with the broken leg on the other, telling his brother to follow him.

Zoe searched around and pulled out a flashlight, but it didn't work either. She took off her mask and examined the plastic cow that seemed to be something used for decor, it was hollow inside and the legs were detachable. She noticed the triggering system, a wire connected from the udder to a leg. It split into multiple places which Zoe followed with her fingers. She told Jin to check out the one on the opposite end of where she was. He followed the wire to see a large electrical machine.

"An EMP!?" exclaimed Jin from the other side.

Zoe turned to him. "To disrupt coms?"

She looked back down and noticed the other triggering wires connected to gas canisters.

"Probably to stop us from communicating and thus making us easier targets?"

Jin walked back toward Zoe. "Or they don't have anything big enough to kill large groups yet," Jin said dryly.

The two started walking back to the farmhouse.

"I know but, why the trap? And having two random normies do the dirty work, it doesn't make sense. Making June's phone ping here. Her scent... Why?"

Zoe tried her communicator again but it just crackled. "Coms are down."

Jin checked his and cursed under his breath. He turned to Zoe and stopped walking. "Double trap!?"

They ran back past the empty barn and through the dry farmland as quickly as possible. Crawling through the thicket and back to the first farmhouse they were in. Jin and Zoe finally made it back and saw several men holding the two teams captive on their knees and with their hands over their heads. The farmer with the broken leg and his brother pleaded with them as the men threw both of them on the ground. They didn't seem to be Bricks by the force they used to push them, but they were all armed with those weapons. One of the men took pleasure in stomping on the man's broken leg. They laughed and pointed the guns at the others. Zoe and Jin gave each other a knowing nod before putting their masks back on. Jin made his way around the tall grass and toward the other side of the house when he heard Officer Manuel protesting.

"Please no!" he said desperately.

Jin tried to hurriedly make his way around the house. By the time he made it to the corner, he could see a man kicking the officer to the ground and pulling the dog by its collar. The dog lunged at the man and he just slapped it to the ground.

The officer's wails could be heard as Furia barked aggressively at the man. Suddenly there was a flash of light and a yelp. "No!" cried the officer. "Monster! You're a monster!" he yelled.

Jin could see him reloading the weapon again. All it took was putting in two marble-sized bolas in a compartment on the top and pressing a button to charge it. That was all Jin needed to see before he lobbed a sleep grenade into the air. At the same time, Zoe threw a canister and the team tried to get up and fight. One of the Zealot mercenaries panicked and shot Hector in the leg, causing him to fall with a yell. Before Jin could make it to the armed Brick, he shot the officer in the chest, causing him to convulse violently. Jin ran and stopped in front of him.

"You just lost your bargaining chip," Jin said with wide, furious eyes. The man, who Jin now noticed had a small gas mask on, threw the weapon, opened his arms, and challenged Jin to fight him. Meanwhile the others had their masks on and managed to knock out the ones who weren't Bricks onto the ground and piled them up. The man glanced over at them and noticed they had all escaped and knocked out his men.

"Huh, I knew there was more of you, but I expected you all to travel together. Miscalculation on my part," he said, putting his arms up. "I'll tell you whatever you want to know."

Jin walked up to him and grabbed him by the collar. "I want you to tell me where June is!"

Zoe looked closer at the man. "Enrique? That's Tomas Enrique!" Zoe charged at him and Freya held her back by the waist.

"Not now, hon, we got him. Let's take him in and have him answer all of our questions," Freya said, pointing at the other team with her head. Zoe nodded reluctantly and cleaned herself off. Jin, still holding Enrique by the collar, pushed him toward the group.

"Come with us," said Ken. "Let's take the officer's truck," he suggested, turning to his team. Isaac, checking on Hector and propping him up, nodded and carried him.

"He's not doing well at all, he's passed out from the pain."

Jin looked down at the officer and his dog. "I'm so sorry." He knelt down and checked Manuel's pocket for the truck's keys.

"Got it. Will we all fit? It's a five-seater," asked Edwin.

"I don't think so," said Ken, picking up Hector as he squirmed and eventually passed out from the pain. "Edwin, your team will stay here with the prisoners, and we'll take these two to get medical attention. I'm sorry, you guys will have to wait out here for longer."

"It is what it is." Edwin shrugged and helped open the rear door to lay Hector inside while the others helped the farmer lay in the trunk.

"Someone will be here soon, I promise."

"Promises are all I get," Edwin said as he motioned for his team to follow him. Ken glanced at the others and they all nodded somberly before getting into the vehicle.

During the ride back, Ken called William. "William, it all went sideways. June's not here but we caught a person of interest. ... Yeah, two casualties. The officer and his canine. Hector's badly injured, as well as a civilian. Several prisoners too; Edwin's team is keeping an eye on them. We have a vehicle, so we'll head to the precinct as soon as possible. Send authorities to the farmhouse. ... Yeah, I know. See you soon."

Ken turned back to see Enrique giving him a wicked sneer.

***

At the police station, Hector and the farmer were taken away in separate ambulances. Isaac, Jin, and Zoe took Tomas Enrique into a room to begin questioning, while Ken and Freya went to the director's office and told them everything that happened.

"It was a trap," Freya said, pushing the door open. Gutierrez, who was speaking with the police chief, closed the door behind her and walked back toward them.

"A family was found in a river a few meters north from where you were. We need to confirm, but..."

William gave a sad nod and Ken cursed under his breath.

"What did we do wrong?!" asked a frustrated Freya, as tears began to form in her eyes.

"Nothing, these monsters are just one step ahead of us."

Gutierrez sighed as he sat.

William held Freya's hands from across the table. "They're much more powerful and connected than we know."

Just then, Zoila walked in. "He wants to talk to you," she said, staring at William with a concerned expression. "He said your name."

William seemed confused, darting his eyes between the director and Zoila, then he turned to Ken and Freya. He sighed and placed his hands on the table. "I'll see what that maniac wants. Hopefully it's something good." After he got up and walked out of the room, they glanced at each other with concern. "Stay by the door with him, *reinita*," said Zoila, putting her hand on Freya's shoulder tenderly. "He might need all the help he can get." Freya nodded and followed him down the hallway to the interrogation room. Ken sat silently, rocking as Director Gutierrez leaned forward and pulled out a notepad. "Ken, tell me everything," he said softly.

***

Freya stood at the door as William walked in. He closed the door behind him and sat across from Enrique.

"Weiss sends his regards," said Tomas Enrique as he sat in the chair with handcuffs chained to the table.

"Who?" asked William.

"They chained me up here like some normal person. Procedure, I guess. I can snap these off whenever I want."

"What do you want?" he asked Enrique as the man studied the handcuffs curiously.

"Um... To rule the world, no? It's what everyone wants, there's even a song..."

William smacked the table and leaned forward. "What the hell do you want!?"

The man seemed taken aback and laughed. "Look at your *cojones*. Maybe this will be fun, after all," he said calmly as he interlocked his fingers on the table. "I work for people that work, worked, and died for you." Enrique sucked his teeth. "I want you to know that the fear, the power, the *peace* you bring..." He made air quotes. "...is a fantasy you cannot sustain. We will not be oppressed and we will use whatever means necessary."

William gritted his teeth. "Then why now? Why here?"

Enrique snickered and looked toward the camera in the corner of the room and then at the large two-way mirror. "You see, it was simple. We found someone who had the following already, who believed in the power." Enrique leaned in. "He believes our power will steamroll the earth and we will become the dominant species. No longer afraid of lions, tigers, or even mosquitoes. We are the perfect organism. We are a juggernaut." Enrique scoffed to himself, seemingly hating his own words.

William's eyes squinted as he analyzed the man. "So, you don't believe in Cesar?"

Enrique laughed. "Supremacy is an illusion. I believe in the failings of human nature. Cesar believes us to be his allies. And before you wonder why I'm telling you all of this, it's because I want you to know..." Enrique leaned in closer and whispered. "...William, that we know... Everything." He then leaned back in his seat. "Where June came from, where she's been, and even where her real mom is."

William's head perked up. "Her mom? Her mom is dead," William said, feeling a sting of sadness.

"William, so smart, yet missing so much information. Head agent of the Nevada branch of B.R.I.C. Agency, handler of the famous Team Alpha, and you don't even know where your sister-in-law is."

William clenched his fist, and Enrique beamed.

"I've said all I was going to say. You think this little police station is going to hold me? Us?" Enrique let out a loud, forced laugh. William felt his whole body shake with fury.

"No one is going to reign supreme, William. No one is above nature. We'll make sure of that. But right now, I've got some temporary friends that want me free. By the way, tell those greedy mercenaries you arrested that they aren't ever going to see a dime."

Enrique closed his eyes with a malevolent smile. William was about to say something when suddenly an explosion was heard from the roof of the building. William ran while Enrique laughed wildly and snapped apart his handcuffs. Freya reached in and pulled William out and the two began running toward the roof.

"What the hell is all of this?!" Freya asked William and he shook his head, grunting as he slammed into the stairwell door.

"They're ten steps ahead. This is a fight for survival now."

Freya swallowed heavily as they made their way up, seeing the members of the Colombian team running up the stairs as well.

"What's happening?" asked a confused Edwin. Freya pointed at the roof and they all made their way up to see several men jumping up and down and punching it. They were causing the floors and ceilings to shake. Once they saw them, they stopped. The men all stood in a line, facing the team, and grinned. The man standing in front opened his arms out and dipped his head. Freya heard a rocket-propelled grenade launch and she dove in front of William. It hit the floor in between both groups, causing them to fly back.

The building began to crumble. Freya looked through the rubble to find William. She heard several coughs and saw Edwin's team shake their heads, confused, and picking themselves up. Marisol was clearing some rubble next to her and pulled out an unconscious William. Juan and Marisol peered through what was left of the walls around them as they came out of what used to be the entrance of the stairway.

"What the heck just happened?" asked a very disoriented Ricardo as Herman helped him push a piece of the roof off of his legs.

Freya shook her head, looking around for the Zealots. "They're after us. All of us."

Marisol asked, "Now what?" as she carried William.

Freya and Edwin glanced at each other while Juan, Herman, and Ricardo searched for survivors. With a loud cracking boom, Juan went flying across the floor and through a wall. The Zealots stood up from the debris and cleaned themselves off.

"Oh, we are not prepared for this." Freya turned to Marisol. "Get him out of here. Find the others."

Marisol nodded and ran toward the exposed stairwell. Juan walked out from the wall he was thrown through. "*Cabrón.* Who hit me?!" The Zealots just laughed and started walking toward them.

Edwin nodded. "No choice. We fight." There were five Zealots against the five of them. Edwin, Juan, Ricardo, Herman, and Freya each lined up in front of an opponent.

They charged at each other and the cracking, booming sounds of punches being thrown could be heard from the ground level, where Marisol ran out and tried looking for anyone who could help. The ambulances and police officers were trying to maintain a perimeter and ushered as many people as they could out of the building. Marisol noticed Ken was helping put people into stretchers and carried William to him. "He needs help!" she yelled, and Ken, startled at the sight of an unconscious William being carried by her, hurried and took him to find an ambulance.

"No!" yelled Zoila from across the street. She waved him down past the barricades. "This way. You too!" She pointed at Marisol. "Over here!" Ken and Marisol ran toward Zoila and a large black SUV. Director Gutierrez was at the wheel, beckoning everyone to get in.

Marisol opened the rear door where Jin and Isaac were already seated and they climbed to the far back seat, leaving space for Marisol and Ken to climb in.

"Where's..." Ken began.

"Freya's with my team, fighting on the roof... or what's left of it."

"What about Zoe?"

"We need to get William somewhere safe, *mi hijito*," said Zoila. "They can take care of themselves until the agency comes to help."

"I'm not worried for my team, if I'm honest, I'm afraid of what they'll do."

***

Sitting relaxed and covered in the dust falling from the roof,

Enrique snapped off the handcuffs and made his way to the door with a big smile on his face. He stopped to give a middle finger to the camera when suddenly the door broke off its hinges and threw him across the room with tremendous force. Zoe stood, breathing heavily at the doorway.

"Where is she?"

Enrique peeked from behind the door to see Zoe standing there, fists clenched and walking menacingly toward him.

"What's a little girl like you going to do to a man like me?!" He laughed.

"Plenty."

Zoe wound up a punch that landed in the center of the door, breaking a hole through it and causing Enrique to break through the floor below.

"I asked politely. Where is she?" Zoe dropped down after him. Enrique coughed, clearing his throat from all of the dust and debris.

"You got cojones, kid, but let me show you how the adults do it."

Enrique threw what was left of the door at Zoe, who pushed it aside, and threw a punch at her. Zoe bobbed under it, throwing a punch into his stomach that caused Enrique to lose his balance. Enrique stumbled back and threw another punch, aiming for Zoe's torso. She performed a pirouette and stood next to him as a right hook landed on his diaphragm, causing him to lose his breath. Enrique grew angrier. Zoe walked up to him and weaved, dodging a left hook and a right jab. Zoe uppercut Enrique in the center of his throat.

"Bitch!" Enrique bellowed, infuriated, as he coughed and tried to catch his breath.

Zoe said nothing as she caught his right hook, twisting the

limb into an arm lock that put him off-balance and fall face-first into the floor. Zoe then kicked his head into the floor repeatedly. She could barely make out what he was saying. "I'm sorry. I can't hear little bitches when they mumble," she said through gritted teeth as she continued to kick Enrique's head into the floor.

"I know where she is!" Enrique yelled. Zoe stopped kicking, but held him tighter.

"Where?" she asked slowly and forcefully.

"A small farmhouse, by the Venezuelan border, near Cucuta."

Zoe squeezed his arm harder and Enrique felt his muscles starting to cramp.

"*Viveros los campos!* Just south of the city!"

Zoe grimaced though bared teeth. "Thanks. Bitch." She then pushed Enrique's arm downward past his chest, causing a loud popping sound, and Enrique began yelling. "Never felt pain like that before, have you? You asshole."

Enrique writhed in pain on the floor, yelling, "How? How did you do this?"

Zoe sneered. "Everything has a weakness. Even if you have unbreakable skin, your joints and tendons still work like a normal person's. They just require the right amount of force. Now I'm going to ask you one last time. Where is June?"

Enrique sobbed as he rolled on the floor. "I told you, I wasn't lying. Please, please, don't hurt me anymore."

Zoe stood up next to him. "You're begging me, like that cop did for his life. You really *are* pathetic."

Enrique grabbed his arm and tried to crawl away. He turned on his back and showed his teeth. "The only thing pathetic here is how you think you're all going to win. We're bigger than you know and..."

Zoe kicked him in the jaw so hard it caused his neck to snap. He fell on the floor, limp. Zoe glanced over at him as she panted. "And we're tougher than you'll ever know. I know."

***

Freya laid on the floor as she held a Zealot by the throat while he continued to punch her in the head. She tried to push him off of her. Herman and Juan were rolling on the ground as well with the other two Zealots, Ricardo was fighting off a choke hold, and Edwin was picked up off the ground and thrown across the room past where Freya laid. Freya rolled her eyes, she was getting tired of this. She let go of the man's throat and put both arms between his legs and hooked them as she lifted herself up. Rolling over the man, she knelt on him. The confused Zealot went to wind up a punch but Freya rolled over him again and off. She turned around and before the man could get his bearings, Freya grabbed him by the hair, lifted and slammed his head into the ground, and caused the floor to shake. She then grabbed him harder and twisted her body, causing him to lift up, and threw him on the other men that were fighting on the floor.

The five men laid there, confused and trying to gather their thoughts, when Freya reached in and lifted Juan, Ricardo, and Herman off the ground. They dusted themselves off just as the Zealots also stood up. Edwin, who came through the door of the room he was thrown into, joined them.

"We are chosen! You will not beat us!" The man who threw him laughed.

Freya rolled her eyes again and turned around. "Do you

guys ever listen to yourselves?" She rolled her shoulders and walked toward the man, putting up her fist.

"You are no match for us." Freya dodged a punch and slapped him in the ear. The Zealot blinked as he lost his balance.

Freya glanced at Edwin's team that were just staring at her, and they nodded. Edwin charged at one of them and tackled him, while the others did the same. The men struggled but tried to target weak points using their knuckles to hit eyes and open palms to box their ears. They struggled for a while, tussling, and the Zealots tried using the same tactics to a lesser degree.

Freya continued to fight with the large man who seemed only an inch or two taller but built wider than her. She had a hard time hitting his head because of his broad shoulders. Finally, she'd had enough and did a split and punched the man in the testicles. The man bent over slightly. "Wow, I... Wow," he said, trying to catch his breath. "Hurts the most when you least expect it."

Freya smirked. She then put her hand under his neck and flipped him onto his back, causing him to lift off the ground as she hooked his neck with both arms and squeezed. The man kicked and struggled but a determined Freya held him until she could feel him go limp. She dropped his unconscious body on the ground and checked for a pulse. He was still alive. Freya shook her head. As much as she wished she could kill him, it felt like the wrong thing to do. She turned to the others and they appeared as if they were all having a playground shuffle.

"Boys..." said Freya, rolling her eyes. She stood up and dusted herself off.

"Right?" said Zoe, walking up behind her.

Freya sighed in relief. "Z, what took you so long? Where's everyone?"

Zoe shook her head. "I... eliminated..." She sighed. "Enrique."

Freya closed her eyes, took a breath, and put a hand on her shoulder. "The others? Where..."

"Everything downstairs is chaotic. Haven't seen anyone since."

"'Kay, it's up to us to finish this then."

Zoe grabbed the guy who was trying to jam his fingers into Juan's eyes and put him in a choke hold. Freya came in and punched him in the jaw, effectively causing the man to lose consciousness. The two then walked up to Herman's fight and pulled the guy by the legs off of Herman before punching him in the back of the head simultaneously. Herman then nodded in thanks to the girls.

"I got this one." Zoe walked up to Ricardo's opponent as he was trying to put him into a choke hold. She punched him in the lower back and kicked the back of his knee, and he fell back onto the floor. She then kicked his jaw, causing him to lose consciousness. Zoe bent down and checked for his pulse. She looked at Freya with a smirk and nodded, letting her know the man was still breathing.

Edwin, who was trapped and locked into a grapple with the remaining Zealot, yelled at the five of them. "A little help... *por favor*." Freya and Zoe sniffed. The Zealot glanced around the room and noticed all of his teammates had been knocked unconscious and let go of Edwin. "Eh, no. Please. I give up!"

Freya and Zoe looked at him with matching wicked grins. "You must be the smart one," said Freya.

"Let's go." Edwin held the man by the arm and the others

picked up the fallen Zealots.

Zoe put her hand on Freya's shoulder. "I think I've got a location. Might be a long shot, but Enrique made it seem very convincing."

"No choice but to check it out, then."

Zoe nodded. "Yeah. Now, let's get these assholes into coffins."

The conscious Zealot's eyes widened as he stared at the man holding him and panicked.

"No one's gonna kill you, it's just a prison," said Edwin with a smile on his face.

"You need a better name for those things. Here we just call them *dormideros*."

Zoe and Freya rolled their eyes.

"Same difference," said Freya.

"We gotta call William."

Freya nodded her head. "I hope he's okay, Marisol took him and never came back."

"He'll be fine," said Edwin. "Marisol is tough. Like you two. She's probably protecting him now, for her not to come back and fight with us."

They all walked out of the stairwell where firefighters and policemen were all running around, clearing debris and trying to find more survivors. A firefighter walked up to Freya and asked her if they were okay in Spanish. The team replied they were and the firefighter walked them to the exit where a paramedic proceeded to check their vitals. Edwin waved down what seemed to be Colombian B.R.I.C. agents that were parked in black vans.

"This is what we were avoiding. A fight with Bricks almost brought this whole building and we're pros who can minimize collateral damage. Imagine a random fight. This city wouldn't have stood a chance," Freya said as she surveyed the destroyed police station. Zoe nodded sadly, then pulled out her phone. "I'll try Ken, I hope he's with everyone else."

Freya agreed as she looked around at the panicked civilians. She couldn't help but imagine the chaos a war of Bricks would bring. The thought chilled her to the bone.

As the chaos died down and the Zealots were placed into the coffins, Zoe managed to contact Zoila from another agent's phone.

"Hey, where the heck are you guys?"

Ken replied, "Zoe? Zoe it's you, are you okay? What happened, is Freya with you? Edwin's team?" Zoe closed her eyes.

"Dude, chill, we're okay, we all made it. We caught the Zealots and Enrique is dead."

Ken, surprised, asked, "Dead? How?"

Zoe breathed out. "I happened. We got a possible location on June."

Ken gasped. "Then we have to follow up. Where at? We're heading to Bogota base."

"Cucuta. Near there. I have the name of a ranch."

Ken sighed. "That's far, but let's see what we can do. Meet us here, and regroup. William's..."

"I know. Keep us posted." Zoe turned to Freya and pointed with her chin to the Colombian team as they sat on the sidewalk.

"We'll meet you there. We need a ride, though."

Ken agreed. "I'll ask Zoila, see what we can do."

The team piled into a police van. The officer turned on his siren and drove as fast as he could toward Bogota. They sat quietly during the trip. Freya held Zoe's hand and gave her a reaffirming nod. Zoe smiled weakly back at her. Edwin's team sat with their heads in their hands, frustrated by the day's events. After what seemed like hours, they arrived at the Bogota base's entrance. A large gray unassuming building. Sandwiched between other unassuming buildings but surrounded by mountains.

"*Vamos,*" said Edwin, breaking the silence. "Let's go."

The six made their way out of the police van and walked in. Herman's stomach growled.

"Same," said Juan. "Hope we get something good."

Freya and Zoe remembered that they hadn't eaten since before their team arrived to meet them. They walked into the lobby and greeted the guards in front. Zoila met up with them and called them in.

The elevator went down from the lobby and opened to a long corridor where a cart was waiting for them. "Get in. Are any of you hurt?" Zoila asked as she turned to Edwin, placing her hand on his back. "Are you okay?"

Edwin nodded and gently shook her hand off. "We're okay, we're all fine. These ladies came and helped us." He motioned to Freya and Zoe sitting in the back of the cart. Zoila thanked them and motioned to the driver, and they drove down the long corridor.

After what seemed like another extremely long ride, Freya and Zoe got off and walked around to group up with Edwin's team and Zoila as they entered a secure door that needed Zoila's card to open. They walked into the base of operations for the Colombian branch. Freya and Zoe never even saw the one back home since it was probably on another floor than they usually came in through. "Is this how hectic ours was?"

Zoe asked Freya, seemingly feeling overwhelmed.

Zoila glanced back at them. "It's usually a little calmer here, but you know, being attacked and all has us all running around like chickens with no heads." Zoila laughed softly and continued leading the group toward the elevators. "Hector and William are in medical, floor three. Everyone else is in the living quarters, which is floor four."

Freya and Zoe turned to Edwin's team. Edwin looked at his team and back at the women. "We'll go to living, we are starving. You go ahead to see your friends. I hope they're okay."

Juan summoned the elevators and got into one with his team while Freya, Zoe, and Zoila waited for the other.

"I'm so sorry, I don't know what happened." Zoila turned to Freya and Zoe.

Zoe shrugged her shoulders and shook her head. "It..."

"It was a trap," said Freya. "Trap, after trap, after trap. They're trying to get us. I don't think they were expecting us to get away from the attack on the station, but we have to be prepared for an attack here too."

Zoila nodded at Freya sympathetically. "We have snipers on the roofs, helicopters ready, and as soon as they get some rest I'll send Edwin and his team to check the perimeter."

"I don't think they were counting on us coming back here. They would have attacked us on the way. You think they're waiting at Cucuta?" Zoe asked Freya, who nodded and thought out loud.

"Maybe they were expecting him to talk? Or..." Freya became lost in thought as the elevator doors opened and the three women walked into a half-full car. The passengers greeted Zoila and talked about what happened in the police station, but Zoila didn't join in. Once they made it to the third floor, the door behind them opened up to a wide space. An all-white sanitary place that couldn't be mistaken for anything other than a hospital. The two of them followed Zoila as she said her farewells to the elevator passengers and continued down the hallways to find a room where a dark-haired woman in a lab coat stood.

"Zoila! Finally! You must be Freya and Zoe. I'm Dr. Cassandra Glendale, head researcher and medical practitioner at B.R.I.C. Agency, well... for the world. William talks so highly of you."

"We've heard of you through William," Freya said, shaking her hand. "He speaks highly of you too, Doctor."

Dr. Glendale bowed her head slightly, her mouth quirked. "Well, he should. I saved his ass... multiple times."

The group let out a weak laugh and walked in to see the two men on different hospital beds beside each other, only split by a curtain. Hector was awake and weakly drinking from a juice box, but William was still unconscious.

"Will he be okay?" asked Zoila with a look of concern.

"He'll live, he just took a heavy hit to the head. Luckily the shock wave didn't do much damage to his organs."

Freya felt relief knowing that she did manage to block some of the damage.

"He might need a few days. As for him..." Dr. Cassandra pointed at Hector, who smiled and waved. "He's almost as lucky as Ken."

"Please tell me he'll be able to play football again, Doctor," said Freya jokingly. The doctor stifled a grin.

"If he's okay playing with one ball."

Zoe's and Freya's jaw dropped.

"Yeah, okay, the volt blew out a testi. Can we not?" Hector said, blushing and holding the juice box closer to his chest.

Freya shook off the shock. "Yeah, no, dude, this is... this sucks. Like, it could have been worse and all, but... shit, I'm sorry. If he lost an organ and Ken's heart almost exploded, what hope do we have against those weapons?"

Zoe seemed to have come to the same realization and the two of them looked at each other.

Dr. Glendale breathed deeply and calmly spoke to them. "I've been trying to do some research on these weapons. All I can gather is, it's European-built, metals and plastics used from facilities around Germany and France. But other than that, I couldn't find any more info. As far as defense goes, I'm lining the suites with heavy rubber. It'll still sting but it's better than the full force of it. All I can say is, don't get shot."

The doctor turned to Hector as he struggled to open a pudding snack. "Anesthesia should wear off soon." Dr. Glendale motioned to the group to leave the room.

"Get better, bud." Freya waved at him. Hector gave a small wave back at the two of them as they walked out behind Zoila and the doctor.

"I'll be frank," said Dr. Glendale in a sterner tone. "You guys are screwed if you get hit. Between the gas in his lungs the volt of electricity that fried his leg's nerves and caused his testicle to rupture, and don't get me started on Ken who is lucky to even be alive, we need to figure out who made these weapons and soon, because I don't think they're just going to stop at this. I know they're European because I looked into the French branch who placed an order for tons, and I mean tons, of a carbon fiber material very similar to this, while the German branch placed an order for an insane amount of

300

metals and materials that line up with everything that's being used here."

Freya shook her head. "We can't just go gallivanting to Europe now, June needs us and we know where she's at. Dr. Glendale, please..."

Dr. Glendale lifted her hand. "Please call me Cass, dear, and no, I'm not making you go there. I've sent word, and another team is going to check it out. If it's true that we have been infiltrated, then we need to be more cautious than ever."

Zoila nodded at the two women. "Girls, go upstairs, eat, meet up with your team, try to rest, and be ready. Around midnight, we will head out. We will find June, and then we will be able to get to the bottom of this."

Freya turned to Zoe, feeling worried. Freya nodded, and they both walked back toward the elevators. Once inside and with no one else around, Freya asked, "What's on your mind?"

Zoe shook her head. "We almost lost both of them, that's three of us that have almost lost their lives. What if June's not... What if something..."

Freya hugged Zoe tightly. "Hey, it'll be all right. She's a trooper, plus that asshole said she was alive, right?"

Zoe took a step back. "But why? Why is she still alive, while they keep trying to kill us?"

Freya shook her head. "I wish I could have heard what that man said to William before the explosion."

Zoe added, "I wish I could talk to him now."

They gave each other a concerned glance before walking into the mess hall.

"I'm worried about her, about everything, Freya. She must be terrified."

"Me too, Zoe, me too."

11

The Shackles That Tear Us Apart

Cesar Villalobos sat cross-legged in front of a dangling June.

"You talk... so much," she said as she struggled to move.

Cesar sneered. "You really think you are alive because I want you to be?"

"I thought you kept me alive because I'm known to make a wicked grilled cheese."

"Right now your friends are dead. We set a trap that should have killed all of them. Despite what my 'partner' wanted, I went ahead and sent a few people to take care of your friends and anyone who survived at the police station. My men must have destroyed that place, uh, to the ground, as you gringos say." Cesar shot a wicked grin at June. She stared at him, grinding her teeth.

"I promise you, my friends are fine. They're gonna come here and kick your ass."

Cesar let out another belly laugh and stood up. "I didn't want to have to do this, it's bad enough my contact is lying to me. Now that I have you, I will wait for them, and have my delicious dinner. It's no grilled cheese, but if you'd like to join me, you'll tell me why you cannot die."

June was confused and finally asked, "What do you mean, I can't die?"

Cesar stopped and turned around. "You really don't know?" He made his way back to the seat. "No gas can kill you. Not even drowning. You seemed to sleep until the water pushed itself out of your lungs. It was fascinating to watch." Cesar shook his head slowly. "I may be invincible, but you may be immortal."

June scoffed. "I think I'd remember being drowned."

Cesar shook his head. "No, *niña*, you slept the whole time. It was incredible. I don't have many other means to kill you but smoke, drowning, even making you drink poison, your body throws it all up. After a few hours, you just continued sleeping like a baby."

"The house explosion..."

"What?"

June glared back up at Cesar. He nodded slowly as he stared at June, her eyes darting as she showed her teeth.

"You are remarkable. I'm holding you here until my partner can tell me what to do with you."

"Do with me!? I'll tell you what you can do, you grandiose hobo, let me down so I can shove my foot up your old ass!"

Cesar shot up and grabbed her by the hair. "That's the problem, child," he said through clenched teeth. "Old. We are invincible, but time is still our enemy. I cannot rule this world if I die of old age!" Cesar screamed into June's face as he pulled on her hair. June, shocked by his action, got an idea.

"Well, because you're not a god, are you? You're not even the chosen one you think you are. You're just an old fart who still needs prostate exams and..."

Cesar snapped again. "YOU LITTLE BITCH!" He shook her head violently as he cursed at her in Spanish, some words June knew and others she didn't. It was working. June felt the chains loosen a bit, just enough so her left arm had some movement. "Guess you'll be dead and your followers will just have to follow me to a better, more peaceful future than you could…"

A thunderous crack was heard as Cesar backhanded June, who went limp for a moment. Cesar cleaned off his shirt and took a deep breath and waited for her to gain consciousness again. June blinked and felt disoriented for a moment.

"Oh, you're still here. I thought you'd have died of old age by now."

Cesar's mouth twitched in anger, but he kept calm this time. "That would have killed a man, maybe even hurt an invincible man, but you, you come back as annoying as ever." Cesar shook his head and turned away from June. "I don't trust my partner, but we require technology to test you, technology I don't have. If we can see what made you immortal, then maybe we can apply it to ourselves—"

June interrupted. "So your old ass can live forever lying to people? You can't turn a normal person into a Brick and you sure as hell can't use my DNA to make yourself immortal! You're a has-been who's getting old, is scared to die, and you've now realized how much of your life you have wasted on this stupid crusa—" Cesar turned quickly and punched June across the face. June grunted but laughed. "Heh… that all you got, old-timer? I've seen tortoises punch harder than you."

Cesar became red with anger. "I get enough insults from my partner and the non-believers, but from a little girl like you, I will bury you in cement up to your mouth and kick you in the head every day until I figure out how to become immortal like you!"

June scoffed. "Can you cover me up to my ears, so I don't have to listen to you go on and on and on and..." June continued until Cesar was so fed up he walked out of the room.

He slammed the door behind him and June quickly tried flexing the arm that came loose after several of Cesar's punches until she heard a snap. She looked around, hoping no one heard. The link fell to the floor with a dull thud. June slowly wiggled around as the chain became looser and fell off in chunks, until only the part holding her up by the armpits remained. June slipped loose and dropped to the floor. She searched for her necklace, but it was lost in the grass below. With a sigh, she made her way to the door to listen if anyone was coming.

June didn't hear anything and peeked out to see a guard fast asleep on a chair holding a cattle prod in his arms. She considered giving him a rude awakening, but decided against it and just walked quietly past him. As June walked around the end of the hall, she noticed she was in a large ranch surrounded by an electric fence with turret towers at each corner. She wished Ken were here so he could take out the towers like he did the last time, but she was going to have to do it on her own now. It was dark and June had no idea how long she'd been here for. She regretted not having her suit on, as the dark color could have helped in the night.

She decided she was going to stick close to the ground and try to make it up a tower to jump over the fence. She'd seen the others leap high, but she still wasn't sure she could. She crawled past the open field and close to another large, elaborate building where she assumed Cesar held himself up. She pressed against the wall and peeked around the corner. She could make out some movement, maybe a guard pacing in front of the door, or a fern; she couldn't tell and she wasn't going to chance it.

June grabbed a rock from the floor and flung it over the building. A loud thud was heard from the roof. She didn't throw it as far as she wanted, but the figure still moved past the other side of the building. June crouched and tried to run as fast as she could toward the tower. She made it, but the guard in the tower was suspicious of the rustling beneath him. June tried to hide behind some overgrown bushes and held her breath.

Eventually, the flashlight passed her and the guard went back to using the spotlight outward. A loud slam could be heard from the building June came from. It was the guard, he came out from behind the building cursing in Spanish and cursing the birds. June had to be especially quiet now and stick to climbing the tower from the inside of the ladder. She hoped the beam would be enough to block her petite frame from the guard's view. June climbed up swiftly, trying not to make any noise. She made it halfway before she heard someone shouting.

Gunshots fired and suddenly everything went quiet. June glanced around to see that the guard from the other tower had shot into the jungle, killing a large cat. All the other guards laughed at him and he cursed at them in Spanish. June continued climbing the thirty-foot tower and made it to the bottom side of the floor. She climbed to the other side of the ladder and slowly peeked over the railing to see the catwalk and a door were all that stood between her and freedom.

June saw a military truck approaching that honked its horn and was let through the massive gates between the towers. She tried to peer inside, but it was too dark. She climbed over the railing and onto the catwalk, standing by the door. She closed her eyes and planned a way to get the guard's attention without making a ruckus.

"*Cabrón* gringo," said the guard to himself.

June pondered for a moment before noticing the radio PA system inside the room. If she could make it loop, it should give her enough time to jump and run into the jungle without them noticing. Now, if only she could open the window and mess with it without the guard noticing. He was leaning against the floodlight. June waited for him to move the light toward the left and she carefully pulled the large sliding window open. It was heavy, clearly made to be bulletproof. She reached in and grabbed the mic and placed it in front of the speaker. The loud sound echoed all throughout the compound and June saw her chance.

The guard covered his ears and turned to the other tower, yelling at them. June seized the opportunity and jumped past the fences and into the bushes below. She ran as fast as she could, keeping parallel to the road but staying off of it just in case there were more guards along the way. June kept running before realizing she had no idea where she was. The mountain and jungles obscured her view and she couldn't tell how far the nearest city was. She stopped for a moment, caught her breath, and continued running as thunder boomed through the jungle.

June ran for over an hour, stopping along the way to catch her breath. While lost and still trying to make her way back to civilization, June began reflecting. She gritted her teeth and stood in the dark jungle. "That asshole killed me!" June fell to her knees and punched the mud. "I'm going to kill him." June couldn't see her tears fall on the dark jungle floor but she shook her head and tried to get up. Her knees buckled under her and she fell in the mud again, her sobs drowned out by the heavy rain.

The thick, humid fog of the jungle cleared as the morning sun broke over the mountains. The sunlight made the path clearer. June made her way into a small town quietly, past the shanty houses, making it to a road. Covered in mud, the few people she spotted tried their best to ignore her and keep walking past. June spotted a bike she could take, but felt guilty as she grabbed it, sighed, and kept walking. She kept looking for any sign of where she might be. Finally, after hours of walking, June came up to a sign. "Cucuta?"

***

Both teams—or what was left of them—met up in the mess hall, sitting on a bench. They were the only ones left in there. Everyone in this branch of the agency was running, in a panic, trying to cover up or explain away last night's chaos in two different parts of the country. Edwin sat eating a piece of bread, slowly, more pensively than hungry.

"These guns, these weapons that landed your friend in the medical station, how do they work?" he asked.

Freya shook her head. "They... They cause massive electrical shocks to the body, sometimes causing the lesser organs to erupt, or explode."

"How... How is he?" asked Marisol timidly.

"He'll be okay. He just needs to recover for some time."

Zoe reached into a bowl of fried plantains that no one was eating, and asked, "Where are Ken and Isaac?"

The team shrugged their shoulders without looking up.

"Probably..." Juan said after a moment. "Probably in the showers. I was thinking of going there soon, but..." He trailed off.

Freya and Zoe gave each other worried glances. "We should go take showers too. Where..."

Edwin shook his head and put down the piece of bread. "Of course, of course, uh, Marisol, could you..."

Marisol nodded and motioned the two to follow her. "I needed to go too, I still smell like mud."

The three women left the guys sitting at the table barely picking at their food. Zoe noticed the men slouch farther and lean on the table.

"This way," said Marisol as she led them to the elevator on the other side of the mess hall.

"Thanks," said Freya. "How are you guys doing?"

Marisol shook her head slightly and closed her eyes. "You mean now, after knowing that there's a gun out there that can kill us?"

Freya nodded solemnly, and Zoe scratched the back of her neck. The doors opened and Marisol walked in first, greeting the other passengers. The ride up became quiet. Finally reaching their floor, Marisol led the way as soon as the doors opened.

The three women walked down the concrete corridors and made it to a large opening. There were red doors on each side, one for women and the other for men. Zoe tried to listen to the men's area to hear for showers, but couldn't hear anything. Freya looked at her and Zoe shook her head. Marisol held the door open and the three walked in.

"You can put your suits to wash here." She pointed along the right wall at a line of washers and dryers. "Spare clothes are in those boxes there." She pointed past the lockers to cubbies along the opposite wall filled with labels marking types of clothing and sizes. "Showers are past here," she said, pointing at an archway at the end of the room.

Marisol went to her locker and started grabbing her own clothes, while Zoe and Freya sifted through the boxes to find something to wear. Zoe found a yellow T-shirt with a macaw on it and some loose-fitting jeans. She sighed in relief when she found a belt to hold them up. "Any luck?" she asked Freya, who was indecisive between a very large, gray shirt with an air-conditioning company logo and a pink camouflage T-shirt that fit her well with the words "Bad Bitch" in big, white letters. Freya glared at her and Zoe giggled softly, causing her to sigh.

***

Ken laid down in a bunk bed, looking down at the shirt he found, a generic cartoon on a red T-shirt, and adjusted his cargo shorts before staring off into the ceiling, pondering.

"Bruh, it's almost midnight. Where is everyone?" Isaac asked as he rolled over on his bed toward him.

"We've been here for hours, man. I can't take this, especially…"

"I know! I know!" said Ken, frustrated and putting his palms over his face.

"This situation is trash," Jin said, sitting up on the bed across from them. "Isaac's wearing a floral-patterned polyester shirt and Bermuda shorts and I'm wearing a navy blue button-up shirt with khakis! We look like tourists! This is a crime of fashion, no wonder these clothes are in the abandoned bin! What are we supposed to do now?!" He eyed Ken, expecting an answer.

"What do they expect us to do, we can't even..." started Ken, before he was interrupted.

"Can't even, what?" said Zoila, walking in through the door.

Ken, Jin, and Isaac turned to her. "Hey, hi, hey..." said Ken, palming his face. Isaac gave her a nod with a worried expression and Jin gave her a small wave. Zoila sighed.

"The girls are here. They're taking a shower now. Our information says that there is a compound near Cucuta a few miles south, practically on the Venezuelan border. We sent a team to investigate now, so we have to wait for a while before we hear back." Ken and Isaac sighed. Zoila gave a sympathetic nod and continued. "We need to get you guys ready, so grab your suits and meet me outside as soon as you're done."

The guys hurried to the foot of the beds and grabbed their suits. A moment later, they were dressed and meeting Zoila outside the dormitory.

"Good, *vamos*, the girls should be ready soon and will meet us in my office."

The four walked into an elevator and Zoila took a deep breath.

***

Freya and Zoe finished drying their hair and got dressed. Zoe noticed Freya putting on the pink camo shirt and giggled.

"Don't judge me." Freya sighed.

"I didn't say nothin'." Zoe shook her head and tightened her belt. She appreciated that at least the length of the jeans was right, but didn't feel comfortable with the way they bunched around her waist. Zoe noticed Marisol speaking to someone by the washing machines, then she turned and walked toward them with a grave look.

"We have new orders," Marisol said, almost robotically. "Zoila wants us to meet her at her office."

"What about our suits?" asked Zoe.

"I guess we'll come back to pick them up before we go. They're still only drying now."

Zoe grinned at Freya. "I hope the guys look worse than we do." Freya let out a soft laugh.

"Okay, let's go see what they want."

Marisol nodded and started walking away. Zoe and Freya turned toward each other, confused as to why Marisol seemed much more agitated and worried than when they first met.

"Are you okay?" asked Freya.

"Fine. I just... I miss home," replied Marisol "But now the danger seems to be getting worse, and I'm afraid I'll never see it again."

Zoe placed a hand on her shoulder. "Same, lady. We're all terrified."

***

At Zoila's office she, Ken, Isaac, and Jin walked in to see Director Gutierrez sitting at her desk. "Hi..." Zoila began, but the director lifted a finger and made a motion to wait while he spoke on the phone. He seemed worried and leaned back in his chair, defeated. He glanced at Zoila and then the others. The director hung up the phone softly as Zoila sat on the desk next to him.

"What happened, Guille?" she asked the director.

He rubbed his palm across his face and looked up at her with a sad expression. "Mexico—a Mexican team—was just wiped out. They had info that Villalobos was there. The team, their leader, all taken out at the same time. Director McAfee called me, told me to be careful about false information, and to make sure who we are getting it from."

Zoila stiffened. "We just sent a team to Cucuta to check rumors..."

The director nodded. "I gave them the warning. Told them to make contact in two hours or we will consider them missing and send the military."

Zoila shook her head and stood up. "That would be war, we can't do that!"

The director nodded again. "I know, call it incentive, but I won't actually send the military. We can't risk more lives. Especially so close to the border. Last thing we need is for Venezuela to think we are going to war with them."

Zoe, Freya, and Marisol walked in and the mood felt grimmer than before. Ken, Freya, Zoe, Jin, and Isaac all gave each other tight hugs but didn't say anything to each other. They all turned to Zoila. She was looking at them sympathetically.

"I hate to ask this of you so soon but, it's time you get ready and head out to back our agents up."

"Count us in. Whatever we can do to bring back June and stop Cesar, we're in," Ken said with determination.

Zoila and Director Gutierrez nodded in agreement.

"Let's go save the world... again," Jin sighed.

***

June made her way through the city, it was early in the morning and the foggy mist was clearing. She made her way to a bar that was still closed. She thought to herself she should call someone, but she didn't know anyone's numbers. So June continued walking. She looked for a taxi, but the roads were mostly empty. Checking her pockets, she realized she didn't have any money on her either. If she could only figure out how to send a signal to Ken or Zoila or anyone. Maybe find a police station, but June couldn't spot anyone to ask. It was dawn and the town seemed abandoned.

June found a convenience store and tried searching for a map but didn't have any luck. Grunting in frustration, she walked up to the clerk, asking him bluntly how to get to Bogota.

The man laughed, eyed her up and down, then replied in Spanish. "What's a little girl like you doing in a city like this?"

June raised an eyebrow and glared at the man. "I was kidnapped, captured, tortured, escaped—and now I'm here asking an idiot how to get back to where I need to go."

The clerk's eyes widened, and he apologized. "I'm so sorry, are you serious!?"

June glared at him, unamused. "Do I look like I'm kidding about this? Why else would I be covered in leaves and mud with torn clothes?"

The clerk, feeling bad, pulled out his wallet and gave her some cash. "Please, I'm so sorry. Do you need an ambulance?"

June shook her head. "I just want to get home."

The clerk pulled out his phone. "Anyone I can call to pick

you up?"

June shook her head again. "I lost everyone's number, but if you can call the Bogota police station and ask for Zoila De Armas, that would help."

***

As the team was getting dressed and preparing to head out, a woman in heels was heard running down the hall toward them yelling, "Zoila! Zoila!" Zoila turned around and walked toward her, and they both began speaking in Spanish.

"She's in Cucuta!"

Zoila, confused, asked, "Who?"

"She's in Cucuta, the girl—the missing girl." Zoila turned to the two teams with a shocked expression on her face. "She called the police station, asked for you, and that triggered our systems."

Zoila thanked her and rushed back to the group. "They found her, she managed to escape somehow. We don't have much time. Hurry to the address I'm about to send you. Be careful! It could be a trap." Ken gave her a nod and led everyone into the vans. Ken's team took the one in the back while Edwin's team sat in the leading van.

***

June sat outside of the gas station, waiting to see if anyone got her message. The clerk told her it was about a twelve-and-a-half-hour drive; two hours by plane. She sat there and watched the cars pass by. The clerk gave her a bag of chips and a soda can to hold her over. While she ate, the clerk came

315

outside.

"They called back. There will be an officer to pick you up and take you to the station. They said they will meet you there."

June thanked him and finished the last bit of her soda before placing the empty can and bag in the bin by the door. As other customers came in and gave her weird looks, June rolled her eyes and leaned against the wall.

After half an hour, a police cruiser came in, and the officer sitting in the passenger seat asked, "June? June Romero?" June nodded at the female officer and walked toward the car just as the male officer opened the door for her. She sat in the rear seat, thanking them, before she laid her head back and fell asleep.

12

Reunited

June was woken up gently by the female officer. She thanked the officers as they walked inside the station. The officer continued to ask June questions, but June felt dizzy and disoriented as she struggled to walk. They finally made it to a waiting room where the officer sat June down on a chair. June weakly thanked them both before falling asleep again.

"...And no one gave her any food or water?" June could barely open her eyes when she realized Zoila was arguing with the officers in Spanish.

"She was sleeping..."

Zoila waved her arms around. "Of course! She's exhausted! She has run for miles and is dehydrated! She needs medical attention!"

June fell asleep, this time waking up on a stretcher in a white hallway before passing out again. Finally, June woke up in a hospital room attached to heart monitors and a needle in her arm. June's mouth opened to yell, but a voice told her to relax. "It'll snap if you move it and it'll be almost impossible to get it out." June nodded and passed out once more.

"Who…" June started to ask, her vision still a bit blurry.

"Dr. Cassandra Glendale, I specialize in superhuman physiology."

June remembered William calling her back at the Nevada military base.

"In case you're wondering, I used very specific, high-powered tools to fix you up. It takes a very focused and powerful laser to penetrate your skin, but it has to be done in layers and I'm not gonna bore you with the details. Let's just say, a needle in the arm which should take a second becomes an hour's worth of work. So please, don't move until we get it out. You needed it. I've never seen such a dehydrated Brick who still had traces of water in their lungs."

June wished the clerk would have given her water instead. "What happened? Where am I?"

Dr. Glendale pulled a seat next to June and sat down with her legs crossed, leaning close to her. "I could ask you. We ran MRIs and X-rays and, well, what did they do to you? As to where, you're at our Bogota base. Safe. But tell me what happened to you."

June tried to remember, but it was too painful. "They, uh, they said they killed me." The doctor sat up straight with a shocked expression on her face. "So it's true. You have the gene."

Bits and pieces came back to June. "He said he wanted to study me, figure out why I'm immortal."

Dr. Glendale faced June with a sad expression on her face. "You are a rarity, indeed, but the traces of chemicals and liquids in your lungs, I was hoping it wasn't that. Some damage in the neck ligaments too…"

June put her hand on her neck, remembered the sucker

punch that snapped it, and winced.

"It's healing, but it'll take time." June nodded her head gently and laid back down. "I'll keep an eye on you. And just so you know, your friends are worried about you, but they'll have to wait to see you until after the IV has finished and we get that needle out. Don't want an accident." Dr. Cassandra got up and put her hand on June's head with an empathetic look. "Okay. Take care." With that, she walked out of the room. June could only close her eyes now. Her body felt heavy and finally, her eyes closed and her breathing evened out.

***

June awoke to voices in the distance. Dr. Glendale put her hand on June's cheek.

"It'll feel like a small prick, but you're gonna be okay." June felt a stinging sensation in her arm. She glanced down to see the needle being withdrawn and her own blood seeped out. Dr. Glendale cleaned her with alcohol pads and put a bandage on her.

"All done now, hon, you'll be okay. Your friends are here to see you."

Ken was the first through the door, followed by Zoe, Jin, Freya, and Isaac. They gathered around June, concern on all of their faces.

"Girl, you look like shit," said Jin, sitting at the foot of her bed. Ken went to give her a hug but ended up just caressing her shoulders, and sat down on the chair next to her while the others sat around her bed.

"What happened, are you okay?" asked Freya, concerned. "The doc didn't tell us anything, said it's up to you to let us know."

June put her hands up and with a groggy, raspy voice, she tried to slow everyone down. "Whoa, whoa, one at a time. Okay, one, I'm okay now, I guess. I was dehydrated, chained up for a day, and running through a jungle all night apparently did a number on me. Two, you'd look like shit too if you had the day I had. And three, where's William and Hector?"

The team lowered their gaze. "Hector's okay, he just lost a... well, he's a little lighter now," said Jin. "Also, sorry for the comment on..."

June held up a hand and gazed up at Jin. "Dude, I expect nothing less. We all gotta look our best to be the best, right?" She smirked.

Jin forced a smile as well. "You know it, girl." They both held each other's hands. June glanced back at Zoe, hoping to hear about William. Zoe averted her gaze and Freya sighed, she gazed down at the floor then glanced at June.

"William's in a coma. He was in an explosion at the police station in Cali, where we were attacked. He'll be fine, but the doc says we gotta wait for him to wake up. Nothing more we can do."

June nodded sadly and debated her follow-up question. "When... So, was the doctor here all last night?"

The team turned at each other, confused. "We think so, I'd have to ask Zoila, but..."

June remembered the clerk telling her it was about a two-hour flight from Bogota to Cucuta. "She wasn't missing for more than a few hours, was she?"

"No," said Zoila, walking into the room holding some flowers. "*Mi hijita*, she spent all night at William's side. I'll double-check, but between Hector's operation, William's coma, and checking on you, she hasn't had time for anything, why?"

June shook her head. "Just a theory."

Zoila put the assortment of flowers on the table next to June. "Does the doctor have anyone who helps her that may have left and come back?"

Zoila cocked her head and scrunched her eyebrows. "*Mi hija*, what are you saying?"

June looked at everyone in the room. "When I was escaping, a big camo truck showed up and I heard the guards saying the 'gringo' was there. I figured it might be the person who betrayed us."

Zoila grimaced, puzzled. "Okay, you're going to have to tell us how you escaped, but also, Americans here..." Zoila scratched her chin. "From the agency it's only Cassandra, everyone else is regular staff here. It's just you guys and William." Zoila gave June a kiss on the head. "I'll do what I can to find more information, but you rest, *mi hijita*, I'll come back later to check up on you. You guys catch up. I'll let you know if I find anything." Zoila then hurried out of the room, waving goodbye.

"You think she'll find anything?" asked Zoe, and Freya nodded her head.

"I hope so. We don't have much to go on other than they're some military American dude..."

June interrupted. "With Brick physiology knowledge and is capable of producing weapons."

Freya nodded slowly as what June told her sunk in. "So, someone way up in the ranks?" Freya scratched her head and seemed even more worried.

Ken held June's hand, and asked, "Dude, how? Did they

hurt you? What did they do to you? Did you see Cesar?"

June couldn't help but smile. Her mind was still only able to take in a few things at a time. She grabbed his hand. "I saw the asshole. He likes to monologue." June didn't want to tell them how she was killed over and over again, they seemed to have enough on their plate. "So, when he had me tied up I made him hit me enough to loosen the chains. When he left, I broke 'em, snuck out, and hauled ass." Ken held her hand more tightly and drew it closer to her. June could tell something was boiling up inside of him.

"Jesus," said Freya, shaking her head. "Is that... is that all they did?" she asked cautiously.

June looked down and her face became more somber. "He..." June searched for the words, but didn't want them to know, and she definitely didn't want to relive the experience.

"He was an asshole, hell-bent on ruling the world forever. He talked so much I tuned him out, it was better getting hit than putting up with his monologue," June said jokingly, but she knew it wasn't funny.

Ken's grip on her hand became even tighter. "I'm going to kill him..." he whispered. June thought she heard wrong and turned to him, making a questioning sound. "I'm going to wipe him off the face of the earth," Ken vowed with an expression that scared June. He stared at their clasped hands, the anger and fury reflecting off Ken's eyes scaring even his team. "He broke us. He killed our friends. He put William in a coma, Hector was injured, and he hurt you," he said, turning back to June. "He's going to pay for messing with us. And I'm going to be the one who snaps his neck and watches the light leave his eyes." Ken got up and walked toward the door.

Freya got up after him. "Where do you think you're going?"

"I'm going to help Zoila with the investigation. June, how far did you say you ran from his farm to the city?"

June, still shocked by Ken's anger, shrugged her shoulders lightly and tried to remember. "Maybe about two miles. I feel like I ran for hours, and the main road I appeared on didn't really have a lot of signs to go by."

Ken nodded with his eyes closed. "We got the gas station they picked you up from. From there, I think we can retrace your steps. Then we'll get his ass." Ken opened the door and walked out. The rest of the team sat there and turned back toward June.

"That happened. Seemed like this has been boiling up since Nevada. Girl, you're lucky you didn't die. I think Ken might be the 'scorched-earth' type and if anything happened to you, he might be the one we'd have to stop," said Jin in a loud whisper as soon as Ken was out of earshot.

June knew she couldn't tell them. If this was Ken with her safe, how would he be if she wasn't?

"Ken was unbearable," said Isaac, "the whole time we were in the showers, but I gotta admit, I was worried too." The team stared at him with concern. "I just wanna get this over with, and the waiting, not knowing where y'all are at and..." Isaac swallowed. "Bruh, these Zealots have gotta pay for what they did. I'm gonna choke the life outta 'em."

"I get it, but you're all way too violent for my taste." Jin shook his head. Isaac paused for a moment and nodded his head. "But, I get it. They took everything away from us, and have us living in constant fear. We're in a foreign country, fighting for our lives, and some of us ain't even old enough to drink."

"Yeah, and I'm with Ken. Maybe not the brutal murder part,

but yeah. I want Cesar to pay. He killed a lot of innocent people. He killed my..." Freya fought back a sob.

"But we have to know who he's working with. June's right, some religious farmer from nowhere ranch couldn't have planned something so elaborate *and* made some crazy guns to do major damage." Freya put her hands on her hips and walked closer to June. "What else happened there? I know you're not telling us everything."

June lowered her eyes and spoke softly. "Don't tell Ken," she started, before telling them what she endured during her captivity.

An hour had past and the team was sitting around the bed until Jin broke the silence. "What the hell..." Zoe put her hand on his shoulder and looked at June.

"You—you don't remember the parts underwater or with the gasses?"

"No, I don't, but the doc said there are traces of water in me that should clear out over time."

Zoe shook her head slowly. "And your neck, like..."

June nodded. "Dr. Glendale says it'll heal—slowly, but it'll heal."

Freya crossed her arms. "I regret asking. Okay, so, no one tells Ken, because he might set the whole jungle on fire to find Cesar." Freya turned to June and sat in the bed next to her, giving her a tight hug. "I'll never let them take you again. I promise."

Zoe joined in next to her. "Same, Bee. You're under our constant eye now."

Jin sniffled and rubbed his head. "You're all getting too sentimental. We got a psychotic megalomaniac to find, remember?" Jin turned to Isaac as he was sitting on a chair in

324

the corner.

"Oh, we know, and we're gonna obliterate his ass and send him to hell," Isaac said through gritted teeth.

"Well, we're all in agreement. When Ken comes back, we're gonna go out there, find Cesar, and punch his face into the ground until he's on the other side of the planet."

"Yeah, let's go kick his ass," June said.

Freya and Zoe put their hands on June's shoulders. "No way we're letting you back out there," Freya told June with a motherly expression. "You've been through enough. I can't let you go back out there. You've only been with us for a few weeks and you weren't prepared for any of this."

June shook their hands off her shoulders. "Listen, I know, but I'm pretty capable on my own, 'kay? I know I have a lot to learn, but I'm your handler, remember? William picked me because he knew I had potential, and he's all the family I have left, so I'll be damned if I sit back and do nothing while you guys risk your butts for me. I'm a part of this and I want Cesar and Bovo to pay."

Freya gave a half-hearted grin and nodded. "Well, William did pick you to lead this team. We're all fighters to the end, aren't we?"

Isaac nodded and Jin stood up and placed his hands on his hips as he addressed the team. "This is all fine and dandy, but what are we going to do? Grab a taxi, drive, like, six hours to Cucuta, and hope we find the trail that June took from the evil enemy lair?"

Freya and Zoe gazed at each other, looked back at June, and turned to Jin, and said simultaneously, "Yeah."

Jin threw his hands up. "Well, all right, but we're down a man, who's down a boy, and we need adult supervision, and all we have is a caffeine-addicted boomer, who brings flowers to someone in an underground medical facility."

June snorted and looked at the said flowers, which were now withering. They were pretty and colorful, but she knew the lack of sunlight would shorten their already short lifespan. "We do it ourselves. As soon as Ken comes back with any info, we'll grab our car and make our way into the city."

"Did you forget? Betsy is in the great garage in the sky. They totaled our van, how are we going to..." Freya said.

"They totaled Betsy?!"

Freya grinned nervously at June. Just then, the door opened gently and Ken peeked in.

"Good, you guys are all still here. Uh..."

"What happened, buddy?" asked Jin.

The team stared at him in anticipation. Ken walked in and crossed his arms.

"Zoila got a location, and it could be where they kept June. We read the list of owners along the paths. There aren't that many ranches or plots of land down there, but we found a few, and..."

Jin raised his hands. "Imma need the TLDR, bud."

Ken shook his head. "Yeah, sorry, we think we know exactly where Cesar's held up." He glanced at them. "Anyway, um, got a big-ass plot of land with sat images. A ranch, building, barn, and a few towers along the perimeter, similar to what June described back at the police station."

June blanched. How out of it was she that she didn't remember telling anyone anything, anywhere.

June shook her head and spoke to Ken. "So now what? Are they sending us in?"

The door opened behind Ken, and Zoila walked in with Dr.

326

Glendale. "You look much better. Drinking plenty of water?"

June noticed a bottle that was next to her bed, still full, and turned to face the doctor with an apologetic smile.

"Still, you're fine. You're good enough to get out of here. All of your vitals seem well. Just take it easy on the neck."

Ken turned to Dr. Glendale, puzzled. "Neck?"

Dr. Glendale glanced at June. She grimaced at her worriedly, and then turned back to Ken. "She had a few injuries, nothing to worry about. She's good to go. Hector, though, he needs to take it easy for a few more days. I need to keep an eye on him. Never seen a Brick with a missing organ."

"So, I know you're all desperate to get back in the fight," Zoila mused. "Give us a day, go sleep tonight, because tomorrow you'll fight."

Dr. Glendale addressed everyone in the room. "I'll keep an eye on William, so you all better come back and see him when he wakes up." Dr. Glendale gave them all a hopeful nod and walked out the door.

Zoila stepped out from behind Dr. Glendale and spoke to the team. "The base is near the location we thought it was going to be. My team is already setting up a base of operations near there." She took a breath. "You got your doctor's orders. Get some sleep, I'll do the same." She turned to June. "June, I washed your suit and you should have it by tomorrow morning." Zoila addressed the others. "Same for all of you. So go to bed." She turned back to June. "June, you can join them if you want."

June, who'd just realized she was in a hospital gown under the sheets, considered it would be better to just stay until she got something more modest. "I'll need some clothes if I'm going to walk the halls, please."

Zoe winked at June. "I gotcha, lady. You are about a size smaller than me, so I'll see what I can dig up."

June thanked her and the team walked out, but Ken stayed behind. "Hey, uh, I..."

June shook her head. "It's okay, I'm okay now. We'll get this guy and give other people like us a better future."

Ken sat next to June on the bed. "We deserve to live, Mouse. I hate living in fear of what I am, and now the fear that we're going to be killed at any moment. I'm lucky to be alive, and all I could think of was missing the chance of us being together. I really like you. I know we haven't had a lot of time..."

"I like you too," said June with a bit of a bashful smile. "Let's not die, and see where this goes."

He smiled back. "Thanks, I-I'm glad you're okay. I couldn't live with myself if anything had happened because of..."

"Hey, it wasn't your fault. You did what you could, dude. It was a shitty situation, and we all got screwed."

Ken nodded sadly and knelt beside her. "I promise, I won't let them get you again."

June shook her head and put her hands on his cheeks to meet his eyes.

"Don't make promises we can't keep. This is a lot bigger than us. I'll try to have your back and you have mine, but let's just promise to do the best we can for each other."

Ken gave her an emotional nod. "I can promise that."

"Okay, you big sap, get to bed. Hopefully Zoe can bring me something that won't show my whole backside and I'll meet you guys in the dorms then."

Ken snickered mischievously.

"Oh, you perv! Get out!" yelled June playfully.

"I'm just saying, I wouldn't be opposed to it. I'm okay with whatever you choose..."

June swiped at him with a pillow.

"Out now! I'll see you later!" she said, pressing the pillow against her face and hiding her blushing cheeks.

"All right, all right. Hey, it'll be all right, that I do promise." Ken looked at her and swallowed. June beamed at him while hugging the pillow.

"Yeah, I know it will."

Ken closed the door behind him and June laid down in bed, staring at the ceiling, and pressed the pillow against her face, hiding a big smile.

A while later, the door to June's room opened and Zoe walked in.

"June, I found a few junior-sized stuff. I hope it fits."

June sat up, thanked her, and grabbed the clothes. "So, what happened with you guys when I was... you know?" June asked, scrunching her eyebrows and looking up at Zoe.

Zoe took a deep breath and put her hands on her hips. "We got pummeled, is what happened. June, we got decimated. Cops are dead or in the hospital, but we got the guys who messed us up, most of them anyways."

June stared at her with concern.

"Also, the other dude that was there when..." Zoe paused and turned away. "When Melody... We got him. I got Tomas. He tried to take us out at the police station in Cali and, well, I messed him up real good. He kind of gave me the location to where you're at—well, was at."

June riffled through the pile of clothes to see what fit. June stopped on a red plaid shirt.

"So, he's... dead?"

Zoe nodded. "We were going to go find you—heck, we were

on our way there, when Zoila told us, and we went to pick you up. Her team's setting up base near where we thought the location was, so we'll join them when we get our bearings and—"

"Good. I want to pay him back." June held Zoe's hand. "I was really scared. Not gonna lie, especially when he told me he attacked you guys and you were all dead. I-I was prepared to die... until he told me I couldn't."

Zoe shook her head and put her hands on June's shoulders sympathetically. "Also, you can't freaking die. But can you die of old age? Cancer? Like, what are your limits?" Zoe caught herself and sighed. "Sorry, it's just, with so much happening, and then this bombshell... Like, I miss the days of sitting in my room playing with dolls. Now I'm stuck in some crazy life with invincible megalomaniacs and immortal friends."

June laughed and gave Zoe a nod. "I know, right? I just want some lavender tea and to listen to a podcast, but here we are. But I'm happy you're all okay. I'm serious, I... I didn't want to lose anyone else. I'm glad Hector and William are alive, but they're not okay, and..."

Zoe took her hands off of June's shoulders and sat beside her. "We're gonna be okay. We just have to stop the world-ending megalomaniac, with his super-secret American partner, and their European weapon-distributing supplier. That's all."

They both let out a dry laugh and then sat quietly on the edge of the bed for a moment.

"It'll be okay, though. We know what we're fighting now. No more surprises. We keep our ears to the ground, eyes looking straight, and we're gonna mess any fool up who gets in our way. Right?"

"You bet."

Zoe stood up from the bed and walked to the door. "All right, get dressed, I'll wait for you outside and we'll go to the dorms, 'kay?"

June gave her an acknowledging nod and separated the clothes. Zoe stepped out and June dressed in a plaid shirt and dark blue skinny jeans that didn't have deep enough pockets, but she just shrugged and put on the hospital sandals. She picked up the rest of the clothes and chugged from the water bottle before grabbing the flowers. June struggled to open the door but finally managed it when Zoe eyed her up and down. "Lady, you can leave all of that here. Zoila said the staff will pick it up, wash it, and put it back in the locker rooms for anyone else who needs it. Also, the flowers?"

June smiled. "What? I think they're cute."

Zoe returned the expression and shook her head. "All right, flower child, let's get your hardcore self to bed. We all need some rest if we really are gonna fight tomorrow."

June nodded and threw the clothes onto the bed and closed the door behind her, but she kept the flowers.

"It's gonna be intense, isn't it?"

Zoe's face grew somber and she nodded. "I hate fights. I prefer spy missions where we just bag and tag. This shit, I ain't big enough to be intimidating and I'm just not cut out for this. I still see Tomas's face when I close my eyes. I did that, I killed him. It's not something you forget."

June glanced at Zoe as they made it to the elevators. "I wanted to kill Cesar, and Bovo, and him, because of what they did to me—to us. I don't know if I could when it comes down to it. But the rage is there, and if it was you or him, I'm glad it was you. We need to stop monsters like him from destroying lives. It sucks for us but we're the only ones who can."

Zoe nodded as she pushed the button.

June shook her head. "I saw them kill Melody right in front of me. And smile." Zoe's lips pinched downward into a frown. "They smiled, Zoe. If anything, you did the world a favor. He needed to be stopped. And when this is over, we'll find Ryan and stop him, too. Hopefully we won't have to end them, but we can stop them. The world's not gonna get any better without us."

The elevator doors opened. "You... you sound like William. He'd be real proud of you." June's lips quirked. "I mean it. You inspire and speak from the heart. Not a lot of people I know do that. I'm glad I can call you a friend."

"Thanks."

The pair entered the elevator and Zoe pushed the button for their floor. Zoe leaned against the wall next to June, crossing her arms, and stared at the ceiling.

"We all do what we can, but we're distracted by the future, what we'd do when we get out. It's nice to hear someone who actually believes in what we do and doesn't treat it like a bad job."

June leaned against the rail and turned to Zoe. "I-I don't think..."

Zoe put her hands up. "Lady, you might just be what we need to rally us together, with William out of play, and one of us injured. We need a strong leader like you. Smart, rational, and inspiring. Ken, he does his best, but the boy's hardheaded and impulsive. Dude would have gotten himself killed twice over if not for us trying to hold him back. Also, side note, he's got it hard for you."

June felt her face get hot as she tried to hold back a grin. "I... Yeah, he..."

"He was ready to rush in to save you. He was almost at the rooftop when they shot him with that electric gun."

June's face turned to a frown. "The what?"

"Yeah, these electric gun things they use. It basically causes our organs to pop. Ken got hit, but the padding saved his life. Hector lost a nut because of it during another mission where we thought they had you."

June's eyes widened. "Wait... What?!"

Zoe shook her head and turned to June. "I have a lot to catch you up on."

After a few minutes of the elevator ride, and walking down the long hallway, Zoe finished telling June everything that happened.

"Girl, Zoe, I... I'm so sorry."

Zoe shook her head and placed a hand on June's shoulder. "It's all right, listen. Shit happens, it's chaotic, mistakes were made, but we all made it out in one piece." Zoe shook her head and glowered. "Most of us made it out in one piece."

June rolled her head. "Hector, man, I'm so sorry."

Zoe nodded. "Yeah, but I know he'll be okay. I've heard guys can still have kids, with just one, and..."

June put her hand up. "That's enough of this conversation. Regardless, though, y'all almost died because of me."

Zoe shook her head. "No, June, we almost died saving the world. You did, though, multiple times, apparently." June shook her head and took a deep breath. "You put your life on the line. Heck, you tried to warn us before all this hell broke loose. So, from here on out, we open up, talk, and watch each other's backs. I know we're gonna be besties, but first we gotta survive tomorrow."

June snickered at that. "You got it. We'll be biffles." Zoe

glared at June, confused. "Best friends for life. B.F.F.L. Biffles."

"Nah, that's so lame. I feel the cringe eating at my core!"

"I know, I heard it from some girls at school once and thought it was cringe too, but it's funny."

Zoe laughed and opened the door to the dorms. "Okay, okay, but never say that again!"

June laughed along with her and followed her in. "Okay, no promises, though." The two giggled before noticing the team staring at them.

"What's going on?" asked Zoe.

Jin sighed and turned to the others. "Not much, girl. We just can't sleep. We're worried about tomorrow. Plus, we're worried about Zoila's team. Last we saw them..."

Freya picked up from where Jin left off. "They didn't look too good, and I haven't heard from them since they got in the other van."

Zoe sat down on Freya's bunk. "Well, Zoila's got them. I'm sure they're resting. They should be all ready and waiting for us, right?"

Freya nodded. "That's the plan, which Zoila and the director are probably trying to work out at the moment."

Ken sighed and rubbed his face with his palms. "We need to sleep," he said, lying down in his bed. "But how are we going to get any sleep, knowing this guy might be getting away as we speak?"

"He's not. We've got drones flying overhead. And our information says he's angry and has Zealots searching for June in the city. So, count yourself lucky you're here, *mi hija*," Zoila said, walking in.

The team sat up in their beds and faced her.

"I'm sorry, kids, I tried to get all the information I could before telling you anything. The director and I, and a few other agents, got together and discussed this. The fight will be close to Venezuela, so we had to bring them into it too. They'll be guarding the border in case anyone tries to run. It's up to us to make sure we catch all of them, so we can't really show military strength so heavily there, because any show of force could be seen as an act of war, and we don't want that..." Zoila glanced over each person in the room and said with a somber tone, "So sleep, *mi niños*, tomorrow is going to be a big day. Especially you, June. You've been through a lot, but hopefully after tomorrow it'll all be over."

Zoila then wished everyone a good night and walked out. The team laid restlessly in their beds. Ken waited until everyone stopped rustling and took the opportunity to hold June's hand. She looked up at him and smiled. He had a melancholic expression in his eyes, but he managed to look gently at June and softly told her, "It's all right, it's all right."

13

Trouble in the Jungle

The next morning, the team was abruptly woken by an energetic Zoila who came in with her assistant carting a tray of coffee and handing them out. The team grumbled for a moment. Ken was the first to shoot up out of bed and grab his suit from Zoila. The others followed suit and walked toward the lockers to change. June felt disoriented but Zoe held her hand and pulled her along. June noticed she was holding her suit but didn't remember when Zoila gave it to her. Zoila was speaking but June was still too tired to comprehend what she was saying.

At the lockers, Zoila held June by her shoulders and gave her a sympathetic nod. "I wish you didn't have to do this, but you know this place better than any of us. Good luck, *mi hijita*." June nodded and the realization of what was happening sunk in. She gave Zoila a weak smile and walked into the lockers to change.

"Hey, all."

"Zoe, you think I'm ready for this?"

"Lady, as ready as any of us. We're all they got, and they're not gonna take no for an answer."

"If— When we get out of this," said Freya, getting up and standing in front of June.

"If you need to talk to someone, I..." Zoe shrugged.

June gave a soft smile. "Thanks, I, uh, I'll hold you to that someday."

Freya swallowed and nodded before hurrying away to the exit. "Yeah, hopefully when this is over, we can chat. Hell, when this is over, we definitely need to just hang and forget all of this."

Zoe took a deep breath. "We better, lady. We need a vacation, pizzas, and copious amounts of therapy after this."

June let out a dry chuckle. "We seriously do."

After everyone was geared up, the team met up at the elevators with Zoila. Zoila nervously paced and quickly typed into her phone.

"Everything okay?" asked Ken.

"Yes, Ken. Just something I'm looking into."

"Anything we can help with?"

"No, no, no. *Vamos! Vamos!*" She pushed the button for the elevator and started pacing again.

"Is Hector coming?"

Zoila shook her head. "He's still recovering. It's just you six for now. My team is already there waiting on orders. Aye, I'm worried about them. The director is also on his way but we need to catch our flight soon." Zoila paced as she sipped from a disposable cup that was clearly filled with coffee.

"How many of those have you had?" asked Freya, and Zoila just shrugged. The elevator doors opened and Zoila rushed in and began pressing a button. The others hurried in before the doors closed behind them.

"We're so close," said Zoila. "Our information says he is still in his mansion. We captured several of his followers in the city and they talked in exchange for protection." Zoila continued talking quickly while pacing inside the elevator. "So, if we hurry he might still be there. They say he was expecting the attack last night, but since nothing happened, he thinks June got lost in the jungle and is hiding. This is our chance. In two hours, we will have him captured." Zoila stopped pacing and became rigid with wide eyes staring up. "He will pay for what he's done to all of us."

The way Zoila spoke made June want to ask her if something else happened to her, but the doors opened up to a hangar similar to the ones used in the Nevada base. A dual-propeller plane was being prepared.

"Aye, let's go." Zoila hurried to the plane and the team rushed behind her. "We can't use gas so close to the border, but you put your mask on just in case they do," Zoila instructed as she stood at the doorway, bringing in the team. "Strap in, let's go!" she said, with June the last one into the plane.

Zoila rushed into the cockpit. The plane took off and June peered out of the window, seeing the mountain they came out of grow smaller and farther away. June swallowed and laid her head back against the window. The bench chairs were a little more uncomfortable than the ones from the last jet she was in. June glanced around at the team as they all sat nervously. Zoe, while sitting next to June toward the back of the plane, held her hand.

"Are you sure you're ready for this?" Zoe asked.

"Yeah. Yes." June nodded pensively. "First this, then pizza, 'kay?"

"Yeah, lady, this then pizza."

Freya sat across from the two of them and stared with a puzzled face.

"We're having a girls' night after all of this. You, me, June, pizzas, and a whole venting session.

Freya's lips quirked. "Hell yeah."

The three women glanced at the guys who then looked at each other. "Beers? Beers! Football? Yeah!" they said in mockingly manly tones.

"Manicures?" asked Jin in a gruff voice.

"Hell yeah!" said Ken enthusiastically, but keeping it gruff, and the other guys agreed with grunts and hollers. The girls rolled their eyes but smiled genuinely for the first time all day.

The sun was rising over the mountains, and the cabin lit up as Zoila spoke to the team over their headphones. "*Niños*, ten minutes to drop zone. Okay?"

Ken gave her a thumbs-up and took off the headphones and put on his mask. Everyone else did the same and stood up to see Zoila opening the door. The wind almost sucked June out of the plane, but she managed to keep her footing.

"You need help?" asked Isaac, putting his hand on June's back and leaning into her ear so she could hear him.

June shook her head. "I've already died before, what's a free fall going to do?" she said but Isaac couldn't hear her. She patted Isaac's back, thanking him for the offer, and prepared to drop.

"Three, two... one!" yelled Zoila as she stared at her phone's map.

Ken dove first, followed by Freya, Jin, Isaac, Zoe, and finally June took the plunge as Zoila gave her a thumbs-up. June loved this feeling of weightlessness. The world became smaller and more manageable in her mind. Her problems went away and for that moment in free fall she was truly free. She waited to see Zoe tuck in so she could too, but tried to line herself up with Isaac. June felt all the leaves and branches feebly breaking her fall until she fell in the river.

She got out of the water and removed her mask, searching for her teammates, when she heard a loud thud. "That must be Zoe..." She walked toward a grumbling Zoe who landed a few feet away from the river and was lying there in frustration. "Hey..." said June hesitantly. Zoe sighed and picked herself up when June held out her hand. "Let's find the rest." The pair started to walk eastward, following the river. June and Zoe met up with the others as they walked alongside the river and they all made their way to the road. As the team made their way to the gated area, Ken radioed in.

"Board is set and ready to play a gambit."

Zoila replied, "Okay, King, all pieces are in position. Make your first move."

June saw the tower that she jumped from, took a deep breath, and put her mask back on. "That one." She pointed at the tower and gave him a thumbs-up.

"Let's go then," Isaac said before he grabbed June by the arms and spun her around, flinging her over the gate. She dove straight into the tower, crashing through the window and terrifying the guard. June got up and saw a blur hit the other tower. The guard tried to ready his assault rifle but June pulled it out of his hand with such force, he fell to the ground. Ken dove in behind her and saw the terrified guard. "This is one of the guys who held you hostage?"

June nodded, wanting to rip him apart for everything that happened in this place, but she took a deep breath. "Yeah, knock him out, I'll get the gate." June pushed the button she saw him use to open the gate that night, while Ken knocked the guard out with a flick to his jaw. Almost instantly, a small military unit consisting of several large transport trucks and many black agency SUVs swarmed into the place.

"We need to get into position, now!" Ken and June jumped out of the tower and headed toward the mansion where an army of raggedy-clothed Zealots rushed out by the dozens, armed with assault rifles and shotguns. The two forces met near the gates, clearly trying to block the paths to the buildings.

Team Alpha ran around them and met up near the entrance of the mansion where Edwin and his team were waiting. They all removed their masks to get a look at each other and Edwin placed his hand on Ken's shoulder. "Okay, Ken, we follow your lead."

Ken faced June. "Any ideas, future leader?"

June scrunched her brows. "He's here. He's in the mansion, which means he thinks he's going to make a narrow escape. Probably hit Venezuela, so we can't follow. We need to block him off here, but there're probably some Bricks in that band of crazies that rushed our military, so they need help too. Plus, the barn. A pair of us should scope that out."

Ken agreed and split up the teams. "Okay, June and I will go in through the front door. Edwin, you and Zoe go back, Jin and Marisol, left, Freya and Juan, right. Isaac, you and Herman go help our guys. Ricardo, go check out the barn, and be careful! Now, let's go!" Ken clapped his hands and everybody rushed to their positions, putting their masks back on. Ken put his hand on June's back, stopping her before they took off.

"You're smart, have a lot to learn, but you're picking it up quick."

June appreciated the compliment, but it didn't feel right to be complimented on surviving and making it up as she goes. She wanted to go home and forget all of this ever happened.

She gave Ken a nod and they made their way to the front of the mansion. As they stood in front of the main doors of this expansive building in this wide field, Ken spoke over the radio. "Everybody ready?" When the whole team acknowledged him, Ken counted down. "...Three, two, ONE!" Ken and June rushed in through the front doors to find two men, one tall and slender and the other short but stockier, both with scruffy beards and tattered clothing. They stood, shocked that anyone dared to charge in through the doors, and got ready to fight.

At the other end of the mansion, Zoe and Edwin busted through the rear fence and into the backyard which comprised of a two-story deck and pool.

"The heck is this place?" asked Zoe, and Edwin grunted in response. Over the radio, they heard Ken ask if everyone was in position. Zoe and Edwin lined themselves up to see into the large glass sliding doors and responded simultaneously with the others. They heard Ken count down and the pair rushed toward the sliding doors that opened as soon as they got close, Cesar standing there with four other Zealots around him. Zoe reached for her earpiece. "We're gonna need some help..."

"Copy!" yelled Jin over the radio. She nodded at Edwin and they both got into fighting poses. Cesar was escorted by his group of Zealots and they stood before Edwin and Zoe, about to charge, when suddenly, Marisol and Jin came crashing from the wall. Marisol, screaming furiously, tackled the man standing behind Cesar, while Jin charged and punched the other. Zoe charged at Cesar but was stopped by the other man who stood in front of her. Edwin was going to charge in too, but was stopped when he made eye contact with the woman in Cesar's group. She sneered at him and raised her fist to fight.

Cesar snuck past them during the scuffle and Zoe screamed out that he was getting away, but was lifted in the air and slammed by the Zealot who mounted her and was about to punch her face, when Zoe pushed his leg out and flipped him over, putting him in a leg lock. He tried to twist Zoe's foot, but she pulled away and rolled onto her back, before landing on her feet.

The Zealot got up and dusted off before getting into a brawler pose. Zoe charged in low and shoulder-rammed him as he tried to grapple her. She lifted him up into the air and she grabbed him by the collar, throwing him headfirst onto the floor and cracking the concrete. As the Zealot tried to recover laying on his belly, Zoe straddled him and put him in a choke hold until he lost consciousness.

Zoe looked up to see Edwin and the woman throwing punches at each other, loud cracking sounds reverberating whenever they managed to land one. Zoe rushed to help him but turned back to hear yelling. Jin was placing his opponent in a choke hold, but Marisol was straddling her opponent, hammer fisting his head underwater. His legs squirming erratically, but his arms were held tight by Marisol's legs. She wailed and cried as she continued to keep the man's head underwater. Eventually the man kicked both of them into the water and Zoe ran toward her, only to see her emerge a moment later.

Jin and Zoe reached her at the same time and helped pull her out of the water. Marisol just broke down crying, falling into the fetal position. Jin held her as Zoe turned around to see Edwin was now in a choke hold, the woman continually kneeing his back. Zoe locked eyes with Jin, who nodded and pointed at them with his chin. Zoe ran and grabbed the woman by her dark hair and slammed her backward into the side of the house. Unfortunately, that caused Edwin to fall as well and land at the Zealot's feet. She pushed herself off of the wall and went to stomp on Edwin, but he rolled out of the way and swiped her legs from under her. She fell on her shoulder and Zoe, seizing the opportunity, threw herself onto the Zealot and immediately put her in a choke hold. Edwin thanked Zoe then ran toward Marisol as fast as he could.

Zoe knocked out the Zealot and chased after him. "Is she okay?" Edwin shook his head.

Jin ran to Zoe and grabbed her by the hand. "We got a fish to catch, girl!" Zoe's eyes widened and the two of them ran toward the barn.

***

Freya, who was in position with Juan, heard the countdown and prepared for someone to run past the large concrete wall, or jump out the window, but none of that happened. Instead, Zoe's call for help made her rush quickly past Juan and as soon as she made it to the back of the mansion, she saw Cesar already making his way toward the barn. Freya saw the group evenly matched and grabbed Juan by the arm. "Let's go get him!" The two ran toward the barn where they saw Cesar go inside through the door. Freya slammed the door open and Juan followed behind her.

Standing in front of them stood Rafael Bovo, holding a cattle prod and smiling menacingly. "You've got a lot of nerve being here."

"Well, you have a lot of nerve being alive," Freya retorted, putting up her fist. She turned to Juan. "Go to the plane, I've got this."

Juan looked at her, confused, but Freya never broke eye contact with Bovo. Juan ran past the pair that were slowly walking toward each other. Bovo seemed to ignore him too, so Juan ran and opened the door, hearing a propeller plane getting ready for takeoff. Freya heard Juan radio for Ricardo, but got no answer. Freya would have to worry about that later. She needed to stop this guy. Make him pay for what he did to them, to June, to June's mom. To Sebastian and Tabitha. Freya's eyes watered in rage. She yelled and charged at him.

Bovo swung the cattle prod and Freya ducked quickly under it and went to punch Bovo, but he kicked her away, making her fall on her back with a loud thud. Freya picked herself up and stood in a fighting pose again. "Come on, asshole. That's all you got?"

Bovo grimaced. He lunged with the prod, thrusting it at Freya. Freya sidestepped the prod, grabbing it by the side and trying to spin it out of Bovo's hands, but the large man lifted it higher and caused Freya to lose her balance. He kicked her to the ground again. Freya picked herself up and dusted off her backside. The two stared at each other and Freya lifted her fists once more. Bovo let out a booming laugh. "Little girl, just go home and play with your—"

Freya threw a small rock she had picked up from the floor right at Bovo's face and, in the split second of confusion, Freya pirouetted past the prod, twirled under Bovo's arms, and uppercut him so hard he was lifted about a foot off the ground. Bovo stumbled backward and became furious. He swung the prod wildly toward Freya and she kept dodging.

Suddenly the door flew open again and Bovo shot up to see Zoe and Jin walk in. Freya took the opportunity of distraction to punch the cattle prod, snapping it, and Bovo leapt back dropping it quickly as some sparks flew.

Zoe realized who it was, and told Jin, "Go after Cesar, Freya and I have got this guy."

Jin nodded and rushed past them. Bovo looked back at Jin and turned to the women. "You think you two can take me on again? It didn't work out so well the last time!"

Zoe snarled at him. "This time you don't have your chubby friend to help you."

"Enrique will be with us soon enough. I didn't think he'd get caught by you, but he will be here."

Zoe gave him a dry chuckle. "You'll meet in the afterlife." She stood up straight with her fists to her sides and Freya looked inquisitively, before realizing what she was doing. "I stopped him from killing William. I stopped him from getting away. And I stopped him... from living."

Bovo's face filled with fury. "No! You liar!"

Zoe took off her mask and beamed defiantly. "It was him or me, asshole. So, guess who's still standing."

Bovo screamed and lunged at Zoe, but Freya tackled him by the legs, causing him to fall forward. Just then, Zoe prepared an uppercut that sent him flying backward. Freya hurried up and held him by one side and Zoe rushed in and put him in a choke hold. An explosion caused the foundation to shake and Zoe lost her grip. Bovo sat up and pulled Zoe off by her head and smashed her body against Freya's before running away. The two women shook it off and chased after him, only to be stopped by another explosion. This time a vehicle landed at the building's entrance, separating them from Bovo as he made his escape over the rear fence.

Jin, having rushed past the girls, saw two men talking over what appeared to be one of the Colombian team members. He saw Cesar and the other man wearing fatigues climb into the plane and he tried to reach them as fast as he could. But the plane was already taking off. He was going to rush in, but heard a groan. It was Juan. Jin didn't know what to do, but luckily he saw Ken busting through a wall and chasing the plane down the runway.

Jin knelt beside Juan as he gurgled under his mask. He pulled off Juan's mask and then his own. Juan stared wide-eyed and tried to talk. "Ge... gu... grrr..." Jin shushed him and held him in his arms. He tried to carry him over his shoulder but before he could move him, Juan went limp in his arms. Jin cursed softly and held him tight. With explosions all around him, Jin carried Juan's body as he ran out the same way Ken came in.

Rushing outside he saw the soldiers and Zealots shooting at each other. Jin laid Juan's body on the floor near the gate and ran toward the battle. "You assholes... You freaking assholes!" Jin rushed toward the battle, joining Isaac and Herman, who were fighting off a few Brick Zealots. The brawl lasted until helicopters started flying over and fired warning shots around the teams. The Zealots dropped their weapons just as Jin held a screaming woman in a choke hold. She became calm when all the fighting had slowed.

Jin was still full of furry. He let her go by pushing her to the ground and walked away. He made his way toward the main gate. Isaac and Herman joined him.

"You all right, bruh?" asked Isaac.

Jin stared at Herman. "I'm sorry. If I had gotten there

sooner, maybe I could have done something." Herman turned to Jin, confused, but Isaac knew and stood quietly next to Herman, placing a hand on his shoulder.

"*Que dices?* What are you saying? What do you mean?"

Jin tried to find the words. "Juan... he..."

Herman shook his head and pulled off his mask. "No, no, no... no..." He fought back tears. Jin went to hug him and as he did, he looked back at the battlefield littered with bodies. Jin closed his eyes as tears ran down his face.

***

Moments earlier, Ken and June stood in the foyer of the mansion, a large area with a walkway connecting both wings of the house, and under it was a large marble fountain decorated with griffins pouring water from their beaks. Beyond that seemed to be large double doors that lead to the rest of the place. The two guards that stood near the fountain stared at June and Ken with matching shocked expressions, dressed in ragged clothes and with long beards.

June noticed the one on the left had a knife in his belt. She began to rush at him when, from the balcony above, two more Zealots appeared and jumped down. June tackled the Zealot that dropped down, causing him to land on the Zealot behind him and effectively breaking his leg. The man screamed in agony and the Brick apologized. June managed to put him in a choke hold as he got up. She held tight and tried to do it the way she saw the others do.

Ken yelled from across the foyer. "I'll get him, just help me!"

June was scared of letting go and held on tighter as the man squirmed and panicked. June heard a snap and the man went limp. He caused his own neck to snap as he tried to slam June onto the ground.

She breathed heavily, in a state of shock, until Ken screamed her name. "June!" He was being held down by the other Zealots. June looked around and the man with the broken leg watched her in fear and began crawling away while crossing himself. June shook her head, got up, and ran toward Ken, pushing off a man with her knee and kicking him on his side.

Ken then grabbed the other man and used a kip-up technique to throw him off. Next, he slammed the guy's face into the ground with his foot, then grabbed the man holding him in a choke hold until he passed out. June, struggling to keep the other man off of her, found herself backed in a corner when Ken grabbed the guy and threw him into the fountain past the archway. The force caused the pipes to burst and shower the area. Ken walked up to him and held his throat and choked him until he was unconscious. Then over the radio they heard Cesar was running away.

June and Ken ran out the front doors again and saw Freya and Juan running after him. June froze and Ken asked her, "You all right, Mighty Mouse? Mouse?" June couldn't move. Her legs felt heavy as she stared at the barn. The flood of memories rushed in her mind. Glimpses of her underwater, being chained up and gassed, Cesar screaming in her face. June breathed heavily.

Ken cursed through his mask and ran toward the barn, but once he heard the plane taking off, he decided that it would be better to just break through the walls. He made it as the plane was getting out of the barn and tried climbing onto it, but tripped over a body and fumbled. Ken glanced up to see June running at full speed past him and making it onto the plane just as it was turning. She crashed through the side of the plane as it took off, and Ken didn't bother looking back to see what, or who, he tripped on. He jumped as far and ran as fast as he could to try to reach the wing of the plane that was having a hard time keeping itself straight.

Ken landed on the tail and tried to punch off the wing, but as the plane took off, he almost slipped off. Mustering all of his strength, he pulled himself up and began punching through the hull of the rear. He suddenly saw someone in fatigues dive out of the plane and into the jungle. Ken punched through and made a hole big enough on the plane to peer inside and see Cesar and June locked in combat. He yelled for her, but the pilot pulled the plane upward and caused Ken to lose his grip and the fall into the jungle.

Ken lost sight of the plane over the mountains and figured they probably passed the Venezuelan border already. The sound of a distant loud crash made him scream out June's name. He wanted to rush in, but a helicopter flew over his head and called out his name. Ken turned on his emergency flare and the helicopter dropped down a ladder for him. He held on to it and gave them the okay to lift.

"Hey, thanks for the help. We're heading toward the crash, right?" Ken asked as he stared outside toward the smoke.

Zoila shook her head and yelled out, "Venezuela."

Ken became furious. "No! We need to find her!"

Zoila tried to calm him down. "International incident."

Ken scrunched his face and turned back to face the smoke past the mountains and closed his eyes. "Not again."

The helicopter landed back at the compound. Zoila and Ken stepped out to join Director Gutierrez as he was waving them down. He was standing with a general and surrounded by several soldiers and agents assessing the damage and collecting the fallen. Zoila greeted them and Ken waved his hand in acknowledgment.

"What's happening?" Jin asked Ken.

In response he just shook his head angrily.

Zoe asked Ken, "Dude, where's June?"

Ken lowered his head and shook it slower this time.

"Venezuela," replied Zoila, pursing her lips as she held back her anger and turned to talk to the director.

Zoe clicked her tongue and cursed through her teeth.

"So what are—"

Ken interrupted Freya with a burning fury in his eyes. "International. Incident," he said, grinding his teeth. The team looked defeated as Zoila turned around after talking with the director.

"*Vamos, niños.* The quicker we go, the quicker we can get June back."

Freya shook her head in confusion. "Go... where?"

Zoila sighed heavily. "Base."

Freya threw her arms up while the others protested. "Back to base!?"

"I know, I know, *mi hijita*!" Zoila said as she raised her hands and shook her head.

"This is horrible, but we need to find out what happened as soon as the Venezuelan authorities capture Cesar. We need our story straight and we can extradite him here to pay for his crimes."

The team was disheartened, but knew they couldn't protest much.

"What about Edwin and his team?" asked Zoe. "Marisol? Juan?"

Zoila wiped a tear from her eye and Jin put his hand on

Freya's back. "Juan didn't make it. He... I-I held him..." Jin said, holding back tears.

"We found Ricardo nearby, too. Both shot with those electric guns," Zoila said, trying to stay calm. The team glanced around and saw all the vans and vehicles carrying the dead and injured, and they looked at each other with the realization that they had just survived the greatest battle they've ever had.

"We're used to being subtle. This... this is too much," said Jin, putting his hands over his head. "This is way too much."

Zoila nodded. "We lost Juan and Ricardo, and June is missing, plus Cesar got away... Again. I hope they catch him."

"I hope June kills him," said Freya through gritted teeth.

Zoila was taken aback but leaned in toward Freya. "Me too, *mi hija*," whispered Zoila. She looked around to see if anyone else was listening. "Frankly, I think he deserves it. After what he did to us..." Zoila trailed off, lost in thought.

From a distance they heard the director giving orders in Spanish. *"Vamos! Nos vamos!"* He waved the team down. "We're leaving!"

Zoila motioned to the team to follow her. They all piled into the large helicopter, along with a general and the director. Director Gutierrez turned to the team as they took their seats. "You guys did good. I'm sorry about your losses, but we'll get this mess taken care of and get you home soon."

The team sat quietly, not replying to him. The director and Zoila exchanged a sad expression as the helicopter flew off. Zoe stared out of the window to see the remaining Zealots being rounded up and placed into Brick transport coffins and carted into paddy wagons. The whole compound was a crumbling mess of broken walls, smoke, and fire. As the helicopter flew farther away, she just saw the smoke rising over the trees and thought, *What a horrible devastation a handful of Bricks caused in the middle of the jungle. A smaller group destroyed several buildings and practically a whole city block. What would an actual all-out war look like? Maybe the agency was correct in keeping Bricks safe away from large populations.*

Jin put his hand on Zoe's shoulder and gave her a nod. "It would suck if something like that happened in a city. I'd hate to see what happens when governments start using us as weapons." Jin contorted his face, deep in thought. "I hope June is okay. It's been a hell of a month for her."

Zoe nodded sadly. "Yeah, she's had a rough few days, that's for sure. And now lost out there, Lord knows where, with you-know-who. I really do hope she finds her way back."

Freya joined the conversation by leaning over Jin. "She's a trooper, she'll be all right. Plus, the Venezuelan team is on their way to find her. I'm sure this will be over soon, with Cesar captured and June with us again. It'll be girls' night before you know it."

Zoe dropped her shoulders and turned to face back out the window. "I hope so."

The three of them glanced up at Ken. He was sitting quietly with his leg shaking and fidgeting with his hands. "It'll be okay," said Freya to him. Ken seemed to snap back from his thoughts and blinked. "It'll be okay," repeated Freya firmly.

Ken gave her a half-hearted smile and nod as he kept fidgeting with his hands. "I lost her. I lost her again. I tried to promise her I wouldn't, but she knew I couldn't keep it. She knew I'd lose her. She..." He covered his face with his hands and bent over. Isaac put his hand on Ken's back and tried to console him.

Freya, in a commanding voice, spoke to Ken. "Hey, I know it sucks, but we did the best we could. She rushed into that plane to stop a madman. We couldn't be prepared to know that they took out two of Edwin's team, 'we could've this' and 'we could've that' isn't going to bring anyone back. This was a mess. It absolutely was, but we did the best we could. Now all we can do is hope she can get out of this mess like she did before, Ken. She didn't need us to save her from Cesar the first time. She's a halfheartedly, and she clearly doesn't need you to be her white knight. What she needs is a friend after what she's gone through, and we'll do our damn best. That girl has lost her life, literally—she's lost her mom, and has been sent into the deep end of a conflict she didn't even know existed a month ago."

Ken nodded and wiped a tear from his face. "Yeah. Yeah, you're right."

Freya cocked her head a little. "I'm always right. Now, let's just try to join June as soon as we can."

14

Keep Your Enemies Close

June awoke sprawled out on the floor of what seemed to be the remains of a plane as the hull sat creaking and dangling precariously off the side of a tree. She could smell the smoke filling the cabin and make out bits of what used to be a wing out the window. She turned to see ahead, to what was left of the interior of the cockpit smashed into the side of a rocky cliff. June jumped down and headed toward the smoky cockpit to see if there was a radio or something she could use since the earpiece she had fell out during the fight with Cesar inside the plane and she didn't know where her mask was.

She shook her head, trying to remember how she even got here. She peered past the smoke and saw a silhouette of a man and blood splattered by what used to be a chair. It was Cesar, and what remained of the pilot. June's stomach turned. No sign of a radio between all the mess of metal and tree branches. She held her breath and grabbed Cesar, pulling him out of the smoke. She threw Cesar out of the plane and placed him sitting up against a tree and sat next to him.

"I should... I should kill you," June said, catching her

breath. She glared at Cesar with tears in her eyes. "You took everything from me." June shook her head. "You take, and take, and take, and for what? Immortality? Followers? A grandiose sense of self-aggrandizing that requires constant affirmation of your ego?" June cursed and Cesar coughed and looked at her with one eye open.

"Maybe that last one." He tried to laugh, but ended up coughing. June didn't move. She stayed sitting next to him and stared at him, angrily. "I, my girl, have always... felt like nothing. My family, especially mi mamá, said I would never accomplish anything in my life. They believed God chooses those who fight for him, and well, after I punched that doctor's heart through his chest, I realized I had been chosen. Chosen to be more than just a follower of my family's teachings. A leader." Cesar coughed again. "Ugh, uh, I was always given nothing and worked for everything. You, you're young. You don't know the pain of waking up and having to gather water for your family, while they ignore you. While they tell you that this is how you are supposed to be. Subservient and ignored. That God's plan is for you to serve them because you're the oldest, so you have to go get water, food, move heavy things everywhere. That no one will love you because you are not chosen. Having a family is for those who have a future. My future was to be there when my family grew old and take care of them in their deathbeds." Cesar laughed dryly.

June glared at him with a raised eyebrow. "Why the hell should I care? Boohoo, you had it rough, and you walked both ways up a mountain to go to school. You're still an asshole."

Cesar laughed. "Ha ha! Yes, I did have to go up a big hill to go to school, but it was only a few months. My family took me out of school because they thought it was taking away from my brother's and sister's ability to learn and I was the only one capable of doing all the chores at home. Do you know what teaching all of that to a ten-year-old does to the mind? I was taught I was a tool. And now, I am someone. I showed my family that I was indeed chosen. That I was indeed worth something. That all the sacrifices I made, were in service of that great and vengeful God we serve." Cesar leaned forward from the tree and nodded his head. "I showed them vengeance. Vengeance as our God would have wanted it. With fire."

June squinted at Cesar. "Shit, dude."

Cesar scoffed dryly. "Ignorant youth. I watched them burn. I watched as the life was taken away from them and cast upward to heaven. I stood in the flames just as Joseph had done and was not harmed."

June shook her head in disbelief. "And this was okay to you? You thought murdering your family was... okay?"

Cesar nodded as he stared at the smoke billowing from the crashed plane. "Yes." He continued, "Yes, and I was justified until I found you. Ever since they found you, you have destroyed all of my plans. You have turned my strongest ally against me and taken all of my followers away. Probably back to those sleeping boxes and tortured with gas and electricity to keep us calm instead of allowing us to reach our full potential as God's chosen fist. The hand of God to bring judgment to all of those who think that they are free of sin, or that they can get away with it."

June shook her head. "Listen, people do bad things. You, you crazy shit, are doing a bad thing. Even if it's with good intentions. You've killed and sent to be killed so many people that were nice, loving, and caring, and—"

Cesar interrupted. "I was following my partner's orders. I just wanted to get word out and get my followers to put their trust in me. Immortality would have ensured that I have all the time in the world to get that done. Save as many sou—"

Now June interrupted him. "Shut up, asshole. I know you meant well, but you and your partner are clearly trying to cause genocide. Killing so many people—children! My mom... " June held back her tears of anger. "You took, and continue to take. I'm glad that I can't give you immortality. I'm glad your plan failed. Because that means you're wrong. I was sent in to stop your great evil from taking over. And I'll be damned if I let you keep hurting anyone else."

Cesar nodded and sneered. "This will be our battleground then." He stood up and dusted himself off, his clothes in tatters from the crash and darkened by the smoke. His beard and long hair singed by the fire. "This is where the fate of the world shall be decided."

June raised an eyebrow and stood up as well. "Illusions of grandeur it is."

Cesar turned to her. "One day, you will believe in the afterlife. One day you, will see there is more to this world than movies and makeup, little girl." Cesar wound up a punch and swung at June, who dodged quickly.

"You're insane, dude." June ran around the tree.

Cesar let out a booming laugh. "This will be grand!"

"Authorities will be here soon!" At least, she hoped.

"No, little girl. There's no one coming to save you. My followers made sure that the Venezuelan government gets distracted." He bared his teeth. "Explosions in their city would do that. I shall spread my message here farther and become more powerful than I ever have! I will end corrupt leaderships. I will bring a new world ruled by the hand of God!"

June ran around a few more trees and doubled back to Cesar.

"I will be the immortal ruler of this wo—"

June punched Cesar so hard it caused him to go careening through some trees and against a rocky wall. "You will shut up! You talk too much, jeez." June knew what she had to do. "If you're not going to stop. If you... If you don't stop, then I have to do this."

Cesar dusted himself off and stood up before facing June. "Good, now we both know what our purpose is. Come! Let us fulfill our destiny."

June rolled her eyes and charged at Cesar. Cesar feigned a punch and twisted his hips to throw the punch with his other hand, causing June to have to take the hit to her shoulder. June, not having had the fighting training the others did, felt out of her element, but from what it seemed, Cesar's fighting style wasn't that much better than hers. June went for an uppercut with her left arm that Cesar blocked with his arms and she used the momentum to bring down her right fist quickly and landed the punch on Cesar's collarbone. Cesar's face contorted with discomfort, and June used the opportunity to punch his head again with her left fist.

Cesar lost his balance, but came back at June, punching wide first with his right hand, then his left. June put up her arms to protect her head and took both punches, and it sounded like thunder coming from the jungle. She swung her leg and front-kicked Cesar in his lower abdomen, causing him to stumble back. June lost her balance and had to hop backward to gain her footing again.

He laughed. "We can do this forever!"

June squinted her eyes at him. "I can, but you'll die of old age."

Cesar's demeanor changed, and he grew angrier. June got what she wanted. Cesar was headstrong, easily angered, and had a fragile ego combined with illusions of grandeur; June was going to use all of that against him.

As Cesar charged at her, she dodged out of the way and that caused him to lose his balance and fall face-first into a muddy stream. Cesar wiped his face angrily and got up to turn to June, she was waiting for him and delivered a haymaker punch that sent him back onto the ground. The echo boomed throughout the jungle around them.

June felt something she had never felt before. A fire burned inside of her. A fire that did not want to be quenched, that wanted to consume and destroy everything in her path, and right now it focused on Cesar. She wanted to eradicate him off of the face of the earth, and she was going to enjoy it. June balled her fist and as Cesar tried to get up again, she threw her whole body weight and momentum into smashing her fist on the back of Cesar's head. The loud, thunderous sound echoed through the jungle. Cesar grunted and tried to get up but choked on the stream. He rolled over on his back and put his hands up.

"Wait, wait, niña, wait. I... We can work together, we can be gods toge—" June grabbed him by a leg and used all of her strength to fling him toward some rocks.

"Don't give me that 'we're the same' super villain mono-logue, we are nothing alike!" June seethed as she walked toward him and grabbed him by the shirt collar. "Nothing!" June dropped on her back and used her legs to fling Cesar into the air behind her. Cesar flew several feet into the air and came

360

crashing down through the mangroves. He landed face-first onto the ground and tried to get up, but as he shook his head, June had already walked up to him and pulled him by the hair. She knelt down and got close to his face. "Sucks feeling so helpless, doesn't it!?" she seethed as she pulled him up and threw him at a large tree. The tree fractured with the impact but stayed standing. Cesar rolled on the ground and tried to get up quickly but staggered. June, having already caught up to him again, charged in with another punch to his face that knocked him back toward the same tree, but this time the tree fell from the impact and June jumped and rolled out of the way. Cesar seemed to have been crushed. June stood there, staring at the old tree that smashed onto the jungle floor.

She heard people rushing toward her yelling in Spanish. "There they are!" The raggedy dressed men pointed and ran toward June. Her eyes widened. She knew these weren't the team she was expecting.

"Get her!" yelled another man in Spanish.

June turned and ran through the jungle as fast as she could. She didn't care to look back, she didn't care that she killed Cesar. She wanted to run, as far as she could, away from here. Wherever here was. June couldn't make out where the sun was under all the jungle foliage. She found herself cornered on the side of a cliff and a small rural road toward the bottom, and glanced back to see them chasing her. There were four of them, along with someone familiar. "Cesar!" she yelled. June couldn't believe he survived getting crushed by the tree. One of the men leaped at her and held her by the waist, but June took the leap. "Get off, you nut!" June yelled, trying to push him off during the forty-foot drop.

The man seemed desperate and tears escaped his eyes as

he screamed. June came to the realization he might not be a Brick. The two landed and June saw his body bounce, then lay limp on the ground. As she laid on her back, she saw Cesar and one other Zealot had sprang behind her while the other two searched for another way down. She got up as the two men landed with a loud boom. June ran along the small jungle road and tried to get away as fast as she could. She made it to a small wooden bridge next to a waterfall.

The smell reminded her of when Ken took her to see the waterfalls near the Panama Canal. "Ken..." She took a deep breath and found the motivation to keep running. "I need to see them again, I need to see him again..." She took a deep breath and ran harder and faster. Up ahead, June saw a small village and ran toward it. Looking back to see Cesar and the Zealot had reached the bridge, June tried to find a place to hide when suddenly she ran into what felt like a steel wall.

A booming voice greeted her and June craned her neck to see a tall, gentle man who smiled and spoke slowly to her in Spanish, asking if she was okay. "Hi..." June said as she walked around him and continued to find a place to hide. June ran down the road and saw a pile of hay. She tried to hide in it but felt so uncomfortable and could barely get in it. She scanned the area and found a small pickup truck with wooden boards around the bed that was about to drive away, filled with chicken cages. June hopped in the back and sat on the floor, trying to hide. The driver peered back to see what the noise was but just waved his hand, ignoring the sound, and drove off. June saw the jungle thicket getting clearer and noticed they were on the open road, leaving much of the mountains and jungle behind. She hoped that she wouldn't see Cesar again, but she knew she had to stop him. But for the moment,

June laid down and closed her eyes and caught her breath.

June awoke to the sound of people arguing and saw that the chicken farmer was fighting with a merchant over her. She got up and jumped over the two men, apologizing and walking away as they both stopped, looked at her for a moment, and then continued arguing. June was in a city, but she couldn't tell which one. It was getting dark. June wandered around and tried to find a phone, but didn't even know where to start.

Dressed in her B.R.I.C. Agency gear, she stood out like a sore thumb and, with everyone giving her weird stares, she didn't want to stop to ask for directions as everyone avoided her and the traffic in the street was pretty congested. "It's probably five or six by now, what the heck am I going to do now?" She continued walking and finally realized she was in a park where there was a statue of a man with a horse. "San Cristóbal?" June wondered aloud to herself. A family walked past her, huddled closer together, and walked away, giving her suspicious glances. June couldn't help but find it funny and sat down at a bench in the park and waited to see if a police officer or anyone would talk to her.

Eventually, as the sun was setting, June saw a patrol vehicle pull up beside the road and a pair of Venezuelan police officers got down and walked toward her. June started thanking them in Spanish and telling them what had happened. The police officers raised their hands and turned to each other in confusion.

"You're a superhero, little girl? You look like you belong in school," said the officer jokingly. "Now come on, let's take you home in your little costume and your parents can take care of you."

June shook her head. "You don't understand, there's a crazy

terrorist running around here. He escaped from Colombia in a plane, we crashed, and now I need help to stop him. Call your superiors, someone has to know about the... the..." June lost the word and said it in English. "B.R.I.C. Agency."

The men laughed and went to reach for June but before she snapped back, the other officer looked up and screamed. A car was flung in their direction and just barely missed the statue. June glanced back to see Cesar and now several more men following him. One seemed to be the large man she saw at the farm.

"Please, you have to help me!" The officers began speaking on the radio when a car door was thrown in their direction, smashing through their patrol vehicle.

"Oh, my God!" yelled the officer. The other cursed, crossed himself, and prayed. Cesar approached them with his arms wide.

"Pray! Pray that today you meet your creator!" he yelled at the men in Spanish.

June faced him and yelled back, "Screw you!"

She ran away. Cesar motioned to the two men to chase after her while he walked to the police officers. June ran down the street packed with cars and peered back to see the vehicles being flung in all directions. She didn't want anyone else getting hurt, especially because of her. So, she ran toward the markets and tried to find a way up, but the buildings were too far apart and not a viable way to travel, especially since she hadn't mastered leaping yet. She tried to find an alley she could escape through, but as she did, a Zealot crashed through the building and stopped in front of her. June turned around to see the large farmer standing behind her with a sad and confused look on his face. June figured it was now or never and jumped as hard as she could. She managed to clear about ten feet and almost missed the roof of the building as she fell. June dug her hand into the concrete and climbed toward the second story. The farmer made a surprised sound while the Zealot jumped toward the wall and began climbing it.

On the rooftop, June could barely see the mountains off in the distance because the sun had set behind them. She knew she had to go westward and reach Colombia, but she had to figure out a way to get Cesar to cross too, not just these goons. June jumped down to see that the farmer was waiting for her, standing on the sidewalk, and tried approaching her with open hands. June ran and heard the Zealot land and berate the farmer for letting her go. The two men chased June down the narrow street.

Eventually they ran into police that had blocked off the road. June didn't know if she should stop and ask for help, causing the officers to be harmed in the process, or keep running and potentially causing more harm along the way. She put her hands up and walked slowly toward the officers. The two men behind her seemed confused. The Zealots charged in anyway. One of them took June by the waist and lifted her into the air, carrying her over his shoulder. June struggled and tried to break free when one officer fired at the Zealot, causing the bullet to ricochet and land on the floor. The officers all glanced at each other, perplexed, and the one leading the barricade walked out slowly and asked the Zealot what he wanted.

The Zealot responded, "A new world! Where the strong survive!" He then began walking away.

The officers rushed in to surround the man and despite June's protest to stay back, they attempted to rush him. The Zealot kicked an officer so hard in the chest his spine seemed to have cracked through because June saw blood drenching his uniform and pool under him as he laid on the ground. The other officers backed away, but the Zealot grabbed one by the hand he was holding his gun up with and crushed it. The officer fell to his knees, crying out in pain. June began yelling at all of them to stay back. June, unable to see in front of her, only heard the familiar deep voice of the farmer.

"No!" He yelled for the man to stop, while the Zealot asked him what he meant. He tried to kick the farmer in the leg but June saw an opportunity and wiggled at the right time, causing him to lose his balance. Free from his grasp, June almost went for his throat, but figured it would look bad if she just killed a guy in the middle of the street, despite the mayhem he had caused. June grabbed the farmer by the hand and they both ran back, past the police car barricade, and continued on. The Zealot got up and chased after them.

"Do you talk?" June asked the farmer as he was trying to keep up with her. He let out a grunt as he shrugged. June scanned the area and saw a market. She glanced back to see if the Zealot was behind them, but didn't see him, so she pulled the farmer into a convenience store. The clerk stared at them strangely, but continued tapping on her phone. June looked around and pulled the farmer toward the back of the store and told him to sit on the floor. The nearly seven-foot man was about June's height sitting down.

"What's your name?" asked June softly, holding the large man's hand that dwarfed her own.

He grinned. "Oh— Oh— Oscar," he said, struggling to get the words out.

"Oscar, that's a nice name." She smiled back at him sympathetically. "My name is June," she said, placing one

366

hand on her chest. "Oscar, are you scared?"

Oscar looked back at the door they came from and nodded his head nervously.

"I won't let them hurt you anymore, okay?" June put her hand on his shoulder as she stood up. "Stay here. I'll be right back." His lips turned down but he stayed sitting as June walked around the aisles and back toward the clerk. "Hey, we need your help." The clerk gave an acknowledging "Mm hmm" but kept staring at her phone.

"Listen, there's bad people looking for him. Can you keep him safe? He's from a farm, a few miles away, if you can let the police know he's missing..." June talked but wasn't sure she was being listened to. The clerk nodded her head without ever lifting her gaze.

After a moment of June standing there, the clerk gave her an uninspiring "Yes" and waved June away.

June's face pinched as she reached over the counter and grabbed the clerk by her shirt. "Listen. Help him or this store, this whole city, will be up in flames. You're in danger as much as we are and if you don't help I'm going to crush your skull with my bare hands!" June threatened, holding the clerk. She was wide-eyed and shocked at how June pulled her and held her up in the air. "Got it?!" June said, pulling the clerk closer to her face. The store clerk nodded and called the police.

June walked back to the farmer who was still sitting and staring at the floor. His face lit up when he saw June. "Hey, Oscar, this nice lady is going to help you, okay? Just listen to what she has to say." Oscar nodded. "I have to go." Oscar shook his head and held June by her hand. "I'll be okay, you need to go back to your family. They need you." Oscar pouted and shook his head. "You're gonna be okay. Just go back to the farm where you'll be safe." June let go and ran out the door while the clerk started asking Oscar his information.

June walked outside and saw that the Zealot was ahead of her, peering into the stores through the window. She got lucky he must have passed by when they were all in the back. June then rammed into the man's shoulder from behind, causing him to fly several feet and hit the sidewalk so hard it cracked and lifted. June ran up to him and tried to put him in a choke hold, but he flipped her over his shoulder and slammed her to the ground. She tried to scurry away before the Zealot could get his hands on her again. With no idea how she was going to get out of this, she had to figure out a way to knock him out without destroying the city. June ran, almost getting hit by a car, across the street and toward another alley and past a very aggressive dog that tried to bite her.

She kept running as the Zealots followed just a few yards away. June heard the dog yelp and knew what happened, causing her to get angrier. "I hate superiority complexes," June muttered aloud as she stood in the dead end of an alley she turned into. "I'm so tired of running," she said angrily to herself.

"I got you now, little girl!" said the Zealot as he turned into the alley.

"I'm so tired of running!" June repeated as she yelled at the Zealot who was taken aback. June rushed him and before he had time to get into a fighting stance, June had tackled him onto the floor and began punching so hard the ground shook and it sounded like thunder cracks echoing through the alley. The Zealot grabbed June's hair and pulled her off of him. June punched him in the face, causing him to stumble and loosen his grip on her hair. She pulled away and grabbed him by the shoulder, slamming him to the ground.

"How do you like it?!" She then put her knee on his chest and started punching his face. "How do you like being beaten?! OVER! AND OVER! And over! And over!" June continued yelling with every punch until the Zealot used his legs to hook onto June's head and caused her to fall to the floor. June yelled in anger and went feral as she swiped at the Zealot as they were trying to grapple with each other to the ground. "Just leave me alone!" June started screaming as the Zealot managed to pin her hands over her head with one hand and tried choking her with the other. June squirmed and tried to push him off, but he kept using his knee to pin her down. June felt things going dark when a large shadow loomed over her.

Suddenly, all the pressure she was feeling was lifted and she could cough. Her eyes widened when she realized what was happening. Oscar had lifted the Zealot up into the air by clasping his neck with both hands and despite the man's squirming, he eventually went limp. Oscar dropped the Zealot with a loud thud and gave June a big smile. "You, you saved me," June said, surprised. She coughed as she rubbed her throat. Oscar grinned and nodded as he helped her up and carried her, placing June on his shoulders. June felt like a five-year-old being straddled over this large man's neck.

"J-J-June is... June is safe." June felt like that was true for the first time in a long time.

"Yeah. Yeah, I am. Thank you, Oscar," June said, rubbing his hair and holding him by the top of his head. "Let's go home, friend."

Oscar nodded and carried her out of the alley. "Fr-friend." As the pair walked out of the alley, they could see some people gathering outside of the stores and businesses, trying to see where all that loud noise was coming from. June gave a half-hearted smile as some people started to stare at them. "Okay, friend, you can put me down." Oscar nodded and gently let June off of his shoulders. Then in the city lights, June saw a large group of people walking toward her from down the street, with Cesar leading the group.

Ken sat on a metal chair across from the agent asking him questions in the interrogation room, fidgeting his fingers. "Look, I told you, I think it was him, but I don't know. I was running toward the plane. I saw June jump into it and I needed to go help her."

The officer wrote down on the clipboard and gave an aloof "Mm hmm."

Ken rolled his neck and put his hand up. "Look, man, what else do you want me to say?! June is out there and needs our help!"

The agent shook his head. "So, you never saw Juan or Herman enter or exit the plane hangar?"

Ken slumped his shoulders and leaned back against the chair. "No. I didn't. Please, we have to help my friend."

The agent nodded indifferently and walked out of the room. Ken sat there for a moment before the door opened again. "Okay, you're free to go."

Ken shot up. "Finally! Thank you!"

The agent motioned with her head to Ken, suggesting he follow her. Ken followed the agent down the hall and toward the elevator where a moment later Jin appeared.

"Bro!" Ken hugged Jin. "What happened?! Did they keep questioning you too?"

Jin dropped his gaze and nodded. "Yeah, 'cause I'm the

one who found Juan, they wanted to know why I didn't find Herman."

Ken shook his head. "Dude, I'm pretty sure I tripped over Herman. Because of that stupid overgrown barn, I didn't see him." The two of them glared at the agent, who could not be bothered to look up from her clipboard.

"The others?" asked Ken. Jin just shrugged his shoulders. The elevator doors finally dinged and opened. They all walked in and the agent pressed two buttons. Jin and Ken sat on the bench and the agent sat across from them with her legs crossed and writing on her clipboard.

"The weapon they used on you, Ken, why didn't it kill you?"

Ken's eyes widened. "'Cause it, um, it hit my chest protector and caused the electricity to disperse instead of bursting my heart."

The agent nodded. "And Hector? He survived as well?"

Ken and Jin looked at each other, and Jin replied, "Barely, I think he got shot in the leg padding and it caused his, um, his testicle to explode." The agent raised her eyebrows for a moment before turning stoic again. The elevator doors opened and they were on the floor with the lockers and dorms.

"Rest, and get ready in a few hours. Your handler will come and inform you of our findings." She stayed seated in the elevator and Jin and Ken walked out. The doors closed and the two walked toward the dorms.

"Dude, that was messed up."

Jin nodded. "We've never lost anyone in our missions. That, and we've never had an all-out war before," Jin said with a grimace.

"Nah, dude, this was contained with a few hundred people. Can you imagine an actual war? Especially with hundreds of

Bricks. It would be insane."

Jin shook his head. "I'd rather not." Jin and Ken walked into the dorms to see several people laying there and the rest of the team huddled up in the same area they were in previously.

Freya waved at them ecstatically. "Finally! Get your asses over here." Ken and Jin walked over and saw that Hector had joined as well.

"Dude! You're back! How're you feeling!?" said Ken enthusiastically.

Jin laughed and asked, "So how does it feel?" Hector blushed a little as he glanced quickly at Freya.

"It, uh, it feels normal. The doc put in a prosthetic or something, so I would feel like it's never, you know, like I never lost it," said Hector shyly. Jin quirked his lips and sat on his own bed, while Ken sat down on his.

"So, did they keep you guys for long? They kept asking me questions about Herman and Juan and..." He trailed off.

"No, not really, mostly about Cesar and Bovo. Can't believe those two got away. We freaking had them," Freya said, holding the sides of her head.

"I wonder who the other guy in the plane was," mused Ken, more to himself than expecting an answer.

Isaac, who had been lying face down with his head buried in the pillow, glanced up at Ken. "Pilot, maybe?"

Ken shook his head. "Nah, the pilot was the one who caused me to fall off the plane. Dumb-ass pulled up so hard he lost control and caused the crash over the mountains. He must have been important, more than Bovo, to be heading out of the country with Cesar. I wonder if that was the supplier of the weapons." Ken cursed under his breath. "Bro, she's out there with these madmen and their insane weapons. I don't think I can lose her." Ken curled up, putting his knees to his chest. Freya and Zoe glowered.

"Dude, she'll be okay. She's a fighter," Freya assured him. "I've never seen you like this. Are—"

Ken shook his head. "I'm not. We almost lost him." Ken held his hand out, pointing at Hector. "We lost two on Edwin's team. June's lost in yet another country. Like, man, it's been one thing after another, and I still haven't gotten over Maria, and Mr. B, and, and..." Ken began sobbing.

Freya cursed softly as she jumped out of her bed and hurried to hold Ken. The others gathered around too. The group stayed huddled as Ken quietly sobbed.

Zoila walked into the dorms to see the refugees they gathered from the ranch battle talking amongst themselves and at the team huddled quietly together. She had seen this before. She wanted to give them time to feel their feelings again, but this was important.

"Niños. I'm sorry," she interrupted, turning away as Ken dried his tears. Zoila was not expecting it to be Ken crying this time. She swallowed and faced the team, trying to keep a composed expression on her face. "We have news. The good news is, June is alive and in San Cristóbal. The bad news is... Cesar has already found his army of Zealots and is destroying the city. He used them to distract the teams and military over there and I reached out to the Venezuelan branch. They said their team is working on it but want us to send backup. Since my team is down two—three, since Marisol is under psychological evaluation—I was hoping you—"

"YES!" said Ken before Zoila could finish. "Let's go! Let's go now!"

Zoila's cheek twitched. "Bueno, muchachos. Let's get going.

Good thing you're still in your suits. Hector, I'll get you yours."

June ran, holding Oscar's hand, as fast as they could both go, vehicles and other large items crashing around them. Oscar began yelling nervously.

"I know, I know!" yelled June "Welcome to my life."

They tried running out of the city but every turn felt like a labyrinth. June and Oscar kept running with the new Zealots behind them. Finally June made it to a road that seemed to lead out of the city. It was already dark and she hoped this would get them as far away from civilization as possible. The two ran down the road as the jungle began getting thicker around them. June knew it was the right choice. She turned back to see the Zealots following them. "How? How do these megalomaniacs always get followers so quickly!?" she said, out of breath as she kept running. Oscar looked back and gave a scared-sounding grunt.

Suddenly a truck landed in front of them, setting ablaze and blocking them from the narrow road. June surveyed the thick jungle around them and debated which way to go, but they were already surrounded. The Zealots with cell phone flashlights shining in June's and Oscar's faces confused them, and Oscar yelled angrily, holding June behind him. June felt herself press against him as he covered her with his arm to protect her. "Who's saving who?" she said with difficulty, feeling like a rag doll as Oscar moved her about.

"My little girl. My June. Please, don't make this worse. Save him, save yourself. Join me. The world is changing and I will be its architect," Cesar said as he walked past his followers. "These people know their place in the new world. They know of what we're capable of. They have been waiting for me. For they—"

"They know you talk too much, you grandiose maniac!" She peeked from behind Oscar. "You talk too much, and your fake false promises of a new world are dead! You failed in Colombia, you failed in Mexico, and you're going to fail here!"

The followers questioned each other.

"Child, I still stand and these people have seen my miracle. They know I'm chosen and—"

June screamed. "Ahhh! You don't shut up, do you?! I'm this, I'm that, I'm God's golden testicle. Shut up, you asshole! You killed my mom, you took Oscar away from his family, you lied to your followers who are all now either dead or in jail. You are a devil!"

The Zealots started talking amongst themselves, doubting Cesar.

Cesar, undeterred, continued, "You are my key to immortality. You will help usher in a world with no pain, no suffering, no cancer, and no old age. We have defeated death and will live forever with your sacrifice!" June rolled her eyes and walked toward Cesar, Oscar feeling unsure and trying to hold her back.

"You're a liar. A murderer. And you are an insane, senile, decrepit, old man."

Cesar lost his temper and backhanded June so hard she flew toward a tree that cracked with a thunderous boom on impact. The Zealots all gasped and took steps back. Oscar rushed angrily toward Cesar. Cesar rolled his eyes and flipped the large man and slammed him on the ground behind him. Cesar then put his knee on Oscar's back and pulled his hair, causing him to arch and expose his neck. Cesar then grabbed and twisted his head, and Oscar fell limply on the ground. June lifted herself up from the tall grass and saw Oscar's body. She yelled so loudly that no one else made a sound. It was quiet for a moment, and then the Zealots began to back away.

"If you hadn't run away and had just given me your DNA—"

"SHUT THE HELL UP!" June interrupted. She breathed heavily, tears forming in her eyes as she stared at Oscar's lifeless body. "YOU TAKE EVERYTHING FROM ME!" she yelled so hard the veins on her neck started to bulge.

"This guy is just an asshole," shouted one Zealot.

"He's just abusing this poor girl," added another.

Helicopters could be heard off in the distance as well as the faint sounds of sirens. The group around them began to murmur and disperse, running back into the city as the sun had fully set. Cesar and June stood in the dark, only lit by the fire of the burning truck. June faced Cesar and stood in front of him. "We end this. Now!" June said coldly. Cesar went to backhand her again, but she jumped back to dodge it and lunged forward, reaching for his neck. Cesar, not expecting her to dodge, opened his eyes wide and jumped to the side. June grabbed onto his shirt and tugged on him as she threw a punch toward the back of his head. Cesar blocked it with his arm. June kept punching and used her other fist to land another blow to his face. Cesar put his hands up and pushed her away. He yelled at June but was unable to stop her despite being well over a foot taller than her.

June wasn't thinking anymore. She was full of fury. She walked up to him again and dodged a hit, then she began punching Cesar in the gut rapidly, causing him to lift off of the ground as he held on to her head. She kept punching so hard he flew up several feet after her last right uppercut. Cesar lost his grip and landed with a loud thud several feet away. He growled, baring his teeth, and charged at June, who sidestepped out of the way, twirling behind him. She grabbed his shoulders, pulling him down on his back.

Cesar, beginning to lose his own cool, crawled on the ground and struggled to get back on his feet before he charged June. She managed to get up and ax-kicked him in the head, causing him to slam face-first into the ground. An infuriated Cesar yelled in the mud and rushed toward June. She hopped over him and wrapped her arms around his waist, hanging upside down on Cesar's back. She began using her legs to kick him in the back of his head and Cesar grabbed her by the ankles, trying to pull her off. June held tighter and wrapped her legs around his head. Cesar grunted and tried to unwrap her legs while June let go of his waist and punched him in the back of the knees, causing him to lose balance and kneel. Then June let go, dropped on the ground, and quickly got up to wrap her arms around Cesar's neck as he tried to get up and turn around. Now June had her arms around his neck and her legs around his waist. Cesar grunted and punched her in the face. June flinched but continued to hold tightly.

Cesar yelled in Spanish for her to let him go. "Release me! I am... The future... Guh—"

June squeezed harder and whispered in Cesar's ear, "You're just playing pretend."

June tensed her abs, then shot back. His neck snapped. Cesar's head dangled as June let go and watched his body flop to the ground. She knelt alone in the dark road as the fire and smoke continued to spread. She crawled toward the flickering shadow that was Oscar's body. "I'm sorry. I'm so sorry. I can't save anyone. You saved me, and I couldn't save you." She put her knees to her chest and sat in the dark, crying by herself.

After a moment June saw the helicopters flying over toward the city, shining spotlights at what she assumed were the Zealots still causing chaos. Another helicopter flew over to her direction, shining a light at the flaming car and then down toward her. She covered her eyes and put a hand on Oscar's chest. She said through her tears, "I just wanted to get you home. Y-you deserved to be home." June looked at the helicopter backing away and making its landing on the open area farther away. "I need to stop wishing." June caressed Oscar's face and kissed his forehead before walking to the helicopter. She saw six shadows running toward her and heard voices that made her feel a little better.

"June!" yelled Ken, taking off his mask.

The team surveyed the area and put away their gas grenades.

"June, what... happened?" Jin saw the pair of bodies on the ground and the burning vehicle up ahead. June shook her head and hugged Ken. He put his arms around her and walked her back toward the helicopter. Freya glanced at Zoe and they both took off their masks.

"Is that..." started Zoe, pointing a flashlight at the motion-less body of Cesar Villalobos.

"Who's this?" asked Hector, leaning over Oscar's body. June stopped walking and turned to him.

"A friend." She lowered her head, held Ken tighter, and continued walking toward the helicopter.

In the helicopter, Zoila waited for June to get in and helped her inside, sitting her down and giving her a headset.

"I'm glad you're okay," said Zoila, her eyes softening, though she had to yell because of the noise.

"'Okay' is a relative term," June said, glancing at Ken who

sat down and put on his own headset. The others joined in after.

"We need to clean up," said Freya.

"And Cesar?" asked Zoila. Everyone glanced at June but didn't say anything.

"Ah," said Zoila, crossing her legs as she began typing on her phone.

The ride was silent with only the sound of the helicopters flying toward the city. Through the window, June saw the Venezuelan agents gathering the Zealots with cattle prods and placing them in black vans. June closed her eyes and leaned back on the seat. She felt Ken hold her hand.

If June could feel anything right now it would be happiness, but with everything, these past few days had been enough to make June feel numb. She just wanted to forget this whole month. June felt a tear escape, but was too tired to wipe it, so she turned her head and stared out the window of the helicopter. She hoped it was finally over. Though she learned that wishing was a waste of time. She'll have to live with these memories for the rest of her life. She closed her eyes again and hoped she could sleep until they got to their destination.

***

June opened her eyes to see she was in an airport surrounded by soldiers and agents gathering up coffins and splitting the normal people from the Bricks. Zoila held out her hand and beckoned June to get out of the helicopter. The team was already making their way toward a large white van. June and Zoila met up with them.

"This thing looks like it has someone offering free candy in it," said Jin suspiciously, eyeing the old panel van.

"It's what they had. They're using everything they have to gather all the new people they found today."

"Were there many, uh, Bricks?" asked a groggy June.

Zoila nodded and grimaced empathically. "A lot more than we could have thought. Probably about a couple dozen or more."

June's eyes widened. A couple dozen out of the group of almost thirty people that was gathered around her. "If just a handful of them would have been loyal enough to Cesar the outcome of tonight would have been very different." June shook her head, trying to shake off the thought of what could have happened.

"With Cesar dead, we don't have to worry about extraditing him. And the prisoners here can be handled by the authorities. The government is trying to cover it up, but the video of Cesar mounting the San Cristóbal statue after knocking the man off the horse is going viral. We're teaming up with the U.S. tech department to get it removed."

The team piled into the van and buckled in. June shivered as the buckle clicked. Twice already she had snapped a person's neck. She felt disgusted with herself as the sound reminded her of that feeling of something clicking under the skin that caused someone to lose control of their body and die immediately. She tried not to think of it.

She just wanted to go home.

15

What the Future Holds

The sun was rising as June was awoken by Zoila clapping her hands. "Okay, we're here. A short flight back to Bogota, a quick debrief, some food, maybe breakfast, then, after some sleep, you guys can finally go home!"

The team gave a weak and unenthusiastic cheer. June peered out and noticed the van had stopped at the airport near Cali and stayed quiet, just focusing on her hands.

Zoila faced June with concern, but her phone buzzed and she turned to check it. "Hey, I've got some better news."

Jin, who had his head in his hands, looked up. "We're entitled to a lifetime supply of pork rinds?"

Zoila beamed with excitement. "No, *mi hijito*, William is awake!" The team shot up and June finally felt her heart swell up with something other than misery.

"He... he's up? Is he okay? What is..." June asked, realizing she was too excited and noticed the others were smiling at her.

Zoila replied softly, "He's okay, *mi niña*. He's out of intensive care, but he's still being monitored, so you might not see him until tomorrow, but he'll be okay."

Zoila tapped the driver on the shoulder and thanked him for the ride. She checked her phone again, smiling. June wondered who Zoila was talking to, but was too excited to see William again, more than she thought she would be. She didn't know him much, but he was the closest to a dad she's ever had. June saw the others were all smiling and much happier.

Ken turned to her. "Dude, I know you've been through it but I'm so glad we found you, and now William waking up, I'm—I'm—"

June grinned, though her eyes still showed sadness. "Yeah, I get it. I'm happy you guys found me, and yeah, I'm glad William's up. Just want to know what happens from here. Will he be okay to still help us? Am I even still part of the team? Are we even still a team?"

Ken's smile slowly disappeared. "I don't know, Mouse. I think we'll probably just end up in Texas with Quinn as our handler."

"Most likely," said Freya, turning back toward them. "We'll probably be shuffled off to Texas, like William said originally, and they'll keep a close eye on us, until we can root out the traitors and moles in the agency."

June felt those words sink in. The Cesar attack seemed to be over, but the mole, the reason she was in this mess to begin with, they were still out there. She closed her eyes as Freya continued.

"...with that shit going on. We'll probably be allowed less time outside. Heck, we probably won't even be allowed to hang out without any supervision. Ugh, they're gonna go full 1984 on us and it sucks."

Jin chuckled dryly and joked, "Yeah, how's a girl gonna flick her bean comfortably with Big Brother watching?"

Zoila slowly turned around with a confused look on her face then turned back. Jin beamed at Freya, whose red face seemed like she was going to burst out in laughter and anger simultaneously. June just smiled and hid her face behind the seat. Zoe couldn't hold it in and just started laughing, causing Jin to laugh louder. Freya closed her eyes and joined. While Hector, who was trying to contain himself, snorted and laughed, causing Isaac to shake his head.

"Bruh..." Ken smirked at June, placing his arm around her. June tried to hide her face in her hands, leaning on him but trying to look away. She felt conflicted. She wanted to laugh with her friends, but people were dead. Innocent people. Because of her. Her shoulders slumped and she clicked her tongue as she pulled away from Ken. He was confused, but he gave her space and turned to talk to Jin. "Bro, how long have you been sitting on that one?"

Jin snickered and turned away. "It just came to me, knowing they won't be able to."

Isaac tossed his hands. "Bruh!"

Hector blushed and put his hands over his face as he tried to stifle more snorting laughter.

"Ha ha," said Freya. "Laugh it up, but when they have us chained up with cameras everywhere, you'll remember this day, boys."

June leaned her head against the side of the van as Freya opened the door. It was nice to feel like a family again, but she felt like she didn't deserve it.

I let so many people die. She clenched her fist, but then the thought hit her. "What happened after I got on the plane?"

383

The team stopped laughing and turned to her. Zoila looked back at the sudden silence.

Everyone turned to June, and Ken shook his head. "All right, I'll—we'll fill you in on everything that happened."

The team took turns explaining to June what happened as they sat in the plane. All the while, June nodded and said nothing. After a few hours, they finally reached their destination. Everyone waited for June to say anything. After another moment, Ken put his hand on June's shoulder. "You okay, Mouse?" June sat motionless for a beat and then lifted her head while her gaze was still on the floor.

"I... You all came for me, again, and I don't know how to thank you guys, but... If you would have come sooner, if I hadn't gotten so preoccupied with catching Cesar, if I had just..."

Ken had both hands on her shoulders now. "Don't do this to yourself, Mouse. You did what you thought was right. Your plan worked, but we weren't ready for shock guns and—and Bovo, and Marisol having a nervous breakdown. Heck, you had a moment too, didn't you?" Ken asked, immediately regretting it. June tried to find the words.

"Hey, it's okay, you've been through some shit, June, you don't have to explain it. We all freeze sometimes," said Zoe, while sitting on the other side of Ken in the row.

"You don't have—"

"It's my fault. If I had the team stick together, we wouldn't have been split up and get people killed and..." rambled June.

"No, lady, stop it." Zoe reached over and grabbed her hand.

Freya reached over from the row in front and held out her hand toward June. "Listen, it's never simple, okay? Sometimes you can make every right decision and shit will

384

still go sideways."

June looked up with watery eyes. "I couldn't save them." She put her face in her hands, beginning to cry.

Ken reached over and hugged her tightly. "It's all right. I know I felt the same every time I let you down, Mouse."

June squinted her eyes. She was tired of the nickname but didn't want to argue. "You didn't let me down, though, you guys always come through..."

"Bullshit," said Jin. "Girl, every time we're going out on a mission to rescue your ass, you've gone and saved yourself. You've been with us less than a month and we need you, more than you need us."

June stared at him skeptically.

"That's absolutely true," said Freya. "June, we'd be lost without you. You helped us find Cesar, you weakened him, you made him lose focus, and got him running scared. You helped us kick ass!" Freya faced June with a soft look in her eyes. "And then you can tell us all about your adventure in Venezuela."

June's lips quirked but her gaze remained solemn. "Yeah, maybe later."

Zoila stood outside the small propeller plane's open door. "*Vamos!* Let's go!" The team walked out of the plane and saw that they were in the Bogota airport. "Let's go, we got ourselves a private plane! It'll take us to the airport near the main base," said Zoila excitedly.

The small white plane had a blue stripe along the side and seemed luxurious. June had never seen anything like that before, but she never really knew a lot about planes until recently. She'd already lost count of the different types of planes she had been in since this all started. Zoila motioned for everyone to get in. Ken saw June sit far back in the plane and sat next to her. He held her hand and tried to comfort her.

"Hey, um, I'm sorry if I..."

June shook her head. "It's okay. I just... I've had a hell of a week, so..." Ken nodded. "I just need some me time, if it's okay?"

Ken agreed. "You got it. I-I'll be... yeah." He walked away and sat in the row next to Hector and Isaac. June watched him for a moment then turned back to face the window and closed her eyes.

"She just needs time to process," said Freya, whispering to Ken as she sat next to him. "She'll be okay, just give her space."

"I..." Ken felt lost for words and quietly agreed.

Freya glanced to where June was sitting but couldn't see her behind the seat, she imagined her still staring out of the window. Jin and Zoe sat behind Freya and gave her forced smiles. "She's gonna need time..." Freya whispered to them. They both nodded knowingly and leaned back in their seats. The team sat quietly, waiting for Zoila. Freya eventually leaned over to see out the window, seeing Zoila talking with the pilot. She couldn't make out what they were saying but saw Zoila give the pilot a thumbs-up before they both made their way into the plane. When she turned back she noticed Hector was focused on her, but he quickly turned toward his window. Freya felt a little bashful but tried to conceal her grin while turning to the window again.

A moment later Zoila came from the cockpit and said they were taking off soon. She sat in the seat across from Zoe and Jin. "*Muchachos!* You're almost home!" The team let out a soft cheer but June stayed quiet, hiding in her corner. As soon as the plane began to take off, June closed her eyes and hoped it would all be over soon, though she kept telling herself it's pointless to wish. The flight so far was pretty event-less, at least by this week's standard. She was looking forward to seeing William again and she couldn't help but want to actually have that girls' night Zoe kept talking about.

June felt emotional at seeing them all talking and laughing, but Oscar's and Melody's faces kept popping in her head, Cesar yelling at her. Threatening her. The way she felt snapping that Zealot's neck, she didn't even know his name. The way Cesar's body went limp in her arms, how her fury died with him. How she felt sick all of a sudden. A stab under her belly. "Shit." She ran to the bathroom. Everyone stopped talking amongst themselves and Freya and Zoe locked eyes. Freya pointed at the bathroom with her chin so Zoe would follow June. Zoe hastily walked up to the door and knocked.

"Yeah," answered a sad-sounding June. "Yeah, it's my time."

Zoe let out an acknowledging sound. "Do—do you need... Is there any in there?"

June checked around and saw a small dispenser. "Yeah, they actually have some here." June hoped they weren't too rough on her. She cleaned herself up and washed her hands. She stepped outside to a worried Zoe. "It's just some before-time stuff. I think I'm finally not so stressed that my body decided it still needs more stress."

Zoe let out a sympathetic chuckle. "A'ight, lady, anything you need, lemme know."

June shook her head. "No, I'll be okay, just need some rest."

Zoe nodded and June smiled at her and turned to go sit in her seat. Zoe kept walking and sat next to Jin. "Tom," Zoe said as she got comfortable in the seat. Jin raised his eyebrows in acknowledgment. Zoila, still confused as to what's going on, closed her eyes and leaned back in the chair.

Freya felt Ken's leg bouncing next to her. "Ken, just relax, it's an eight-hour flight. Lean back and rest, she'll be okay."

Ken shook his head. "I know, I just..."

Freya opened her eyes and turned toward him. "Time. Just give her time. Let her come to you. We'll probably be locked up in a room together when we get back after the debriefing. Let her have her space now." Ken nodded and Freya closed her eyes and leaned her head back again. Ken peered out the window, past a sleeping Hector. He was too far up to really see anything but the occasional cloud.

***

The plane landed and the team woke up from their sleep. Zoila hurried up and told the team to get out of the plane. Most had passed out and June was gently awoken by Jin stroking her hair. Outside there was a team of agents waiting for them. The team groggily climbed out of the plane and were greeted with cheers and claps from the agents. June noticed this was the airport where she first met Zoila and Director Gutierrez. The director climbed out of his vehicle and walked up to them as they stood on the tarmac.

"You kids—you kids are something else. Especially you." He pointed to June. "*Sólita*, you took on a madman and a group of people that were following him, but you convinced them otherwise. *And* you took him out all by yourself." The team turned back to look at June with concerned expressions on their faces. "Ah, she's modest! She didn't tell you what she did, did she? Bah, come, come, get in the van, I'll debrief you along the way. We've set up a breakfast for you. You kids must be starving."

June, now realizing it was well past noon, realized she slept the whole plane ride. "Get in. Zoila, you too, come, come. *Vamos.*" The director climbed into the passenger seat while the driver slipped out and opened the sliding door for everyone to climb in. June climbed in first and sat toward the back. Freya held out her hand, holding Ken back, and let Zoe climb in and then Jin. The driver moved the chair back so the others could sit in the middle benches, with Zoila climbing in last. The driver shut the door and the director turned around, addressing the team.

"Tell me everything, *muchachos*!"

Zoila, despite being a little sleepy, was sitting next to Ken and slapped his back. "You first!"

Ken started, "I, sir, well..."

The director held up a hand. "Please, please, you guys have done so much, call me Guille. Please continue." Ken glanced at Zoila, who was happily peering out the window, and turned back to the director. "Well, er, Guille, when we got to the border—"

The director shook his hands at Ken. "No, no, I mean from the Nevada incident to now. All the information I have is secondhand. I want to know what each of you went through," he said as he pulled out a tablet and began writing on it. Ken's eyes widened and he looked back at Freya. Freya's eyes were wide too, but she shrugged her shoulders and tossed her hands up. Ken explained everything that happened, up until he landed in the hospital, all the while the director continued writing.

"What happened in the hospital?"

Ken turned to Zoila and she gave him a nod as she rubbed his back. "Um, Dr. Glendale helped me. She, uh, she flew down from the States and helped me get better. She used her laser technology to hook me up to an IV for a bit, and checked my heart the whole time to make sure it was healing properly, and after a few days she left and I was good to go."

Director Gutierrez nodded his head. "Mm hmm. Please continue."

Ken felt weird talking, but continued anyway. June started to feel sick to her stomach because she knew this story. How she was kidnapped and because of that Ken ended up in the hospital. June lowered herself and put her head on her hands, elbows on knees, and just stared at the ground. Zoe put her arm around her and despite June flinching at first, she held her tight and June eventually leaned into her. Ken continued telling his side of events. Once Ken had finished he glanced up at Zoila, and she proudly nodded. Director Gutierrez then moved his attention toward Hector.

Hector shot up nervously, but Zoila held out her hand and told him it'll be okay.

"Speak from the heart, *niño*, let us know everything that happened to you."

Hector swallowed and took a deep breath. He told his version of events, similar to Ken, up until the hospital, and continued. June heard all the events from his point of view and felt bad, hearing how they all went through so much just to find her, though the way Hector spoke about Betsy the van you'd think it was a person. He made it to the part where they attempted to rescue June at the decoy farm and was captured. Hector's face grew grim. "That's when they shot me in the thigh, with, you know, the shocky gun thingy." Hector made spark gestures with his hands.

The director nodded and continued writing on his pad. "And then what?"

Hector lowered his head and shot a quick glance at Freya. They, um... Zoila called Dr. Glendale again and she operated on me. As soon as she came in, I had a hemorrhaging test... testicle." Hector cleared his throat and didn't look up as he continued with his voice getting lower. "I-I sat out the ranch mission because the doctor thought I might pull a muscle in my weakened state and cause more internal bleeding."

"Mm hmm," murmured the director without much facial expression other than a furrowed brow and occasionally biting his tongue as he wrote. Hector continued nervously and Freya noticed this and spoke up.

"Why are we doing our debriefing here?"

Zoila and the director turned to her with concerned looks. "Because, *mi hija*, there is a mole, possibly in the base, and we want to get you home as soon as we can. The longer you stay here the more danger everyone is in. Our resources are thin enough as it is, and after the fight at the ranch, we lost a lot of good people there."

Zoila grimaced. "So, the sooner we get you back home the better it will be for all of us. Sorry if you're not used to this, but we really want to get you home. I think your flight is scheduled tomorrow at seven in the morning, so let's get this over with. It's about an hour drive to the base, so let's hurry it up.

The team continued telling their sides of events. Isaac told of his experience when he went to fight the Zealots in the ranch and accidentally punched a guy he thought was a Brick, causing his head to snap, and how he felt nervous with all the guns firing around him. Isaac's watery eyes reminded June of when he was tasked to take on the Zealots and he seemed to dislike the idea of charging in. He made his disdain for guns subtle but June noticed how he would almost struggle to say the word. Then Freya spoke and she had a hard time bringing up Ryan. She would shoot glances at June every time she brought him up. June was surprised when Zoe blatantly told them how she went into the police station interrogation room to stop Enrique and killed him during the tussle.

Jin was his usual carefree self, up until the incident at the farm when he rushed in and saw the plane take off. He decided to stay with Juan until he passed away, but regretted not trying to get on the plane with June and Ken. He sounded sad as he recalled that part of his story and just stopped talking as soon as he mentioned seeing Ken again. Zoila looked at him with sad eyes, but finally turned to June.

"*Mi amor*, tell us everything." Zoila and the director exchanged glances and turned to June attentively.

June cleared her throat and focused on the floor between her feet, the bare metal of the van providing no comfort for what she was about to recall. She mentioned how everything was the same as what everyone else had said until the hotel. "I got knocked out, taken to that madman's farm, and apparently experimented on."

Zoila couldn't help herself. "What? How? Why?!" she exclaimed, and June hugged herself.

"Cesar... He mostly tortured me, and said something about how his partner lied to him, but I don't know many of the details. I barely caught a glimpse of him, while I was on the plane fighting Cesar." June lifted her legs and put her feet on the chair and hugged her knees against her chest. The director faced Zoila and she gave him a nod.

"What about in Venezuela?" asked the director.

June explained everything. The director concentrated and wrote on his tablet. Zoila crossed her arms and stared out the window. The team glanced back at June sympathetically and Freya reached back to hold her hand. Ken felt guilty about trying to make a move on her and was glad Freya made him give June her space.

"Hon, you're getting a girls' night as soon as we get home!" said Jin as enthusiastically as he could. Everyone laughed nervously and June turned to him.

"I better. And there better be some freaking pizza."

***

Arriving at the base, the team exited the van, quieter than usual. Zoila told them to go on ahead. "I'm going to go get some mangoes. You go ahead and eat. I'll be back soon." She left along with the driver while the director addressed the team.

"I really appreciate everything all of you did," he said sincerely. "You're all heroes who have been through really terrible things. No matter what I say, it won't change that fact, but I hope you can recover and someday be happy again. But we will be forever grateful to you," he said as he placed one hand over his heart and gave them a thankful nod. The director then walked away, following the driver, and the team walked toward the elevators.

"Well, that was... something," said Jin with uncertainty. "The heck, like yeah, we saved our asses, their asses, and all we get is a 'good job, now go home'?"

Freya shook her head. "No, no, you simpleton. We get a short trip on a private plane, dinner, then a coach flight to Texas where we'll be treated like nothing happened," she said sarcastically.

Jin rolled his eyes. "Oh, yeah, how could I forget?"

The elevator doors opened and they made their way down to the mess hall where the whole facility was waiting for them with banners saying "Congratulations!" and a large cake.

"Wha..." said Jin, confused at everyone cheering them.

"We never got this back home," said Ken, rushing in with his hands out in the air celebrating.

"When in Rome..." scoffed Jin, following Ken's lead.

Hector and Isaac looked at each other and shrugged. They all walked toward the tables full of food. Freya and Zoe put their hands on June's back.

"Do you want to join, or go up and we'll take you something to eat?" asked Freya, and June nodded.

"The second one, please," she said, not making eye contact.

"We gotcha, June. We'll be up soon."

June made her way back to the elevators and up to the dorms. She grabbed her plaid shirt and jeans, fresh underwear, pads, and made her way to the showers and put her suit in the wash.

After freshening up, June went back with her suit in hand and just sat on her bed. She felt numb, like the events of the past week had happened to someone else. She heard the term home, but it didn't mean anything to her. Despite her wanting to be with her new friends, they felt distant—she felt distant. June couldn't find it in her to care. She wanted Ken's warmth to hold her, but that was it. The crush, the fun, it was gone. June didn't know what she was feeling.

"Depression sucks, dude." Freya appeared behind her.

394

A startled June turned to see Freya bringing her a plate of steak, rice, and beans, with a side of tostones.

"Here, you're probably not gonna wanna eat much, but you gotta try. Food helps keep blood flow, which means your sadness chemicals get flushed out and recycled and, well, honestly I'm not a doctor, so take that with a grain of salt. And these tostones, they got salt."

June raised an eyebrow and grabbed the plate. "Grain of salt, eh?"

Freya laughed and sat beside her. "That's what the experts say." The two smiled and bumped each other's shoulders gently. "Listen, I can't imagine what you're going through. This whole thing from when you joined until now, it's been wild." Freya sat back, lifting a leg onto the bed, and turned to June who was eating crossed-legged with the plate over her ankles, but not looking at Freya.

"I'm sorry. About it all. Like I've told you before and tell everyone, if you wanna talk, just let me know, but right now I just need you to listen."

June paused for a moment then continued eating.

"I... I know what it feels like to be violated. To feel helpless while someone has their way with you. And even though I... I know it's not the same to say that I was some pervert's plaything before he tried to kill me, to you literally being killed over and over again. It's all messed up. The hard part is then being lauded as a hero, or being strong for living your life after that when all you want to do is forget it. To pretend it never happened and move on with your life. Survivor's guilt is hard, and not a lot of people are going to get it."

June kept staring at her plate but ate much slower.

"People don't understand that being a victim means having

to live a life where you constantly fear being a victim again, and it's always on your mind. And you wake up and go to sleep with those thoughts in your head. So, I guess what I'm saying is that it doesn't get better, but it just becomes more manageable. The loud voice inside your head quiets over time, but never really goes away. It desperately wants to keep you safe while keeping you locked in a cage in your mind. Feeling nothing is easier than pain. So I get it. I'll be here if you ever want to talk.

"I'm glad you listened. It probably won't hit you yet, but when you get that rush of pain and feeling, then you can start the healing process which, honestly, is more of a compartmentalizing of your emotions than just getting better, but you'll hopefully find a reason to live again."

June nodded slowly, placed her plate on the bed, and dove into Freya's arms. Freya wasn't prepared for this, but wrapped her arms around June as she burrowed into her chest, sobbing softly. Freya stroked her hair and placed her chin over June's head as her own tears escaped.

After a few minutes, Freya gently laid a sleeping June down and picked up her plate as she made her way back down to the mess hall. Freya hadn't eaten since she made the plate for June and told Zoe to keep everyone there as long as she could until she came back.

The guys were sitting at the table talking about their adventures with a group of women who seemed enamored by them. Zoe and Jin sat surrounded by a group of people who were hanging off of every word.

Freya went to the food table and served herself a small plate of rice and some fried plantains. She sat far from the groups but watched them with a melancholic expression on her face.

"For you, Seb and Tabby." A tear rolled down her face as she lifted her cup and poured a little juice onto her tray.

***

The next morning, Zoila came into the dorm and woke everyone up. Freya, wearing her pink camo shirt again, grabbed her backpack. The team all prepared last night before bed, and put June's next to her as she slept. Freya then gently nudged June awake.

"Come on, June. We gotta go." June woke up with a start, but rubbed her eyes as she let out a silent yawn. Freya could tell whatever she was dreaming, it was hurting her.

"Come on, I got your stuff in the bag. Let's go brush our teeth and get to the elevators."

Zoe was shaking a heavily sleeping Jin awake when she looked up at Freya with a grin. The others groggily woke up and grabbed their backpacks before heading toward the restrooms.

"Come on, you don't want to be late," Zoila said as she walked off in high heels that sounded loud against the concrete floor. The team freshened up before making their way to the elevators where Zoila was waiting.

Ken rubbed his eyes as he asked Zoila, "When are we going to see William?"

"He's waiting for you when you get back to Texas."

Ken and the others exclaimed, "What?!"

Zoila was smiling and handed Ken a small box. "These mangoes are for him. He woke up yesterday during the Venezuelan incident. These are for you guys, but take some for him, okay? He's a lot better and he had to fly out before we got back yesterday." Zoila was giddy with excitement and the team, though still processing everything, was much happier now knowing William was better. Even June found a reason to smile. Freya held an arm around her and June nodded, knowing that Freya was right; it'll take time, but June will both live with the pain and find reasons to live.

***

The van carrying Zoila and the team stopped in front of a restaurant. "Here, here!" She tapped the driver's shoulder. "Breakfast!" The team got down and walked into a cozy, classic-styled restaurant.

"Old-school, I dig it," Zoe said as the team looked around.

Zoila sat the team down at a large bench table. The waitress came and asked them what they wanted.

Zoila enthusiastically asked for, *"Huevos perico y chocolate caliente."*

Zoe's eyes widened. "Oh! Same! But coffee with milk please."

Jin read the menu. "Bandeja paisa, please! Daddy needs his pork rind fix before leaving this place!"

The others laughed and put in their orders. Freya looked at June and placed a hand on her shoulder, a worried expression on her face.

"I'll, um... Whatever you have I'll get too."

Freya nodded and lifted her hand. "Two fried eggs with arepas, and two hot chocolates." Freya squinted at June. "With cheese." June shot an eyebrow up. "Trust me, it's weird, but I like it."

June shrugged her shoulders. "If you say so."

Zoe turned to June. "It is, I usually get it when I'm here, but I wanted coffee to get me going for the next eight-hour flight."

"It's more like six hours," said Isaac, digging into the plate of fried plantains the waitress left on the table. Zoe turned to him, waiting for him to say something else, but he just kept enjoying the chips.

June looked around as everyone got their orders and enjoyed their meals. June actually started to feel a little better, almost happy, and knowing she'll see William soon meant some normalcy in her life, though she had a million questions for him. She took a sip of her hot chocolate that tasted surprisingly good. Right now, she was going to enjoy this moment.

After breakfast, the team gathered up in the van again and headed to the airport. Ken carried the box of mangoes to customs and got it through. They all said goodbye to Zoila who was about to cry.

"The director sends his love and wished he could be here, but he's meeting with government officials to give them your reports. I love you guys. Please be safe. Don't forget to write to me. We'll figure out a way to chat, okay?"

They said their goodbyes at the airport terminal as the team boarded their plane. Zoila walked back to the van that was waiting for her at the terminal and sat down in the passenger seat. "These were difficult times, but we did it. I never told them that my team was let go and sent to live on farms under supervision. They couldn't handle everything that happened. Those kids are tough. Hopefully they'll be okay. You never really know what's going on in someone's head. But, David, an early retirement from the agency? Ah, what a dream, if only we were so lucky."

The car kept driving down the road and made a left into an abandoned alleyway. "Where are we going, David?" Zoila asked, realizing he hadn't said a word, and turned to get a good look at the driver. "Wait, you're not David... you're—" Blood splattered on the passenger window and the driver walked away, adjusting his hat as the black van started to burn.

***

During the flight, the team was spread out in separate seats. June wasn't bothered by it. She got a window seat and was very grateful for the view. The world seemed small, and it made her feel free for a moment. June sighed, closed her eyes, and tried to repress her pain.

***

Opening her eyes, a woman shot up out of bed, grabbed her phone, and called the number she knew by heart. No answer.

After pacing around and breathing heavily, the woman knew something was wrong. She walked out the door of her isolated farmhouse in a hurry. She then made her way through the busy Mexican streets and eventually walked into an unmarked building.

She stood at the front desk as suited agents encircled her.

"I need to speak to William Saturnino. My name is Harmony Romero."

End

About the Author

G. S. Cifuentes was born to immigrants in the decade where pop culture was truly taking off. Raised with public broadcast shows and being mystified by animation and storytelling, he grew up having to push that all to the side to become an acceptable functioning member of society. But as an adult, the rules have changed. Imagination and fantasy are valid pursuits. Writing, cinema, video games, it's all a sought after commodity. People want to escape from the drab mundane grind of life, and G. S. Cifuentes, like everyone else, loves to be swept up in a good story. Until one day he decided he was going to put his own imagination to work. After failed attempts at a normal life, he decided that writing his cinematic thoughts would be a healthy outlet while grinding his day jobs. Finally putting pen to paper after almost a decade of working a superhero styled spy thriller. G.S. Cifuentes hopes to reach others who feel as trapped as he did and will continue working on other stories and genres like fantasy and horror!

You can connect with me on:

🌐 https://cifuenteswrites.com